THE FORGET-ME-NOT SONATA

The Hurlingham Club in Buenos Aires is home to the small Anglo-Argentine community where gossip is devoured as eagerly as the scones and Earl Grey tea. Here Audrey Garnet loses her heart to Louis Forrester, the talented, troubled young man who sets tongues wagging with his eccentric behaviour and chequered past. Finding in Audrey the one woman who understands him, Louis composes for her a brilliant piece of music: the Forget-Me-Not Sonata. To the hypnotic melody of this magical tune they embark upon a secret love affair. But a family tragedy brings their romance to an abrupt end and Audrey thrills her parents by accepting Louis's successful, respectable elder brother, Cecil, as her husband. It is a sacrifice she bitterly regrets. Despite the pleasures of family life and, in time, beloved daughters of her own, Audrey hears the sweet, plaintive notes of the sonata echo through the years as a reminder of the love that she has lost.

THE FORGET-ME-NOT SONATA

Santa Montefiore

CHIVERS PRESS
BATH

First published 2003
by
Hodder & Stoughton
This Large Print edition published by
BBC Audiobooks Ltd
by arrangement with
Hodder & Stoughton Limited
2003

ISBN 0 7540 1943 8

British Library Cataloguing in Publication Data available

Printed and bound in Great Britain by
Antony Rowe Ltd., Chippenham, Wiltshire

To Lily Bathsheba

I would like to extend my deepest gratitude to my cousin, Anderly Hardy and my friend, Sue Nicholas, who both had the good fortune to grow up in Hurlingham, Argentina. Thanks to their lively descriptions and razor-sharp memories, I have been able to bring to life this little corner of Englishness that has changed so dramatically since their childhood. I would also like to thank my mother for her stories, my father for his wisdom and my aunt Naomi for her constant encouragement and interest. Dr Stephen Sebag Montefiore MD and his wife April gave me invaluable help on medical and psychiatric matters that helped bring my characters to life. My editor, Sue Fletcher, deserves a medal for such meticulous editing and sound advice and my agent, Jo Frank, merits a thank you for she is so wonderfully dedicated and unwavering in her support. Without my friend, Kate Rock, I wouldn't be writing at all, so I owe her an enormous debt of gratitude. Lastly, but most importantly, I would like to thank my husband, Sebag, for his wise counsel and boundless enthusiasm, because whenever my imagination runs dry, he's always there to water it.

THE LEGEND OF THE FORGET-ME-NOT

In Austrian legend, a man and his betrothed were walking hand in hand along the bank of the Danube River the night before their wedding. As the young woman looked into the water, she saw a lovely blue flower being washed away by the current. So sad was she that such a beautiful flower should be lost, that her lover heroically leaped into the river to save it for her. However, the river ran mighty and wild and as he was swept to his death, he threw the flower onto the bank and cried 'Forget me not, I will love you for ever.'

PART 1

PROLOGUE

The sky was almost too enchanting for a day such as this. An October sky that blessed the countryside below it with a dazzling golden radiance as if the autumn trees and neatly ploughed fields had been set alight by God Himself to mark this great day of passing. Brazen strokes of flamingo pink and blood red slashed the heavens in a bid to render them as impressive as possible while the dying sun descended slowly like lava, melting into the evening mists on the horizon. Nature was triumphant, but the humble soul of Cecil Forrester seemed quite undeserving.

Grace was the only one of Cecil Forrester's daughters who didn't cry at his funeral.

Alicia cried. She cried with the same sense of drama that characterised every other aspect of her life, as if she were permanently on a stage, her beautiful face always in the spotlight. She cried glittering tears and sighed long-drawn-out sobs that caused her black-gloved hands to tremble as she dabbed at her cheeks with an embroidered hanky. She was careful enough not to allow her display of grief to contort her features, expressing her emotions in the pretty quiver of her lips and in the gentle tilt of her head, enticingly obscured behind delicate black veiling attached to the brim of her hat. Leonora cried too, quietly. Not for the father she had lost, but for the father she had never had.

3

The man in the coffin might just as well have been a stranger to her, a distant uncle perhaps or an old school teacher. He had never allowed her more intimacy than that. She looked across at her younger sister who watched impassively as the coffin was lowered into the tidy hole in the ground and wondered why she showed no emotions when out of the three of them she had the most cause to grieve.

Grace was more than ten years younger than her twin sisters. Unlike her siblings who had been sent away to be educated in England at the tender age of ten, Grace had grown up in the leafy English suburb of Hurlingham in Buenos Aires. But it wasn't due to the age gap that they felt they barely knew her, or the many years of separation that had forged an insurmountable wall between them, but because Grace was different. As elusive as the garden fairies of their childhood, she was not of this world. Alicia said her ethereal nature was due to the fact that their mother had held onto her and spoiled her having suffered so much after they had been sent away, leaving her alone and adrift. But Leonora didn't agree. Grace was just made that way. Their mother had been right not to be parted from her. Grace would have wilted like a wild prairie flower in the cold English schoolrooms where she had sobbed tears of homesickness onto hard pillows.

Grace watched the coffin with little emotion as it was lowered into the ground against the exaggerated sobs and sniffs of her sister who had increased the volume for dramatic effect. It seemed all the more tempting to play the role on such a spectacular evening, beneath such a magnificent

4

sky. Grace didn't judge her. She just watched with serenity knowing that her father wasn't in the coffin as everyone else thought. She knew because she had seen his spirit leave his body at the moment of his death. He had smiled at her, as if to say, 'So you were right all along, Grace.' Then accompanied by his deceased mother and favourite uncle Errol he had floated off into the other dimension leaving nothing behind but a wilted carcass. She was tired of telling them the truth. After all, they'd find out in the end when it was their turn to go. She shifted her eyes to her mother, who stood beside her with her soft face betraying a mixture of regret and relief and linked her fingers through hers. Audrey squeezed her daughter's hand with gratitude. Although Grace was now a young woman she had a purity and innocence that gave the impression that she was still a child. To Audrey she always would be.

To Audrey Grace was special. From the moment she was born in the hospital of The Little Company of Mary in Buenos Aires, Audrey knew she was different from her other children. Alicia had screamed her way into the world with characteristic impatience and Leonora had followed submissively in her wake, trembling in the face of such uncertainty. But Grace was different. She had slipped out of her mother's small body without any fuss, like a contented angel, and blinked up at her with a knowing smile that played upon her pink lips with a confidence that took the doctor so much by surprise his face flushed before the blood drained away altogether, leaving him ashen with fright. But Audrey wasn't surprised. Grace was celestial and Audrey loved her with an intensity that almost

5

suffocated her. She held the tiny baby against her chest and gazed adoringly into her translucent face; surely the face of an angel.

To Audrey Grace was a blessing bestowed upon her by a compassionate God. Her hair was a wild halo of untameable blonde curls and her eyes were like a deep green river that held all the mysteries of the world in their depths. She enchanted people and frightened them at the same time for she seemed to look right through them, as if she knew them better than they knew themselves. But she frightened no one as much as she frightened her own father, who did his best to avoid contact with this creature who was as foreign to him as a being from another universe. She possessed none of his qualities or physical features and was impervious to the force of his will and the might of his temper. She just smiled with amusement as if she understood his nature and the reasons he constantly fought against it. He had never understood her, at least not until the end. After all their differences he had suddenly smiled in the same way that she smiled, knowingly, almost smugly and embraced her with love. Then he had died, leaving an uncharacteristic grin on his face that had never been there in life.

Audrey released her daughter's hand and stepped forward, holding her silver head high with a dignity that had supported her through many tumultuous years, and dropped a single white lily into the grave. She whispered a hasty prayer then raised her eyes to the shrinking sun that descended behind the trees casting long black shadows over the churchyard. It was at that moment that her thoughts lost their focus and drifted nostalgically

6

back to a time when love had blossomed with the jacaranda trees. Now she was old she would never love again—not in the way she had loved in her youth. Age had robbed her of such innocent expectations. Before the dark grave of her husband Audrey finally succumbed to the might of her memories and watched them rise up in her mind like ghosts. They shook themselves free of their bonds and suddenly she was a young girl again and her dreams were all shiny and new and full of promise.

CHAPTER ONE

The English Colony of Hurlingham
Buenos Aires 1946

'Audrey, come quick!' Isla hissed, grabbing her sixteen-year-old sister by the arm and tugging her out of her deckchair. 'Aunt Hilda and Aunt Edna are having tea with Mummy. Apparently, Emma Townsend has been discovered in the arms of an Argentine. You have to come and listen. It's a hoot!' Audrey closed her novel and followed her sister up the lawn to the clubhouse.

The December sun blazed ferociously down upon this little corner of England that resisted with all its might integration with those nationalities that had come before and fused into a nation. Like a fragile raft on the Spanish sea the English flew the flag and flaunted their prestige with pride. Yet the heady scents of eucalyptus and gardenia danced on the air with the aromas of tea and cakes in an easy tango and the murmur of clipped English voices and tennis echoed through the grounds against the thunder of Argentine ponies and the chatter of the gauchos who looked after them. The two cultures rode alongside each other like two horses, barely aware that they were in fact pulling the same carriage.

Audrey and Isla had grown up in this very British corner of Argentina situated in an elegant suburb outside the city of Buenos Aires. Centred around the Hurlingham Club where roast beef and steak and kidney pie were served in the panelled dining room beneath austere portraits of the King and Queen, the Colony was large and influential and life was as good as the cricket. Palatial houses were neatly placed behind tall yew hedges and English country gardens and joined together by dirt roads that led out onto the flat land of the pampa. The sisters would compete in gymkhanas, play tennis and swim and tease the neighbouring ostrich by throwing golf balls into his pen and watching in amusement as he ate them. They would ride out across the vast expanse of pampa and chase the prairie hares through the long grasses. Then as the sun went down and the clicking of the crickets rose above the snorting of ponies to herald the dying of the day, they would picnic with their mother and cousins in the shade of the eucalyptus trees. They were languorous, innocent times untroubled by the pressures of the adult world. Those pressures awaited their coming of age, but until then the intrigues and scandals, passed about the community in hushed voices over scones and cucumber sandwiches, were a great source of amusement, especially for Isla who longed to be old enough to create ripples such as those.

When Audrey and Isla wandered into the Club they became aware at once of the faces that withdrew from their cups of china tea and scones to watch the two sisters weave their way gracefully through the tables. They were used to the attention but while Audrey lowered her eyes shyly Isla held her chin high and surveyed the tables down the pretty slope of her imperious nose. Their mother told them it was because their father was a Chairman of Industry and a very important man, but Isla knew it had more to do with their thick corkscrew hair that reached down to their waists and glistened like sundried hay and their crystalline green eyes.

Isla was born fifteen months after Audrey and was the more striking. Wilful and mischievous, she was blessed with skin the colour of pale honey and lips that curled into a witty grin, which never failed to charm people even when she had done little to deserve their affection. She was smaller than her sister but appeared taller due to the joyous bounce in her step and the large overdose of confidence that enabled her to walk with her back straight and her shoulders broad. She relished attention and had adopted a flowing way of moving her hands when she talked, like the Latins, which never failed to catch people's eyes and admiration. Audrey was more classically beautiful. She had a long, sensitive face and pale alabaster skin which blushed easily and eyes that betrayed a wistfulness inspired by the romantic novels she read and the music she listened to. She was a dreamy child, content to sit for hours on the deckchairs in the grounds of the Club imagining the world beyond the insular one she belonged to, where men were passionate and unrestrained and where they danced with their lovers beneath the stars amid the thick scent of jasmine in the cobbled streets of Palermo. She longed to fall in love, but her mother told her she was too young to be wasting her thoughts on romance. 'There will be plenty of time for love, my darling, when you come of age.' Then she would laugh at her daughter's dreaming, 'You read too many novels, real life isn't a bit like that.' But Audrey knew instinctively that her mother was wrong. She knew love as if she had already lived it in another life and with an aching nostalgia her spirit yearned for it.

* * *

'Ah, my lovely nieces!' Aunt Edna exclaimed when she saw the two girls approach. Then she leant over to her sister and hissed, 'Rose, they get prettier every day, it won't be long before the young men start courting. You'll have to watch that Isla though, she's got a naughty glint in her eye, to be sure.' Aunt Edna was a widow and childless but with typical British stoicism she managed to smother the tragedies in her life with a healthy sense of humour and satisfy her nagging maternal instincts by embracing her nephews and nieces as her own. Aunt Hilda stiffened and watched Audrey and Isla with resentment, for her four daughters were thin and plain with sallow skin and insipid characters. She wished she had had four sons instead, that way the odds on a good marriage would have been more favourable.

'Come and sit down, girls,' Aunt Edna

continued, tapping the chair beside her with a fleshy hand made heavy with jewellery. 'We were just saying . . .'

'*Pas devant les enfants*,' Rose interjected warily, pouring herself another cup of tea.

'Oh, do tell, Mummy,' Isla pleaded, pulling a face at Aunt Edna who winked back. If she didn't tell them now she would later.

'There's no harm in relating this tale, Rose,' she said to her sister. 'Don't you agree, Hilda, it's all part of their education?' Hilda pursed her dry lips and fiddled with the string of pearls that hung about her scraggy neck.

'Prevention is better than cure,' she replied in a tight voice, for Aunt Hilda barely opened her mouth when she spoke. 'I don't see the harm in it, Rose.'

'Very well,' Rose conceded, sitting back in her chair with resignation. 'But you tell, Edna, it makes me too distressed to speak of it.'

Aunt Edna's blue eyes twinkled with mischief and she slowly lit a cigarette. Her two nieces waited with impatience as she inhaled deeply for dramatic effect. 'A tragic though utterly romantic tale, my dears,' she began, exhaling the smoke like a friendly dragon. 'All the while poor Emma Townsend has been engaged to Thomas Letton she has been desperately in love with an Argentine boy.'

'The worst is that this boy isn't even from a *good* Argentine family,' Aunt Hilda interrupted, raising her eyebrows to emphasise her disapproval. 'He's the son of a baker or something.' She burrowed her skeletal fingers into her sister's packet of cigarettes and lit up with indignation.

11

'The poor parents,' Rose lamented, shaking her head. 'They must be so ashamed.'

'Where did she meet him?' Audrey asked, at once moved by the impossibility of the affair and eager to hear more.

'No one knows. She won't say,' Aunt Edna replied, thrilled by the mysterious nature of the story. 'But if you ask me he's from the neighbourhood. How else would she have bumped into him? It must have been love at first sight. I've been told by a very reliable source that she would creep out of her bedroom window for midnight rendezvous. Imagine, the indecency of it!' Isla wriggled in her chair with excitement. Aunt Edna's eyes widened with the fervour of a frog who's just spotted a fat fly. 'Midnight rendezvous! It's the stuff novels are made of!' she gushed, recalling the secret meetings in the pavilion that she had enjoyed in her youth.

'Do tell how they were discovered,' Isla pleaded, ignoring her mother's look of gentle disapproval.

'They were spotted by her grandmother, old Mrs Featherfield, who has trouble sleeping and often wanders around the garden late at night. She saw a young couple kissing beneath the sycamore tree and presumed it was her granddaughter and her fiancé, Thomas Letton. You can imagine her horror when she failed to recognise the strange dark boy who had his arms wrapped around young Emma and was . . .'

'That's enough, Edna,' Rose demanded suddenly, placing her teacup on its saucer with a loud clink.

'Dear Thomas Letton must be devastated,' Aunt Edna went on, tactfully digressing to satisfy her

12

sister. 'There's no chance that he'll marry her now.'

'From what I hear, the silly girl claims she is in love and is begging her poor parents to allow her to marry the baker's son,' Aunt Hilda added tartly, stubbing out her cigarette.

'Good gracious!' Aunt Edna exclaimed, fanning her round face with the menu in agitation, but clearly savouring every detail of the affair.

'Oh dear,' Rose sighed sorrowfully.

'How wonderful!' Isla gasped with glee, wriggling in her chair. 'What a delicious scandal. Do you think they'll elope?'

'Of course not, my darling,' Rose replied, patting her daughter's hand in order to calm her down. Isla always worked herself up into a lather of excitement over the smallest things. 'She wouldn't want to bring shame upon her dear family.'

'How sad,' breathed Audrey, feeling the full force of the lovers' pain as if she were living it herself. 'How desperately sad that they can't be together. What will happen to them now?' She blinked at her mother with her large, dreamy eyes.

'I imagine she'll come to her senses sooner or later and if she's lucky, poor Thomas Letton may agree to marry her still. He's so fond of her, I know.'

'He'd be a saint,' Aunt Hilda commented, dismissing the girl with a swift sweep of her knife as she spread jam onto her scone.

'He truly would be,' Aunt Edna agreed, extending her arm across the table to help herself to a piece of Walkers shortbread. 'And she'd be very fortunate. There's a great shortage of men now due to the war, it'll leave an awful lot of young women without husbands. She should have had the

13

sense to hold onto hers.'

'And the poor boy she's in love with?' Audrey asked in a quiet voice.

'He shouldn't have hoped,' Aunt Hilda replied crisply. 'Now, did you know Moira Philips has finally dismissed her chauffeur? I think they were right to do so considering there was a high chance that he was reporting their conversations to the government,' she continued in a loud hiss. 'One can only imagine the horror of it all.'

Audrey sat in silence while her mother and aunts discussed Mrs Philips' chauffeur. She didn't know Emma Townsend well for she was a good six years her senior, but she had seen her at the Club. A pretty girl with mousy hair and kind features. She wondered what she was doing now and how she was feeling. She imagined she was suffering terribly, as if her whole future was a bleak, loveless hole. She looked across at her sister who was now playing with her sandwich out of boredom; Mrs Philips' chauffeur was extremely dull compared with Emma Townsend's illicit affair. But Audrey knew that their shared interest in the scandal differed greatly. Isla was riveted by the trouble the girl had caused. The romantic, or tragic, elements of the story couldn't have interested her less. She delighted in the fact that no one could talk of anything else, that they all spoke with the same hushed voices that they adopted when talking about death and that they devoured each sordid detail with hungry delight before passing it on to their friends. But most of all the glamour of it enthralled her. How easy it was to rock their orderly lives. Secretly Isla wished it were she and not Emma Townsend who basked in the centre of

14

such a whirlwind. At least she would enjoy the attention.

*   *   *

It was a good two weeks before Emma Townsend was seen at the Club. Like a forest fire the scandal spread and grew until she was wrongly accused of being pregnant by the gossiping Hurlingham Ladies. The Hurlingham Ladies consisted of four elderly women, or 'Crocodiles' as Aunt Edna wickedly called them, who organised with great efficiency all the events held at the Club. The polo tournaments, gymkhanas, flower shows, garden parties and dances. They played bridge on Tuesday evenings, golf on Wednesday mornings, painted on Thursday afternoons and sent out invitations to tea parties and prayer nights with tedious regularity. As Aunt Edna pointed out, they were the 'protocol police' and one knew when one had fallen short when the little lilac invitation failed to find its way to one's front door, though it was at times a relief not to have to think of an appropriate excuse to decline.

Audrey and Isla had spent the fortnight looking out for poor Emma Townsend. She hadn't appeared at church on Sunday, which infuriated the Hurlingham Ladies who sat with their feathered hats locked together in heavy discussion like a gaggle of geese, criticising the girl for not showing her face to the good Lord and begging His forgiveness. When Thomas Letton walked in with his family the entire congregation fell silent and followed his handsome figure as he walked up the aisle with great dignity, his impassive features betraying nothing of the humiliation that Audrey was sure burned beneath his skin. The Hurlingham Ladies nodded in sympathy as he passed, but he pretended not to see them and fixed his eyes on the altar in front of him before settling quietly into his seat next to his mother and sister. Emma hadn't been seen at the polo either or at the picnic which followed, organised by Charlo Osborne and Diana Lewis, two of the Crocodiles, who spent the entire afternoon muttering that if she so much as showed her face at their event they would send her home in disgrace while secretly longing for her to appear to give them more to gossip about. Then finally after two long weeks she arrived on Saturday for lunch with her family.

Audrey and Isla sat in the lounge with their brothers and parents and, of course, the indomitable Aunt Edna, when Emma Townsend crept in with her head bent, staring with determination at the floor in order to avoid catching anyone's eye. Audrey looked about as the chattering ceased and every eye in the room rose to watch the solemn procession file in and take their seats at a small table in the corner. Everyone, that is, except Colonel Blythe, who was too busy with his grey winged moustache buried in the *London Illustrated News*, smoking his Turkish cigarettes, to notice the silent commotion that made a small island out of him. Even Mr Townsend, a large-framed man with silver hair and woolly sideburns, seemed to swallow his indignation, choosing silence over confrontation which would normally have been his response at such a moment. He meekly ordered drinks and then turned his back on the rest of the community who were waiting like jackals to

16

see what he would do next.

'Well,' Aunt Edna exploded in a loud hiss, 'so unlike Arthur not to growl at us all.'

'That's enough, Edna,' Henry chided, picking up a handful of nuts. 'It isn't our place to comment.'

'I suppose not,' she conceded with a smile, 'the Crocodiles do enough of that for all of us.'

'They'll be furious they're missing this.' Isla giggled and nudged her sister with her elbow. But Audrey couldn't join in the merriment. She felt desperately sorry for the family who all suffered so publicly along with their daughter.

Just when the Townsends' shame threatened to suffocate them a gasp of astonishment hissed through the room like a sudden gust of wind. Audrey turned around to see Thomas Letton striding across the floor with his chin jutting out with resolution. Isla sat up with her mouth wide open as if she were about to scream with excitement. Albert, hating to miss an opportunity to pay his sister back for years of teasing, grabbed a peanut and flicked it down her throat. She stared at him in surprise before turning as red as a beet as the nut caught in her windpipe and prevented her from breathing. Pushing her chair out with a loud screech she swept the glasses off the table where they shattered onto the floorboards causing everyone to avert their attention from Thomas Letton and the Townsend family to see what the disturbance was. Isla's bloodshot eyes rolled around in their sockets as she choked and waved her arms about in a frantic attempt to get help. Before Audrey knew what was happening her father had grabbed Isla from behind, pulling her off the ground and wrapping his strong arms

17

around her stomach, thrusting his wrists into her lungs, again and again. She spluttered and gasped, all the time turning redder and redder until the whole lounge had formed a circle around their table like a herd of curious cows, anxiously willing Henry Garnet to save his daughter from a hideous death. Rose stood petrified with terror as the life seemed to leave her little girl's body in agonizing spasms. Silently she prayed to God. Later she would praise Him for His intervention because with one enormous thrust the peanut was dislodged and the child gulped in a lungful of air. Albert collapsed into tears, throwing his arms around his mother with remorse. Aunt Edna rushed to embrace Isla as she lurched back from the brink of death and began to shake uncontrollably. The crowd of onlookers clapped and cheered. Only Audrey noticed Emma Townsend leave with Thomas Letton. It didn't escape her notice, either, that they were holding hands.

'Great Uncle Charlie died from choking,' Aunt Edna remarked solemnly when the clapping had died down. 'But it wasn't a peanut. It was a piece of cheese, a plain piece of farmhouse cheddar, his favourite. After that we always referred to him as Cheddar Charlie, didn't we, Rose? *Dear* Cheddar Charlie.'

CHAPTER TWO

Much to the indignation of the Hurlingham Ladies, Thomas Letton and Emma Townsend were married in the autumn. Rose was delighted that at

18

last the Townsend family could hold their heads up again but Aunt Hilda felt very strongly that the girl was undeserving of such a decent young man. Aunt Edna called her an 'honorary Crocodile' and made snapping noises with her tongue behind her back, which made Isla giggle and copy her. Though Isla was less tactful, she would buzz about her aunt like a dragon fly singing 'snap snap' with her eyes wide with naughtiness. 'What's got into the child, Rose? All this snap snapping, what on earth does it mean?' Aunt Hilda complained. Even Rose found it hard to contain her amusement and reassured her sister that it was a game she had brought back from school.

'Oh good,' Aunt Hilda replied, 'I thought it had something to do with me.'

'Of course not, Hilda. Ignore her, she'll move on to something else soon enough,' she said. Of course she was right. Isla had a short attention span and soon the 'honorary Crocodile' bored her.

Emma Townsend's love affair had made a deep impression on Audrey. She was unable to forget. She observed the wedding from a distance, imagining the bride's passive resignation to her fate as she dutifully took her vows and embarked on a life without love. To Audrey such a bleak destiny was unspeakable, worse than death. But when the couple returned from their honeymoon, a fortnight later, the young wife seemed happy enough in her new role. The scandal was erased by time and the willingness on the part of the community to forget. Soon even the Hurlingham Ladies set aside their disapproval and received the new Mrs Letton with gracious smiles, delivering once again those little lilac envelopes with the same tedious regularity as before. But Audrey believed she heard muffled cries of pain in the light ripple of her laughter. She believed she saw suffering behind her eyes that revealed itself only in the rare moments when she would lose concentration and stare into space as if recalling those tender kisses beneath the sycamore tree. To Audrey, Emma was a tragic figure and her tragedy endowed her with a solemn beauty she hadn't had before.

*　　　*　　　*

When Audrey turned eighteen in January 1948 her mother took her shopping in the grand Harrods store on Avenida Florida, accompanied by Aunt Edna and Isla and then for tea in the Alvear Palace Hotel. Aunt Edna, who like her sister Rose had never been to London, shuffled about the shop complaining that it was nothing like as glamorous as the original, which was much larger and as magnificent as Aladdin's cave. But to Audrey and Isla it was a treat they always looked forward to, not only because of the clothes their mother bought them, but because it was an adventure to watch the elegant ladies in tidy hats and gloves totter up the carpeted departments on precariously high heels, browsing among the cosmetics and fashion imported from Europe. Isla watched with envy while her elder sister tried on grown-up dresses and silk blouses and sulked when she wasn't allowed a pair of earrings until she was eighteen. To appease her, Aunt Edna bought her a Pringle twinset, which immediately managed to put the smile back onto her face because she knew her mother disliked it when Aunt Edna undermined her weak attempts to discipline.

The heat was insufferable as they marched up the dusty streets, ignoring the dirty little beggar boys who leapt out of the shadows like monkeys to ask for money or sweets. They passed a magazine stand where Eva Peron's luminous face smiled out at them from the front page of every national newspaper. The dyed blonde hair pulled back into a severe bun, the cold brown eyes and the triumphant smile reflecting the ruthless ambition of a woman who would never be satisfied. Aunt Edna and Rose walked briskly on, keeping their opinions to themselves for fear of being overheard. There were too many stories of people being lynched by angry mobs of Peronists all because of a careless remark. The streets of Buenos Aires were not the place to speak ill of the First Lady. One no longer felt safe even within the walls of one's own home.

Audrey adored the city. It gave her a taste of freedom to bathe for an afternoon in the sweet anonymity of this urban labyrinth. She loved the bustle of people, striding purposefully to their jobs or to meetings, or ambling nonchalantly up the avenues, gazing into shop windows or lingering on sunny corners watching the world dash by. The cars and the noise excited her, the frothy squares and grand ornamental buildings enchanted her and she yearned to be a part of it, to weave her way quietly into this other world like a thread of silk in a vast tapestry. She adored the romance of the little cafés and restaurants that tumbled out onto the pavements and served as tranquil watering holes before the frenetic hurry would begin all over again. The quaint shoe-shiners and flower sellers

21

who enjoyed breaks together in the shade, discussing politics and trade, sipping *mate* through ornate silver straws. The air was thick with the smell of diesel from the buses and caramel from the pastry stands and punctuated with the animated voices of children that rose above the busy hum of activity. She didn't miss a single detail as she followed her mother's rapid footsteps up the pavements. Noticing the young couples wandering hand in hand beneath the palm trees in the Plaza San Martin her mind drifted once more to love. Her heart stirred with longing as the rich scents of gardenia and cut grass clung to her nostrils and transported her into the languid world of the novels she loved to read. She imagined that one day she might walk hand in hand like those lovers did and perhaps steal a kiss beside the fountain. But then they were in the tea room at the Alvear Palace Hotel and Rose was telling them about the two young men who had recently arrived from England to work in their father's company.

'Cecil and Louis Forrester,' she said, clearly impressed for her mouth twitched into a small smile.

'Brothers?' Aunt Edna asked, unbuttoning her blouse an inch and fanning her damp flesh.

'Yes, brothers,' Rose replied. 'Cecil is the elder, he's thirty and Louis is twenty-two. Louis is a bit . . .' she paused to find the right word, anxious not to appear malicious. 'Eccentric,' she said with emphasis then moved swiftly on to his brother. 'Cecil's so handsome and refined. A charming young man,' she gushed.

'Can I have *dulce de leche* pancakes, please?' Isla interrupted, eyeing the trolley of cakes as it was wheeled past by a white-gloved waiter, clearly taken with the two young girls who shone prettily in the smoky tearoom.

'Of course you can, Isla. Is that what you'd like too, Audrey?' Audrey nodded.

'Have they come alone?' she asked her mother.

'Yes, they have. Poor Cecil, he served in the war. Played an important part, I believe.' Rose sighed heavily. She wanted to add that apparently Louis had refused to fight, stubbornly remaining in London playing melancholic tunes on the grand piano, even during the raids, but she held back. It was unfair to turn her daughters against him even before they had met him. 'They've come out here,' she continued to Aunt Edna, 'to get away from Europe and all that depressing post-war gloom. Their father, who has done business with Henry in the past, suggested they come. We owe him a favour or two. He's been very good to Henry. I'm so happy he can help them. They're staying at the Club.'

'Well, there's a great shortage of young men,' Aunt Edna said, pouring herself a healthy cup of Earl Grey tea. 'War robbed us of the cream of our youth. What a tragedy war is.'

'Isn't it?' Rose agreed, quietly resenting the young Louis for not playing his part when her husband and many others had made that precarious journey across the waters, risking their lives, to defend a country they believed was theirs even though some of them had never even stood on British soil. She had even contributed herself by joining the Hurlingham Ladies Guild who met in the ping-pong room at the Club producing sweaters, socks, balaclava helmets, sea boot

23

stockings and scarves for the war effort. Once the war was over Rose had vowed never to knit another stitch, for each click of the needles reminded her of those tortuous days of waiting and of the agony that hope brought with it.

'Will you invite them to Audrey's party?' Isla asked, taking an interest now that her plate was full. Rose straightened and tilted her head to one side.

'I don't see why not,' she replied, looking to her sister for approval.

'Of course they should come,' Aunt Edna exclaimed with enthusiasm. 'It'll be the perfect way for them to meet nice English people. Besides, Hilda's girls are all on the look out for husbands, so are the Pearson twins not to mention poor June Hipps, if she doesn't find one soon she'll be left gathering dust on the shelf, she'll be *twenty-nine* next spring.' Rose hadn't considered Cecil Forrester for anyone else's daughter, even if her own daughters were still too young to think about marriage. Hilda's girls were no competition, neither was June Hipps, but the Pearson twins were slim and pretty and eager to settle down. She pursed her lips and swallowed the competitive ache that rose in her throat.

'That may be so,' she said tightly. 'But it's Audrey's party, Edna, not a marriage market.'

Aunt Edna looked hurt and blushed right down to her wobbling chins.

'Oh, Rose, I didn't mean . . . well,' she stammered. 'You've met them, Rose, what are they like? Do you think your girls will like them?'

Rose smiled and put down her teacup. 'I'm sure they will. Louis is closer to Audrey's age, but then he seems a bit . . . well, *wild* would be fair. He has yet to settle down. Now Cecil's entirely different. He's responsible, conscientious and handsome. An utterly charming young man, though a good deal older than Audrey. I don't think that matters, it's nice to be in the company of a man who's seen a bit of the world. Well, Audrey, would you like me to ask them to your party?' She turned to her elder daughter. Audrey attempted to contain her excitement by buttering a pastry she didn't want. She nodded her thanks then nibbled the corner nervously.

'I bet those Forrester boys fall in love with Audrey.' Isla giggled. 'Oh, I bet they will,' she insisted when her sister shot her an embarrassed look. 'Don't be coy, Audrey. You're prettier than all the other girls, even the Pearson twins. Anyway,' she added mischievously, 'I shall dance with them both.'

'You have to wait until you're asked, Isla,' her mother replied. Then she turned to Aunt Edna with a smile. 'What will the Crocodiles say when Isla rushes around asking all the men to dance?' she chuckled.

'Snap snap snap!' Aunt Edna replied and her chins wobbled so much that they all laughed heartily.

*   *   *

Audrey and Isla didn't have to wait long to meet the Forrester brothers, for a few days later their father invited them both for dinner at the house in Canning Street. The table was set beneath the vines on the terrace, illuminated by large hurricane

25

lamps and small candles that served as decoration as well as light. Audrey and Isla picked fresh flowers from the garden and made a pretty arrangement for the centrepiece while Rose discussed menus with Marisol the young cook. She had invited Aunt Edna out of kindness but also because she wanted her sister's opinion on Cecil Forrester, who might one day make a good husband for Audrey. She had decided against allowing her young sons to join them at the table, it would be too much of a distraction and Isla always behaved badly when Albert was around.

Audrey and Isla waited in the garden, both in new dresses their mother had bought them at Harrods. Isla noticed how her sister was already looking like a young woman and felt gauche by her side. She was only fifteen months younger than Audrey and yet, tonight, Audrey held herself differently, with more dignity, and looked leagues older. For the first time in her life Isla experienced a sense of wistfulness. Their childhood was clearly coming to an end.

'Girls, you both look delightful,' Aunt Edna exclaimed as she stepped out of the house in an ivory silk blouse and skirt, playing with a long string of pearls that hung over the swell of her large bosoms and swung down to her waist. She smelt strongly of Christian Dior and had powdered her face leaving a heap of dust on the ridge of her nose like a white snowdrift. Isla had no intention of telling her. It would have been amusing to have watched her sit the whole way through dinner like that, in blithe ignorance. But Audrey wasn't so unkind. She told her aunt immediately and then brushed away the offending snowdrift with gentle fingers. 'You are a sweet girl,' Aunt Edna breathed gratefully, pulling her powder compact out of her bag to check that she hadn't overlooked anything else. Satisfied that she had made the best of what Nature had given her she reapplied her lipstick before clipping her bag shut and looking at her watch. 'They should be here at any minute,' she said. 'I must say, I'm very much looking forward to meeting them. The Club is positively buzzing with excitement. Only today I heard that Cecil helped old Diana Lewis into her car yesterday afternoon and dazzled her with his charm. I bumped into Charlo at the *panadería* who told me that Colonel Blythe dined with him last night and played cards well into the early hours of the morning; they've become great friends. The old Colonel loves to witter on about the war, which we're all dreadfully bored of, but *dear* Cecil talked to him for hours about what he had experienced. I believe he proved himself quite a hero, the Colonel says he has a shining reputation in London—unlike his brother, who's something of an idler, so I'm told. I understand that Louis played the piano all night long, which didn't go down very well with the other residents. It would have been fine had he played something sensible, but he was apparently playing the most extraordinary tunes. Haunting melodies, gave everyone nightmares.' She sniffed and turned expectantly towards the house.

At that moment Henry and Rose appeared on the lawn followed closely by two young men. 'Ah, at last,' Aunt Edna sighed, smiling a broad smile that sent her plump chins expanding like marshmallow. 'Ready, girls?' And she proceeded to walk across the grass to meet them. Audrey and Isla glanced at each other excitedly. Isla was unable to control the wide grin that extended across her monkey face, even when she was introduced to their guests. But Audrey managed to compose herself, lowering her eyes shyly as she shook their hands.

What struck her immediately was the difference between the two brothers: Cecil was tall and slim with perfect, symmetrical features, lucid blue eyes and a long, aristocratic nose. His alertness was accentuated by the contrast with his brother whose vague and wandering eyes seemed lost in a world of their own. Cecil's dark brown hair was neatly combed into a side parting and shone with the same brilliance as his shoes. He smiled with confidence and nodded his head as he greeted the two girls, noticing at once how pretty and graceful the elder daughter was. Louis was shorter than his brother with softer, irregular features, revealing in the unsteady curl of his lips his changeable nature and intense sensibility. He wasn't handsome, but his face was alive with laughter lines and lines of pain and when Audrey caught his eye she was alarmed to find that she sunk into his gaze, as vast and consuming as a whirlpool. Stunned, she quickly shifted her focus to the ground and immediately noticed that his shoes were scuffed and beneath his trousers he wore one blue sock and one black one. His fingers were long and pale and moved ever so slightly as if he were touching the keys of an imaginary piano. When she lifted her gaze once more she saw that he was still blinking at her with curiosity through a sandy fringe that he hadn't bothered to brush. To her shame the heat rose up her throat, stinging her cheeks, exposing the inner turbulence that sent her heart pounding. She turned her face away and hoped no one had noticed. Louis wasn't beautiful, he wasn't particularly charismatic but there was something in his stare that unsettled her. He had a dark presence that drew her in although she felt instinctively that it was to be resisted at all costs.

Taking their champagne glasses with them they proceeded to stroll around the garden. Cecil walked with Henry, Rose and Aunt Edna while Audrey and Isla found themselves a few paces behind on either side of Louis. Only Rose noticed that Cecil made a swift backwards glance to check on his brother, in the same way that a father might look out for an awkward child. Audrey began a stumbling attempt to ignite the conversation, wishing she were walking with her parents. 'Mummy tells us this is your first time in the Argentine,' she said, hiding her unease behind a veneer of politeness.

'Yes,' he replied and sighed heavily, his face suddenly sagging with wistfulness. 'Europe seems to be suffering an eternal winter. Here it's spring, and with spring comes new life and hope. One forgets misery when the sun is shining.' Audrey looked at him in puzzlement, silently wondering what he meant and how to respond. Isla giggled and smirked across at her sister who pretended she hadn't seen in case they offended their guest.

'Spring is very beautiful here,' she said, hoping that she didn't sound stupid. Then she added impulsively, 'Spring always follows winter, even in Europe.' At that Louis turned to look at her, his face suddenly flushed pink. Audrey swallowed as his expression softened with surprising tenderness.

'You're right, it does,' he replied, frowning at

29

her, trying to work out whether she really did understand him or whether she had spoken without thinking. 'But why the winter in the first place?' he continued. 'Sometimes I wonder why God put us all down here if all we do is fight each other.'

'That I don't know,' she said, shaking her head, 'but I do know that if it was spring all the time we'd never appreciate it, human beings have to suffer to know what happiness is. I don't think life is meant to be easy. War is a terrible thing, a terrible thing. But it tests the human spirit to its limit and can bring out the very best in people,' she added, recalling the incredible stories of human kindness her father had told her.

'And the very worst,' he retorted cynically. 'It should never be allowed to happen.'

'Did you fight in the war?' Isla asked brightly. Audrey winced because one only had to look at him to know that he hadn't. A sudden blush of shame stung his cheeks pink and his lips twitched in discomfort. Cecil's shoulders hunched but he continued to talk politely to his hosts.

'No, no, I didn't,' he replied quickly. Audrey tactfully changed the subject to avoid any further embarrassment.

'I gather you play the piano most beautifully,' she said with enthusiasm. He regained his composure and his eyes smiled down at her with gratitude.

'Aunt Edna said you kept the whole Club awake and gave them nightmares,' Isla interjected with a laugh.

Louis chuckled. 'I was playing from the heart and even I don't understand my heart.'

'You say the strangest things!' Isla remarked,

30

curling her lip and looking at him quizzically.

'Isla!'

'Don't worry, Audrey, I like people who say what they think. Very few people do.'

'Well, I'm afraid Isla always says what she thinks. Or rather,' Audrey added, smiling, 'she often doesn't think at all.'

'Audrey thinks too much. Much too much,' Isla giggled.

Once more Louis looked down at her, probing her features with distant eyes. 'So I see,' he mused and Audrey stared at the ground in front of them, embarrassed by the intimacy of his gaze that she felt was inappropriate and intrusive. Yet she found to her horror that it excited her. Isla filled the heavy pause that ensued.

'Did you leave a sweetheart behind in England?' she asked, gulping back another swig of champagne.

'If I had a sweetheart I would not have come,' he replied. 'After all this is a Latin country. The land of tango and romance, is it not?' Isla giggled again. Audrey felt herself blushing and sipped from her glass in an attempt to hide it. There was no breeze, just the humidity, thick with the fertile scents of nature and Audrey's tumultuous spirit.

'Aunt Edna says we're short of suitable men because so many went off to fight in the war and never returned,' she continued. Audrey wished their mother hadn't allowed her to drink champagne. It had clearly heightened her senses.

'Really, Isla!' she protested. 'Poor Mr Forrester has only just arrived, you'll have him married off before dinner.' Louis laughed and shook his head.

'Don't worry, Audrey, I'm getting the measure of

your sister. She says what's on her mind, a bit like mine.' Then he turned to her and added softly, 'Please call me Louis, Mr Forrester makes me feel very old. Mr Forrester belongs to someone else— Cecil, for example, he carries Mr Forrester very well, very well indeed.'

'Does your sister live in England?' she asked, following her parents who were now making their way to the dinner table under the vine on the terrace.

'Cicely, yes, she does. She lives in a freezing old farmhouse,' he replied.

'She must be terribly sad to lose you both to the Argentine.'

'I don't think she is,' he said with a grin. 'If you knew my sister, you'd understand. She's not the warmest of women.'

'My sister's very warm,' said Isla, now beginning to slur her words. 'She's in a world of her own though. She's a dreamer.' Louis looked down at Audrey with eyes the colour of cornflowers and smiled at her reflectively.

'I'm a dreamer too,' he said and for a moment Audrey was sure she saw a sudden gloominess pass across his face as if the sun had briefly disappeared behind a cloud.

'I would die of grief if Audrey left me to live in a foreign country,' Isla interjected melodramatically. 'Promise you won't, Audrey.' Audrey caught eyes with her mother who noticed to her dismay that her younger daughter had already drunk too much.

'I promise I won't,' she replied indulgently. When she looked at Louis again the cloud had passed and his face was untroubled once more.

'Isla dear, please will you go into the kitchen and

tell Marisol that we are ready to eat,' Rose said. Then she added in a whisper as Isla floated past her, 'Have a large glass of water while you're out there. Your father will be furious if he sees that you're tipsy.'

*   *   *

The two guests sat on either side of Rose, then Isla was placed beside Louis and her father while Audrey had Cecil on her left and Aunt Edna on her right. She looked across at Louis and wished that she could swap places with her sister. Louis raised his eyes and caught her gazing at him with ill-concealed fascination. Audrey at once stared into her bowl of soup before turning to talk with Aunt Edna for her mother was already discussing the war with Cecil, clearly enraptured by him. Had she allowed her eyes to linger a moment longer she would have seen Louis' face crease into an enchanting smile.

'Isn't he charming?' Aunt Edna commented under her breath. Audrey knew she wasn't referring to Louis.

'Very,' she replied automatically, humouring her aunt.

'He's very handsome. A handsome army officer, desperately romantic, don't you agree? I think he likes you, my dear, I saw him gazing at you.'

'Oh, I don't think so,' she protested. 'Besides, I'm too young for love, apparently.'

Aunt Edna laughed. 'You're eighteen now, Audrey dear. I was your age when I fell in love with Harry. *Dear* Harry,' she said with emphasis. 'He was a good man.'

33

'Did you love him very much?' Audrey asked, changing the subject.

'Very much,' Aunt Edna replied, but she refused to allow the thought of her late husband to dampen her enjoyment of such a pleasant evening. She smiled through her melancholy, once more conquering it with humour. 'Harry was a great mimic,' she began. Audrey cast her eyes across the table to where Louis was laughing boisterously with Isla, who giggled back flirtatiously. To her frustration she suffered an unsettling twinge of jealousy at the sight of their mirth and turned back to her aunt, desperate to ignore those feelings that were both unfamiliar and primitive. 'He could mimic my mother, your grandmother, to perfection,' continued Aunt Edna, oblivious of her niece's turmoil. 'Once when my father shouted in from the garden "Elizabeth, what do you suggest we do with this cherry tree?" Harry replied in my mother's voice before she had time to, "Rip it out, darling, rip them all out." My father was left greatly puzzled.'

'How did you know Harry was the one?' Audrey asked, fighting her impulse to stray once again across the table. Aunt Edna looked at her and frowned.

'Aren't you a curious child?' she mused. Then her chubby fingers settled onto the ruby engagement ring she still wore and she sighed pensively. 'Because he was different from everyone else I had ever met. He made me laugh more than anyone else. I suppose I just knew. An instinct, quite animal really, very primitive. He made me feel wonderful. With Harry I was always facing the sun. My sunshine Harry. The sun has never been

34

quite the same since,' she added, then smacked her lips together, wrenching her thoughts back to the present. 'You'll know, Audrey dear. When it happens, you'll know.' Audrey felt certain she knew already. She glanced across at Louis aware that there were unsettling forces at play drawing them together.

When the main course was served Rose turned to Louis leaving Cecil free to talk to Audrey. With Cecil the conversation was light and easy. His expression was kind and his attention unwavering as he gazed upon her with the full force of his beautiful face and if it hadn't been for his brother, who sat opposite them like a wild dog, one moment buoyant the next sinking into melancholy, her heart might have been captivated by this dazzling army officer. But Audrey found Louis compelling. Her ears strained across the table in spite of herself. She knew she shouldn't and battled to control her feelings. But the more she sensed the danger the deeper into it she sunk.

'How long do you both intend to be in the Argentine?' she asked.

'About a couple of years,' he replied. He settled his steady eyes upon her and knew that he could be persuaded to stay longer. A piece of bread caught in his throat and he coughed then dislodged it with a swig of water. Disarmed by the loveliness of this serene young woman he felt self-conscious and clumsy.

'Then you'll return to England?'

'That's the plan.'

'You might lose your heart to the Argentine. So many have,' she remarked and noticed his lips curl into a small smile. He had already lost his heart but

Audrey was unaware that she held it.

'You don't know England, do you?' he asked. Audrey shook her head.

'No, but Daddy talks about it often, I feel I know it quite well.'

'There's no place quite like England. Perhaps you'll find the time to go there one day.'

'I'd like that. But I can't imagine living anywhere but here.' Then she chuckled. 'Colonel Blythe has a strange fascination with the weather in London. He reads the *London Illustrated News* and comments on it a week out of date. It appears to rain all the time.'

'Ah, the inimitable Colonel Blythe.' He chuckled, sitting back in his chair. 'What a wonderful eccentric he is. A true Englishman, for like the rest of us he talks of little else—the weather and the war.'

'Does it rain all the time?' she asked.

'My dear fellow,' said Cecil in the Colonel's deep plummy voice, 'I should think it'll be a wet summer again, bloody bad luck for all those at The Races.' Cecil laughed and was delighted that Audrey's shoulders quivered as she bubbled into laughter too. 'Colonel Blythe isn't wrong. It does rain a lot of the time, I'm afraid. You feel wet right down to your bones. It's that damp cold in winter that's so unpleasant, but springtime in England is lovelier than anywhere else in the world, even here. The rain makes it all so green. And when it's sunny you can imagine everyone's joy. That's why they comment on it, because it's such a rarity and therefore such a pleasure.'

As Cecil talked to Audrey he was unaware that during the pauses that punctuated their dialogue

36

her attention was diverted across the table to his brother. Due to Audrey's polite laughter and spirited commentary he felt he was being entertaining, but then he had a way with people. Everyone loved Cecil Forrester; mothers wanted him for their daughters and some secretly yearned for him for themselves. Young girls knew instinctively that he was eligible and did their best to attract his attention. But Audrey was different. She robbed him of his self-confidence. She had the same detached air as his brother yet in Audrey Cecil found it desperately attractive. It placed her out of his reach and gave her an ethereal quality that he had never encountered in anyone else.

He looked across at Louis and cringed with embarrassment. He hadn't even bothered to dress up for dinner. Cecil was sure he had let his good manners slip in order to irritate him. But Louis was untameable and wild, a liability wherever he went. Cecil remembered his parents' relief when he volunteered to take him to South America. They pretended to be saddened but he knew they were happy to see the back of him. He had let them down, badly.

Rose led her sister and daughters inside while the men smoked on the terrace, discussing the pros and cons of privatisation. Isla grabbed Audrey by the arm and hissed into her ear, 'Isn't he the most attractive man you've ever met?'

'Who? Louis?'

Isla shook her head with impatience. 'Don't be silly. Louis is odd! No, Cecil. He's so handsome he makes my eyes burn.'

'Yes, he is,' she said lightly. 'He's a gentleman.'

'You're so lucky, you talked to him all through

dinner. I could only look on longingly. I'm so glad he's coming to your party, Audrey, I'm going to be the first to dance with him.'

'If you like.'

'Just for fun. I'd like nothing more than to annoy all the other girls. He's the most eligible man in Buenos Aires, Audrey, and he's yours if you want him.'

'Oh, Isla, you're still tipsy!' She laughed.

'Perhaps, but not too tipsy to notice the way he looked at you.'

'Rubbish. He was just being polite.'

'There are limits to politeness and he far exceeded those!' Audrey couldn't help but feel flattered, after all, she wasn't immune to the attentions of such an attractive man and his interest caused her spirits to soar.

It wasn't until they were on the point of leaving that Audrey found herself alone with Louis beneath the soft light of the street lamp. She glanced anxiously back up the path to see the rest of her family lingering at the door with Cecil, pointing to the strange tree in the corner of the garden that had no known name and always baffled everyone, even the many expert botanists who had come from all over South America to identify it. Louis swept his sandy hair off his forehead with an unsteady hand and settled his eyes on the nervous young woman who shuffled from foot to foot beside him, suddenly unsure of herself now that she was on her own. 'Do you dance?' he asked. It struck Audrey that his question wasn't motivated by politeness but by genuine curiosity, for he looked at her intensely as if her answer was of great importance to him.

38

'A little,' she replied, unable to help but smile through her shyness. 'I don't think I'm a very good dancer.'

'I think you'd be a very good dancer. You have a natural grace when you walk. You see,' he mused, watching her shift her weight from one foot to the other. 'You're already dancing and you're not even aware of it.'

She glanced down at her feet. 'I don't think I am,' she said. 'I don't dance very often. I don't have the opportunity.'

'I'd like to learn to dance the tango,' he said and flicked his fingers as if to the time of a melody that only he could hear. 'I'd like to dance over the cobbled streets of Buenos Aires. I'd like to dance with you.' Audrey bit her lip and then watched in amazement as he began to hum, moving his body in time, lifting his hands and knees with the fluidity of a trained dancer. Audrey laughed and this time she saw his face open into the widest and most captivating grin she had ever seen. He was never happier than when he was giving way to the constant rhythms that played in his head and his enjoyment lit him up from thc inside like a lantern. Audrey thought of Aunt Edna's sunshine husband and knew what she meant.

'You certainly know how to dance,' she said truthfully, wishing she had the nerve to dance with him.

'Yes, but not the tango.'

'It's a beautiful dance.'

'Beautiful,' he agreed. 'It's formal yet simmering with sensuality. It's the most romantic of dances. So close yet not close enough. It makes my hair stand on end just to watch it, but to dance it, now

39

that would be truly something.' His eyes widened with excitement.

'They dance the tango in Palermo,' she said. 'Have you been to Palermo?' He shook his head. 'There's a little café there where they hold tango evenings. I know because Aunt Hilda's maid has been. That's a secret by the way, Aunt Hilda would be appalled. She considers the tango as intimate as . . . as . . .' she blushed.

'As making love?' he interjected.

'Yes,' she replied tightly, swallowing hard.

'She's right, it is. That's why I like it. Your aunt must be a dry old thing.' Audrey laughed, touching her hot cheeks with her hand, hoping to cool them down. 'Perhaps one day some lucky man will take you to tango in Palermo,' he said quietly.

'Not if my aunt has anything to do with it, or my mother for that matter. I don't think it's something that a nice young lady is expected to do.'

'How boring to have to be a nice young lady. Nice young ladies should only have to perform up to midnight, after that they should be allowed to step off the stage and have some fun. I'd like to see you leave the theatre by the back door and tango your way into the sunset.' Then he added in a quiet voice, 'You're a dreamer like me. People don't understand dreamers. We frighten them. Don't be afraid to dream, Audrey.'

There was a heavy silence while Audrey struggled past her embarrassment to find something to say and Louis watched her, enthralled. He was certain that they were two of a kind, that she was the first person who understood him. With the instincts of a child Louis perceived Audrey's big heart and vast capacity to love and he

40

was drawn to her with a need that made his whole body tremble.

Just when Audrey was on the point of floundering, her parents led the small group down the path to join them. They were still laughing and discussing the strange tree. 'So what do you call it?' Cecil asked.

'The bird tree,' Henry replied.

'Because for some reason it attracts all the birds in summertime,' said Rose, linking her arm through her husband's.

'Well, it's a delight, whatever it is,' Cecil concluded. 'Thank you so much for inviting us, Rose, we've had a charming evening.'

'It's been a pleasure,' she replied enthusiastically. 'And welcome to Hurlingham. Please come as often as you like. You're almost family after all.' She noticed Cecil pay special attention to Audrey before he and his brother started up the street towards the Club. She had been pleasantly surprised to see how well they both got on and it hadn't escaped her notice either that while they were talking under the bird tree, Audrey had not once, but twice, cast her eyes across the garden to Cecil. She inhaled the sugary air and sensed the blossoming of young love.

*   *   *

That night Audrey lay in bed and brooded on the sudden infatuation that had, quite inadvertently, changed the colour of everything. She couldn't sleep and she was too restless to read. She could hear the ghostly whistles of the policemen who patrolled the streets as they signalled to each other

41

and a warm breeze now slipped in through the open window, carrying with it the scent of the orange trees and jasmine, but neither the sweet smells from the garden nor the reassuring whistling could soothe her tormented spirit. It was humid, too hot to find a comfortable position to lie in. So she threw off her covers and tiptoed down the stairs, across the blue shadows into the silent hallway. Once out in the garden she could breathe again. The dew seeped in between her toes, cool and wet and pleasurable. Following their earlier footsteps through the orange orchard she recalled the brief conversation with Louis that had so unsettled her. She conjured up his easy smile and the distant light in his eyes and dwelt on his frightening unpredictability and delicious impulsiveness. He seemed beyond the rules that everyone else lived by, following his desires with little regard for protocol and etiquette. Audrey was captivated by this man whose vague charm was in sharp contrast to his direct speech. She couldn't work him out—there was no one else like him to set a precedent. In spite of her instincts that warned her against him she was unable to harness the cyclone that whipped her emotions into foam. There was something terrifyingly unstable about him but at the same time oddly familiar. She felt at ease with her fear.

When she returned to her bed sleep no longer eluded her but wrapped her in dreams so pleasant she longed to hold onto them. In the twilight gloom of her imaginings she danced with Louis across the old cobbled streets of Palermo. Their bodies were united, so close she could feel the heat of his skin through her dress and the warmth of his breath on her neck and they both knew the steps as if they had been dancing them all their lives.

CHAPTER THREE

When the Garnet family returned to Buenos Aires at the beginning of March after six weeks in the Uruguayan resort of Punta del Este they discovered to their disappointment that while Cecil Forrester had continued to grow in everyone's esteem his brother had done little to win people's affection. Of course, his antics hadn't escaped the notice of the Crocodiles, who were only too delighted to discuss them during their Thursday afternoon painting session in Diana Lewis's overgrown garden.

'He does play the strangest tunes on the piano,' Diana said, dipping her brush into a jar of murky water before bringing it up to her mouth to lick it dry. 'He goes into a trance with that serious look on his face. Most peculiar.' Of the four Crocodiles she appeared to be the most innocuous, innocently making comments for the others to interpret and seize upon like hyenas, thereby distancing herself from the actual kill. But she enjoyed the ripping of flesh no less than the others. 'Sky, I find sky so dreadfully difficult,' she complained airily, waiting for the others to pick up the bait she had just laid. She could always count on Charlotte Osborne.

'Diana, ever the queen of understatement. He's positively loopy. The piano is the least of it, after all, he's a gifted musician, there's no doubt about it. It's his whole manner I find disturbing. I don't

43

believe his mind is all there.' She lowered her voice and hissed, 'Loopy, quite loopy. He didn't lose it in the war like all those brave heroes. No, Louis Forrester is mercurial and bohemian without good reason. I am not prejudiced against people who are different; poor Dorothy Franklin's son is simple, born that way, and one has complete sympathy. But Louis isn't simple, just arrogant. Yes, it is a form of arrogance not to wear a tie for dinner, for example, not to bother with one's appearance. He displays an open disregard for convention and it's convention that shapes our society and keeps us all civilised. Louis Forrester isn't very civilised, is he?' Charlo sniffed her disapproval. 'You've got a blue mouth, Diana,' she added curtly, observing her friend over her glasses with eyes as narrow as a serpent's. 'I just wash the sky in.'

'What do you mean, wash?' Diana retorted, forgetting to wipe her mouth.

'Well, I just dip the brush in water and wash it all over the page, then add a tiny bit of blue, tiny, tiny. Look, like this.' She demonstrated with exaggerated strokes across the paper. 'There, rather effective don't you think?' She sat back and admired her painting in the same way that she admired everything she did in her life, with total confidence. Still attractive at sixty-eight with a handsome face, intelligent blue eyes and fine silver hair, she believed that allure was dependent on self-assurance not beauty. It didn't matter what one did; as long as it was done with utter decisiveness one would always be admired.

'Very effective, Charlo,' breathed Phyllida Bates deferentially, passing a dry tongue over thin, scaly lips. Possibly the most poisonous of the four,

44

Phyllida was cowardly yet utterly ruthless. With the spine of a reptile she always twisted in whichever direction the majority turned and relished the spilling of guts more than anyone else. 'Are you suggesting, Charlo, that Louis Forrester is, to put it delicately, mentally unstable?' she asked, rubbing her arthritic hands together with pleasure.

Charlo laughed out loud. 'Trust Phyllida to be delicate. Delicate but incisive.'

'Mad,' Cynthia Klein interjected from behind her easel. The least malicious of the Crocodiles, Cynthia's only vice was to say things as she saw them, good or bad. 'He's definitely mad.'

'I agree,' said Charlo, nodding her head. 'It's the look in his eyes that unsettles me. There's something very unpredictable about him, not to mention self-indulgent. He's handsome enough, but the dishonour of not fighting for one's country negates anything positive about him. Do you know I saw him dancing all by himself the other night after dinner? I was on the point of leaving when I saw his silhouette in the moonlight. It was unmistakeably him. That hat set crooked on his head, no one else wears it like that, especially at night! Imagine dancing all by oneself without any music. Most peculiar. His brother is clearly embarrassed by him and I don't blame him. Cecil is a decent, beautifully mannered young man who returned from the war a hero. A true hero. It's because of men like him that we've been saved from the horrors of Nazi Germany. He risked his life for all of us while his silly brother danced the war away. The shame of it! One wonders why on earth he came out here in the first place.'

'I think it's obvious why he came out here—

because he had disgraced himself in London.' Diana chuckled, wiping her clumsy hands on her painting smock.

'Well, he's got off to a bad start,' said Charlo. 'We all know his secret. He can't run away from such shame. What do you think his excuse is, pacifism?'

'For certain—or some mad religion,' said Diana, taking pleasure in adding another dimension to the subject.

'Oh yes, he's probably a member of some sect,' Phyllida agreed in a thin voice. 'Black magic under the guise of pacifism.'

'Come on, girls, this really is taking it too far. He's not a bad person, just a little too unpredictable for us old people,' said Cynthia, tearing the paper off her easel and discarding it on the grass with the other painting she had started and grown tired of. 'One can't blame him for not fighting without knowing why. Perhaps he has a perfectly legitimate reason. Besides, I think he's attractive, in a roguish way. I'm rather partial to that vulnerable look in a man. He clearly needs looking after. One wants to mother him.'

'In your case, Cynthia, you'd be grandmothering him,' said Charlo with a sneer.

'Pot calling the kettle black, Charlo, my dear. You're so many years beyond your prime one can barely remember it.'

'Those poor girls, all waiting hopefully for marriage, what with such a shortage of young men.' Diana sighed, bringing the brush up to her mouth, adding a touch of green to her blue lips. Charlo watched her put more paint on her face than on the paper and smirked.

'No mother in her right mind will want him for a son-in-law,' said Cynthia. 'If I were fifty years younger I'd put my money on his brother Cecil. Now he's a sensible young man.'

'Oh, he most certainly is,' Diana gushed, remembering his gentle manner the day he had helped her into her car. 'Such a gentleman. He possesses true nobility.'

'Unfortunately, girls can be very stupid,' said Charlo loftily, 'they don't always know what's best for them. Some poor fool will fall for Louis' vague charm.'

'Fine for a flirt but not for life,' Cynthia added. 'One wants a man who's reliable and solid, like an oak tree. My Ernie was an oak tree if ever there was one.'

'An oak tree!' Charlo exclaimed. 'More like a twig. After you'd whipped him into shape there was precious little left of the man.'

'Really, Charlo, sometimes you go too far,' Diana chided. 'Don't bother getting into the ring, Diana,' said Cynthia with a smile, 'I'm more than capable of defending myself and Ernie, God rest his soul. Charlo, not one of your three husbands was an oak tree.'

'Well, you're right about that,' she agreed, dipping her brush into the paint and resuming her work. 'Perhaps I'll have better luck with the fourth,' she added provocatively.

Cynthia raised her eyebrows. 'Ah,' she sighed, unable to resist the bait. 'Colonel Blythe is more of an oak tree. Fourth time lucky, perhaps.' Charlo's pale face smarted with embarrassment beneath her sunhat.

'Colonel Blythe?' exclaimed Diana and Phyllida

47

in unison, rising to peer over the top of their easels as quickly as their old legs could lift them.

Cynthia was triumphant. 'How many times has he asked you to marry him?' she demanded. 'Come on!' Charlo stiffened on her stool and lifted her chin in an effort to maintain her composure. She had no intention of marrying the colonel. He only asked her for sport. He enjoyed the game, that was all.

'Twice,' she replied nonchalantly. Phyllida and Diana stared at each other in amazement.

'And what did you tell him?' Cynthia continued.

'Oh, really, this is all very childish,' Charlo protested, putting down her brush and standing up.

'Well, Charlo, what did you tell him?' Diana insisted, then turned to Cynthia, 'What did she tell him?'

'I told him,' said Charlo, articulating her words with emphasis, 'that I have a nasty habit of burying my husbands. I don't think he'll ask me again.'

'Poor Colonel Blythe,' Phyllida sighed, sitting down again. 'What has an old man like him got to look forward to?'

Charlo rolled her eyes and strode into the house.

*   *   *

Audrey had spent those six weeks by the sea in a wistful, romantic vapour, placing herself among the whimsical heroines of the novels she read. She had lain on the sand, silently playing out scenes in her imagination where Louis loved her, acting out each moment of their courtship in exhaustive detail until her desires had penetrated her dreams and she had longed to stay in bed in the mornings to make them last. No one had noticed the faraway look in her eyes because she had always been distracted, ever since she was a child. Her mother put it down to the romantic novels she consumed while Aunt Hilda complained that she shouldn't read such rubbish for it was turning her mind into cotton wool. 'Love never did anything for anyone,' she commented sourly. 'Look at Romeo and Juliet.'

Audrey had returned to Hurlingham full of anticipation. Excited and nervous at the prospect of seeing Louis again she was thrilled to be back in the same city as he, breathing the same air. But Audrey was to be bitterly disappointed. When she heard from her mother and Aunt Edna that Louis was fast disgracing himself at the Club she hid her mortification behind a determined smile then cried later when she was alone in the garden. She sat on her mother's rose bench and sobbed with frustration. Her dreams were felled before they had even had time to grow. A romance with Louis was impossible and there was precious little she could do about it. The first she heard of her mother's hopes for her and Cecil was when she overheard her talking with her sisters beneath the leafy vine which now reminded her of Louis like everything else in the garden.

'But he's only just arrived,' Rose protested, shaking her head and frowning. 'I believe everyone deserves a chance. After all, appearances can be deceptive.'

'Sometimes appearances are a true reflection of the person's character,' Aunt Hilda insisted, pursing her thin lips together in disapproval. 'In Louis's case he's as sloppy as those funny trousers he wears. You can imagine what the Crocodiles are saying.'

With agitated fingers Aunt Edna tapped the string of round amber beads that dripped over her bosom like shiny pebbles and snorted in irritation. 'Those crocodiles are so malicious,' she declared. 'It's because he didn't fight in the war. I'm sure he had good reason.'

'Does he look like he has a legitimate reason? A limp, one hand?' Aunt Hilda interjected briskly. 'No excuse.'

'Oh dear, poor Cecil, he must worry terribly about his wayward brother,' said Rose.

'Dear Cecil,' Aunt Edna sighed with a smile. 'I noticed how taken he was with Audrey the night they came to dinner.'

'So did I,' Rose agreed meekly, unable to contain her pride that suddenly flowered across her cheeks. 'I can't help but hope,' she added, shrugging her shoulders anxiously.

Aunt Edna fanned herself with the red gypsy fan that Harry had bought her in La Boca during those heady, newly wed days. 'Me too. What a good match he would make,' she gushed. 'How fortunate he has come to live in Hurlingham.'

'Isn't he a bit old for Audrey?' said Hilda tightly, her voice thin with resentment for Cecil hadn't yet met her daughters.

'Oh, Hilda, one can't dwell on details,' Aunt Edna snapped impatiently. Aunt Hilda never missed an opportunity to dampen everyone else's pleasure out of bitterness at the lack of pleasure in her own life.

Aunt Hilda stiffened. 'But he's twelve years her senior,' she protested. 'Audrey's far too young to be thinking of marriage. Dear me, my Nelly is already twenty-five and marriage is very far from her mind.'

'Sour grapes, Hilda,' Aunt Edna sniffed tactlessly. 'I do love Nelly but she isn't the most enchanting of your daughters and she doesn't help herself. Perhaps if she managed the odd smile occasionally she might encourage the young men to court her.' Hilda had to admit that for once Edna was right. Nelly was eye-wateringly plain.

'As if age has ever made a difference in the affairs of the heart,' said Rose. 'Anyhow, I did notice the beginning of an affection between them. I just pray it grows into something stronger. I've invited both boys to Audrey's party on Saturday,' she added. 'Cecil, because he's an asset anywhere, Louis out of generosity. One must be kind.'

'You're a good person, Rose,' Aunt Edna declared. But Aunt Hilda was unable to compliment her sister because her jealousy had formed a cork at the top of her throat and the words, as much as they bubbled up, were unable to advance higher.

Audrey retreated into the house, blinking away her tears. She didn't want a party any more. She didn't want to see Louis ever again. She wished she had never laid eyes on him. But as her father always said, 'everything comes to pass' and in spite of her resistance Saturday dawned, bringing with it the dreadful anticipation of seeing the Forrester brothers.

'What's the matter with you, Audrey?' Isla asked over breakfast. 'It's your party tonight, you should be smiling from ear to ear. Just think of all that attention. I'm going to dance until sunrise!'

'Nothing's the matter,' she replied flatly. 'I just don't feel like it.'

51

'You will by this evening. You've just got out on the wrong side of the bed.' Then she narrowed her green eyes at her sister and grinned knowingly.

'You're in love, aren't you?' she said. Audrey nearly dropped her cup of coffee.

'Of course I'm not in love,' she protested, putting the cup down so as not to expose her trembling hands.

'Yes, you are,' Isla laughed. 'I can tell. You've been mooning around all summer. Ever since you met Cecil Forrester.' Audrey's shoulders dropped with relief and she sat back in her chair.

'Is it that obvious?' she heard herself responding.

'I'm afraid it is. But only to me, because I know you so well.'

'You won't tell, will you?'

'Of course not. I promise. Why, if you're in love with Cecil, are you dreading your party?' Audrey played for time by bending down and pretending to pick up her fallen napkin. Isla had a point; if she was meant to be in love there was little logic to her ill humour.

'Because my feelings aren't reciprocated,' she replied carefully, amazed by her own capacity to lie.

Isla sighed melodramatically. 'You are so unaware of your own appeal, Audrey,' she exclaimed. 'For goodness sake, all the boys fall in love with you and Cecil more than anyone. He made it very obvious that night at dinner.'

'But it's been weeks, he's probably forgotten all about me.'

'I doubt it. Absence makes the heart grow fonder and all that. I bet he's longing to see you,' said Isla confidently. 'He's very correct. Not like his brother,' she added, her voice heavy with admiration. 'You'll see him today at the Club for sure. Let's go early, play some tennis and swim. Daddy's taken the boys riding and Mummy's got golf with Aunt Edna. We can spend the whole day there. Gosh, isn't it nice to be back!'

'Don't you think I should just wait until my party?' she began weakly.

'Absolutely not,' Isla retorted. 'Hurry up and finish breakfast then we can go immediately.'

*   *   *

They set off on their bicycles down to the Hurlingham Club. The streets resounded with barking dogs, squeaking children and the shrill cries of the maids as they chatted to one another in Spanish across the garden fences. Audrey confided to her sister about her infatuation and the torment she was suffering because of it. To her surprise it was a relief to be able to speak openly of her feelings, in spite of the fact that they were both talking about two entirely different men. As they approached the gates Audrey's heart accelerated and she suddenly felt hot and uncomfortable. 'Calm down, Audrey,' said Isla in amusement, jumping off her bicycle and leaning it up against the wall. 'Gosh, you have been badly hit, haven't you!' she exclaimed, taking her sister by the hand. 'Perhaps we should swim first and then play tennis. That way you can cool off a bit first.' Audrey agreed and they made their way straight to the swimming bath. It was early and the grounds appeared deserted, drenched in the dazzling light of morning. A few people could be seen in the distance walking their dogs or riding up the avenue of tall plane trees but otherwise they were quite alone, able to enjoy a swim undisturbed.

All the while Audrey glided up and down the pool she had her eyes fixed on the park and her heart suspended in her chest, anticipating Louis' appearance at any moment, longing for it and dreading it in a conflicting mixture of emotions. Each time someone appeared up the steps her stomach lurched with expectation, only to be disappointed, until Isla suggested they play tennis before the heat became too much, thus dragging her away from her anxious vigil.

But Audrey was barely able to concentrate on her tennis game either. Isla was much the superior player and began to get irritated when Audrey missed the ball or hit it into the net out of sheer inattentiveness. Audrey wished she had stayed at home to read her novel under the bird tree and dream. Suddenly dreaming seemed so much more pleasant than reality. Finally, in exasperation, Isla insisted they go to find Cecil at the clubhouse. 'No, we mustn't!' Audrey exclaimed in horror. But Isla was unwavering. Nothing would give her more pleasure than hunting him down before slaying him with one of cupid's arrows.

'We'll go and get a drink, have a look around, I'll be subtle,' she insisted. But Isla and Audrey had very different interpretations of the word 'subtle'. Isla had never once kept any of Audrey's secrets, not out of malice, but out of an exuberant inability to keep anything to herself. Now Audrey faced the possibility of being thoroughly humiliated in front of Cecil. She wished she had denied the whole thing. But Isla was enraptured by the state of her sister's heart and was determined to be the one to sort it out. Audrey knew very well that it wasn't the romance that seduced Isla but the excitement of the challenge. Audrey had now provided her with a most enthralling mission.

She reluctantly followed her sister's buoyant steps towards the clubhouse, hoping both brothers had gone away for the day, or better still, returned to England on the ship they had come out on. But to her acute embarrassment she heard a familiar voice, followed by Isla's shrieks of excitement. 'Cecil!' she exclaimed. 'How lovely to see you again.' Audrey raised her eyes to encounter the diffident smile of Cecil Forrester who, on seeing the young woman whose face had dominated his thoughts and dreams for almost two months, now flushed with joy. He felt awkward in her company and struggled to compose himself. Audrey couldn't help but cast a quick glance over his shoulder to see whether he was accompanied by his brother. He was not.

'Hello, Audrey,' he said, nodding formally. 'You've been playing tennis, I see.'

'Yes,' she replied. 'Not very well, I'm afraid. We were just coming in for a drink.'

'Why don't you join us?' Isla trilled happily. Cecil's face revealed his enthusiasm in a dazzling smile and Audrey found it impossible to be angry with Isla or irritated by him. His enthusiasm was very flattering.

*   *   *

The three sat at a small round table in the tiled

55

corridor, drinking lemonade and Audrey tried her utmost to be spirited when all she wanted to do was lie on one of the deckchairs in the shade and think of Louis. While she answered Cecil's questions and fielded Isla's unsubtle comments she secretly contemplated Louis in the quiet halls of her imagination. She recalled the sudden fire in his eyes when he had talked about the tango, when his body had moved to his humming as if he had been powerless to stop it, when he had told her not to be afraid to dream. She smiled outwardly so that Cecil believed her to be smiling at him and not at his unseen rival. Isla was triumphant. They were clearly enjoying each other's company. But neither Isla nor her sister realised that Cecil's heart was also in turmoil. For weeks he had been agonising over whether to ask her out for dinner, just the two of them. After all, she was the boss's daughter and he had only just arrived in Buenos Aires. He knew it wasn't appropriate to jump in so quickly. He had to earn Henry Garnet's respect before declaring his feelings. He only hoped that no one else would win her heart before he had time to try.

After about an hour the heat had intensified and Isla had grown restless. Her sister's infatuation with Cecil no longer entertained her for the challenge had been met and won. She had brought them both together, made suggestive comments and encouraged their friendship—the rest was up to them. Then a strange melody wafted in from the hall, a doleful tune in a minor key and Audrey recognised it at once because it was Louis' melancholic spirit translated into music. Her cheeks prickled with yearning as she realised suddenly that it was also a reflection of her own rootless spirit striking a chord within her. Unable to remain a moment longer at the table she muttered a hasty apology and fled, following the hypnotic sound of the piano.

* * *

When Audrey stood beside the piano, watching Louis' long fingers gliding across the keys, she noticed that he wasn't reading a score but inventing the music as he went along. His eyes were closed and he was following his feelings as if he were riding a wave on the sea, aware of her presence without needing to see her. His fingers trembled slightly and his mouth curled into a small smile. Then little by little as his spirit rose, the minor chords were transformed into major ones until his melody was surprisingly happy and full of hope.

After a while Louis opened his eyes. He rested them on the blushing young woman who swayed to his music without even realising. Then his mouth extended into a wide smile and Audrey found herself smiling too because Louis had the artlessness of a child, jumping from melancholy to joy in a single moment. Audrey found such spontaneity disarming and her spirits lifted with his.

'Come and play with me,' he said, making room for her on the stool.

'No, really, you play so well,' she protested. 'I can't improvise.'

'Of course you can. Come, I'll show you.'

Audrey sat down beside him and immediately felt the warmth of his body against hers, burning through her clothes. She rested her nervous fingers over the keys and waited for his instruction.

'These are the notes we're going to use, G minor,' he said, playing a chord. Audrey copied him and played the G minor scale. 'There, that's not too hard, is it?'

'I spent years learning the scales.'

'You play them beautifully. Now, I'm going to invent a tune for you, "Audrey's Sonata", and once you've familiarised yourself with the melody I want you to close your eyes and slowly let your feelings move your fingers. Don't worry if you make mistakes, it doesn't matter. Soon your fingers will be an extension of your heart and you won't think in terms of notes but feelings. You'll feel the need to express them. Now close your eyes.'

Audrey obeyed and listened as he began to play slowly, a sad, engaging tune that stirred her restless soul. Then he spoke over the music in a soft, hypnotic voice, drawing her away from the hall in the Hurlingham Club, to a faraway place where they were alone beneath a dark sky in an enchanted valley. Tentatively her fingers began to touch the keys. Falteringly at first, a note here a note there until they lengthened into phrases that threaded into his and united with them; a doleful sonata of dreams.

As the strangely alluring tune resounded through the hall the old colonel, who was sitting in his usual leather chair reading the *London Illustrated News*, put down his paper and listened. He sat as if petrified while the music melted the frost that old age had sketched upon his heart and felt a thawing in his joints so that when he finally pushed himself up he did so with the agility of a much younger man. He snorted in puzzlement and

58

shook his head as the echo of that melody still rang in his ears. When he looked around the world looked softer. He blinked, then blinked again. It remained soft as if an invisible hand had buffed away the sharp edges. 'Curious,' he mumbled to himself. 'Most curious.'

*　　　*　　　*

Later in the day when Audrey joined her family for lunch in the tiled corridor her body was still swaying to the music they had made and her eyes had glazed over with imaginings inspired by Louis and his wandering soul. She no longer feared him. On the contrary, she felt she understood him.

She knew she shouldn't love him, but he was the most loveable human being she had ever met. He was otherworldly and he had captured her spirit with his music, with his passion and with his impulsiveness that somehow made him vulnerable. She ceased to hear the small voice of her conscience for the internal melody of her love had muffled it.

'Are you excited about your party?' Aunt Edna asked Audrey when they all sat down to eat.

'Yes,' she replied. Aunt Edna frowned at her lack of enthusiasm.

'She's nervous because she's in love,' Isla explained in a loud whisper. Audrey's face throbbed scarlet with mortification and she shot her sister a wounded look. 'I'm sorry, Audrey.' She laughed. 'But it's written all over your face, they were bound to find out in the end.' Their three younger brothers sniggered into their hands.

'Don't embarrass your sister,' Rose chided

gently, silencing her sons with a reproachful glare, though she longed to ask her daughter with whom she was in love. Audrey lowered her eyes and wished for a miracle to magic her away, but Isla's ebullience was by now totally out of control.

'She's in love with Cecil Forrester,' Isla blurted, her thick curls swinging about her face as she bounced in her chair with delight. 'But she doesn't think her feelings are reciprocated. Only Audrey could be so modest.'

'Let's change the subject,' said Henry firmly. Rose caught her sister's eye and without even moving her eyelids she communicated her pleasure with the utmost discretion. Aunt Edna responded in the same code. After a lifetime of mute messages the two sisters understood one another perfectly. Cecil would indeed make a good match for Audrey.

CHAPTER FOUR

Audrey sat alone in the shade of a eucalyptus tree, gazing out across the grounds of the Club with weary resignation. She knew she should never have trusted Isla, but like a fool she had once again been lured into confiding in her sister. Now her parents thought she had lost her heart to Cecil. If they knew the truth, they'd be mortified.

Her mind drifted then to Emma Letton. She wondered how very different Emma's life would have been had she married the Argentine. Happier, or had it been no more than an infatuation that would have died in time? Perhaps

60

she had been expressing a subconscious yearning to break the rules. To experience what life was like outside the sheltered confines of their insular community.

She knew Cecil was the right man to fall in love with. Not only because she instinctively understood what was expected of her but because she had heard what people were saying about the brothers. Cecil was the sensible, responsible one with good looks and charm and a solid, prosperous future. Louis was the wayward and impulsive one. The one who had failed to fight for his country.

'Are you all right?' came a deep voice from behind her. She turned around to see Cecil standing over her, his face in the sun, squinting at her through his dark glasses.

'I'm fine,' she replied, then sighed apologetically. 'I'm sorry I rushed out like that this morning. It was the heat, it suddenly made me nauseous.'

'Well, I hope you've recovered. It's cool here in the shade.' He grinned at her so that the lines around his mouth creased into his skin, already tanned from the hot Argentine summer. 'Do you mind if I join you?' Audrey shook her head and watched as he sat down beside her. It was then that she noticed he was in his riding clothes. Shiny brown leather boots over white jodhpurs and polo shirt.

'You play polo?' she exclaimed in surprise.

'I played a little in England,' he replied, then chuckled. 'I'm not very good, though.'

'You'll improve here. This is the land of polo.'

'I know. I play racket sports well, I've got a good eye for the ball, so polo should come naturally. Practice makes perfect.'

'Yes, it does,' she agreed, gazing out into the distance. 'Don't you just love it here?'

'It feels like home already. Charming people and an idyllic way of life. No grey skies in this part of the world and no post-war gloom.'

'I hear you came back a hero,' she said, wondering how she could steer the conversation around to Louis. 'You must be very brave.'

'One never knows how one is going to react in a war. I worried I might discover I was a secret coward. But it made a man out of me.'

'Everyone's talking about your heroism, especially Colonel Blythe, you have a true admirer in him.'

Cecil chuckled, 'I like the Colonel very much.'

'Louis didn't fight in the war, did he?' she asked, knowing the answer but wanting an excuse to mention his name. Cecil's face turned grey and his mouth twitched at the corner.

'He's not like others, I'm afraid.'

'That's part of his charm,' she said, turning her face away in an attempt to hide the light that burned through her cheeks.

'You're unique if you think he's charming,' he said, amazed and grateful that she looked for the good in Louis and found it. This sympathy encouraged him to confide in her. 'Oh, Audrey, I despair sometimes,' he groaned. 'I worry for him, for his future.'

'But, he's doing all right in Daddy's company, isn't he?'

He shook his head and laughed. 'You're so sweet, Audrey. He earns a salary because your father is a very generous man. Louis just wants to dream and play the piano. If it wasn't for his music

I'd think he was a lost cause, but he's very gifted. It's a shame he can't channel that talent into other things. But he doesn't want to work. He could be a concert pianist, one of the very best. He could teach music, compose, but he lacks the will and the discipline. Instead he sits in a stuffy office in the city behind a desk sketching everyone's faces in caricature. He's in a world of his own where no one else can reach him. Not even me.'

Audrey's heart stumbled at that moment because she knew that she had reached Louis, that he had invited her into his world, that she had made herself at home there. Cecil looked so strained when he spoke of his brother she wanted to reassure him by telling him of their shared love of music and their piano playing, but she held back. When Cecil looked at her steadily she saw how he admired her and she didn't want to crush him. He hadn't appeared vulnerable before, but now, talking about his brother, he looked defeated.

'Has he always been like that?' she asked, picking up a fallen leaf and rubbing it between her fingers to release the medicinal scent of eucalyptus.

'Yes. He was always happier on his own than with other children. He didn't seem to relate to anyone. The only time he came to life was when he played the piano. My mother had a large grand in the drawing room at home and he'd sit playing for hours, inventing tunes even before he began to learn to read music formally. He could play anything, you'd only have to hum a tune and he'd transform it into something incredible. I don't know where that gift came from, neither of my parents are particularly musical. My mother plays only because her parents forced her to learn when she was growing up, but she isn't a natural, not like Louis. Then he didn't enlist when all the other young men of his age volunteered to fight. That was an awful blow for my father, who fought in the Great War and was awarded an MC. He's a proud man, a military man, he's never understood Louis. Mama, being a woman and more sensitive, did her best, but then gave up when Louis drifted further and further away.'

'What about Cicely?'

'Ah, Cicely, she's a female version of Papa. Louis was always an embarrassment. She pretended he was adopted. She used to say it so often I almost began to believe it, so unlike the rest of us is Louis.'

'How cruel,' Audrey gasped. 'Did Louis know?'

'I'm afraid he did, but he didn't seem to mind. I don't think he wanted to belong to us. He doesn't want to belong to anyone. I brought him out here because I thought a new place would be good for him. A place where no one knows him, where he can start from scratch.'

Audrey looked at him, her faced aglow with admiration. 'You're a very kind man,' she said, her eyes brimming with gratitude. 'Louis is so lucky to have you to look after him.'

'I do my best, but at times I wonder why. I get little thanks and it hurts me to hear people criticise him.'

'They're rude because they don't know any better. It's a small community, if you don't conform to their standards you're an outcast. I've seen it,' she said, thinking of Emma Letton.

'I'm afraid Louis doesn't stand a chance.'

'Oh, but he does. He'll win them all over in the end. I've never heard anyone play the piano more beautifully—anyway, he's not odd, just eccentric and artistic. He's unique, a very gifted, very special human being.'

'You're sweet,' he said, losing his heart to her all over again. 'If I tell you a secret, will you promise to keep it, no matter what?'

Audrey nodded gravely. 'I promise,' she replied.

Cecil stared into the hazy blue distance. 'Louis wanted to fight. He wanted desperately to join the war effort but he wasn't allowed to. It's his health you see.'

'What's wrong with him?' she asked in a thin, anxious voice.

Cecil sighed heavily, aware that he was divulging something that only his immediate family knew. He hesitated a moment, fighting with his conscience. Then pushing aside his reservations he said in a low voice, 'He had a psychotic breakdown a few years ago.'

'What's a psychotic breakdown?'

'A nervous breakdown. He was hospitalised for a few months with severe depression. He's unable to cope under pressure. He can't be relied on, you see.'

'I see,' she said slowly, her heart flooding with affection for this deeply troubled young man. Then she added after a moment's thought, 'I'm sure love would cure him. He needs someone to love him and look after him.'

'We all need that,' said Cecil softly. He looked at her with steady eyes.

'He's obviously too sensitive for such a cruel world,' she concluded.

'You understand so well and you're so young. Where does this wise head of yours come from?'

Audrey laughed bashfully. 'I don't think I'm particularly wise.'

'Yes, you are.'

'I read a lot. I read everything. Novels, hundreds of novels. You learn a lot about human nature through literature.'

'Well, it's taught you well.'

'Thank you.'

'No, thank *you*, Audrey. I've been feeling so low recently. You've made me very happy today. I shall enjoy your party tonight.'

'Me too.'

'Will you promise me a dance?'

'Of course.'

'May I ask you a favour?' he said suddenly, his head tilted on one side, a frown creasing his forehead. She nodded.

'I hate to ask this of you . . .'

'Please do, I'm sure I won't mind,' she replied, hoping that she wouldn't.

'Will you dance with Louis?'

Audrey blinked at him in amazement. 'Of course,' she replied, barely able to restrain the smile that tickled her lips.

'If you set a good example, Audrey, I believe the rest of the community will follow. Everyone thinks so highly of you.'

'Don't worry, Cecil, I'd be pleased to,' she said confidently.

Cecil relaxed his shoulders and sighed with gratitude. 'You have a very sweet nature, Audrey. No one else has been so generous to Louis. I'm afraid he won't thank you, but I thank you on his behalf.'

'I don't need thanks, everyone deserves a

chance,' she replied, not knowing what else to say. But Cecil thought her the kindest, most gentle human being he had ever met. Later when he thundered up and down the polo field Audrey was on his mind and in his heart and he didn't care that he kept missing the ball because he had finally met the woman he wanted to spend the rest of his life with.

*   *   *

For Audrey a bath was always a sensual experience. Scented with rose and lavender oils she lay in the pink water surrounded by steam, left alone to sink into her secret world of dreams. Isla's shrill voice rang down the corridor as she argued with Albert but Audrey was far away with Louis, sitting on the top of a green mountain where they could lift up their hands and touch the sky. She hadn't been able to stop thinking about the music they had created together at the piano and his words that had transported her into his world of make-believe. She closed her eyes and recalled every moment with such intensity that she might as well have been living them again. She pictured his sandy hair and dared to run her hands through it, feeling with her fingertips the texture and breathing in the spicy male scent which clung to his scalp. She touched his face, the lines that extended out towards his temples from his eyes and those that happiness had imprinted on his cheeks with each smile and with each burst of laughter. Then she found the furrows that melancholy had carved deep into his skin and she kissed them lightly in a bid to erase them and the memories that lived in them. She lay in the bath until the water had cooled and the steam had condensed. She opened her eyes and reluctantly emerged from the realm of fantasy. She had read all about the pain of love in literature but now she understood it. Her limbs ached and her heart strained against the excess of emotion that flooded into it. She knew her mother would be appalled and she didn't even risk imagining what the Crocodiles would say if they knew how her soul longed for Louis. But she was unable to arrest her growing affection. She could think of nothing else but him.

*   *   *

The dining room at the Hurlingham Club spilled over with an abundance of arum lilies and gardenia, lilacs and honeysuckle, drowning the musty smell of old wood and formality with their intoxicating perfume. The tall doors opened out onto the gardens which were bathed in the amber light of evening and misty with humidity. Audrey stood on the threshold with her sister and watched the sun set into a pink sky. Contrary to fashion Audrey and Isla wore their hair in long bouncing curls that fell thickly down their backs to their small waists and gently curving hips of blossoming womanhood. Their silk dresses reached the ground and rustled likc autumn leaves when they walked, showing off the gentle slope of their bare shoulders and the luminosity of their skin. Isla's dress was ice green to match her eyes while Audrey had chosen duck egg blue. They both wore long gloves and grown-up faces, aglow with excitement. 'I love this time of day,' Audrey sighed, thinking of Louis. 'It's so romantic, you long for it to last, but suddenly it's gone, taking all this beauty with it. I suppose part of the attraction is its transient nature.'

'Who are you going to dance with then?' Isla asked, much too animated to dwell on such a commonplace thing as a sunset. 'I'm going to dance with everyone. In fact, I'm going to dance all night without stopping. I suppose you'll dance with Cecil till dawn.'

'Perhaps,' she replied cagily and a small smile caused her lips to quiver at the corners. There was only one man she wanted to dance with.

'As the birthday girl, you can dance with whoever you choose.' Isla laughed.

'I'm very proud of you both,' said their father, appearing behind them, his shiny black shoes tapping across the floor with characteristic precision. The girls turned around and smiled at him with affection. 'Beautiful young ladies,' he added, noticing their flowering figures and their poise. 'You do me credit, both of you.' Audrey and Isla swelled with happiness, for their father didn't often give praise and when he did he meant it. Even Isla, who enjoyed testing the boundaries, couldn't help but feel a certain delight in pleasing him. 'It wasn't so long ago that you were two very little girls,' he continued, reflecting on the rapid passing of time. 'As you know, Audrey, the year of your birth was marked by the visit of The Prince of Wales and his brother, Prince George. It only seems like yesterday that I danced with your mother in this very room while you slept in your cot back at home.'

'And Mummy danced the best of all,' Audrey added with an indulgent smile; she had heard this

69

story a thousand times. Henry Garnet drew himself up with satisfaction.

'Indeed she did,' he replied, sniffing his admiration. 'There's no one who can waltz like your mother.'

'Not even Aunt Edna and Aunt Hilda?' said Isla, grinning provocatively so that her face suddenly lost its poise and creased into a childish smirk. Henry was unable to hide his amusement as he recalled Aunt Edna's solid body swinging clumsily off the arm of some generous-spirited man who had asked her to dance and Aunt Hilda who was so thin and dry she looked as if the vibrations of the music alone might snap her.

'They're not natural movers like your mother,' he replied diplomatically.

Isla laughed out loud. 'Nothing natural about either of them,' she giggled.

Her father chuckled. 'Now, Isla, that's a little unfair, don't you think?' he said, then added, 'You are both fortunate to have inherited your mother's grace. Audrey, I would like to have the first dance with you tonight.' Audrey's face broke into a wide smile and she blinked up at him with pleasure.

'I would love that,' she said.

'The young men will just have to wait,' he added when he saw how delighted his daughter was. She made him feel twenty years old again.

*   *   *

As the guests arrived, leaving their gifts on the table at the entrance, Audrey searched the faces for the only one that mattered. Aunt Edna entered with Rose and Aunt Hilda with her four pasty daughters and her husband Herbert striding pompously ahead in white tie and tails. The Pearson sisters tumbled in, twittering like two spring sparrows followed by Colonel Blythe and Charlo Osborne, who still managed to dazzle in a long silver gown with her shiny white hair pinned on top of her head, twinkling with lustrous pearls. When the other Crocodiles saw her arrive on the arm of the Colonel they immediately formed a tight circle, where they remained gossiping fanatically until the Colonel rushed at them as if he were a lion, scattering them like a trio of vultures picking at a piece of old meat.

*   *   *

The band played and the guests mingled and Audrey tried her best to concentrate as she greeted them all, extending to each a courteous remark or a flattering compliment on the dress or the hairstyle, so that no one left her company without commenting on her charm and goodness. 'Rose, I really must commend you on your daughters. Utterly enchanting girls, especially Audrey,' Phyllida Bates gushed with genuine admiration. Before Rose could thank her, Cynthia Klein, who had her back to the group, turned around swiftly in order to give them the benefit of her opinion.

'I agree with Phyllida,' she said vigorously. 'It's a joy to see such refinement and class. There are enough plain girls here to send the young men back to war. Really, their insipid little faces make my eyes water,' she commented loudly. Rose blushed and glanced about anxiously to see if anyone had heard.

'You're so right, Cynthia, though I would never have said it with such candour,' Phyllida agreed, her beetle face pinching with pleasure.

'Beauty is only as deep as one's skin,' Rose objected tactfully, attempting to laugh off her unkindness, hoping someone might come and rescue her.

'But, my dear, it's the skin we all have to look at,' said Cynthia with a snort. 'What use is a sweet nature if it doesn't show through one's skin?' she continued with the insensitivity of old people who feel it is their right to say exactly what they think. Then to Rose's relief the tall, starched figure of Cecil Forrester stepped in to break up the conversation and save Rose from her embarrassment.

'Good evening, Rose,' he said, bowing slightly. Then he turned to the Crocodiles and greeted them both by name. 'What a beautiful evening,' he commented by way of complimenting the hostess on the magnificence of the room. Rose, who understood such reserve, thanked him gratefully.

'Now, *this* is a decent young man,' said Cynthia, who had by no means finished with Rose Garnet. 'Cecil, there's one young woman in this room worthy of you and I suggest you snap her up before somebody else does.' Rose blushed again.

'You're putting me on a pedestal, Mrs Klein, I fear I do not deserve,' he replied with delicacy.

'Absolutely you do,' Phyllida insisted.

'I hope you have booked a dance with the birthday girl,' said Cynthia, raising her eyebrows expectantly.

'I have,' he asserted then turned to Rose. 'It will be a great honour.'

'I'm so glad,' she replied, a little flustered. 'Don't listen to Cynthia, she's being far too kind.'

'Come, come, Rose, you know me better than that. Phyllida, tell Cecil how I never say things I don't mean.'

'If you're referring to Audrey, Mrs Bates, you don't need to convince me of her qualities,' said Cecil, raising his eyes above the crowd in search of her.

'Come, Cecil, I know my husband would like to see you,' said Rose, seizing a good moment to extricate themselves. 'Please excuse us,' she added to the Crocodiles, who, the moment she had gone, scanned the room for their next prey.

*   *   *

When Audrey saw Louis through the vibrant froth of silk and bow ties she was filled once again with the familiar sense of buoyancy that she had felt earlier, after their duet on the piano. Unable to control her features, a broad smile illuminated her face and her cheeks flushed with excitement. Then he saw her too and he smiled back, a smile disarming in its honesty and tenderness, as if he had come only for her. In that brief and fleeting moment, when the candour in their gaze revealed feelings they could no longer suppress, they both felt that they knew the other more intimately than they knew anyone else in the world. As the party bubbled about them Louis and Audrey declared their love, silently but undeniably, and neither wanted to be the first to pull away.

*   *   *

When the music played the first waltz, Audrey was obliged to dance with her father. But she didn't mind, for as she glided about the floor she could feel Louis' eyes watching her and carrying her through her steps, giving her more energy and grace so that her father had to focus on her face to reassure himself that he wasn't dancing with his wife, eighteen years before. But Audrey didn't feel Cecil's eyes following her from the other side of the room. Greatly encouraged by his conversation with her mother he felt that in time, when they knew each other better, it would be appropriate to invite her out for dinner. Of course, he would ask her father first, out of respect, but his intentions were honourable; they were for life.

*   *   *

When the dinner began, Audrey was seated between Cecil and James Pearson, the twins' elder brother. She still hadn't spoken to Louis. She hadn't had a moment as she was swung from the arms of her father into those of her Uncle Herbert, who had insisted on holding her in a lecherous clinch for two dances and then into the awkward embrace of Cecil who had patiently awaited his turn with the discipline of an army officer, shoulders square, back straight and chin high. Audrey hadn't needed to look past him to check that Louis was still watching, for she knew; his gaze rested on her like the heat of the sun and she smiled because of it, a deep smile that affected the whole of her face. Cecil was certain she was smiling at him, for her eyes didn't waver once from his, but

74

stared into his soul as if she understood him completely.

Dutifully Cecil filled Audrey's plate from the buffet and then talked to her with animation until dessert. Audrey was anxious to find Louis and scanned the room for him while Cecil did his best to entertain her. Alarmed that he was nowhere to be seen she excused herself and rushed off to the Ladies Powder Room where she bumped straight into Isla, giggling wickedly. 'Audrey,' she screeched, 'I danced with Uncle Herbert and I swear to you he had a nut in his pocket.'

'A nut in his pocket?' Audrey asked in confusion, pacing with agitation up the floor.

'Yes, you know, a *nut!*' she repeated, her green eyes wide with mischief. She then collapsed into laughter again. Audrey suddenly understood and shook her head.

'How disgusting,' she exclaimed. 'He's your uncle.'

'It was a pathetic little nut, no wonder Hilda's bitter all the time.' Isla smirked.

'Isla!'

'She is. Uncle Herbert's little nut wouldn't satisfy a mouse.'

'I think you've had too much to drink again.' Audrey sighed, suddenly forgetting her frustration and focusing her attention on the feverish face of her sister.

'I'm not going to dance with him again, ever,' Isla continued. 'What good is a man with a small nut? I must go and tell Aunt Edna, she'll love it!' and she flounced out of the bathroom, leaving Audrey alone in front of the mirror, gazing into her pale face in anguish. The evening would be over soon and she still hadn't danced with Louis.

Suddenly Louis' cheerful face appeared around the door. Audrey sat up with a start. 'Louis!' she exclaimed in horror as if she had been caught thinking out loud. His eyes settled on her with tenderness and his mouth curled up at the corners as if he had heard her thoughts.

'I know this is strictly off limits for men, but you've been in here for ages and Cecil says you've promised me a dance,' he said, raising an eyebrow. Audrey couldn't help but laugh. She stood up, her cheeks aflame and walked toward him. 'I've been waiting all night,' he added, taking her by the hand. They both felt an inner jolt as they touched for the first time, and Audrey was relieved her satin gloves came between them, as if the sensation of his skin against hers would debilitate her completely. But the heat of his hand melted through the satin and seemed to rise up her arm and into her chest as he gently led her across the room. She was sure her body glowed like a Chinese lantern. 'You didn't doubt me, did you?' he asked seriously, stepping onto the dance floor and pulling her into his arms with confidence. Overwhelmed by the proximity of his body pressed against hers, she could only shake her head and smile, blinking up at him as the scent of his skin invaded her senses and set her mind alight with thoughts she knew she shouldn't have.

They allowed the music to lead them, gazing mutely into each other's eyes. As they moved smoothly around the room they were unaware of the ripple of admiration and surprise that vibrated through the party, for no one had expected the 'eccentric' Louis Forrester to dance with such grace. For a moment even the Crocodiles saw past the unpolished shoes and dusty tailcoat and were struck by his handsome face and the intense light in his eyes as his spirit soared on the waves of the music. 'My dear fellow,' muttered the Colonel to Cecil, shaking the ice in his empty glass with an unsteady hand. 'He might not know one end of a gun from the other but he's bloody good on his feet. Who'd have thought it, young Louis of all people!' Cecil felt a stab of jealousy before remembering that it had been he who had suggested Audrey dance with his brother. Suddenly he wished he hadn't.

Audrey felt nothing but the pressure of Louis' hand on her back and the warmth of his chest against hers. She knew she had never danced so well. They glided as one complete being, as if they had danced together through many lifetimes and knew the other's responses as well as they knew their own. When the dance ended Louis didn't wait around for the next but without a word led Audrey out into the privacy of the gardens beyond where they could finally be alone.

The lawn was lit by a bright crescent moon which smiled down at them from a clear, starry sky. It was humid and the air was heavy with the dulcet scents of dew-soaked grass and gardenia. Louis didn't let go of Audrey's hand but held it tightly as they walked away from the party until the music was little more than a low murmur in the distance and they were engulfed in the mysterious silence of the night. He stopped at last and took both her hands in his. 'I'm deeply in love with you,' he said, squeezing her fingers to emphasise that he meant it. Then he shook his head and sighed heavily. 'I feel elation and yet, at the same time, a deep sadness, like one does in the face of a beautiful sunset or a magical view. I feel melancholy.' Audrey was touched by his honesty and vulnerability.

'I feel it too,' she replied, amazed by her boldness.

'Melancholy?' he asked, blinking down at her fondly.

'No, love,' she said and to her surprise she didn't blush, or tremble or stammer. With an impulsiveness that made her laugh he threw his arms around her and drew her into a tight embrace. Then his lips touched the soft flesh of her neck and the sensation of his bristles against her skin rippled all the way down her body like a pebble thrown into a pond and she wound her arms around his shoulders to steady herself.

'Why do I feel melancholy?' he asked into her ear.

'Because beautiful things always make us sad,' she replied, closing her eyes and nestling her head against his.

'Why?'

'Because we can't hold onto them forever.'

'No, they're transient, like a rainbow or a sunset. Nothing beautiful lasts. Or perhaps because they remind us of where we come from and our spirits long to return,' he whispered.

'Perhaps.'

'Do you believe in God?' he asked.

'Yes, I do.'

'So do I. Do you believe in Fate?'

'Yes.'

'I believe that God created us for each other. I believe that Fate brought me to the Argentine for

78

you.' Audrey laughed softly. 'I knew it the moment I saw you. It was like lightning. Sudden and unexpected. I thought about you while you were away. I thought about you every moment of the day. My heart ached for you. I don't know why, but I feel you're the only person here who understands me. The only person I can be myself with. With everyone else I'm someone different. I had a lot of time to think, Audrey, while you were in Uruguay. I wondered whether you were looking up at the same sky and thinking of me. I tried to ignore my feelings, hoped they'd go away, but they only got worse. I had only met you once and yet, your face stayed with me. As if it was meant for me. I tried to ignore it, after all your father is my boss and I'm not the sort of man he would appreciate courting his daughter.'

'I know,' she sighed sadly. 'You're too impulsive for your own good.'

'I couldn't ignore my heart, Audrey. I tried to. But I couldn't,' he explained. 'When we talked that evening in your garden, I knew you understood me. When we played the same music today, that confirmed it. You do understand me, don't you, Audrey?'

'I do understand you, Louis,' she repeated quietly, knowing how much it meant to him to be understood.

'You don't realise how alike we are. You dream impossible dreams and your heart is too big for your body. Oh, Audrey, your heart is as big as the ocean and mine is as big as the sky, I thank God that I've found someone with a heart big enough to accommodate mine.'

Audrey swallowed as her emotions caught in her

throat. 'You say such beautiful things,' she whispered.

'Because with you I feel such beautiful things. With you the music in my head no longer torments me because I'm creating every tune for you.'

'I was frightened at first. You scared me. The intense look in your eyes, your boldness, your impulsiveness and yet, now you don't scare me at all. I want to wrap my arms around you and take care of you. You're like a rare beast, a beautiful rare beast of the forest and I want to nurture you and love you and look after you.'

'Now you're saying the most beautiful things,' he said and tears glistened in his eyes because no one had ever cared about him before. His parents had always been ashamed of him because he was different, but Audrey loved him for his differences. He felt like a little boat in a rough sea finally drifting into port. With Audrey the real world felt a safe place to inhabit.

As the music from the party reached them, dancing on the air with the scents of the pine trees and damp grass, Louis held her close and moved in time to it. 'Oh, Audrey, how have I lived so many years without you?' He took her face in his hands, paler and even more lovely in the silver light of the moon, and softly kissed her forehead, her eyes and then finally her lips. She knew it was wrong to kiss him so soon but she didn't care. She shut her eyes and allowed him to kiss her the way lovers kissed in her novels, the way Emma Letton was kissed beneath the sycamore tree. She didn't feel nervous, she just felt an exquisite sadness, the type of sadness that comes when one is faced with something of great beauty. She wrapped her arms around him and followed her senses like that afternoon on the piano and all the while she was holding him the tune he had composed for her replayed itself again and again, hypnotising her with a strange magic that vibrated between the notes, casting an indelible score on her mind.

CHAPTER FIVE

It was five in the morning when Audrey and Isla crept across the shadows in the hallway. Dawn was singeing the horizon and illuminating the sky that only moments ago had been dark and impenetrable. Audrey had floated back, her body still swaying to the music that had been carried across the lawns from the party by a warm, sugar-scented breeze. Overcome by the beauty of the fragile morning light that cast the streets and houses in a pale amber glow and filled once again with that sweet melancholy, Audrey's spirit brimmed with love. She wasn't tired. She could have waltzed all night, out there among the clicking crickets and watchful plane trees, who like sturdy sentinels had hidden their forbidden dance behind the leafy screens of their branches. There he had kissed her. Now she felt different, as if that kiss had opened her eyes to a more beautiful world. Looking about her everything was more defined, more brilliant and she wanted to embrace the God that had given her Louis.

Isla wasn't tired either. She had danced without pause, oblivious of her sister's sudden disappearance as she had swung from partner to partner, aware that she was one of the most enchanting girls in the room and relishing the admiration she received. She followed her sister into her room and flung herself down on her bed. 'Oh, Audrey, I have had the most heavenly night.' She sighed melodramatically, flicking off her shoes. 'I wish it hadn't ended.'

'Me too,' Audrey replied truthfully, hiding her secret behind a knowing smile.

'I saw you dancing with Cecil.'

'Yes.'

'And you sat next to him at dinner.'

'Yes.'

'You must be very happy. He's got love written all over his alarmingly handsome face,' she giggled.

'It is handsome, isn't it?' Audrey agreed, unzipping her dress and slipping into her dressing gown. 'But there's something very sweet about him too. He has a vulnerability I hadn't noticed before,' she added, reflecting on the conversation they had shared that afternoon.

'If you say so.' Isla laughed. 'He's not my type.'

'Who is then?'

'No one,' she answered nonchalantly. 'I'm not interested in romance.'

'But of course you are, Isla,' her sister insisted. 'You're attractive and spirited, there must be someone you admire.'

Isla sighed and raised her eyes to the ceiling in thought. 'No, I've tried, really I have, but no one has the power to move me,' she stated with arrogance.

'Yet,' Audrey said, sitting down at her dressing table and brushing her long, brandy-coloured hair.

'I'd rather a dog,' she said. 'I'd love a big, shaggy

dog. You see, dogs don't demand too much, they don't get jealous and they don't want to be kissed other than chaste kisses on their muzzles. Yes, I'd much prefer a dog.'

'Isla, you are ridiculous sometimes.' Audrey laughed.

'Mummy's really excited about Cecil. She thinks he'd make the perfect husband for you.'

'Well, I think her excitement is a bit premature,' said Audrey. 'After all, we haven't even held hands.'

'But you've danced.'

'Yes, but . . .'

'Dancing can be like making love,' Isla said provocatively, watching her sister through narrowed eyes.

Audrey's brush hesitated on her hair and she stared into the face in the mirror, barely recognising the woman who now returned her stare with self-awareness. With the right man, a dance could be a physical act of love. Two bodies moving together. Two souls separated only by skin. Two hearts calling to each other through the bars of their ribcages. Isla didn't know just how right she was.

'Can I share your bed tonight?' Isla asked, snuggling deeper into the pillow. Audrey frowned at her.

'We haven't shared a bed since we were children.'

'I know. But I want to. You're my sister and I feel you're growing away,' Isla explained. 'Soon you'll be married and we won't be on our own any more. You and me against the world. It'll be me against the world and you and Cecil somewhere else, in the blissful land of marriage.'

83

Audrey laughed. 'All right. If you want to.'

'Hardly seems worth going to bed,' Isla said and yawned. 'If Albert wakes us up I'll be furious.'

'He'll find your bed empty and think you're still dancing.'

'I will be, in my dreams.'

Audrey slipped beneath the sheets and closed her eyes. She too was still dancing, dancing with Louis down the leafy passages of her imagination. When Isla's hot body wrapped itself around her sister's, Audrey was almost asleep. As she hovered on the brink of slumber she felt the reassuring sensation of another being next to her, heard the gentle rise and fall of breath and the occasional movement as her sister arranged herself into a comfortable position. She wondered what it would feel like to lie in Louis' arms. She wondered so intensely that she closed her mind to reality and opened it to the random world of dreams.

*   *   *

She was lying in Louis' arms in a small attic at the top of a house, oddly familiar to her in the illusory realm of her subconscious. Louis' face was staring tenderly into hers, caressing her features with his eyes and with his fingers. Loving her with kisses and unspoken words expressed in a language forged over many lifetimes. She heard the distant music of the tango as if the musicians were settled beneath the window, playing only for them. She basked in the warm reassurance of his embrace and in the certainty that she belonged to him and he to her in an eternal bond that no one could break. Then the music seemed to fade into the distance, replaced by the cold, methodical drumbeat of a march. Suddenly Louis' face became Cecil's and his caresses were at once unwelcome. She squirmed and yet she didn't try to get away because she knew it was what she had chosen.

An icy claw scratched her heart and awoke her with a jolt. She opened her eyes to the reassuring sight of her pale blue bedroom, the linen curtains billowing at the window, the early morning light tumbling in with the breeze and the cheerful dawn chatter from the bird tree. She heard the seven a.m. siren from the Goodyear factory in the distance and her sister's deep breathing and remembered where she was. Her heartbeat slowed but the dream continued to haunt her. She was afraid to close her eyes in case the image of Cecil returned with the ominous sense of destiny that hovered in the wings ready to snatch her future away.

*   *   *

As Audrey embarked upon a secret and dangerous romance with Louis Forrester her dream receded into the shadows of her memory until it no longer troubled her, so certain was she of their future. However, they had to use all their resources and ingenuity to see each other. Louis worked every day in the city with his brother, taking the train early in the morning from the small station in Hurlingham. Not to be defeated by the seemingly impossible nature of the situation he devised a way of communicating through little notes that he would hide in a hole in the brickwork of the station house as he left in the morning and retrieve her reply from the same place at the end of the day. He spent evenings at the Garnets' house quietly sketching caricatures of Aunt Edna and portraits of Audrey and Isla while Cecil sat on the terrace with Rose and Henry oblivious of the tender glances that passed between the young lovers. Then at night, when the long hours of waiting were finally over, Audrey would creep out of the house and into the garden where Louis would be waiting for her in the orange orchard, hidden beneath the umbrella of a cherry tree.

To mask her feelings for Louis she devoted more attention to Cecil. As long as she shared the same air as Louis she was prepared to welcome the attentions of his brother, for if everyone suspected her heart to be attached to him her true feelings would naturally go unnoticed. So absorbed was she in her secret world that she failed to realise Cecil's growing confidence and her parents' increasing speculation on the gentle progress of their affection for one another.

*   *   *

'Why doesn't he court her?' Aunt Edna sighed one Saturday afternoon while the girls lay in the sun up at the pool with Cecil and two of Hilda's insipid daughters, Agatha and Nelly. Rose smiled hopefully, leaning on her golf club.

'Henry says it's because he's a correct young man,' she replied. 'You can understand, poor Cecil, being in love with the boss's daughter. I imagine he wants to take his time, assure himself of her affection, before asking Henry's permission.'

Aunt Edna nodded her head in approval, picking

up her golf club again. 'What beautiful manners he has. Most other boys would dive straight in there without asking.'

'Not Cecil,' said Rose. 'He's a different type of man altogether. I know it's only been a short time since he arrived in the Argentine, but I'm so terribly fond of him.' She bent down to place the ball on the tee.

'So am I,' Aunt Edna agreed. 'But I'm also fond of Louis.'

Rose stood up and positioned herself for the drive. 'Oh, me too. I've got to know him better over the last few weeks. He's a wonderful artist and plays the piano most beautifully. He's just not the sort of man one would want for one's daughter.'

'True. Isn't it lucky Audrey's so sensible,' Aunt Edna commented.

'Oh, Audrey wouldn't fall in love with Louis, she's much too intelligent. No, she needs a strong man with a stable job and a good, solid personality. Now Isla's more of a worry, she's likely to fall in love with the most unsuitable man just to cause trouble.'

'You're going to have to watch that one,' Aunt Edna chuckled.

'So are you,' said Rose with a smirk. 'We all are.' Rose swung the club a couple of times to get her eye in, then shuffled her neat feet, pulled the club back and swung down upon the ball. 'There, much better than yesterday, don't you think?' She laughed as the ball was launched into the air in a perfect arc.

'Goodness me, Rose, that was awfully good,' her sister congratulated with admiration. 'The thought of Audrey and Cecil is really improving your game.'

Rose tried to hide the smugness in her smile, but she was so confident of their attachment the effort proved too much and she grinned openly.

'It's improving everything,' she replied.

*　　　*　　　*

Cecil was confused. One moment Audrey was giving him her full attention, walking with him around the garden in the evening, sitting talking to him up by the swimming bath, laughing with him while they watched his brother play the piano in the hall, always with animation as if there was no one more important to her than him. Then the next moment she would appear distracted, gaze out into the half-distance lost in thought as if he wasn't there. During those interludes he knew there was nothing he could do to reach her. It was those brief dives in the steady rise of their friendship that delayed his asking her out properly. They threw his mind into doubt. He longed to discuss it with Louis, but Louis wasn't the sort of brother one could confide in, he wouldn't understand. Louis had never been in love and probably never would be. His mind was elsewhere. So Cecil resolved to keep his anxieties to himself and be patient; after all, her actions suggested that she preferred his company to any other, so he had all the time in the world.

While Cecil brooded on the object of his desire, Louis and Audrey believed there was nothing that could come between them and they congratulated themselves on their powers of deception.

'I want to take you to Palermo,' Louis announced one night in early April. 'I want to dance the tango with you.' Audrey frowned apprehensively, she felt very safe behind the wall in her garden. The idea of sneaking off into the city in the middle of the night filled her with fear.

'Oh, I don't know, Louis,' she began. 'How will we get there?' Louis took both her hands in his and kissed them, one at a time.

'You don't have to worry, my love, I'll never let anything happen to you.' He watched a small smile alight across her troubled face. 'Your problem is you think too much.' He chuckled, brushing her cheek with his fingers. 'Do you remember when I told you not to be afraid to dream?' She nodded. 'Well, I'm not afraid to dream, or to turn my dreams into reality.'

'And I so want to,' she replied, anxiety and excitement rising together in her chest and making her shiver in spite of the humidity. 'I'm worried we'll be seen.'

'In Palermo?' he exclaimed. 'Who's going to see us there at one in the morning?'

'I don't know.' She laughed. 'I don't know what I'd do if we were discovered.'

'We're not going to be discovered until the time is right. In the meantime, I want to dance with you.' He watched her blush as she recalled her sister's shameless analysis of dancing. Then as if he read her thoughts he added, gazing at her with eyes made heavy by the weight of his emotions, 'I want to be close to you, Audrey, and here on this bench is not close enough.' She knew what he meant and blushed a deeper crimson.

'All right,' she conceded. 'Let's go to Palermo.'

Louis jumped to his feet, pulling her up with him and gathering her into his arms where he pressed his body against hers, one hand in the small of her back, the other threading his fingers through hers and holding it against his chest. Humming softly he proceeded to dance with her on the glittering grass in the orange orchard. At first she giggled at his impulsiveness but then, when his forehead leant wistfully against hers she no longer laughed, but felt as he did that familiar melancholia that is the weight of love on one's soul. Neither spoke. They just moved slowly to the low murmur of his voice as he sung the sonata he had composed for her.

*　　　*　　　*

The following morning Audrey cycled as usual to the station to retrieve Louis' note. It was another hot day in a relentless string of hot days. The sky was a cornflower blue, almost violet and the sun seemed to pulsate as if barely able to cope with its own force. The station was quiet. Only a couple of bony mongrels trotted up the track, sniffing the ground for scraps like a pair of wild prairie dogs. She leant her bicycle against the wall and walked hastily onto the platform. Finding the hole in the brickwork she pulled out the little piece of white paper that in the last few weeks she had come to depend on.

> Tonight we'll dance the Tango together in the cobbled streets of Palermo. Watch the clock and think of me for today every minute will drag. I long for you with every muscle in my body. I'll meet you tonight in the same place at the same time. Don't be afraid, my love will protect you.

He always signed it 'From he who loves you most' and she in turn signed hers 'From she who loves you dearly' as a precaution against the notes being discovered by someone else. She smiled as she read it over and over, running her thumb across the paper that he had held in his hands only a couple of hours before, then she brought it to her mouth and passed it over her lips, closing her eyes as if it had the power to transport her closer to him. Finally she folded it away and placed it at the very bottom of her pocket, pulling out her own note that she had written in the early hours of the morning, when sleep had seemed to her an unnecessary waste of time when she could spend it better, thinking of him. She opened it and read it again, taking pleasure from the thought of him returning home that evening and reading it himself. It said simply:

Today I love you more than I did yesterday, which I never thought was possible. There is no limit to my devotion.

Satisfied that her words would please him she rolled it up into a tiny scroll and pushed it into the hole. She then stood back and looked at the wall to make sure that it wouldn't catch anyone's eye unless they were looking for it.

'*Todo bien, Señorita*?' said Juan Julio, staggering out into the sunshine from the cool shade of his office. Audrey sprung around guiltily, hoping he hadn't seen her place the paper into the wall.

'Oh, fine, thank you, Juan Julio,' she replied in Spanish. He straightened his hat and pulled his trousers up over his round belly. His face was red and sweating. He was too fat for this heat and too lazy for a job such as his. He sighed heavily as he waddled slowly towards her like a penguin having just feasted on a sea full of fish.

'How hot it is today,' he commented without caring that he had said the same sentence to everyone he had come into contact with for the past two months.

'Yes, it is.' She nodded. 'I like the heat.'

'Oh it doesn't suit me,' he lamented, mopping his forehead with a grubby hanky. 'It's always hotter on the platform. Not good for my blood pressure. Not good at all.' He walked past her towards the signal box. Audrey's shoulders relaxed with relief. He was too deep in his own stupor to notice the notes or to even ask what she was doing there. She skipped off to where she had left her bicycle and bumped straight into Diana Lewis and Charlo Osborne, dressed in cream hats, silk dresses and long pearl necklaces as if off to a garden party.

'You're looking very happy today, young lady,' observed Charlo, when she saw Audrey's bright eyes and smile.

'It's a lovely day,' she replied, picking up her bicycle.

'What are you doing here of all places?' Diana asked, removing her gloves. 'Far too hot for these,' she muttered to herself, squashing them into her handbag. Audrey decided it was best to avoid the question and diverted their attention to themselves.

'Are you going into town?' she asked.

'Charity luncheon in the city,' Charlo sighed. 'But one must do one's duty,' she added sanctimoniously, looking Audrey up and down with her sharp blue eyes.

'One certainly must,' Diana agreed. 'Mind you, it's too hot to be in the city on a day like this. Good God, I'm already glowing. Still, one must think of all those poor people and do what little one can.'

'How is that dear Cecil Forrester, Audrey?' Charlo asked silkily. 'I gather he spends an awful lot of time at your house.'

'Yes, he and his brother both do,' Audrey replied innocently. 'They're both very well.' Charlo's mouth twitched with frustration. But Diana wasn't going to leave without throwing a piece of bait into the water.

'You look full of the joys of life, Audrey,' she said. 'Oh to be young and in love again!' She sighed, shaking her head so that her chins wobbled like a fat chicken. Audrey frowned at her.

'Come on Diana, I can hear our train, we wouldn't want to miss it.'

'And do the poor out of precious funds, no we certainly wouldn't,' Diana added. They waved good-bye to Audrey as she cycled up the road then entered the stationhouse gossiping about Audrey and Cecil's advancing friendship, which they were both certain would amount to marriage at some time in the near future. 'She'd be a fool to let that one go,' Diana said, pulling out her purse.

'She's no fool, that I assure you,' Charlo sniffed confidently. 'She knows what's good for her. Always done the right thing, ever since she was a child.'

*   *   *

93

Audrey dreamed the day away while Isla and her brothers were at school and her mother was at the Club playing golf with her sisters. She sat on the bench in the shade reading, but although her eyes followed the lines of prose her mind was in another realm, the one inhabited by Louis, the place where she was happiest to be. As irritating as the Crocodiles were she had to congratulate herself on the success of her deception. Everyone thought she had lost her heart to Cecil and as much as she longed to shout her true feelings from the rooftops she knew that her patience would pay off in the end, when at last they would be able to declare their love to the world without facing disapproval and prohibition. They'd all see the good in Louis in time.

The hours passed as slowly as Louis said they would and she watched the clock and thought of him watching it too, willing the time to fly. Finally day succumbed to night and darkness flooded in to hide their secret in cool pools of shadow that even the moon was unable to penetrate. Once again Audrey removed her shoes and tiptoed down the stairs, taking care to avoid the floorboards that she knew creaked. As she left the house she was too excited to notice the pair of eyes that silently watched her from the upstairs window.

*   *   *

Louis met her beneath the cherry tree in the orange orchard as usual. Sometimes she'd go there in the daytime, when he was at work, and sit in a daze, feeling with her senses his vibrations that lingered in the boughs and in the leaves as if part of him was still there. After embracing her and kissing her ardently he led her out into the street where a car awaited them, hidden around the corner like a crouching puma. The driver knew where to take them and Audrey sat in Louis' arms, watching the mysterious world of the night pass by the window. As they drove into the city she noticed at once that far from being sleepy the streets were throbbing with activity. The lights dazzled and the cars tooted their horns, impatient to reach their destinations. The smoke-filled restaurants heaved with people and music reverberated across the leafy avenues and plazas where couples walked hand in hand in the warm glow of the streetlamps. She squeezed Louis' hand to show him how pleased she was that she had come and he squeezed it back in silent agreement.

As they drove into Palermo the scenery changed completely. The wide avenues were reduced to narrow cobbled streets which ascended a hill and opened into a small square around which little restaurants and cafés tumbled out onto the pavements next to the dark windows of antique shops, closed for the night. The car stopped and Louis told the driver to come back for them in a couple of hours. They walked around the square, happy to step out together in a place where no one knew who they were and no one cared. They kissed in the plaza then embraced to the music that seeped out from beneath the door of an old tavern. 'Now, we're going to learn how to dance tango,' he said, leading her towards the music. Audrey held back.

'Do you know this place?' she asked apprehensively.

'Yes, I've been here a few times already and Vicente is expecting us,' he replied.

'Vicente?'

'You'll love Vicente, he's a character.' He kissed her fingers. 'Don't be afraid, I've already compromised you by bringing you here, we might as well enjoy ourselves.' He grinned at her and once again the charm of his smile disarmed her and she found herself following him willingly into the tavern.

Vicente recognised Louis immediately and shuffled over, weaving his way through the clutter of round wooden tables crammed with smoking guests. An old man with silver grey hair, small brown eyes and a nose that one could hook a fish on, Vicente revealed his eagerness to please and his sensibility in his jovial expression. Known in Palermo for his tango nights and good wines he beckoned them to follow him to the back of the house where he gave them a glass of his best *vino tinto*, complimented Audrey on her beauty and grace then indicated with an impatient nod that his wife should start the music again, from the beginning. 'The steps aren't so important at this level,' he began, rolling up the sleeves of the white shirt that he wore beneath a black waistcoat. 'You have to feel the music and let it lead you.' He beat his chest with his fist to illustrate his point and emphasised the word 'feel' by closing his eyes. Audrey grinned up at Louis, who smiled back, understanding from her expression that they had mastered that step already. 'Now hold each other close,' he instructed as Louis pulled Audrey into his arms. 'Closer, the tango is a dance of passion. It is like making love.' Audrey blushed and tried to hide her face in Louis' neck. 'Don't be bashful, Señorita, the tango is a sensual dance so release all those inhibitions and follow your heart.' He pounded his chest again with his fist. Louis chuckled and kissed her temple reassuringly.

'I'm following your heart, Audrey, because it's ensnared mine,' he whispered into her ear.

'Then we have no choice but to dance together,' she replied and began to move to the soul-stirring notes of the violin and accordion.

*   *   *

At first Audrey was nervous. Each time she felt herself pressed against Louis' body she giggled and stiffened, aware that they were indeed experiencing a physical intimacy they hadn't experienced before and they weren't alone to taste it in private. But once the complicated steps had been repeated over and over and finally mastered she closed her eyes so that all she could feel was Louis and the music and the impassioned notes of her own internal melody.

For the next hour and a half Louis and Audrey learnt to tango under the guidance of the ebullient Vicente, who with great delight led them through each step with the passive assistance of his sullen wife, Margarita, who never once smiled but danced with the agility of a woman twenty years younger. Promising to return the following week they skipped out of the tavern and into the square where they fell on each other again and danced beneath the moon out of the shadows, eager to put into practice what they had just learned.

'I'm so glad we came.' Audrey sighed with

happiness as they moved in time to the distant music from the tavern.

'I dreamed of bringing you here,' he replied, resting his cheek against her hair. 'I knew you'd love it. You see, you've left the theatre by the back door and isn't it fun?'

'I love the sense of freedom. No one knows us here. No one judges us. We're just two strangers like everyone else, dancing in our own secret world. When I'm close to you like this I feel that nothing else exists but us.'

'You've made life beautiful for me, Audrey,' he said, moved once again by that familiar sense of melancholy. 'As a child I only felt secure when playing the piano. Without music the world was a grey and frightening place. No one understood me. It was as if I was living in a different dimension to everyone else. I felt like an outcast. So I retreated into my music and gave up trying to relate to my family and their friends. But you, Audrey, you've given me the courage to love. You've opened my heart and now I'll never close it, ever. It will always be open and you'll always be in it. There's no turning back now. We belong together.' He pulled away so that he could look down at her earnest face illuminated in the golden glow of the streetlights. Then he traced the line of her jaw with his fingers and kissed her on her lips. Aware that time was running out they clung to each other with the fierceness of two people destined to part for years. But Louis and Audrey were storing up their kisses in order to last only a day, for the following night they would meet again beneath the cherry tree in the orange orchard and they didn't dare think further ahead than that.

Audrey crept back up the stairs with a light bounce in her step as she continued to hear the music in her head. She had felt free for the first time in her life and tasted adventure and rebellion in one delicious feast. It was early morning and her clothes smelt of cigarettes, more noticeable now that she was in the clean air of her home. Quietly she opened the door of her bedroom and stepped into safety. To her surprise she found Isla asleep in her bed. She closed the door behind her as softly as she could but Isla slept with one ear alert, waiting for her sister to return even in her dreams. She opened her eyes at once and sat up. 'Where have you been?' she hissed in excitement. Then smiled mischievously. 'Have you been out with Cecil?'

CHAPTER SIX

Audrey found it incredibly difficult to lie. She had managed to tell half-truths so far, which didn't seem so bad and didn't weigh as heavily on her conscience as full lies, but now, looking into her sister's enquiring face, she knew she would tell her everything and regret it as she always did. She was unable to stop herself. She was too happy and happiness made her reckless.

She threw herself onto the bed beside Isla and stretched like a contented cat. 'I've been to Palermo,' she breathed, delirious with joy. 'I'm so in love, I feel it's consuming my entire body like a fire. There's no putting it out, it just grows and grows. Oh Isla, it really is like they write in novels. It really is wonderful. My heart feels as if it's going to burst with happiness.'

Isla's smile widened. 'Cecil took you to Palermo?' she repeated, amazed. 'I thought Louis was the adventurous one.' Audrey's face coloured with shame as she hesitated on the brink of telling her sister the truth. But Isla knew Audrey well enough to sense when things weren't quite what they seemed. She shook her head and narrowed her green eyes suspiciously. 'It's not Cecil, is it?' she said slowly, studying her sister's features with the rigour of a doctor. 'It's Louis.' Audrey pulled a thin smile, aware that Isla might be offended that she hadn't confided in her earlier and nodded her head. 'Oh, Audrey, I can't believe it. This puts a whole different colour on things,' she exclaimed in a loud whisper. 'Louis all along, eh. Aren't you a dark horse! You of all people, Audrey. I didn't think you had it in you.'

'I love him,' she replied simply, hoping honesty now would make up for lying to her.

'As Aunt Hilda says, what's love got to do with marriage?' she replied softly. 'You know Mummy and Daddy will fry you alive if they ever find out. They've got their hearts set on Cecil.' Her eyes glistened with delight as the full extent of her sister's rebellion reached her understanding and ignited in her mind all sorts of possibilities.

'I know,' Audrey replied with a groan. 'That's why we're keeping it secret for the moment, so that they can get to know him and like him. After all, he's nothing like his reputation suggests. He's been very wronged by everyone.'

100

'You know this place, once a reputation is made it's very hard to unmake it. Mind you, if you get caught he'll be seen in an even worse light for having led you astray.' Isla shook her head again. 'I can't believe you, Audrey. Without any encouragement from me.'

'Am I wicked?'

'Deliciously so.' Isla giggled and threaded her fingers through Audrey's hand that was hot and trembling. 'I'm so happy you're happy,' she added truthfully. 'You look radiant and to think I thought it was all thanks to Cecil.' She suddenly turned serious. 'But, Audrey, Louis is mad. He's eccentric and artistic. I know he plays the piano beautifully and I know he draws like Leonardo da Vinci, but he's got that crazed look in his eyes, terrifying. One minute he's sad, the next minute he's happy, you never know what he's going to do next. Oh Audrey, I hope you know what you're doing!'

'You don't know him like I do. He's gentle and kind, sensitive and generous. I'm sorry I didn't tell you before, I was so worried you might let it slip.' She fixed her sister with beseeching eyes. 'You won't let this slip, will you, Isla? You don't know how important this is to me.'

'Oh, I do,' she replied. 'I do.'

'So you won't tell?'

'I won't . . .' she began, 'on one condition.'

Audrey sighed. 'What might that be?'

'You tell me every detail right from the start and confide in me every step of the way.'

Audrey smiled and sat up. 'I'll tell you everything if it means I can go on seeing Louis in secret,' she said, climbing off the bed and slipping out of her clothes.

'I'll cover for you,' Isla suggested enthusiastically, longing to be included. 'Oh, what fun we'll have hatching plans and fooling them all.' Audrey hung her dress over the back of her chair. 'You'd better get up early tomorrow and have a bath, you reek of smoke.'

'Do I?' she pulled a clump of curls in front of her nose and sniffed it.

'Yes, you do,' said Isla. 'But I like it. It smells like forbidden fruit. Come on, get into bed and tell me how it all began. Did it start that first night when he came to dinner? Did you know he was The One then? When I engineered that drink with Cecil at the Club you weren't in love with him at all, were you?' Isla sighed in amazement. 'I can't believe I didn't notice. Well, I'm not going to be kept in the dark any longer, am I?' Audrey slipped between the sheets and curled up against her sister.

'I lost my heart to Louis the first moment I saw him smile . . .' she began, as if she were reading from a romantic novel. Telling Isla was a release. The unburdening of her conscience made her feel less guilty. It also enabled Audrey to relive each moment in vivid detail, setting it into the poetry of words and thereby making it more real. Isla listened to Audrey's adventures without the slightest twinge of envy. Certainly she would have liked to be taken to dance in Palermo, to sneak across the garden at midnight for secret rendezvous, to lead a clandestine existence which ran parallel to everyone else's without them having the slightest knowledge of it. But the very idea of love left her squirming with repulsion. Wet kisses, clammy hands, physical intimacy were enough to make her skin crawl with a hundred ants. The fun

102

was in the flirt, the flattery and the flouting of rules. What fascinated her about Audrey's romance was that it went contrary to everyone's expectations of her. Audrey was the sensible sister; this sort of behaviour would have hung better on *her* shoulders. Not one to be overly sensitive Isla was aware of the role reversal and she couldn't help but worry for Audrey if she got caught.

'What are you going to do?' she asked after her sister had finished describing the dance in the square in Palermo.

'I don't know. I'm trying not to think of the future,' she replied, but the future was all she ever dreamed about. 'I'm going to spend the rest of my life with Louis, though,' she said resolutely. 'Whatever happens.'

'Daddy won't be too happy to give you away to *him*. I heard him talking to Mummy in the garden a few days ago, while you and Cecil were playing chess on the terrace. They think Louis is frighteningly unreliable.'

'Just because he's not like other people,' she exclaimed in frustration. 'He hasn't murdered anyone. Goodness, people here are so narrow minded and petty.'

'I'm only preparing you, Audrey. They'll be heartbroken. Mummy adores Cecil.'

Audrey breathed in deeply as a heaviness sunk upon her shoulders like a pair of invisible hands. 'Give them time. I don't care how long it takes. They'll love Louis like I do in the end,' she argued.

'I hope so,' said Isla.

*   *   *

103

Both girls closed their eyes, but neither found it easy to sleep. Finally, they both resigned themselves to Fate, relieved to step out of the struggle and leave to destiny what neither could control. Entwined like lovers they slept with their long, corkscrew hair spilling over the pillows like silk. That is how their mother found them in the morning. But because it was Saturday and there was no school she decided to let them both sleep in. As she closed the door softly and walked away she smiled to herself; Audrey and Isla enjoyed a rare bond. As well as sisters they were friends and the thought of them asleep like a pair of puppies delighted her. She made her way down the stairs towards the commotion of her three sons and husband eating breakfast outside on the terrace, under the vines.

*   *   *

The next couple of months Audrey and Louis were able to see so much more of each other, thanks to the shrewd plans concocted for them by Isla. While Henry and Rose harboured ill-disguised hopes for Audrey and Cecil, interpreting their increasing closeness as a sure indication of their affection, Isla helped plant the notes at the station, accompanied Audrey to the Club and covered for her so that she could be alone with Louis. She rode out with them across the plains and they didn't ask her to leave because they enjoyed showing off their affection for each other and besides, they owed her so much. Without Isla their liaison would have been limited to the orange orchard. Isla was thrilled by their romantic nighttime trips into the city and kept

104

watch from the landing until they had disappeared round the corner into the shadows. Then she slept in Audrey's bed with half an ear on the door, ready to spring up the minute she returned from Palermo, her eyes sparkling with excitement, the adventures of the dawn spilling out in dreamy words like poetry. Isla loved these moments best of all. She lived the romance through her sister without having to experience the horrors of physical intimacy. They'd lie in the pale morning light, their arms casually draped over each other, and whisper until their throats ached and their eyes stung with tiredness. This was an intimacy Isla treasured. An innocence she clung onto for fear of the adult world. That was one secret she couldn't reveal to anyone, not even to Audrey. She didn't want to grow up, ever.

*   *   *

As the days shortened and winter set in, Cecil gathered his courage to ask Audrey out to dinner. The more he rehearsed how he was going to do it, the more nervous he became, until his confidence seemed to retreat with the autumn. He felt like a clumsy giant: his hands were too big for his body, his tongue too large for his mouth, his nose too hefty for his face. He had never felt inadequate before but Audrey undermined his self-assurance. There was something about her; a faraway look in her eyes, an ethereal quality about the way she floated when she walked. If he didn't know better he would have said that she was simply going through the motions out of politeness, but then he considered her nature; less passionate and

105

impulsive than her sister's. So he consoled himself that she was probably as nervous as he was.

It wasn't until the end of June, when winter had robbed the bird tree of its leaves and its song, that Cecil finally asked Audrey out.

'Isn't it bare this time of the year?' he said as they strolled through the sleeping orange orchard. Audrey felt a wistfulness wash over her as she walked past the naked cherry tree that had hidden her and her lover on so many sultry summer nights, a silent witness to their illicit love. In spite of its nakedness it still held tender memories within its frozen branches.

'Yes, isn't it,' she replied. 'But I like the change of seasons. The summer was so hot and humid, it's a relief to feel the chill of winter and snuggle up in front of the fire.'

'It is indeed,' he agreed, rubbing his hands together nervously. 'It's not as cold as England though.'

'Or as wet.'

'That too,' he chuckled. Audrey noticed his unease and the strangled tone of voice and wondered what had come over him.

There was an awkward pause as they walked through the gate at the end of the orchard and back into the main garden. The flowerbeds lay dormant under rotting foliage, like a botanical graveyard, thought Audrey, beneath which the spirits of the plants still lived and waited for their springtime reincarnation. Cecil coughed. He saw the house loom up at the end of the lawn and knew he had better get on with his task.

'Audrey,' he began. She looked at him and smiled. A smile of encouragement, he thought and

106

bravely plunged in. 'I would like to ask you out for dinner.' Her eyes flickered with surprise and her cheeks reddened to the colour of *membrillo*.

'Oh,' she said.

'I haven't asked your parents' permission, I wanted to ask you first,' he explained. She looked down at her shoes and laughed lightly. How formal and serious he was all of a sudden.

'That would be very nice, Cecil,' she replied. 'How sweet of you to ask.' He didn't know whether she understood the gravity of his request, that he was asking her permission to court her.

'I've grown tremendously fond of you over the last few months,' he persevered, hoping to leave her in no doubt about his intentions. This time a tighter laugh escaped her throat.

'Well, you and Louis have become part of the family,' she said, deliberately misunderstanding him. 'Mummy and Daddy treat you both like sons, almost.'

'They're very kind,' he agreed, watching her fold her arms in front of her chest. He found her bashfulness endearing and felt more confident as a result.

'Yes, they are,' she replied, knowing how happy they'd be that he had started to court her formally. She felt out of her depth and walked faster in order to cut the conversation short. She needed to consult Louis and Isla. They'd know what to do.

When they entered the house, Louis noticed the strained expression on Audrey's face and the proud smile that played about the corners of his brother's mouth and sensed that something monumental had taken place while he had been sketching Isla. Hastily he indicated with his eyes that she go and talk to her sister somewhere private. Audrey blinked at him with gratitude and left the room in a flurry, leaving Louis shuffling anxiously in his chair, wondering what was afoot.

Finding Henry alone in his study writing letters, Cecil asked, with his usual politeness, whether he might interrupt him for a few minutes. 'Please,' Henry replied, gesturing for Cecil to take a seat by the fire. 'Dismal day, awfully cold,' said Henry, putting his pen down and turning to give Cecil his full attention.

'I'd like to ask your permission to court Audrey,' he said.

Henry chuckled good-naturedly. 'You don't need my permission, Cecil. Audrey's got a mind of her own, it's her you should be asking.'

'Oh, I already have, and she has agreed to allow me to invite her out for dinner.'

'I'm delighted,' Henry exclaimed. 'She's not a child any more but she is inexperienced. I'm glad she's fallen into your capable hands.'

Cecil was flattered. 'I've spent months deliberating on this, Henry. As I work for you, I was worried it was inappropriate.'

'What nonsense, my dear Cecil. Rose and I have been watching your friendship blossom for a while. You have our blessing and if you have Audrey's then you have nothing to be anxious about.'

'Well, I'll go and beat my brother at chess now,' he said cheerfully, getting up from the armchair, his heart as weightless as a cloud. Henry watched him close the door softly behind him and thought how very different he was from Louis. 'Chalk and cheese,' he said to himself, shaking his head. For a horrible moment he thought of Isla and Louis as a couple and shivered. It would be typical of his wilful daughter to fall for a man like Louis. Not that there was anything overtly wrong with the boy, just that he'd make a most unsuitable husband. 'Now, he's irresponsible, that one,' he said, picking up his pen and dispelling the thought. Henry never worried about things until they happened, that was his gift. But Rose did and she had noticed Isla's growing closeness to Louis with dread. She had voiced her fears to Aunt Edna, but there was only one person who could possibly have any influence over the girl, and that was Audrey.

*   *   *

'Oh, Isla, I don't know what to do,' Audrey wailed, falling onto her bed. 'Cecil's asked me out for dinner.'

'Oh God!' Isla exclaimed. 'That's not good.' She shook her curls until they bounced about her face like springs.

'He's so formal. Straight out of a Jane Austen novel. You have to laugh. He's gone to ask Daddy's permission.'

'Oh God! Sounds like he wants to marry you.'

'Don't joke.'

'I'm not.'

'Well, that will never happen.'

'Of course not. You don't have to marry anyone you don't want to,' Isla reassured her. 'Did you agree to go?'

'I had to,' she explained, sitting up. 'I couldn't say no, not after I'd led him a merry dance for all these weeks.'

'Your acting must be better than we thought,'

said Isla with a smirk.

'Thank you.'

'You have to tell Louis,' Isla instructed, opening a drawer and pulling out a pad of paper and a pen. 'Write him a letter now and I'll slip it to him as he leaves.'

'Oh dear, I feel so helpless.'

'You'll have to go, of course,' said Isla, sitting in front of Audrey's dressing table and picking up her hairbrush. 'Anyway, it's the perfect cover. As long as Cecil courts you no one will suspect the truth. It's all part of the game, Audrey.'

'What if it goes too far?' Audrey asked anxiously.

'That depends on you,' Isla replied, watching her sister's reflection. 'You mustn't let him get too close.'

'I feel so mean, Isla. He's so sweet and kind. I'm very fond of him. I really am. I just don't want to marry him.'

'It's a dangerous game, Audrey,' said Isla, who felt like a spy in the war. 'But, you have no choice. If you turn him down now you'll be in danger of exposing your feelings for Louis. After all, just look at yourself. You look like love personified. No one's in any doubt that you're infatuated, they've just got the wrong man. Imagine looking like that with no one to cover for you. They'd all start speculating and then they'd surely guess, just like I did.'

'Oh, Isla, you make it sound so scary,' she moaned.

'It *is* scary. This is real life, Audrey, not one of your novels and the stakes are high. Now hurry up and write that note. I think you'd better meet him

110

tonight in the orchard. I'll cover for you.'

Audrey finished the note, composed herself and returned to the sitting room with her sister. Isla was puffed up with self-importance and strode purposefully across the floor. Rose watched them enter, but her focus was on her younger daughter who immediately took the seat next to Louis to watch the game of chess he was playing with Cecil.

Albert lay on the floor in front of the fire building houses out of cards with his two younger brothers. Audrey didn't dare sit near Louis, she was too agitated and feared she might give it all away so she joined her brothers and tried to distract herself with card houses. It wasn't until Cecil and Louis got up to leave that Rose's anxieties were confirmed. She saw Isla pass Louis a note. It was a subtle gesture, done with the utmost secrecy and swiftness. Rose wouldn't have noticed had she not already suspected something to be going on between them. Once they had left she summoned Audrey to her room under the pretence of wanting her advice on an outfit for Aunt Hilda's cocktail party.

Audrey followed her mother into her bedroom then closed the door behind her as instructed. Rose leant against the windowsill. She was suddenly pale and her lips twitched with worry. 'I need to ask you something, Audrey,' she began in a grave tone. Audrey felt sweat tickle the skin under her arms and her knees grew faint with anticipation. She sat down on the bed and played with her nails.

'What is it, Mummy?' she asked, trying her best to act normally. Rose was too busy fretting to notice Audrey's unease.

'I'm afraid that Isla and Louis are . . .' she

111

hesitated, searching for the words. 'Affair' was too sophisticated, 'romance' too playful. 'I think they're in love,' she said finally. Audrey could have cried with relief.

'What makes you think that, Mummy? It's absurd,' she exclaimed.

'I could have sworn I saw Isla pass Louis a note this evening.'

'I don't think so,' she reassured her. 'It certainly wouldn't be of the romantic kind, Isla's not interested. She tells me everything and I would know if she was.'

'You really think so?' Rose asked, stepping away from the window and sitting next to Audrey on the bed. 'You really think so?'

'I know so,' she added with emphasis.

Rose wiped her eyes. 'You've lifted a great weight off my shoulders, Audrey.' She sighed. 'You really have.'

'But, Mummy, what's so wrong with Louis?' She ventured bravely.

Rose shook her head. 'There's nothing wrong with him, dear,' she explained lightly, happy to be generous now there was no danger of him courting her daughter. 'He's just rather irresponsible. You know, Henry's heard all sorts of things about him from friends in London. He's a loose cannon. He's unreliable and he's got a reputation as long as a ball of wool. He's a charming young man, and handsome too, there's no doubt about that, I just wouldn't want him courting a daughter of mine. I simply wouldn't tolerate it. He isn't a man of honour, my darling. Imagine not fighting for your country. It's a disgrace.'

Audrey felt tears sting the back of her eyes and

112

swallowed hard. 'I don't think he's anything like as bad as you all say,' she protested angrily. 'I think you're all being unnecessarily cruel.'

Rose believed Audrey was defending Louis because he was the brother of the man she loved. She patted her daughter's hand and smiled indulgently. 'My dear girl, no one has the slightest doubt about Cecil's integrity and good character.'

'But Louis is a good person too. He's spontaneous and impulsive, outspoken and unconventional but that doesn't make him a bad person.'

'Of course it doesn't,' she agreed. 'He's a pleasure to have in the house.'

'Just as long as he doesn't get romantically involved with one of your daughters.'

'Well that doesn't seem likely, does it?' she replied, her cheeks now glowing with relief. 'Tell me, what did Cecil talk about on your walk? He looked very happy when he came in.'

Audrey sighed heavily, aware that she had to play the game. 'He's asked me out for dinner,' she replied in a small voice.

'Oh, how kind of him,' Rose responded, trying not to look too hopeful. 'Will you go?'

'He said he had to ask your permission first.'

'Really, how very correct,' Rose exclaimed with admiration. She stood up and began to arrange the small Victorian boxes on her dressing table in order to calm her hopping nerves. 'He has our permission. I can speak for Henry,' she said calmly. 'It's what *you* want, my dear, that's important.'

'Oh, I'm happy to go,' she said, trying to inject some enthusiasm into her voice. 'It's only dinner.'

'Of course,' said her mother. *She must be afraid,*

113

she thought, *after all it's her first dinner alone with a young man.* Then she said out loud, 'I'm sure he'll take you somewhere nice, he has very good taste. Ah, what to wear? I think we need to go into town, don't you?'

*   *   *

That night, behind the cold wall of the orange orchard, Audrey pressed her body against Louis' in a bid to stay warm. He had spent the entire evening bashing out his fury on the piano until Diana Lewis had asked him to either play something harmonious or not play at all. 'I don't want you to go, my darling, but if it means we can still go on seeing each other, it's worth it. Please tell me your parents are coming around to me.'

'They are slowly, give them time,' she replied, not wishing to hurt him by recounting her conversation with her mother.

'Time is what we don't have,' he moaned.

'What do you mean?' she asked.

'Well, Cecil's very serious about you and you're leading him on,' he explained, biting into the name of his brother with venom. 'You can't play games with him forever. You can't deny me forever either.'

'I'm not denying you, Louis,' she gasped, hurt by his accusation.

'Then let's just run off together.'

'You know I can't do that.'

'What other choice is there?'

'Damn my parents!' she hissed angrily, pulling away and looking up into his eyes. 'Why do I care so much about what they think?'

114

'Because, my lovely Audrey, you've grown up with their love,' he said, running a warm hand down her face with tenderness. He kissed her forehead. 'It's natural that you don't want to hurt them. You need them too. Oh Audrey, you're not the sort to elope, are you?'

'Are you?'

'Of course. I'd run off with you at the drop of a hat. But then, I'm irresponsible.' He chuckled sadly.

'Oh, Louis. You're perfect. To me you're perfect.'

'I love you, Audrey,' he said softly, pulling her to him again and brushing his lips across her temple. 'I really do love you.'

'And I love you, Louis,' she replied. 'Nothing else matters really. We'll always be together.'

'Of course we will. I'm not foolish enough to let you go. Besides, we've got a lifetime of adventures ahead of us. What about all those dreams of yours? Someone's got to make them come true.'

'We've already danced in Palermo,' she laughed.

'So we'll dance on the top of Machu Picchu and over the Atacama desert when it's in flower. We'll dance across the Atlantic to Paris and Rome and Vienna. We'll dance all the way around the world and I'll never let the music stop. I promise you that, my darling, Audrey. The music will never stop.'

She nestled her face into his neck, sure that he was right.

CHAPTER SEVEN

Audrey dreaded her evening with Cecil, not because she disliked his company, but because she was aware of Cecil's affection for her and knew that what she was doing was wrong and hurtful. She worried constantly about the tangle of intrigue that was slowly winding its way around her and pulling her under. It was against her nature to wound. But Isla convinced her that it was a necessary means to an end. 'Don't be fooled, Audrey, Cecil's too cold to have a warm heart. After all, how much does a fish feel?'

Cecil was unable to focus on his work, his play or on anything else that would have diverted his attention from his impending evening with Audrey Garnet. He had taken great trouble to arrange the evening because he wanted so much to impress her. He had organised to borrow Henry's Ford T to drive them into the city where they would watch the ballet from a gilded box in the Teatro Colón. He imagined them exchanging tender glances through the darkness; perhaps she would allow him to take her hand in his. That wish hung suspended in his thoughts until the telephone rang, shattering his dream and thrusting his attention back to the present moment. But after he had replaced the receiver his concentration wavered once again until Audrey's long, sensitive face surfaced to steady it.

Cecil had never discussed his feelings for Audrey with his brother, but overcome with optimism and the need to share his joy he opened his heart to Louis on the train home after work. As Cecil's face glowed with optimism and pride Louis felt his stomach twist with jealousy. He tried to dodge the subject but Cecil was determined and spoke over him until Louis had no choice but to listen. 'I didn't dare hope that she'd accept my invitation. She's unfathomable. But when she said yes it was as if the drawbridge was finally being lowered for me to step inside.' He sighed, certain that the battle for Audrey's heart was over and that he had won. Louis noticed the self-satisfied smile and was irritated. Cecil's face flushed crimson as if he were ashamed of his own smugness.

'So where are you going to take her?' Louis asked in a strangled voice, drawing his ankle onto his knee in a gesture of defence.

'Audrey's a cultivated young woman who loves music and dancing,' Cecil began in a tone that suggested he knew more about her than his brother. Louis looked out of the window, but it was dark and all he saw was his own grey face staring back at him. 'I'm taking her to the Colón to see *Giselle*,' he replied. 'She loves the ballet, you see, but rarely gets to go.' Then he added with an uncharacteristic twinkle in his eyes, 'It's a surprise.'

Louis repressed a groan and coughed into his hand. 'You've thought of everything,' he said grimly.

'I hope so.'

'But you don't even like ballet.'

'It doesn't matter. She does. It will give me pleasure to see her enjoying it.'

'Don't push her,' Louis added, unable to stop himself.

'What do you mean?'

'She's very young. If you jump in there too fast

117

you'll scare her away. Take your time.'

But Cecil was so certain of himself that he simply smiled knowingly and replied, 'This isn't a game, Louis. She may be young but she's got the mind of a much older woman. My plans for Audrey are long term and I believe she knows it.'

Louis shuddered. His brother was unwavering in his belief that Audrey reciprocated his feelings. He was suddenly debilitated by conflicting emotions. On one hand he felt guilty—Cecil's heart was being deliberately set up to be broken as if he were taking part in a monstrous pantomime. He thought of Shakespeare's poor Malvolio and regretted their wicked game. But on the other hand his guilt was tempered by his jealousy that, in a perverse way, enjoyed the certain knowledge that his brother would be crushed when Audrey finally revealed the truth. He willed himself to be patient. Time would untangle this knot.

When they arrived at Hurlingham station Louis surreptitiously retrieved the small scroll that Audrey had slipped in between the bricks and regained his good humour. Audrey loved him and no amount of courting and wooing would inspire her to change her mind and love Cecil. As they strode back up the bleak winter streets to the Club, Louis' fingers played with Audrey's note. It gave him a warm sense of reassurance. But their secret was beginning to grate on his conscience and his pride. He longed to tell everyone that she was his. He was impatient to show her off. He didn't know how much longer he could dance in the shadows.

*   *   *

Rose was so excited about her elder daughter's flowering romance that she made the grave error of mentioning their forthcoming evening out to Diana Lewis in the bakery. Diana wasted no time in telephoning Charlo Osborne who passed it on to Colonel Blythe over tea at the Club. The Colonel twisted the ends of his white moustache and huffed thoughtfully. 'I don't know a finer fellow than Cecil Forrester,' he said, puffing on his Turkish cigarette. 'And young Audrey is a treasure, always has been.'

'Beautiful girl. Beautiful,' Charlo stated. There was little she admired more in a woman than beauty and nothing she regretted more than the relinquishing of it. 'A girl has to use her looks while she's young because they don't last. Look at me. I was quite lovely as a young woman. Lovely. But now . . .' She sighed, knowing her comments would ignite the right reaction in the old Colonel. He patted her hand with his rough, calloused fingers and blinked at her with undisguised devotion through the thick glass of his monocle. Charlo was aware that since the summer the old Colonel had changed. She didn't know why but it was as if his internal baton had snapped, leaving him infinitely more human and, dare she hope, romantic.

'You mature well, like a good claret, old girl,' he said and his dry lips extended into a mischievous grin. 'Beauty is commonplace, my dear, there's far too much beauty around and not enough spice. You've got enough spice to put the entire Indian subcontinent out of business.' Charlo giggled and shrugged off the lascivious glint that was now magnified through his monocle. Was it possible that love had tamed the old warhorse?

'Really, Colonel, you're too generous,' she

119

protested, smoothing her hand over her thick, silver hair and fixing him with cunning blue eyes that were still hypnotic in spite of the reptilian quality of the eyelids.

'Come, come, old girl, you know how much I admire you,' he continued, puffing on his cigarette with more urgency.

'I don't deserve your admiration, Colonel.'

'You deserve it, but you won't take it,' he bellowed in exasperation, banging his fist on the table, sending the china jumping into the air as if the Club had just been shaken by an earthquake.

'Well . . .'

'You may have buried three husbands already but by God I survived the Great War. Going into battle with you would be the greatest battle of all and the most challenging. Surely you won't deny an old man one final skirmish?'

'I'm like a black widow,' she warned.

'It'll take more than an insect bite to send me to the grave. I'm as tough as a rhinoceros,' he exclaimed in amusement. 'You don't scare me, Charlo, you enthral me.'

'I'm old.'

'So am I.'

'Too old for romance.'

'You don't believe that.'

'I should.'

Colonel Blythe chewed on the end of his cigarette for a moment, chuckling at his inability to coax this woman into submission. 'You're a fine mare, Charlotte Osborne. I'll have you in the end.'

Charlo's handsome face stung with pleasure. 'The end may be closer than you think for both of us.'

'Quite, my dear, that is why I do not wish to waste any more time with the chase.'

'I've always found the chase the most exhilarating part of it all,' she said tartly, clipping the word 'exhilarating' with relish.

Colonel Blythe removed his cigarette from between his twitching lips and narrowed his eyes.

'At this stage in our lives there's little point in playing games. Good God, old girl, you should anticipate the exhilaration that follows the chase and allow yourself to be caught.'

'I've been caught three times, Colonel, and I've been disappointed each time. I'm too old now to withstand another disappointment.'

Colonel Blythe replaced the cigarette and sat back in his chair, temporarily defeated. 'So, young Cecil Forrester, eh? No disappointment there,' chortled the Colonel.

'Not yet,' Charlo replied sourly. 'But there will be. There's always a degree of disappointment in affairs of the heart. The higher the heart flies the further there is to fall.'

'Young people.' He sighed. 'Naivety is a great blessing, as is ignorance.'

'Quite. One grows cynical with age.'

'Only if one allows oneself to, old girl.'

*   *   *

It wasn't long before the whole Club was talking of Cecil's courtship of Audrey. The girls praised her choice in patronising tones, infuriated that he had chosen her above all of them. 'So typical of Audrey to lose her heart to Cecil,' commented Agatha and Nelly, masking their jealousy behind saccharine

121

sweetness, 'she's so sensible. They make the most delightful couple.' The Crocodiles discussed it over Bridge and found to their disappointment that they had little to criticise. Only Aunt Hilda exposed her bitterness in the thin line of her mouth that seemed more sourly pursed together than usual. She would have liked Cecil for one of her daughters.

Audrey was mortified that everyone knew and avoided the Club. Rose, oblivious that it had been she who had started the tirade of gossip, was appalled by everyone's interest in something that had nothing whatsoever to do with them and did her best to comfort her daughter. By the time the evening of the dinner arrived Audrey felt so distressed she almost called it off due to a genuine headache brought on by anxiety. But Isla massaged her temples with lavender oil and reminded her of the reason she had accepted his invitation in the first place. 'You'll be back in Louis' arms tomorrow and if you're clever you can stall Cecil for a little longer,' she assured her.

'I don't think I'll have the strength,' Audrey protested. 'I'm going to speak to Louis tomorrow, I simply can't go on with this charade. I think we should just tell Mummy and Daddy the truth and face up to it. After all, how bad can it be?'

'Bad,' Isla replied bluntly. 'Mind you,' she added, 'if it were me, I wouldn't think twice, in fact, I wouldn't have hidden it in the first place. But you're too decent and too worried about upsetting them. You're too sweet natured for your own good. If it were me I would have run off into the sunset long ago. You've always been a coward, Audrey, that's why we all love you and that's why I'll suffer the wrath of the entire community some day, I just

122

know it.'

Isla was right. Audrey was a coward, she always had been. She was incapable of wounding her mother. She wished she were more like her sister. But, however much she fired herself up in preparation to drop such an unpleasant revelation she knew in her heart that there wasn't much point. Her parents' happiness would always come before her own.

*   *   *

When the fated evening arrived, Cecil appeared at the door crisp and polished as an officer on parade. The scent of his aftershave was so pervasive Audrey forgot her headache and suffered a giddy wave of nausea. Cecil was so nervous his hands were clammy with sweat and his expression so grave he may just as well have been going to a funeral. He knew he had overdone the cologne and the knowledge that it was too late to remove it made him stammer with anxiety. He complimented Audrey on her long lilac dress and wondered why the smooth, debonair Cecil Forrester had deserted him just when he needed him most. Isla sat on the stairs biting her nails while her mother and Aunt Edna spied on their parting from behind the curtains in the living room. 'He's terribly handsome,' Rose gushed as she watched them get into the car.

'He's a real gentleman,' said Aunt Edna, 'and there aren't many of them around these days.'

'I don't think he's at all right for Audrey,' Isla interjected boldly from the stairs. Rose and Aunt Edna turned around in surprise. 'Well, he isn't.

They've got nothing in common. Audrey loves poetry and music while Cecil loves the army and chess, they're most unsuited. The last thing she needs is everyone putting pressure on her.'

'Really, Isla, what's all this about?' Rose asked in bewilderment. Isla stood up and began to march up stairs. Aunt Edna frowned at her sister who responded with a shake of her head.

'She'll end up marrying him just to please you and Daddy!' she shouted down in frustration. She wanted to add, 'And she's not in love with him at all,' but she stopped herself in time, opened the door to her bedroom and stomped inside. Rose shrugged at Aunt Edna as the door slammed.

'Oh dear.' She sighed. 'Whatever's the matter with Isla?' Aunt Edna dug her chins into her neck and glanced at her sister knowingly. 'The green-eyed monster?' said Rose, automatically interpreting her sister's expression.

'I fear so,' Aunt Edna replied. 'After all, Audrey's been enjoying an awful lot of attention and dear Isla has no one.'

'You're right, Edna. I've been most insensitive. Don't worry, I'll put it right,' she said, relieved that there was no truth in her younger daughter's outburst.

*   *   *

Once in the car Cecil opened the window wide and allowed the crisp winter air to rush in, alleviating Audrey's nausea and his anxiety in one pleasant gust. Once the initial embarrassment had passed their conversation gathered momentum and Cecil began to regain his confidence. Knowing that they were away from the hopeful eyes of her mother and aunt, Audrey felt calmer and although she gazed out of the windscreen recalling those illicit and magical nights in Palermo, she found her fears had been exaggerated. Her heart was Louis' but there was no reason why she shouldn't enjoy Cecil's company as a friend.

*   *   *

Audrey was captivated by the Teatro Colón that dominated the wide Avenida 9 de Julio like a grand, ornate palace from the world of fairytales. Lit up with golden lights that dazzled through the winter darkness it exuded the elegance and sophistication of Paris, echoed the romance of Rome and represented to Audrey the culture and art of a faraway world that one day she would enjoy with Louis. Cecil parked the car and then took the liberty of placing his hand in the small of her back to guide her along the glistening pavements and across the roads. The city enthralled Audrey and she felt excitement rise up her spine and inject her veins with passion until she was laughing and talking without reserve, commenting on the people, their clothes and their jewellery, the grandeur of the theatre and her own, unrestrained exhilaration. Cecil was overcome with happiness. Everything about Audrey was delightful, especially her enthusiasm which he was now discovering for the first time. If he had loved her before it had been a paler love. He looked down at her animated face and felt he was seeing her as no one had ever seen her and he was deeply flattered that she had chosen him to come alive for.

They took their seats in one of the many boxes that hung over the edge of the theatre like gilded lifeboats on the side of a ship and watched the steady stream of people pour in through the doors in their glittering dresses, pearl chokers and diamonds. The hum of anticipation rose on the hot air with the heavy scent of perfume and champagne. Audrey placed her gloved hands on the ledge in front of her and peered down at the men in the orchestra who had now begun to tune up their instruments. Cecil opened the programme and handed Audrey a pair of small opera glasses. 'Oh, this is so wonderful!' she exclaimed happily, focusing on the musicians. 'Oh look, here's the conductor,' she hissed as the audience stopped their chatter and dutifully clapped. He took a brief bow before turning to his musicians and raising his arms in the air with great bravado and showmanship. After holding their attention for a long moment he brought his arms down, extracting on the way up the most awesome explosion of music.

From that moment on Audrey was transfixed. The dancers leapt across the stage with the grace of gazelles and her eyes didn't leave them for a single moment. Cecil, who was not so enchanted by the ballet, watched Audrey through the darkness, taking as much pleasure from the ever-changing expressions on her face as she took from the performance.

'That was so beautiful,' she sniffed at the end of the first act. 'When she committed suicide.'

'I'm so pleased you're enjoying it,' he replied, confounded by the intensity of her reaction. 'Can I get you a drink? A glass of champagne?'

She nodded and burrowed in her bag for a hanky. 'Oh dear, I always cry at beautiful music and dancing. But this is so sad.'

'Don't be embarrassed, it's charming,' he said, handing her a glass of cold champagne and his own silk handkerchief.

'Isla thinks I'm oversensitive. She's never cried at anything.'

'She will when she's older, I'm sure. She's a bit young to appreciate this sort of thing,' he said in a patronising tone, knowing that age had nothing to do with it. He was thirty and he failed to recognise the magic of music and dance. Audrey laughed lightly because she knew what he was thinking and she remembered her sister's words: how much does a fish feel? It was quite clear that he was unmoved but she didn't mind. She knew that Louis would have been sobbing with her, holding her hand and feeling the power of the music as much as she. Cecil's lack of appreciation was unimportant. She thought of Louis and her laughter melted into a wistful smile. She sipped her champagne and waited for the lights to dim and the curtain to rise so that she could lose herself once again and imagine that she was there with Louis.

*   *   *

It was during the final act, when Audrey's tears began to spill again, that Cecil placed his hand on hers. At first she didn't notice, she was so enraptured by the ballet. But then her body stiffened and the blood rushed to her head where it caused her cheeks to throb with embarrassment. She didn't know what to do. If she were to

127

withdraw her own hand she might cause unnecessary offence; if she were to leave it there she might give him the wrong impression. Suddenly she was unable to concentrate on the performance. Her hand beneath his lay like a dead fish in her lap, wrapped in her silk glove but not impervious to the warmth of his skin. After what seemed an eternity she realised that there was nothing she could do. She had to try to forget it and concentrate as much as she could on the end of the ballet. She tried to convince herself that it was a simple gesture of friendship. After all she had begun to cry again, what man wouldn't want to comfort a tearful woman? He was only being kind. So she endeavoured to detach herself from the wrist down and focus with all her might on the dancers. Cecil was encouraged that she hadn't found some excuse to move her hand away. He dared to take it a little further and squeezed it reassuringly. The evening had so far been a great success. When the programme was over Cecil led her down the stairs and out of the theatre to a small restaurant nearby. Audrey was subdued. Cecil believed her too moved to speak. But Audrey's hand still burned beneath the silk and her head ached with the idea that her boundaries had been violated—and that she had allowed it.

Audrey didn't want to spoil Cecil's evening, not after he had made such an effort: it wasn't fair to dampen his enjoyment. So with enormous effort she smiled and conversed with enthusiasm, desperately trying to sparkle as she had at the start of the night when the anticipation of the show had filled her with exhilaration. Cecil was too thick-skinned to notice the subtle change in her tone, he saw only the surface of her face and the glimmer in her eyes that reassured him of her affection.

It wasn't until they were standing in the cold on her doorstep that Cecil finally managed to say what he had been intending to say from the moment he had placed his hand on hers in the theatre. 'Audrey,' he began. 'I've enjoyed this evening tremendously.'

'Me too, Cecil, I cannot thank you enough,' she replied, turning to open the front door, relieved that the evening was over.

'Yes, you can,' he replied, suddenly taking her by the arm. She swivelled around in time to notice the fearful intent in his eyes. But there was nothing she could have said to deter him. 'I want to marry you, Audrey,' he said smiling triumphantly as if he were sure that she had been longing to hear those words as much as he had been longing to say them. She reeled backwards and had to steady herself by leaning against the door. 'I know this is a surprise, and you don't have to give me your answer tonight, or tomorrow night. You can think about it. But I know that you are the woman I want to spend the rest of my life with and I think you know it too. You do, don't you Audrey?' Audrey tried to think of something to say, but her mind was suddenly screaming with so many words that she didn't know which to choose. Instead she stood unsteadily with her mouth open, staring at him blankly, wanting to break down and cry.

Cecil opened the door for her and watched her walk into the hall. 'I await your answer with impatience,' he whispered, aware that the rest of the family were upstairs asleep. 'Good night.' Audrey managed to turn around and mumble a confused 'good night' as he closed the door and strode, whistling his favourite military march, down the pathway that led onto the street.

She staggered up the stairs, blinking away her horror, gripping onto the banisters to stop herself from stumbling. Isla, who had been waiting in her sister's bedroom, heard her heavy steps and crept out onto the landing. When she saw Audrey's pale face and blue lips she immediately thought the worst. 'Oh God, he jumped on you?'

Audrey shook her head slowly. 'That would have been a blessing,' she replied bleakly.

'What could be worse?'

Audrey raised her eyebrows. Isla folded her arms in front of her. 'He asked you to marry him, didn't he?'

Audrey nodded and pulled a thin smile. 'I've really gone and done it now.'

'It's fine,' said Isla firmly. 'You did say no, didn't you?'

'I didn't say anything.'

'You didn't say anything?' Isla repeated, screwing up her nose. 'Why not?'

'I didn't know what to say, it was such a shock.'

'You could have said "no".'

'Oh, Isla, what am I going to do?' She sniffed, taking off her glove and wiping her tears on Cecil's silk handkerchief.

'Come inside,' she suggested calmly, 'I think it's time you told everyone the truth.'

130

CHAPTER EIGHT

When Audrey read Louis' next note, she was stunned to learn that Cecil had told him of his proposal. *I am consumed with a burning jealousy*, Louis wrote. *Although I know such emotions are needless, I cannot help but despise my brother for his audacity.* Audrey's spirits sank even lower. She had wanted to tell him herself, that night in the garden, when they could discuss it together and devise a plan. She thought of Cecil and her resentment mounted. Then she shuddered at the possibility that he might well tell someone else. She had hoped she would wake to discover that it had all been a horrible dream. Now there was only one avenue open to her: she must tell Cecil that she wasn't in love with him and that she could never marry him. Then she would simply have to confess to her parents that she had lost her heart to Louis and face the consequences.

Hastily she plugged the hole in the brick with her reply and left the station before Juan Julio spotted her lurking about the platform again. Once she had gone the station master shuffled out of his office like a lazy, overfed cat, scratching his groin and glancing around to make sure that there was no one to see him read the next instalment of a love affair that had him hooked like a girl with a romantic novel. He hovered about the wall, twitching with anticipation, glancing sideways up and down the platform. When he was satisfied that Audrey Garnet had well and truly gone he shoved his podgy finger into the hole and eased the white

131

note out like a snail from its shell. He chuckled as he looked for the word 'love', which was one of the few English words he could understand and any others that resembled Spanish. It didn't matter that the content of the letter remained a mystery to him, the secrecy of it enthralled him and he could barely wait for the following day. After replacing it carefully—he wasn't about to jeopardise his enjoyment by carelessness—he sloped on up the platform to the signal box where he sat out of the cold, picking his nose and pondering on the destiny of these ill-fated lovers.

*   *   *

When Isla returned home from school she was pale and tearful, claiming that she felt unwell. Albert rolled his eyes and accused her of pretending in order to get attention and Rose silently agreed with him until she took the girl's temperature to find that she had been struck down by a nasty bout of flu. 'I ache all over,' she wailed, crawling beneath the sheets and curling up into a ball.

'You'll be fine, Isla dear,' reassured her mother gently. 'I'll make you a nice hot drink of lemon and honey and have you right in no time.'

'I suppose she won't have to go to school tomorrow,' Albert grumbled. It wasn't the first time that Isla had skipped school due to some phantom illness. But this time she had the temperature to prove it and lay in bed soaking up all the attention with the melodramatic air of an actress.

'Oh, darling Isla,' Audrey sighed taking her sister's hot hand in hers. 'You poor thing. Do you feel dreadful?'

132

'Dreadful,' replied Isla. 'But you can cheer me up. Are you going to see Louis tonight?'

'Of course, then I'm going to tell Cecil the truth.'

Isla pulled a face as if she doubted her sister had the courage to be so bold. 'Just Cecil or are you going to tell Mummy and Daddy the truth as well?'

'Everyone, I'm sick of lying and hiding the way I feel, so is Louis.'

'Good!' Isla exclaimed, grinning widely. 'I can't wait to watch the ripples.'

'I feel sorry for Cecil though, you know, he's a very sweet man. He doesn't deserve to be treated the way I've treated him. I've been horrid and careless with his feelings.'

'Oh, goodness me, Audrey,' chided Isla. 'It's his fault, he shouldn't have rushed in like that. It was only the first dinner invitation, men aren't supposed to propose so soon.' Then she looked at Audrey through narrowed eyes that sparkled with flu and mischief combined. 'You must have encouraged him to be so impulsive.' Audrey's face paled with horror.

'I did nothing to encourage him,' she protested firmly, affronted by the accusation. 'Nothing.' She folded her arms defensively, recalling with a shudder that she had allowed him to hold her hand.

'I'm sorry. I didn't mean to suggest that you had encouraged him on purpose, only that he must have read you wrong.'

'He certainly read me wrong,' she replied swiftly, averting her eyes from her sister's intense scrutiny.

'You'll put it right,' Isla reassured her. 'Just prepare for the storm.'

*   *   *

Aunt Hilda sat at her dressing table rubbing cold cream into the cracks in her skin. Like many women who lived in hot climates she had allowed her face to be burned too many times by the sun, but no amount of caring now could erase the rough texture of solar damage or the ever-increasing corrosion of bitterness which scorched her features with equal intensity. If youth had once bestowed on her a handsomeness of sorts, age had robbed her of it. There was little that was attractive in her cold, bloodshot eyes and in the thin line of her mouth, which rarely smiled even during the rare moments when she genuinely had something to be happy about. She was incapable of taking pleasure from other people's good fortune and had settled into the habit of being perpetually disappointed with her own life. To Aunt Hilda her negative world was as dependable as it was reassuringly familiar. When Nelly, her second and least insipid daughter, entered her room with the news that Isla was bedridden with flu, Hilda stopped tormenting her face with cream and remarked that she didn't believe it for a second. 'That child runs circles around Rose,' she sighed. 'I have good reason to believe that she's enjoying a secret tryst with that ghastly Louis Forrester. Flu indeed.'

Nelly, who had been raised on an unhealthy diet of her mother's resentment that her sister's daughters were more beautiful and charming than hers, enjoyed nothing more than to indulge in long conversations tailored to undermine her cousins' perfection and make her feel better about herself, albeit temporarily. The fact that she too was sweet on Louis Forrester made her eagerness to criticise

134

all the more intense. 'What makes you think that?' Nelly asked, concealing her mortification by feigning disgust. Hilda replaced the lid on the cream then removed the excess from her face with a tissue.

'It's perfectly obvious to everyone else, Nelly, except dear Rose and Henry,' she replied. 'They're far too distracted by Audrey's romance with Cecil. I tell you, they'll rue the day those two boys descended on Hurlingham.'

'But how do you know Louis is in love with Isla?' Nelly persisted impatiently. The thought hadn't occurred to her. 'Isla's too young to be interested in boys, I'm certain of it.'

Her mother scoffed and raised her over-plucked eyebrows into her shiny brow.

'My dear, Edna agrees with me. Rose even noticed them passing notes to each other, and apparently a lot of horse play goes on between them.'

'Why would they bother to keep it secret? Isla's no stranger to trouble. She thrives on it.'

'That may be so, but she knows the difference between "trouble" and "scandal". She's as shrewd as a stoat that one. Thinks she's pulled the wool over everyone's eyes. Flu indeed. She's just feigning being ill so she can enjoy secret rendezvous with Louis. Mark my words.'

'If it's true, Louis and Isla are made for one another, they're both irresponsible,' said Nelly in order to provoke her mother to expand on the subject. Her ploy worked for Hilda swivelled around on her stool and drew her pink dressing gown across her bony chest.

'You're so right, Nelly. At least I bred a daughter

135

with a fine mind. Isla's got the cunning of a fox but her mind is filled with goodness knows what. Young men these days respect women who think. To choose to embark on a secret liaison with Louis Forrester is to choose social suicide. Yes, it is, mark my words. The stories that have made their way across the Atlantic, and I suppose he thought his past would never catch up with him.' She raised her eyebrows again to insinuate all sorts of horrors. 'A woman's virtue is her greatest asset, she loses that and she loses everything,' she said solemnly, clearly reinforcing her daughter's education on the matter. Nelly was unable to meet her mother's eyes.

'Are you suggesting that Louis is only after one thing, Mummy?' she asked, blushing deeply at the sensual thoughts that entered her head and served only to make him more attractive.

'I'm afraid that's exactly what I'm suggesting. Thank goodness you and your sisters have too much class to catch his roving eye.' But Nelly longed to catch his eye and secretly she admired and resented Isla's courage. If it were her, she would find him irresistible too.

*   *   *

It was raining hard as Louis and Cecil arrived at the Garnets' house for drinks. Cecil was eager to see Audrey and hopeful for an answer, while Louis was desperate to finish with the whole charade and tell everyone the truth. Isla languished in her bed, her fever rising with such speed and viciousness that Rose had called the doctor. The wind of Fate rattled the window as if threatening to fight its way in and carry Isla off into the darkness.

136

She heard the rain pound against the glass and in her fragile state of mind, debilitated by fever, she believed the scratching to be the clawing of a hideous beast and cried out for her mother. Rose was too distracted by her younger daughter to give any attention to the brothers who shuffled in out of the cold, shaking their wet shoulders like dogs. So Henry discussed business with Cecil in the sitting room by the fire while Louis sulked on the sofa, wishing that Audrey would end his nightmare by telling everyone the truth. But Audrey waited anxiously for the doctor with her mother. Cecil felt it wasn't the moment to press her for an answer and Louis realised that they'd just have to wait to drop their bombshell.

When the doctor arrived the two women fell on him, Audrey taking his soaking coat while Rose almost pushed him in the direction of the stairs. 'She's delirious, doctor, the fever is vicious, vicious,' she repeated, shaking her head with worry. 'She's sweating profusely and mumbling things about a monster. I hope there's something you can do to alleviate the poor child's suffering.' Doctor Swanson, an old Englishman with the thick woolly head of a sheep and the ruddy round face of a man who liked a few strong drinks after a heavy day's work, followed Rose up to Isla's bedroom, clutching his black doctor's case which had always fascinated the sisters as children. Now it merely looked ominous and Audrey was gripped with fear.

When he saw Isla's burning eyes he put down his case and walked to the side of the bed, frowning gravely. 'You have quite a fever, my girl,' he said, placing his cold hand on her forehead. Isla blinked at him mutely, overwhelmed by the force that was sucking the energy out of her with such velocity.

'She was just off colour when she came back from school this afternoon,' said Rose, wringing her hands. 'It's been very quick. One minute she had a temperature, the next minute she was on fire.' Doctor Swanson pulled up a chair and sat down, drawing his black bag onto his knee.

'Am I going to die?' Isla asked suddenly.

Doctor Swanson chuckled in amusement. 'Not from the flu, my dear. No one here has ever died of the flu,' he said reassuringly, taking out a long black stethoscope.

'Really, Isla, don't say such things,' cried Audrey, looking to her mother for support.

'Trust Isla to be such a dramatist,' said Rose, feigning amusement. But she felt uncomfortable as if her instincts were trying to tell her something. 'Come, Audrey, let's give the doctor some room,' she said, leading her eldest onto the landing.

'You go down and talk to the boys, Henry must be boring them with business. That's not why they came over, they have all day to talk business,' she said. But Audrey didn't want to go.

'I want to wait with you.'

'No, dear, Cecil will be disappointed if you don't go down.'

'Isla's more important,' she protested.

'And she'll be fine. She's got a bad case of the flu. As the doctor said, no one's ever died here of flu.'

'All right, I'll go down, but only if you promise to come and tell us what he says the minute he's gone.' Rose nodded her head and pushed her daughter gently by the elbow. Audrey heard her mother return to Isla's room and close the door behind her.

*   *   *

The atmosphere in the sitting room was tense even though Albert and his two younger brothers played whist at the card table in the corner. Audrey sat beside Louis on the sofa while Cecil watched her stiffly from the armchair. 'How is she?' Henry asked in his usual phlegmatic tone as if he were asking as a matter of routine.

'She's not at all well, Daddy,' Audrey replied solemnly.

'Poor girl,' said Louis, holding Audrey's eyes for as long as he could without giving himself away. Audrey knew what he was thinking, but to her surprise she was unable to feel anything but anxiety for her sister.

'She looks dreadful,' she continued. 'She was fine earlier, it's just suddenly taken hold of her.'

'The first night is always the worst with flu,' said Cecil, wanting to be helpful. 'The night is always bad.' Then he added in a low voice, looking from Henry to Audrey, 'Perhaps we should leave you all.'

'Absolutely not, Cecil,' Henry replied, picking up the humidor. 'Cigar?' Cecil leant forward and peered inside. 'Damn fine cigars, fresh from Havana,' said Henry with pride. 'Louis?' Louis shook his head. Cecil chose one and leant back in his chair to light it. 'Isla's made of strong stuff; she'll be right as rain in the morning, you'll see,' he continued, smiling at Audrey. 'It takes very little to worry the women in my family.' He chuckled. 'No one's ever died of flu.'

Audrey sat quietly while Cecil and her father

139

talked about politics and industry and then moved on to discuss the little island miles away that they considered home. Louis longed to hold her hand in order to give his support but she seemed far away, as if for the time being she had withdrawn her love. He felt his throat constrict at the thought of her slowly drifting away from him. He sensed something terrible was about to happen and his face drained of colour until he felt faint with nausea. Finally Audrey heard the doctor talking in a low voice with her mother at the top of the stairs. She strained her ears but was unable to make out what they were saying. They then descended into the hall, hovered while the doctor struggled into his coat then bade good-bye in raised voices that Audrey desperately tried to interpret as positive in tone. Eventually Rose entered the sitting room and forced a smile that quite clearly sat uneasily on her strained face. 'She'll be fine,' she said, directing her words to Audrey. 'It'll be an uncomfortable night for her, but she'll feel better in the morning.'

'Can I go and see her?' she asked.

'Yes, but don't be long, she needs to rest,' replied her mother, sinking into a chair. 'Being a mother is no easy task,' she said and sighed, 'one worries constantly about one's children, even when they're not children any longer.'

Louis watched Audrey leave the room and wanted to go after her. He knew that although the rain wouldn't put her off their midnight rendezvous, Isla's illness would. She was closer to her sister than she was to anyone else in the world and that included him. He watched Cecil smoke his cigar and knew that behind his steely composure he was equally anxious. Yet, Louis resented his brother's anxiety. How dare he entertain such ideas. But as much as he wanted to crush his brother's hopes he knew he'd have to wait until Isla was well again, because, until she recovered, Audrey belonged to her.

*   *   *

The rain continued to rattle down in a seemingly endless deluge. Louis and Cecil rushed back to the Club beneath their umbrellas, both silent, alone with their thoughts. While Cecil worried for Audrey, praying that Isla would be well again in the morning, Louis arrived at the Club disgruntled with frustration. Audrey had barely noticed him. Infuriated that she had treated him with the distance of a stranger he sat in his sodden clothes on the tapestry stool, drunk with misery and alcohol and bashed out his torment on the ivory keys of the piano until his brother and Colonel Blythe were forced to drag him away swearing and lock him in his bedroom.

'My good fellow,' said the Colonel to Cecil as they later shared a double whisky in the lounge, 'what that young man requires is a touch of discipline. The army would have done him the world of good. Made a man out of him. No use crying over a woman. They're not worth it, mercurial vixens.' He knocked back his glass and thought of Charlotte Osborne. 'Mercurial vixens, the bally lot of 'em,' he said with a snort. Cecil wondered whether Louis had lost his heart to Isla, then as the whisky warmed his spirits he ceased to wonder at all and his thoughts drifted once more to Audrey.

141

*   *   *

Audrey remained with her mother in an anxious vigil, watching over the burning body of her sister as little by little the fire consumed her weakening spirit. Finally Henry persuaded them to go to bed. 'You're just going to frighten her,' he said, gently leading his wife away by the arm. 'Let her sleep in peace.'

Audrey couldn't sleep. She listened to the rain and worried about Isla until the tears ran down her nose and onto her pillow, staining it with anguish. Cecil and Louis were far from her thoughts. She clutched the sheets and remembered those nights when she had lain pressed against the warm body of her sister, recounting her midnight rendezvous with Louis and her secret trips to Palermo. Isla had enjoyed every vicarious minute. Audrey wished they could go back in time and relive those moments because something horrid pulled at her gut, something ominous. She dared not listen to it. Tried to ignore it. But the more she attempted to focus her thoughts on the good times the fear that she was losing Isla persisted until she could ignore it no longer.

Softly she padded into her sister's bedroom. The windows clattered beneath the torrent of rain but the light from the street lamps shone through, illuminating the bed and the feverish form of Isla that twitched and turned in its fiery hell. With a suspended heart she sat on the edge of the bed and, taking the sponge out of the bowl of water, she began to dab Isla's sweating forehead with great tenderness. 'Please get well,' she whispered.

142

'Oh, please fight, Isla.' Isla shook her head from side to side and moaned. Audrey began to cry. 'God help her because I feel so hopeless, I don't know what to do.' Then she spoke with more urgency, willing her sister to wake up and listen. 'I feel you're slipping away, Isla. Please don't slip away. I need you.'

At that moment Isla opened her eyes. They were red-rimmed and glistened like wet pebbles. Once so focused they now seemed distant, as if at the halfway house between this world and the next. 'Isla, can you hear me?' she asked in a trembling voice, placing the sponge back in the bowl to rinse it. Isla looked around as if unfamiliar with her own bedroom. Audrey brought the sponge up to her neck and began to pat the hot skin there. But Isla seemed unaware of it and continued to look about her, blinking at the small room that now meant very little to her. Audrey watched her in despair. She wanted to call her mother and yet Isla wasn't in pain. She wasn't crying out. To the contrary she seemed content and serene. Audrey hoped she was over the worst.

When Isla focused on her sister she thought for a moment that she was an angel come to take her on to the next dimension. She had never believed in the world of spirit. That was Audrey's belief, but now, as she wavered on the brink of death she was certain of it. She wondered why she had been such a sceptic, it all seemed so obvious to her now. She laughed and noticed Audrey's face flinch in surprise. Disappointed, Isla realised she wasn't an angel after all, but her sister. It wasn't her time yet. 'Audrey,' she whispered, then wondered why her voice didn't work as before. She didn't have the

143

energy to speak in anything other than a whisper. Audrey leant forward to hear.

'Isla, are you in pain?'

Isla shook her head. 'I feel drunk,' she replied then smiled. 'It feels nice.'

'Oh, Isla, I'm so pleased. You're going to be all right. You'll feel well again in the morning and we'll laugh about it.'

'I'm going to die,' she replied without sentiment. Audrey was shocked.

'No, you're not.'

'Oh, I am.'

'Isla!'

'I want a big funeral. No expense spared. Tears, wailing and gnashing of teeth.'

'Isla, please . . .'

'I'll be watching, so make sure you all give me a good send off. I'll know if you don't.'

'This is ridiculous, Isla. You're being horrid. You're not going to die.' Then her voice cracked. 'You can't die. I need you.'

'You'll be fine without me. You'll have Louis.'

'I don't want Louis if it means sacrificing you.'

'Just promise me one thing.'

'What? I'll do anything.'

'Have the courage to follow your heart, Audrey,' she said, enjoying the melodrama of death. She was aware that she sounded like one of the heroines out of the novels Audrey read and would have liked those to have been her last words. But to her disappointment she didn't die. So she had to continue finding suitable last words to utter until she finally slipped into unconsciousness, distracted by the bright white light and her grandmother who walked towards her with her arms outstretched,

144

radiating a love she knew didn't exist on the earthly plane.

*   *   *

When Rose and Henry entered Isla's room at dawn Audrey was asleep on the bed, curled up behind her sister, her arm wrapped around Isla's waist. Their long corkscrew curls fanned out over the pillows like golden halos that shone through the pale morning light and the gentle rise and fall of their bodies betrayed no sign of the battle they had fought. Audrey's cheeks glowed like ripe peaches but Isla's were grey. The fire had been extinguished and Isla's small body was no longer tormented but at peace. Rose was suddenly struck with fear and she clutched her neck with a cold hand. She hastened to the bedside and fell to her knees, blinking at her younger daughter through eyes misted with tears. 'Isla,' she choked. 'Wake up, Isla.'

Audrey awoke at once and leapt from the bed in panic. Isla showed no sign of life except the shallow breaths that seemed to enter and leave her body like a random wind whistling through the aisle of an empty church. When neither parent managed to resuscitate her, they realised to their horror that she had lost consciousness.

The good doctor was called once again and after examining the patient with a grave face and leaden heart he declared that she had sunk into a coma. As the whole family stood around the bed waiting for the ambulance to arrive, only Albert had the courage to say what was on everyone's mind. 'No one's ever died of flu,' he said then raised his

145

swollen eyes to his mother, silently demanding an explanation. Rose turned to her husband who sighed heavily and drew his lips into a thin line of despair.

'It's not flu, son,' he replied, shaking his head that felt as heavy and solid as if filled with lead.

'Then what is it, Daddy?'

'The doctor says it's meningitis.'

'Why didn't he say that last night?'

'Because he didn't know then. Meningitis has the symptoms of flu, Albert. He couldn't have known.' Henry was unable to look at his wife. They both knew what meningitis meant.

'But she'll be all right?' he asked, remembering the time he flicked a peanut down her throat, she had been all right then.

'She's not going to die, is she?' asked George, one of Henry and Rose's smallest sons. Everyone stared at the little boy who was too young to understand about death.

'No, no,' said Henry bravely. 'Not our Isla.' He patted George on his shoulder reassuringly.

'No, George,' Rose interjected. 'She'll be fine, you'll see.'

'The doctors will make her well again, won't they?' said Albert hopefully.

Then Audrey spoke. 'Isla's gone,' she said in a small voice. She hadn't spoken since the early hours of the morning when she had begged her sister not to leave her and her voice now sounded far away and strange. But Isla had wanted to go. Death had no longer frightened her but welcomed her into its breast like an old, familiar friend.

They all stared at the bed where Isla's body was now still. The random wind had moved on leaving behind an empty shell. No one spoke. A shocked silence descended upon them all. Rose cried quietly, the tears cascading down her cheeks and she held out her hand for her husband to hold. There is no grief like a parent's grief for their dead child and Rose and Henry stood alone with their pain, their fingers entwined, silently struggling with their Faith. Little George and his younger brother, Edward, wept because their mother was weeping; they were too young to comprehend the finality of death. Albert would have liked to cry, but his fear froze his emotions and robbed him of his voice so that only his chin wobbled, silently conveying his anguish.

'We never said good-bye,' whispered Rose. 'We never even told her how much we love her.'

'She knew,' said Henry.

'I was the last person to speak to her,' said Audrey softly, without taking her eyes off her sister. 'She knew she was going to die, yet she wasn't afraid. She was happy to go, impatient even. It was as if she was aware that she was delivering her final words. She told me to tell you all that she loves you and always will and that she was sorry she didn't have time to tell you herself. Then she said she had to go.'

Rose shook her head and brought her hand up to her lips to stop them from trembling. 'Go where?' she asked in a raw whisper.

Audrey shrugged. 'Most unlike Isla.' She smiled at the recollection of her sister's departure. It had been serene. A gentle slipping away. 'She stared into the far corner of the room and her whole face lit up. Then she said, "So that's where you went to, Granny, I've always wondered what Heaven's

147

like.'"

'She said that?' Rose asked in amazement. Suddenly her daughter had transformed in her mind from a fallible human being to a saint or an angel at the very least.

'Yes, and I mustn't forget, she also said she wants a big funeral with a lot of wailing and gnashing of teeth.'

'Really, Audrey!' said her father in disbelief. It was hardly the moment for jokes.

But Rose pulled a fragile smile and sniffed.

'Of course she did,' she said sadly. '*So* like Isla!'

CHAPTER NINE

28th June 1948

News of Isla's death slashed the community to its very backbone. Few could speak, so consumed with grief were they, and those who could were unable to speak of anything else. Peron's acquisition of the British-owned railways, fulfilling his promise in his election campaign to diminish foreign influence in the economy, suddenly seemed so unimportant in the midst of this very human tragedy. Her death was so unexpected. Unexpected and unthinkable. The school closed its gates for the day in mourning and everyone filed into the Hurlingham church hall for the afternoon funeral, filling the rows of chairs like black bats. Everyone remembered Isla for her sense of fun and mischief; for her laughter and her own unique magic. Even the Crocodiles remembered only the good in a child who hadn't had time to be tainted by the temptations of adulthood. She was an innocent and above criticism.

Rose hid her sorrow behind a black veil and led her four weeping children to their pew where they sat staring in awe at the small coffin that was placed beneath the nave under an abundance of white lilies. Isla had always seemed so much taller in life. Henry, who had left his tears behind with his childhood, found them again and made up for the years of restraint by shedding enough for a small puddle. He did his best to comfort his family; after all, one mustn't forget the living, but he felt hopelessly inadequate beneath the weight of such a heavy loss.

Audrey was numb. She barely felt the legs that carried her, out of habit, up the aisle and settled beneath her seat, one foot over the ankle of the other. She gazed transfixed at the coffin and tried to imagine the irrepressible Isla lying in submission within such a small space. It didn't seem possible that the girl who had more life in her than an entire family was no longer living. But then she focused her thoughts on the waxy features of her sister as she had lain on her bed in death and knew that however impossible it seemed, Isla was dead. Extinguished. Audrey suddenly felt all alone in the world and she began to cry, as much for herself as for Isla, who couldn't benefit from anyone's tears. She was in a far better place, a place where she could leap about with her long, corkscrew hair bouncing in the heavenly winds and her mischievous mouth twisted into an eternal smile. She remembered Isla's request but was too aware of the congregation to wail out loud.

For Audrey much of the funeral was a blur. She listened to her father read the lesson and watched him fight against the overwhelming urge to break down with an effort that caused his knuckles to turn white as they gripped the sides of the pulpit. Rose's shoulders shook throughout; Henry had never before looked so vulnerable and she loved him all the more for it. She loved him so much it hurt. The hymns were sung with unsteady, weak voices accompanied by an organ that was played with too much vigour and afterwards the vicar read the prayers before a congregation awed by the volume of their own silence.

Audrey glanced across at Aunt Hilda and Aunt Edna who sat together in the midst of Hilda's daughters, insipid now to the point of disappearing altogether. Hilda's mouth was thinner and more bitter than ever; she was obviously blaming the Lord for striking at the heart of her family once again, whereas Edna just sat with her sad face tucked into her chins, remembering her beloved Harry with gratitude and silently praying that he find Isla and look after her wherever they all were.

Audrey didn't have the courage to glance at the rows behind her. She was sure Cecil and Louis were both there. She had expected to want to be with Louis. But she didn't. If she couldn't have Isla then she wanted to be left alone with her thoughts. Louis seemed unimportant. Cecil seemed unimportant too. Isla's death had taught her a lesson or two about life. Nothing was more important than family.

It was during the final Grace that Audrey noticed Isla's presence in the church. It came as no surprise. After all, she had said she would come. At first she felt a tingling in her bones, a light fluttering across her skin, the presence of someone so close she could feel the breath on her neck. The blood rushed to her cheeks making them burn with amazement. She hastily glanced around to see if anyone else had noticed. They hadn't. They were all concentrating on the vicar's closing prayers. Then she raised her eyes and rested them upon the altar where she intuitively sensed the spirit to be. As hard as she looked she couldn't see anyone. She bit her lip and tried harder. She knew her sister and what she was capable of. Then as if exasperated by Audrey's lack of vision the spirit performed a small miracle. Audrey caught her breath and for a long moment she was unable to move. She just stared at the altar, her mouth agape. Finally, without averting her eyes she gently nudged her mother and whispered into her ear. 'Did you notice, two candles have just gone out on the altar,' she said, clutching her mother's hand with hot fingers.

Rose shook her head. 'What do you mean?'

'Look.'

Rose looked. Audrey was right. The first and the sixth candle in a row of twelve had simply gone out. They smoked away in triumph.

'What are you talking about, Audrey?' her mother hissed between snivels.

'Isla,' she gasped.

'Good God!' Rose exclaimed in amazement. 'You don't think . . . ?'

'Yes! Isla was sixteen. What else could it be?'

They both stared at the altar. But although they couldn't see her they were both sure that Isla's spirit was there somewhere.

Once the funeral was over Audrey helped her mother to her feet. 'Darling Audrey, you're such a comfort to me,' she said, smiling at her daughter with tenderness. 'If it wasn't for you I don't know what I'd do. You're my only little girl now. You were my first; I never thought I'd ever love another child as much as I loved you. But then Isla arrived and I realised that children come into the world bringing their own love and I loved her as intensely as I loved you. But now it's you and me again. I prayed for you today. I prayed that Cecil will look after you and see that no harm comes to you.' Audrey cast her eyes to the floor in shame. If only her mother knew who she really loved. 'I feel your future is safe with Cecil,' she said, patting her daughter's hand. 'Now go and find him, my dear, and ask him back to the house for tea. Everyone's invited, Marisol's made *empanadas.*' Audrey watched her mother walk up the aisle with her father and felt a tremendous wave of sadness.

Slowly the church was drained of its mournful congregation. The hushed voices retreated until Audrey found herself alone at last with the invisible spirit of Isla. Quietly she crept up to the altar where the first and the sixth candle still smoked in proof that a miracle had taken place. Isla had spoken in death in the only way she could. She had always had a keen eye for drama and trickery. With trembling hands Audrey reached up and pulled the two candles out of their silver candlesticks and brought them down to eye level where she could see them better. Then she knelt down and closed her eyes and in the silence of the empty church she believed she could feel her sister's presence as intensely as if she were alive.

'Oh Isla, I hoped you'd come. I'm so lost without you. I feel so afraid, so rootless. How could you leave us all so quickly, without any warning? We didn't even have time to tell you how much we all love you and how special you are. But then you know, don't you? You always knew and now you know better than ever before, because you can see everything clearly from where you are. I wish I were there with you. I don't want to go on living without you. Life suddenly seems so long and so arduous. Where will I be without your friendship, your support, your laughter and your love? I don't think I have the will to go through with it.' She was no longer aware of where she was. The words spilled out without restraint. She wasn't even aware of her tears or the sound of her voice that had ceased to be a whisper. 'You were so vibrant, Isla,' she continued. 'Where did your life go? Why didn't you fight harder? I'll never stop missing you or loving you. None of us will. And one day we'll be reunited. Oh Isla, I can't help but long for that moment.'

When she had finished she kissed the candles before placing them back in their silver candlesticks. Then she turned to leave, wiping her eyes with her gloves, adjusting her small hat and sweeping the hair off her face. To her surprise someone sat in the shadows at the back of the church. She felt the colour rise to her cheeks, embarrassed that someone might have heard her or, worse, seen her kiss the candlesticks. When she got a little closer she realised it was Louis.

'Louis!' she exclaimed. 'What are you doing

153

there?'

'Waiting for you,' he replied, getting up. When he came forward into the light, Audrey noticed that beneath his hat his face was as grey as ash and his eyes swollen and sore.

'Oh, Louis, I can't believe she's dead,' she sniffed, blinking up at him awkwardly. Louis wanted to fold her into his arms and yet something prevented him from acting spontaneously. Audrey seemed to have withdrawn her love. Instead of the warm aura that usually surrounded her, a coolness kept him at a distance. Isla's death had shifted the dynamic. He swallowed his anguish and attempted to speak, but only a rasping hiss escaped his throat. 'She was my dearest friend in the world,' Audrey continued as if oblivious of his pain. 'I don't know how I'm going to live without her.' He watched her, small and vulnerable and pale as if all the colour had been leached out leaving her deflated and waxen. His long fingers twitched nervously at his side as the music grew louder in his head. A feverish, tormented melody. He shook his head to free himself of it, yet it persisted until he could barely hear what she was saying. Then, just as he was about to break down she threw her arms around his neck and sobbed against him. Louis staggered forward and drew her to him, breathing the perfume on her skin as if it was the oxygen he needed to live. He closed his eyes and buried his face in her hair. The music quietened with the frantic beating of his heart until only the tears revealed his hurt and they were shed in silence. They both clung to each other, Audrey for support, Louis for survival. But they both knew that Isla's death had shattered their dream.

'What happens now?' he said after a while. He knew instinctively that it was the wrong thing to say, but he couldn't help himself. His impatience was overwhelming. Audrey pulled away and sank onto a chair. She remembered the scandal that Emma Letton had caused and the venomous Crocodiles rose in her mind like shadowy judges sentencing her to live as an outcast because she had hurt the people she loved the most. Then she saw the gentle face of her mother already scarred with grief and knew that she wasn't strong or selfish enough to swim against such a formidable tide. Louis sat beside her. He looked into her gaunt face and his shoulders slumped with disappointment. He knew what she was going to say by her expression. 'We don't have to discuss this now,' he added hastily, desperate to retract his question, but it was too late.

'Oh, Louis. Don't you see? I can't risk hurting my parents. Isla's death has destroyed them—it's destroyed all of us. I can't think of myself alone. I can't think only of my own happiness. You do understand, don't you?' She looked at him with sad eyes. 'I need time,' she added huskily.

'I'll wait as long as you want.' He took her hand between his but the glove was one more barrier that prevented him from recovering their closeness.

Audrey shook her head. 'I don't know how long it's going to be. I'm their only daughter now. I can't disappoint them.'

Unable to contain his exasperation Louis' face suddenly crumpled with fury. 'What about me?' His voice echoed against the walls of the church. 'Don't I mean anything to you any more?'

She swiftly swivelled around and took both his

hands in hers. 'Of course you do. I love you.'

'Then follow your heart.'

'And break the hearts of all those I care about? I can't. Not now.'

'What about your dreams?'

'I'm afraid to dream, Louis, because my dreams will cause so much pain.'

Louis sat back and stared bleakly out in front of him. It was cold. He shivered. Suddenly he felt as if it were Audrey who was dead and not Isla. His mouth twisted to a thin crescent of despair. He had lived most of his life without love and barely noticed, but now having basked in the radiance of Audrey's love he didn't know how he would survive without it. His future was slowly being swallowed by a swirling grey fog and all he could do was watch it go. There seemed to be no redemption.

'So that's it then?' he asked in a hollow voice. The battle had been fought and he had lost.

'Oh, Louis, please don't sound so defeated,' she implored him. 'I can't think clearly now. Just give me some time, that's all.'

'For what?' He shrugged his shoulders. 'You said so yourself, you can't disappoint your family. I'm obviously a huge disappointment.'

'Louis . . .'

'No, don't, I always have been. I disappointed my parents and Cecil. I seem to disappoint wherever I go. Well, I won't hang around to disappoint yours.'

'Louis, don't talk like this. You're overreacting.'

'Overreacting? I love you, Audrey, that's all I'm guilty of. Of loving you.' His eyes burned with passion and pain and he longed to have the confidence to persevere. But to Louis everything

156

was either black or white. She either loved him or she didn't. There was no in between. And besides, he was now on the defensive. With the strongest will in the world he couldn't have abated his impatience, that rose up to consume him.

'And I love you too, Louis. I love you so much it hurts,' she choked. 'But my sister is dead. My beautiful, vibrant Isla is gone. Do you understand? She's never coming back. How can I think of myself when she is dead?'

'Because you have to think of the living now.'

'Now? Today?' She gasped in horror, searching his features in an attempt to understand him. His impatience and selfishness astounded her. 'Perhaps tomorrow, or the day after. But today? How can I think of anyone else but Isla?'

'I love you enough to fill the void her death has created.'

'No one will ever fill that void. Not even you, Louis my love. Not even you.'

'Let me try.'

'Then give me time. Let us all come to terms with this terrible tragedy.'

'But nothing is going to change. Your family will always find me eccentric. I can't be what I'm not. I can't be a Cecil; it's not in my nature. They'll never embrace me as their son-in-law and I'll never settle for anything else, Audrey.'

'Let's not talk about this now. Please, Louis, let's talk about this when we've had time to come to terms with Isla's death.' She wanted to add that she needed his comfort not his demands but he looked so fragile she feared he might do himself harm so she remained silent, wondering where the Louis she knew and loved had gone.

157

But Louis interpreted her request as a veiled way of delaying the agony. She no longer wanted him and he no longer wanted to be around her, so great was the sting of her rejection.

Audrey begged him to accompany her home for the tea but he insisted on returning to the Club. Audrey knew that he would go straight to the piano and play the most doleful tune he was capable of. She was envious that he had a means of venting his emotions, she longed to convert the agony of her soul into beautiful music but all she could do was cry. She watched him leave, then wrapping her coat about her she hurried home through the icy gale feeling as hollow as a husk.

She looked about her at the bare winter trees and the pale, watery sky and remembered how Isla had cared little for the beauty of Nature. She had barely seemed to notice it. And yet they had understood each other perfectly in spite of the vast differences that would have divided other siblings. She recalled her sense of fun and her wicked humour, the interest she took in the intrigues of other people's lives and how she longed to whip them all up into a lather of indignation. Well, she had certainly whipped everyone up today, but not in the way that she would have intended. As Audrey gazed upon the craggy old trees she thought of Isla, eternally young, while she and the rest of the living would slowly grow old.

Isla's image dominated Audrey's thinking, squeezing out any thoughts of Louis like a mischievous cuckoo. As much as Louis' demands had unsettled her she didn't have enough energy to dedicate to him and his heartbreak. She felt numb and raw and very, very tired. All she wanted to do was curl up beneath the covers of her bed and sleep her way out of her misery. It had been unfair of Louis to try to force her hand when she was so obviously distracted. If she had had more strength she would have felt anger, but all she could muster was a frail disappointment.

She arrived home to find Cecil anxiously waiting for her. The sitting room resonated with the sombre voices of friends and family who had come to give solace to Rose and Henry but Audrey couldn't face them; instead she allowed Cecil to accompany her into the garden. It was dark and the garden lay still and frozen and unforgiving as if in protest at Isla's death. Audrey couldn't imagine a spring without her and her heart was filled once again with an aching sadness. 'Oh Cecil, I feel so desperate,' she said as they walked beneath the black, starless sky. 'The pain of the soul is so much worse than the pain of the body. I can't imagine I'll ever heal.' She hung her head and her face crumpled again with grief. Cecil, overcome with pity, turned and drew her into his arms. Audrey was too tired to resist. To her surprise it was just what she needed and she let her head rest against his chest and her body derive some comfort from his warm and protective embrace. He held her there and let her vent her anger and sorrow into the icy wind until she had no more strength to cry.

'You two were closer than any siblings I've ever known. It's like losing your right arm, isn't it?' Cecil said in a gentle voice. Audrey nodded and sniffed. 'Death is a tragedy even in the old,' he continued. 'But at least they have lived a full life, dear Isla was still a child with all her life in front of her. It makes me spit with anger. At times like this I wonder if

159

there is a God.' Audrey was surprised to hear Cecil speak with such passion.

'I believe in God. It was Isla's time to go,' she replied. 'I know she's in Heaven. I really believe that. I shall miss her so much, that's all. I can't imagine life without her. I'm crying for myself.'

'You won't be without her. If you believe she's in Heaven, then she's a spirit, as Louis would say, and she'll be with you in spirit.' Audrey thought of Louis and felt guilty for allowing herself to be comforted so intimately by his brother. But then she remembered Louis' inappropriate demands and his selfish behaviour that made Cecil's sympathy all the more touching.

'I can't marry you, Cecil,' she said without thinking. 'My heart is elsewhere.' Cecil patted her back and smiled. 'Of course you can't and your heart shouldn't be anywhere else but here with Isla. I understand, my dear Audrey. You shouldn't even be thinking of it. My proposal couldn't be further from my thoughts. At a time like this? Do you really take me for a heartless fool?'

Audrey was suddenly overcome with gratitude. 'You're not a heartless fool. You're the kindest, sweetest man I have ever met.'

'Think no more about it. Let time heal your pain. Then one day, when you feel ready to face the future again, ponder on it a little. I won't mention it again. But I'll wait for you as long as you want.'

'Thank you, Cecil,' she croaked, drawing away from him and pulling a hanky out of her coat pocket. 'You're a very kind man,' she said again, seeing a different side to the person she had always thought of as cold. Fish *do* feel, she thought,

160

remembering Isla's wicked comment, and blew her nose.

*   *   *

When Cecil returned to the Club, he found Louis slumped over the piano, delirious with alcohol and regret. 'I've lost the one woman I shall ever love,' he mumbled without opening his eyes to the cruel light of the real world.

'I'm so sorry, Louis, I didn't realise,' said Cecil kindly, patting him on his back. So the Colonel had been right all along, Louis had indeed lost his heart to Isla.

'You don't know the half of it, you fool!' Louis snapped drunkenly. Then laughed the high-pitched laugh of a madman.

'You'll feel better in the morning,' Cecil sighed, dragging his brother to his feet. He could no longer count the times he had helped him stagger up that wooden staircase and into his small room to undress him like a sick child. Cecil wondered whether he'd ever be free of the responsibility.

'Only death can liberate me from such a hell,' he slurred.

'Come on, Louis, you'll love again, old boy,' Cecil tried to reassure him, but his patience was wearing thin.

'I'll never love again. She's an angel, there's none other like her.'

'She is an angel. She's with God.' Louis looked at him in puzzlement. Cecil frowned. 'Time is a great healer,' he continued. This infuriated Louis even more.

'Time! That's what she wanted too. Time is what

161

I don't have.'

'What do you mean?' Cecil asked, pulling off his brother's shoes and socks.

'I don't want to be here if I can't have her. It'll kill me.'

'Everyone feels like you do today. We all feel bereft, but we can't run away from our pain.'

'She's dead to me now. I might as well leave.'

'Where to?'

'I'll go wherever the winds take me.'

'Don't be ridiculous,' Cecil retorted, helping Louis into his pyjamas.

'I'm leaving to forget.'

'What will you do?'

'Die of a broken heart.' He laughed again, but this time his laughter was empty and hopeless.

'For goodness sake,' his brother chided him gently, tucking him into his bed. 'You won't even remember you said that in the morning.'

*   *   *

But in the morning Louis was gone. Cecil searched the room for some indication of where he had gone and for how long he intended to be away. But he had taken all his belongings with him, except a note, which he had left on the dresser for his brother to find.

Cecil picked it up and opened it. Slowly he read what Louis had written. As his eyes scanned the page his face turned pale and his lips twitched. He inhaled deeply then proceeded to read it again. After a while he sat down in thought, turning the little piece of paper over and over in his fingers. Finally he returned to his own room. There he folded it up and placed it in a polished walnut box he used for locking away things of great importance. Stiffening his shoulders and straightening his back he walked purposefully over to Canning Street to tell Rose and her family. *I survived the war, I can survive this*, he thought to himself. But he knew the greatest challenge of his life awaited him.

CHAPTER TEN

Louis' sudden disappearance only confirmed what everyone had suspected: that he and Isla had been in love. But because Isla was dead and above criticism their clandestine relationship wasn't reviewed with horror; on the contrary, it was seen as a romantic tragedy of Shakespearean proportions and Louis, the grieving lover, was respected in a way that would never have otherwise been possible. If he had been worthy of Isla's affection, they deduced, he must be a very special human being indeed. Unwittingly she had salvaged his reputation, but Louis was unaware of it, sitting miserably on the drizzly deck of a freight ship bound for Mexico.

Rose wept copious tears when she heard the news from Cecil who had hurried over to Canning Street at the first light of dawn. 'He loved my Isla?' she snivelled, crumbling into an armchair in her dressing gown. 'I thought I knew everything about my daughter's life, but I didn't. I've been monstrously unfair to dear Louis. Isla loved him and if dear Isla loved him then I love him too.'

'He left a note explaining that he couldn't bear to be in the same country if he couldn't have her love,' Cecil explained, his face grim. 'Louis isn't like other people,' he continued earnestly. 'But he's a good person. I think he'll regret leaving and be back. Last night he was distraught. We are all distraught and no one more so than you, Rose, and your family. But as I said, Louis is different. He doesn't think things through. He's all feeling and no thought. I told him time would ease his suffering. He can't cope when things go wrong for him. I feel desperate. Before Isla died I don't think I'd ever seen him looking so happy and well. He was a very different Louis.' Cecil looked away and wiped his forehead with a hanky. He felt very strange, as if he were made of air.

'I so hope he comes back, I really do,' said Rose. 'I would dearly love to hear about their friendship. I hate to think there's a part of my daughter's life I haven't shared. Oh, Cecil, do you really think he might come back?'

At that moment Audrey walked in. She too was in her dressing gown with her long curls in disarray about her shoulders and down her back to her waist. Cecil caught his breath because he had never seen her look more beautiful. He was at once energised with determination. But Audrey felt depleted and empty as if someone had sucked out all her insides leaving the wound raw and aching. 'Who's gone?' she asked impassively, wrapping her arms around her body in a subconscious attempt to comfort herself. Cecil hesitated, disarmed by her vulnerability.

'Did you know that Isla was in love with Louis?' Rose asked with impatience.

164

'Isla in love with Louis?' Audrey repeated in confusion. 'No she wasn't.'

'Yes, dear, she was. Cecil's got his note to prove it. Now he's left us. He told Cecil that he can't bear to be in the Argentine if she's not here. What a passionate young man.'

'Louis has gone?' she gasped in horror, finding it difficult to breathe. She turned to Cecil in panic.

'I'm afraid he left this morning,' he replied. Audrey sat down and dissolved into tears. Cecil wanted to hold her again like he had after the funeral, but he knew such a gesture would be unwelcome.

'My dear child,' her mother soothed, reaching out to her. 'This has come as a terrible shock to us all. A part of Isla none of us knew. I must say, I would have thought she would have confided in you.' But Audrey was unable to contain her sorrow.

'Where has he gone?' she sobbed.

'England, I think,' Cecil replied. Then he heard himself saying, 'I should think he'll be back when he calms down. He was very overwrought last night. He had also drunk too much. I should imagine he'll come to his senses when he sobers up. Don't despair, he'll be back, I'm sure of it.' But he was only sure of one thing, that whatever happened now there was no turning back.

*   *   *

Audrey ran upstairs and when she was alone in the bathroom she vomited. How could he leave like that, without even saying good-bye, without at least giving her an explanation? If he loved her, how could he leave her to suffer like this? Then she

165

recalled Cecil's words and with desperation she clutched the small grain of hope. Perhaps he would come to his senses and return when he realised that she was worth waiting for. When he realised that all was not lost. Then she blamed herself. How could she have been so insensitive to his feelings? After all, he needed her too. She had only been thinking of herself.

*   *   *

'You see, I was right all along,' said Charlo happily, studying her cards through her glasses. 'That Isla was a mischief.'

'A very dear mischief,' Diana added, pulling a sympathetic smile.

'Well, we were all wrong about Louis Forrester,' said Cynthia. 'I'm happy to admit when I'm wrong.'

'Me too,' interjected Phyllida, fingering her cards nervously. She wasn't very good at Bridge and every time they sat down for a rubber she felt like a fly about to be devoured by three very large lizards. She cringed and blinked down at her own useless hand of cards.

'Oh, I was never wrong about Louis,' Charlo retorted. 'He's reckless and irresponsible and always will be.'

'Oh, you twisty turny thing!' Cynthia objected, placing her deck face down on the table. 'You said he was mad!'

'No, Cynthia dear, *you* said he was mad.'

'At least I have the decency to admit it, Charlo, you devil. He's not mad, nor is he callous. He's a truly romantic figure and there aren't many of them around nowadays.' Cynthia snorted at

166

Charlo. Charlo lifted her chin and snorted back.

'No, because I buried three of them,' she said and laughed at her own tasteless joke.

'I hope the fourth buries you!'

'Really,' interrupted Diana in a gentle voice. 'We were all very wrong about Louis and now he's gone. I feel desperately sorry for him, poor young man. There's nothing more painful than a broken heart.'

'Quite,' said Phyllida, delighted that the argument was delaying the game.

'We shall all miss Isla dreadfully.'

'Dreadfully,' Phyllida repeated.

'Don't worry, Audrey will marry Cecil and that will give us all good reason to smile again,' said Charlo.

'Or you'll marry the Colonel and that will give us all good reason to laugh again,' Cynthia added with a wicked grin. But Charlo didn't laugh. A frown swept across her powdered brow. There was something different about Colonel Blythe. A sentimental look in his eyes, a faraway expression, a softening of the voice and a sad tune he kept humming to himself. She dared hope that the change in him might have been inspired by her. But she wasn't going to share her thoughts. They'd mock her if she revealed an uncharacteristic soppiness. 'You may be laughing sooner than you think,' she challenged. Cynthia stared at Charlo with her mouth agape.

'I don't believe it,' she said slowly. 'You really are going to bury a fourth.'

'No, no, I think I'll have more fun with a living Colonel than a dead one,' she mused, then added with unexpected gloom, 'I don't think the dead are much fun any more.'

*   *   *

But in the wake of Isla's death no one could care less about Charlotte Osborne's relationship with the Colonel. Hurlingham became a suburb of shadows as everyone shuffled about not knowing what to do with themselves, remembering with disbelief the sunny child whose cheeky grin and bouncy gait had dominated their world. How could someone so alive suddenly be so dead? They all thought of their own fragile lives and felt more transitory than ever. Their time would come and then what?

Louis and Isla's imagined love affair became the stuff of legend—a modern day Romeo and Juliet, which the community feasted on with curiosity grown hungry from so much mourning. Men admired Louis for his heroism and women envied Isla's fearlessness. Suddenly everyone seemed to know so much about their affair, how it had started, where they would meet, their dreams for the future and how, the very night Isla fell ill, they were planning to elope. The more the stories circulated the more outlandish they became, but no one was prepared to stop. In death Isla now belonged to everyone.

'Nelly has been crying now for a month,' Hilda complained. 'Louis has gone and taken her heart with him. Really, I've never known so many tears shed over a man.'

Rose spent most afternoons beside the fire in her sitting room, shivering with a constant chill that resisted the warmth however boisterous the flames were, deriving comfort from her sisters' regular visits which served to prevent her from sinking into a bottomless pit of self-pity.

'Nelly's got nothing to cry about,' Edna snapped impatiently, tired of having to listen to her sister's complaints about her daughter's imaginary heartache. 'How's Audrey, Rose?' she asked in a gentle voice. Rose shook her head while Hilda pursed her thin lips. She resented the fact that everyone was talking about Rose's daughters with the sort of reverence reserved for the Saints. If Isla were alive she'd have caused the very foundations of their community to shake with disapproval, but she was now beyond disapproval and Audrey had been sprinkled with the same holy water. She stared furiously into her cup of tea.

'She's taken the whole thing very badly,' said Rose bleakly. 'She just sits in her bedroom gazing out of the window miserably or pacing the room in fury. Why she's so furious, I have no idea. God,' she added piously, 'it must be directed at God. After all, it is God's doing.'

'And Cecil? Can't he do something to revive her?'

'She needs time to mourn,' Rose replied, lowering her eyes for she was ashamed that all her hopes for her future happiness rested with them. 'He's a tower of strength. He comes around most evenings to see her, but she refuses to leave her room.'

'Oh dear, that doesn't augur well, does it?' Hilda commented with a brittleness of tone that betrayed her jealousy.

'I don't think so, Hilda,' said Rose. 'He's a sensitive young man and understands that she

169

needs time to come to terms with Isla's death before she can possibly focus her heart on him.'

'But surely at a time like this Audrey should welcome his comfort.'

'Everyone deals with grief in their own way, Hilda,' interjected Edna. 'Audrey's always been a bit different from other girls. She's a private person, introverted. Remember she's not only lost her sister, God bless her, but her best friend.' Then turning to Rose she added with a heavy sigh, 'Isn't there something we can do to raise her spirits? Mourning too much is very bad for one's health.'

'Well,' Rose began in a small voice, 'Cecil did make a suggestion.'

'What was that?'

'It sounds a bit outlandish, but . . .'

'I'd try anything once,' said Edna.

'He suggested we buy a piano, just a small one, you know, an upright.'

'Whatever for?' Hilda asked. 'She hasn't played the piano for years.'

'Cecil says that Louis plays to soothe his spirits. He once saw Audrey play with him and she seemed to take great pleasure from it.'

'What a tremendous idea, Rose. What does Henry say?' Edna asked with enthusiasm. *What this house needs*, she thought, *is a bit of gaiety.*

'He's willing to try,' she replied.

'Well, get a piano as soon as possible, before that child ruins any hope for her future. Cecil will only wait so long.'

*   *   *

Rose hastily bought a piano which was delivered

the following week. Audrey still refused to leave her room, so stricken with grief was she. Albert and his two younger brothers delighted in tinkling the keys until Rose told them sternly that it was for Audrey and until she felt like playing it, no one else would. Then just when she was on the point of despairing she awoke one night in early spring to the haunting music of Audrey's tormented soul. She crept out of bed, slipped into her dressing gown and tiptoed down the stairs. As she neared the study the melody got louder until she peered around the door to see Audrey's straight back and trembling shoulders as she wept to the tune that Louis had composed especially for her. Her pale fingers glided over the keys as if she had played all her life and her eyes were closed to allow the music to take her to all the exotic places she had dreamed of visiting with Louis. Rose felt the emotion rise in her throat and placed her fingers over her mouth to prevent herself from gasping. She stood in the shadows watching and listening as her daughter expressed her grief. Then she left as quietly as she had come. Audrey would never know that her mother had shared in this intensely private moment.

*   *   *

Audrey realised now that Louis wasn't ever coming back. She had allowed her regret to eat away at her spirit until she had very little of it left. She had mourned for her sister until thoughts of Louis had begun to dominate every present moment and she had waited and waited and waited until hope had given way to despair and finally resignation. The piano and their music was all she had left of him and once she began to play she was unable to stop.

She bashed out her fury in clashing chords that hurt her ears and sent the furniture vibrating with the very force of her anger. Louis hadn't allowed her a moment to grieve, he had demanded she settle their future at the one time she was unable to. The very day Isla had been taken from her. Then in a fit of impatience and petulance he had deserted her. What sort of a man could behave with such irrationality? What had come over him? Then she played out her sadness in harmonious chords that she stroked with loving fingers until even Aunt Hilda's stony eyes seeped tears. The one man she had ever loved was gone and the notes sung out her pain and her hopelessness. Then when she was alone in the darkness of the midnight hours she would feel him close by, so close she could almost smell him, and her fingers would dance across the keys as if by a will of their own and their sonata would resonate through the room and through the months that ensued. It was their tune, the only expression of their unbreakable bond and she played it to remember him as she willed herself to remember him, before that evening in the church when her dreams had been shattered. And she called it 'The Forget-Me-Not Sonata' for as long as she played it she would not forget him.

But the most surprising thing was that with every tune she began to feel better. Her spirits began to rise and her wounds began to heal.

Then without her even noticing, Cecil earned her friendship and her trust and finally her affection.

172

*   *   *

Audrey sat on the sand and gazed out across the sea that was surprisingly tempestuous for midsummer. The sun was on the brink of melting into the water and she waited as she had always done as a child for the hiss and the steam. But none came. So much had changed since her coming of age. The world looked different somehow. With Isla's death and Louis' disappearance now over two years ago a part of her had gone to sleep. A sure way of dealing with the pain.

'What are you thinking about?' Cecil asked, taking her hand in his. He often wondered what was on her mind, especially when he listened to her playing the piano. Recently, though, the tunes had become less tormented and more harmonious and so had she.

'Isla and I used to sit on this Uruguayan beach and watch the sunset,' she replied. Nowadays she didn't flinch when Cecil took her hand. Ever since he had embraced her in the garden at Isla's funeral she had grown accustomed to his touch, even welcomed it. He had been a constant support, an attentive friend. With Cecil there was no pressure, no demand, just his gentle companionship. She held his hand firmly and took pleasure from the familiar warmth of his skin. 'Isla was never very interested in nature, but she always waited for the hiss and the steam of the sun hitting the water. She used to swear that she heard it. I always felt cheated because I never did.'

'She was a little mischief,' he chuckled affectionately.

173

'Not a day goes by when I don't think about her. We did everything together, everything. I really miss her.'

'Of course you do.'

'But I've come to rely on you, Cecil,' she said earnestly.

Cecil stared out across the sea, afraid of looking at her in case the desperation in his eyes gave away the longing in his heart. 'Good,' he mumbled.

'One good thing has come out of all this tragedy and that is you.' She smiled at him but the smile he returned was fleeting. He kept his focus on the horizon but his hand clutched hers ever more tightly. 'I felt lost without Isla, but little by little I turned to you when I would have turned to her. Your friendship means a great deal to me.'

'I'm pleased.'

'I couldn't bear to think about a future without Isla. I didn't want to live. Everything was so bleak, but you've made it sunny again. I know it's been over two years since you proposed and as you promised, you haven't mentioned it again. I hope I'm not being too bold or presumptuous, but I would like to be your wife, if you'll have me.'

Cecil wanted to cry with relief. Every day of waiting for Audrey had increased the burden of hope on his shoulders so that now he almost stooped beneath the weight. He had begun to wonder whether she would ever grow to love him even half as much as he loved her. His feelings had only intensified with time so that now he couldn't imagine living without her and if he did, he felt the blood in his veins turn to stone. A cold and empty future indeed. Now all the waiting seemed to have passed in a moment. She had agreed to be his and

174

his heart felt as if it were filled with bubbles. He turned to her with eyes that glistened with emotion and smiled with so much enthusiasm it was impossible not to smile with him. 'I never thought I'd be capable of loving as much as I love you, Audrey. You're a unique woman and I'm honoured that you have chosen to share your life with me. Honoured, truly.'

Audrey laughed lightly. He always sounded so formal. 'No, I'm honoured that you will still have me. I've kept you waiting so long.'

'I would have waited for you for ever,' he said, looking at her steadily. She lowered her eyes anxiously anticipating his kiss, trying not to think of Louis. Every morning she awoke with his face emblazoned on her mind, and every morning she willed it away where it hovered awaiting its chance to rise again in her thoughts. She felt sick in the stomach with wearisome regularity so that now she didn't know whether it was because of Isla or Louis—whichever it was, the sharp sense of loss never left her. Her only hope of respite was in a secure future and in time Cecil could give her the former and patience would give her the latter. Then one day she might wake up without that sensation of falling into an abyss, without the bitter dawning of reality and what it lacked.

When Cecil kissed her it was surprisingly pleasant. It didn't burn like Louis' always had but it didn't feel awkward either. It was warm and tender and protective. She wrapped her arms around his neck and felt a reassuring sense of security loosen the knots that misery and regret had tied with determined fingers. With Cecil she had a future, perhaps not the future she had dreamed of, but she was weary of dreaming.

CHAPTER ELEVEN

Charlotte Osborne insisted on a church wedding. Not that she was a virgin bride, she was the first to admit that she was no virgin, having buried three husbands already. But she felt, being a widow, it was correct and proper to have a small, intimate religious service followed by a large tea at the Club. She wanted flowers, champagne, pomp and adulation. The Colonel would have married her on the moon had she asked, for, overwhelmed with gratitude, he could deny her nothing. His dogged persistence had won the final battle and Charlotte had surrendered, waving her white flag with the enthusiasm of a woman who's wanted to be conquered all along. 'Now come here, old girl, and let me kiss you,' he had said, pulling her into his arms and tickling her face with his whiskers.

'How does this old girl taste?' She had giggled like a young girl in the first throes of love.

'Like a vintage champagne, m'dear, once the cork's out it's all bubbles and fizz. There's life in the old girl yet!' Then he had looked at her with tenderness and said bashfully, 'But once the bubbles and fizz die down the wine is full bodied and fruity. I knew you wouldn't disappoint, Charlotte Osborne. You're still a challenge and always will be, but by God you were worth the wait.' And in his ears still echoed the tune he had heard long ago but never forgotten, filling him once again with an exquisite melancholy; the

176

melancholy that is the weight of love on one's soul.

Spring spilled into the church in the pale light of morning, in the flamboyant displays of lilacs and lilies and in the buoyant step of the old Colonel who, in spite of his limp, strode proudly up the aisle, his whiskers twitching with the satisfaction of a military leader reflecting on his greatest victory, an icily beautiful Charlotte Osborne resting haughtily on his arm.

Diana Lewis cast her eyes over the perfectly tailored lilac suit, the wide-brimmed hat coyly lowered over one eye, the silver white hair pulled back into an elegant chignon and couldn't help but admire her friend, who in the autumn years of her life had acquired a handsome beauty. *If it wasn't for her thin lips*, she thought, *one would be led into thinking her beauty extended beneath her skin.* Phyllida Bates sat hunched and shrivelled for her lack of spine had caused her body to sag. She hated weddings because she had never married, but she smiled all the same and no one would have guessed that there was venom in her saliva. Cynthia Klein, who was too lazy to dissemble, gazed upon the old couple who now stood before the altar to make their vows to love and cherish one another and wondered whether Charlo was capable of doing either. Still, she couldn't help but feel a certain tenderness towards them as they stood, aged and grey beneath their fine feathers, vulnerable somehow in the face of God, making the most of the few years they had left.

'*Till death us do part,*' said Charlo in a quivering voice and Diana caught Phyllida's eye, then glanced warily across at Cynthia. They were all thinking the same thing. How long would the

177

Colonel last before he met his Maker? But since Isla's death Charlo had looked at life through different eyes. The final act was now opening to great applause. This leading man would take the bow with her, not before her.

Audrey sat next to her husband and cast her thoughts to her sister as she always did every time she attended church. She remembered the funeral as if it were yesterday and she missed her just as much now. Although the pain was less acute it was still very much there in the form of a constant, dull ache. She missed Louis too, but had resigned herself to the choice she had made and Cecil was a loving husband. She couldn't complain.

*   *   *

Since Audrey's marriage the previous April her mother had come out of mourning and laughter once more reverberated about the walls of the house in Canning Street, though the little spark that was Isla was noticeably lacking. The wedding had been large and extravagant and her mother had thrown herself into its organisation with all her energy and enthusiasm. Aunt Edna had almost moved in and acted as secretary, making lists and amending them, holding meetings with the florist, the caterers, the dressmaker and Audrey had sailed along on automatic pilot not caring that all the decisions were being made for her. She relinquished control as willingly as she had relinquished her heart, but her soul would always belong to Louis.

Cecil had bought a little house a few streets away from the Garnets' and Audrey had done her utmost to make it into a warm home. It was of vital importance to her that she create a small fortress where she could hide away and live off her memories, so she busied herself decorating it, throwing all her love into the rooms until they vibrated with the force of her yearning spirit. She placed her piano in the sitting room and covered it with candles so that when she played at night, the soft, flickering light of the flames served to calm her nerves as well as transport her to a place far away where she still kept her dreams all shiny and new. Rose said it had a magic feel about it and Cecil praised his wife for she had endowed the house with charm and made it beautiful. Only Aunt Edna sensed that her niece had compromised in some way, for she went about the fine tuning of her home with the devotion she should have been dedicating to her marriage. She had done the same thing after Harry had died in order to comfort herself and nurture his memory, but Cecil was very much alive.

As Charlotte and the Colonel walked back up the aisle as man and wife, their faces aglow with happiness, Audrey pulled away from the past and cast her eyes across to where the light tumbled in through the large glass window. She followed its stream until her gaze rested upon the face of Emma Letton who silently withdrew from beneath the sycamore tree to focus her eyes on the dreamy young woman who now stared back at her. They both remained in silent appraisal, wordlessly sensing an invisible bond that drew them to one another. Audrey smiled shyly and was pleased when Emma smiled back with enthusiasm. There had always been something in the young girl's

179

expression that Emma had found curious. She had been slightly afraid of the sensitive child who seemed to understand her in a way that no one else could, as if her penetrating stare would expose her inner unhappiness and the compromise she had made.

'How are you enjoying married life?' Emma asked Audrey as they found each other on their way out of the church. It was an awkward question for Emma sensed that Audrey had shelved her dreams and bowed to convention because she noticed that she smiled only on the surface of her face. Audrey clutched her neat handbag with gloved hands and tried not to look at the wooden pew at the back of the church which always reminded her of Louis.

'Lovely, thank you,' she replied. 'This church has seen so many weddings, if one could see through the eyes of this building one would see the constant cycle of births, weddings, death. It reminds me of my own mortality.' Emma thought of Isla and looked across at Audrey with the deepest sympathy.

'Churches remind me of uncontrollable school giggles, a devastatingly handsome missionary who tried to teach us about God but only served to raise our blood pressure and the time I was a bridesmaid and hid under the altar cloth in fear until the wedding was over and a funeral in full flow.'

Audrey laughed and Emma was pleased that she had lightened their conversation.

'How did you escape?'

'I didn't. I was found by my father, trembling in the dark, convinced that I would go to Hell.'

'You've redeemed yourself since then,' Audrey

180

remarked, 'Thomas has made an honest woman out of you.'

'Yes,' she sighed, then added in a whisper, 'he has, but sometimes I rather wish he hadn't. When you think of your own mortality, doesn't it make you desire to live on your impulses, the way you truly want to live, not the way other people want you to live?' Audrey looked at Emma and recognised the amber light of resignation in her eyes, making them look suddenly sad and defeated.

'We aren't masters of our own destinies after all,' she replied carefully. 'As a child I believed I could be whatever I wanted to be.'

'And you're not?'

'Not entirely. But I'm happy,' she added quickly, glancing over at Cecil who waited for her at the door. 'Marriage is a wonderful thing and you've got a child.'

'Yes, Robert, I'm truly blessed.'

'You are,' Audrey replied, smiling at her husband who waved at her.

'Cecil's so handsome and charming, you know, when you married him you were the envy of every woman in Hurlingham, married or not.'

'I can't believe that.'

'You were and still are. Everyone loves Cecil. Whatever did happen to Louis?'

'I don't know.' Audrey shrugged and looked away for fear that Emma would read her expression and know that she too loved another. 'He sailed away and was never heard of again.'

'Really?'

'I think so.'

'Cecil hasn't even heard from him?'

'No.'

181

'Well, I hope he's found happiness somewhere nice. I always found him rather intriguing. He was a genius, quite misunderstood. Did you ever hear him play the piano?'

Audrey nodded. 'Why don't you walk with us to the Club? Isn't it lovely that the weather has changed and spring is here?'

'Yes, isn't it. I'll go and get Thomas, I think he needs rescuing, he's talking to Diana Lewis and Phyllida Bates. They always manage to corner him and poor Thomas is too polite to walk away.'

'I've asked Emma and Thomas Letton to walk with us to the Club,' said Audrey, rejoining her husband.

'Wasn't she the one who created that huge scandal all those years ago by falling in love with an Argentine boy?'

'Yes, but she's happily married to Thomas now.'

'Of course, those sort of infatuations never last.'

'No.' Audrey sighed and thought how little he understood the hearts of women.

They walked back up the roads strewn with violet petals from the jacaranda trees, breathing in the rich scents of gardenia and honeysuckle that had burst into flower with the warm weather and commenting on the wedding, which united them all in laughter. 'Imagine the old Colonel, finally making it up the aisle,' Thomas said in amusement.

'Wasn't he married before?' asked Audrey.

'Years ago, but she died,' said Emma, raising her eyebrows suggestively.

'Well, that's something they both have in common. I wonder who'll outlive who,' said Thomas.

'I have a funny feeling that this time they'll both

want to go together,' said Audrey. Cecil took her hand in his and chuckled.

'That's typical of you, Audrey, ever the romantic.'

'Emma's a romantic too,' said Thomas, grinning down at his wife with affection. 'She must be the only person here who thinks that hateful Charlotte Osborne . . .'

'Blythe,' corrected Cecil with a laugh.

'Charlotte *Blythe*, the Honourable Mrs Blythe,' Thomas added with emphasis, 'had the radiance of a young bride.'

'She did look quite beautiful,' breathed Emma in admiration.

'The devil has many disguises,' Cecil interjected humorously.

'I agree with Emma,' said Audrey, grinning at her. 'Charlo is a beautiful, elegant woman. If I look half as good as her when I'm an old lady I'll be very contented.'

'Darling, your beauty comes from within and will never wither,' said Cecil seriously.

'Thank you,' Audrey replied, feeling the colour rise in her cheeks.

'That's what I always say to Emma,' Thomas said. 'Why don't they ever believe us?'

Cecil shrugged his shoulders. 'You two have a lot in common, don't you?' he said.

Emma looked across at Audrey and gave a knowing smile. 'Yes, we do,' she replied. Audrey said nothing. She linked her arm through her husband's and lowered her eyes, aware that they had more in common than Thomas and Cecil would ever know.

'I want to say a few words about my new wife,' began the Colonel, swaying slightly, one hand on the stand for support, the other holding a newly topped-up flute of champagne. It appeared as if his bursting belly would topple him over, but he leant back and used the balls of his large feet for balance. He winked at Charlo and his whiskers twitched with sentiment. 'We're old,' he stated, raising eyebrows that resembled two mangy cats' tails. 'There's no doubt about it. Charlo and I are well into our twilight years but for me life has never been better. I thought the rough fields of the Somme were as much excitement as I would have in my life. But then I met Charlo. I had retired from the army and thought my fighting days were over. But Charlo was one territory I couldn't leave unconquered. She doesn't know this, so don't tell her, but she's the greatest victory of my career. It took all my reserves, all my energies, all my courage to win her and never have I held such a prize. She's beautiful, she's elegant, she's wise and she's strong enough to save me from myself. Charlo,' he said, his small eyes twinkling at her with emotion brought on by the alcohol and a strange magic. 'I didn't shed a tear when young Jimmy MacMannus was shot down in the winter of 1916 although I wanted to with every nerve in my body and I didn't shed a tear when Old Bernard Blythe, my late father, died of pneumonia when I was but a wee lad of thirteen, but you, old girl, have the power to make me weep with gratitude that you have chosen to share your final years with an old battle-weary dog like me. I'll make you happy, by

184

God I will and, Charlo, old girl, I'm hanging on here for a good many more years. Life is beginning to get interesting and you've made me feel like a young man of twenty again. Let us raise our glasses to Charlotte Blythe, Charlotte Hamilton-Hughes-Fordington-Blythe and in case you're all wondering, this is about as many names as one woman can carry. There will be no more funerals and no more weddings in the life of the new Mrs Blythe because when I go, old girl, I'm taking you with me.' He raised his glass then added with a smirk, 'We're bloody lucky with the weather, it's snowing in London!' When the applause died down the music began to play and he swept his new bride onto the dance floor where he pressed his sweating cheek against hers. Charlo noticed that his hands were shaking and her thin lips curled into a tender smile.

Aunt Hilda looked across at Nelly and wondered whether she'd ever find a husband. She wasn't getting any younger and there were now few young men available for marriage. Nelly wasn't getting any prettier either; she had never had the luxury of choice, not like Audrey who had had every man in Hurlingham longing to court her. Nelly had to wait until she was approached and at the moment there wasn't a decent young man within fifty miles of her. She watched her husband dance with Emma Letton's little sister, Victoria, and swallowed her resentment as he pressed himself up against her in the most inappropriate way. Poor Victoria visibly cringed and smiled helplessly over his shoulder. Hilda remembered how he had always had an unsuitable fascination with Isla, but now Isla was gone he grabbed the opportunity to dance with any

185

young girl he could lay his hands on. *Disgusting*, she thought wearily, *tragic old man*.

'Why don't you dance?' she said to her daughter when Nelly wandered over, bored and tired and desperate to go home.

'Because, Mummy, no one's asked me. Besides, I don't want to dance with Daddy, he's drunk too much and is sweating like an old pig.'

'Nelly, that is no way to talk about your father,' chided her mother frostily.

'You're a hopeless example, Mummy, the names you call him are much worse.'

'That's not the point. There must be someone you can dance with.'

'No one,' she stated firmly. She glanced around at the chinless young men her mother deemed fit for her to mix with and rolled her eyes in despair.

*   *   *

Audrey was contented with Cecil. He was cheerful, charming, attentive and generous. But they had so little in common. Audrey loved literature, poetry, music and nature while Cecil enjoyed business, politics, economics and people. He wanted the house full of friends all the time while Audrey longed to be alone among the trees and flowers, to ride the gentle waves of her dreams and bring to life those she had loved and lost. Audrey was aware that her husband didn't understand her, that a large part of her was relegated to the shadows of her personality to emerge only when the room was bathed in candlelight and her fingers danced upon the keys of her piano. But Cecil had given her a secure home, she wanted for nothing, and he tried

186

desperately to please her. But one can't teach a blind man how to appreciate a painting and Cecil was blind to Audrey's emotional needs.

Cecil was also content but he longed to recapture the happiness he had enjoyed in those first intoxicating months of their engagement. Now Audrey seemed lost to him, in her own distant world, surrounding herself with an invisible, impenetrable shell where he was unable to reach her. When she played the piano, those sad melodies in the minor key that she would invent for hours and repeat until his head swam, she reminded him of his brother. The same expression would descend upon her face and her skin would drain of colour and glow with the same strange translucence. He had spent his life trying to understand Louis and now he spent much of it trying to understand his wife. But as much as he endeavoured to take an interest in her poetry and her music, converse about the transience of nature and debate the meaning of life and death, the struggle was a useless one. At times she seemed to be talking a completely different language and there wasn't a textbook in the world to teach him the vocabulary. He often felt more at home with Rose and Henry than he did with their daughter.

Rose adored Cecil with the devotion of a mother who has lost a daughter and gained a son. She admired him and looked up to him. He reminded her of Henry when she first met him, the straight back, the square shoulders, the handsome nose and the formal air that she found reassuringly predictable. She enjoyed the way he would sit up with Henry until the early hours of the morning, puffing on a Havana, discussing the sorry state of the economy, berating in hushed voices the dictatorship that both felt would come to a sticky end. Cecil was everything they had hoped for in a son-in-law. Not only had he brought their daughter much happiness but he had also brought happiness back into their lives. She was filled with pride that Audrey had made such a good match although she had never ever doubted her. Audrey had always been the sensible child.

In order to escape the continuing pain of Isla's death Rose had to keep busy, so she cleaved to Audrey and Cecil, Edna and Hilda, Henry and her young sons. Busy busy busy, so that she didn't have time to dwell on the loss. Then Audrey announced one evening in late summer that she was expecting a baby. Never before had Rose been so aware of the cycle of life that continued in spite of Isla's death. It was then that she found peace of mind, in the certain knowledge that birth and death are two sides of the same coin and that one had to think of the future, not dwell on the past. Rose's future was now assured, her sons would grow up and fly the nest but Audrey and Cecil would remain close and fill her days with grandchildren.

Cecil hoped that the birth of their child would give them a common ground on which they could restore their marriage. He also hoped that motherhood would anchor Audrey's mind and cease its dreamy wanderings.

*   *   *

Alicia and Leonora were born in October 1954 in the hospital of The Little Company of Mary where their mother had come into the world twenty-four years before. Audrey gazed in awe upon the two creatures God had entrusted into her safekeeping. They blinked up at her with the eyes of strangers in spite of the nine months that she had carried them and felt them moving and kicking inside her belly. Holding them close she studied their little faces, so full of innocence, so heavenly it broke her heart to think of the painful journey of life that lay ahead of them. Alicia was alert and strong with damp blonde hair that clung to her scalp and a voice that already struggled to communicate her opinions while Leonora made a frail mewing noise and clung with all her might to the towel that she had been wrapped in. Audrey was too moved and too exhausted to speak. She cuddled both babies to her breasts, kissing their wet faces and sniffing their skin as animals do. For the first time in years her heart didn't ache but throbbed with a new energy and a new purpose. The weight of such a responsibility shook her from her dreams. Louis retreated to the back of her mind, taking with him her sadness and her regret so that in the years that ensued she rarely touched the piano except to play jolly songs and nursery rhymes which they would all sing together in the sunny sitting room with the French doors open onto the leafy terrace. Audrey felt Isla's presence throughout the birth as she watched with excitement from the world of spirit, separated only by the intangible wall of vibrations. Audrey felt happy inside, a warm feeling that filled her whole body as if her blood had turned to golden honey. When Cecil entered he was immediately struck by the change in his wife. She reminded him of that first night at the theatre, glowing with exhilaration and optimism. She smiled

189

up at him.

'Twins!' he exclaimed in amazement.

She nodded and her eyes brimmed with tears. 'This is the happiest day of my life, Cecil.' She whispered, for the sound of her voice would surely spoil the divine nature of the moment. 'I feel whole again, as if I've completed a circle, as if with the birth of our daughters I've come to terms with Isla's death. For the first time in years I don't feel pain.' She spoke with such passion that her eyes shone. Cecil was afraid to look into them because the light that burned behind them was unfamiliar. Audrey withdrew and gazed upon the two beings who had suddenly given her life meaning. Then she held her hand out and Cecil took it. Once again her future was painted with the colour of love.

PART II

PART II

CHAPTER TWELVE

The years that followed were swallowed up in the laughter and sunshine of family life so that Audrey was barely aware of the rapid passing of time. Her children brought her much happiness and forged a bridge between herself and Cecil where they were able to meet with total understanding. Cecil recaptured that lightness of being he had so wished for and Audrey's ghosts were locked away with the candles. Rose and Edna applauded the twins regardless of whether they deserved praise or not while Hilda quietly smouldered in the shadows of her bitterness resenting her own daughters for not being pretty and charming and married with children.

Cecil found his wife again; the nights were no longer filled with the doleful music of the piano, but with hours free to love each other in, and Audrey, for whom physical intimacy with her husband had been at the best of times little more than a duty, discovered that a new tenderness had grown up between them. She opened her heart and noticed, to her surprise, that there was a place for him there. It had been wrong of her to constantly compare him to the brother who had created sparks just by looking at her. That kind of magic surely wouldn't have lasted. Besides, she had chosen to marry Cecil and now with hindsight she could appreciate that it had most certainly been for the best. She was happy. Who knows how much unhappiness Louis would have brought?

Audrey was able to enjoy her babies for Emily

Harris, an English nurse shipped over from Brighton, stayed with them for the first couple of years and it was she who suffered broken nights and the exhaustion that comes from the heavy responsibility of caring for infant twins. When she left she was a smaller, greyer version of the rosy young woman who had appeared starched in uniform on their doorstep, full of enthusiasm and energy. As much as she had grown to love the twins, Emily found Alicia uncontrollable and the child sapped her of her juices until she had precious little left for herself. She knew that unless she quit she would grow old before her time, gathering dust on the shelf. She could barely get herself up in the morning let alone go out in her free time and meet people. She missed Leonora dreadfully but she was pleased not to have to deal with Alicia's tantrums and demands any longer.

*   *   *

When it came to her children, Audrey's love was without limits. Sometimes she would collapse into tears beneath the sheer weight of her gratitude and silently thank God for giving her little girls who would love and support each other as she and Isla had. Cecil was a good father, albeit a detached one. He earned well in her father's company and saw to it that his daughters had everything they needed. He wasn't a demonstrative man like his brother for whom touch was as vital as oxygen. Cecil showed his affection with the occasional pat on the back, with a willingness to read bedtime stories and a keen interest in their education. He took great care to ensure that the girls' future was secure while

194

their mother lived only in the present.

Leonora belonged to her mother. Alicia belonged to herself. After Emily Harris left Leonora had cleaved to Audrey, crying hysterically when she was parted from her. If it hadn't been for Alicia's cool independence Audrey would have gone mad with anxiety for she couldn't have taken both girls to her bed at night. But Alicia could sleep anywhere, needing nothing but a nightdress and a mattress—provided the nightdress was smoothed out under her body, for creases made her uncomfortable and furious. This gave Audrey the opportunity to rock Leonora in her arms until the child fell into a contented slumber, her pale face nestled happily against her mother's bosom. Cecil strongly opposed his wife bringing their daughter into their bed, but he was powerless to prevent it, for it seemed as if she was incapable of being on her own. Reluctantly Cecil moved into his dressing room leaving the marital bed free for mother and child, to return on weekends when he insisted that Leonora be put into her own bed, even if it meant that she cried herself into a restless sleep.

*　　　*　　　*

Leonora adored her sister with the same fervour that Audrey had once adored Isla. She rarely took her eyes off her and admired everything she did, for Alicia was a quick learner and extremely gifted. Nothing was too much of a challenge for Alicia; with her beauty and ability she could conquer anything, anything, that is, except herself and it would take her a lifetime to learn that the most

195

testing demon was the one within her.

Leonora on the other hand was gentle and sensitive like her mother but without Audrey's physical allure. She was plain with thin brown hair the colour of parsnips and ears that stuck out but it didn't matter, for she was kind and good natured and loved by everyone except Alicia who despised weakness. The more she tormented her sister the more Leonora admired her and it was that doe-eyed devotion that brought out the worst in Alicia. Their Mexican maid, Mercedes, who herself was not blessed with great beauty, would shake her head made heavy with too many superstitions and claim that good looks were the work of the devil. 'A face like that will be the ruin of many a good man,' she predicted gravely, 'but Leonora will find happiness because her features won't deceive anyone.'

Mercedes hid her stout legs beneath long skirts and her recipes under the parrot cage where Loro learnt to imitate her voice to perfection. So convincing was he that when Oscar, the chauffeur, appeared at the kitchen door claiming that she had summoned him for '*café*' she would waggle her brown finger at him accusingly without realising his innocent mistake was due to the parrot's brilliant impersonation. Furiously she'd shuffle him back out into the yard while Loro sniggered quietly in his cage the way Oscar did when he spied on Mercedes taking a pee in the small lavatory behind the pantry.

Mercedes loved children. She had many of her own fathered by the porters, gardeners and chauffeurs of Hurlingham so that they ran wild about the streets like mongrel dogs not really

196

belonging to anyone. With great pride she would entertain the twins for hours, unlocking for them the mysteries of the kitchen but she learned very quickly that while Leonora enjoyed the whole culinary process from pastry to presentation, Alicia bored easily and only liked the icing and the decoration. Mercedes didn't hesitate to shake her brown finger at Alicia when she attempted to spoil her sister's creations while Loro squawked '*mala niña ja ja ja mala niña!*' at the back of the room with glee, watching through ebony eyes as Alicia retaliated by turning on her astonishing charm and throwing her arms around the maid's thick waist, feigning love; Alicia loved no one but herself.

*   *   *

Much to the relief of many people in Hurlingham Phyllida Bates passed away in April 1960. Only a small number of people attended the funeral and only because they felt they should, or, as in Charlo Blythe's case, because they sensed their own mortality lurking in the lengthening autumn shadows and believed that by proving themselves virtuous and pious they might hold it at bay for a little while longer. Phyllida's decrepit body had finally succumbed to the corrosion of her venomous blood, collapsing into a heap of leathery skin and dry bones. There was so little of her left that the coffin carrying her was unusually small and light. Phyllida's passing interested no one except the six-year-old Alicia who was fascinated by death and the dark allure it exuded. She hovered by the gate in her school apron, her eyes wide with curiosity as the sombre procession left the church.

She sniffed the thick scent of lilies that mingled with the sweet smell of death and felt a cold thrill tingle her spine. 'Come away, darling,' hissed her mother, who held Leonora tightly by the hand, 'let them mourn in peace.'

'They're not mourning,' she said and grinned without taking her eyes off the solemn scene being played out before her.

'Of course they are, Alicia,' replied her mother indulgently.

'Then why is the Colonel stroking Mrs Blythe's bottom?' Audrey raised her eyes into the churchyard and saw, to her horror, that her child was right. The Colonel's withered hand was unmistakeably caressing the skinny behind of his wife.

'He's not stroking it, darling, he's rubbing it better. She fell on it,' said Audrey hastily, striding over and pulling her mischievous child away from the fence.

'Well then, it's working,' she said and giggled. 'Because Mrs Blythe's smiling.'

*   *   *

To Cecil's dismay Alicia's teachers were constantly complaining about her behaviour. They claimed she was too clever for her own good, that she disrupted the class and that she was unkind to the smaller children. In fact, they declared in exasperation, shrugging their shoulders, they weren't able to cope with her at all. Consequently Cecil decided to involve himself more in the disciplining of his daughter and even resorted to smacking her once or twice when she answered him back with a defiance that astounded him. Such boldness in a child of six was inexcusable. But nothing seemed to work, she was spoilt beyond repair. *Her charm might work on her mother and aunts*, he thought, *but it won't work on me.*

Audrey refused to believe that a daughter of hers could be anything but perfect. Alicia would sob in her arms, whimpering pathetically that her father was a beast and that she didn't love him at all, only her mother, whom she adored and with a trembling hand she'd wipe away those crocodile tears, that when needed, came as fast and easily as the garden sprinkler. Audrey would hold her little girl close and remember those nine months of carrying her and promise that she would talk to her father and the teachers and explain that she was just an exuberant, well-intentioned child who was simply too young to control such a formidable nature. Audrey maintained that with a bit of discipline Alicia would develop into an exceptional young woman. But the problem only worsened. They were forced to take her out of school and find a new one. Audrey blamed the teachers, Cecil blamed Alicia and Alicia blamed everyone but herself.

Leonora suffered because of her sister's rebelliousness. She too had to change schools. She cried genuine tears because she missed her friends and her favourite teacher, Miss Amy, who was deeply fond of the sweet little girl who never arrived at school empty handed but came armed with a piece of fruit, a bunch of flowers or a slice of cake to place shyly on her teacher's desk. She still climbed into her mother's bed for comfort, shunting her father back into the dressing room where his own bed was still warm from those early years of exile. Finally Cecil realised that there was only one thing to be done, and he was going to be most unpopular for suggesting it.

'I want to discuss the girls' education with you,' he said to his wife one evening, pouring himself a glass of brandy. It was wintertime; the days were short, gobbled up into the nights that descended early and without warning. The twins were in bed wrapped in blankets and their mother's unconditional love while outside it was cold and blustery and hostile. Audrey smiled at her husband and put down her book.

'I think Alicia's settling nicely into her new school and Leonora is accepting that nothing in life stays the same. A valuable lesson, I believe,' she replied happily.

'I disagree. There's only one thing that will sort Alicia out and teach her to respect her elders.'

'What might that be?'

Cecil hesitated because he knew that what he was about to suggest would ignite a terrible row and he hated the thought of upsetting his wife. He braced himself then fixed her with his pale blue eyes and said quickly and decisively, 'I want them to have a proper English education.'

Audrey froze. For a moment she lost her mind. She just stared at him in disbelief, crushed by her husband's insensitivity and unable to find the words to object.

'A *proper* English education?' she mumbled finally after a long and awkward pause.

'An English education, in England,' he said and watched her features contort. 'The education is simply not good enough here,' he continued,

200

unable to meet her eyes that blinked back at him in terror. 'I think they should board at Colehurst House where my sister Cicely went. There's nothing in the world like an English education.'

'They're children,' she replied slowly in a strangled voice. 'They're six years old.'

'Oh, good God, I'm not suggesting we send them away now. No, no, my dear, they won't go until they're ten. I wouldn't spring something like this on you out of the blue.'

'Ten?' She pulled her cardigan about her shoulders. Gathering together her wits she added slowly and carefully, 'You can't do this to me, Cecil. I won't let you.' She knew of a few families who sent their children away to be educated in England and when they came back they were strangers with new mannerisms, new accents, new expressions. She wouldn't allow it.

'I feared you would take it badly. I've been meaning to discuss this with you for some time.'

'I see,' she replied with forced calmness while trying desperately to keep her balance. 'Cecil, how could you conceive of wrenching away the two people I love more than anyone else in the world?'

Cecil turned his face away. He looked bleakly out of the window. *Women are so emotional*, he thought, *perhaps I've approached this the wrong way*. Then he sighed heavily, and decided on a different tack.

'It is my duty as a father to do what's best, Audrey. I don't want to send them away any more than you do, but one has to think of their future.' His voice was firmer now. She imagined that was the tone he had once used in the army.

'The English schools here are perfectly

201

adequate. Am I ill educated?' She glared at him now with fury.

Cecil lit a cigar and stood in front of the fire. 'Your education was adequate, yes, for your day. But times are different now. The war has changed everything, not least women's place in society. Alicia is headstrong and wilful. They simply can't cope with her over here. She runs riot and if we don't instil in her some sense of discipline she'll turn into an exceedingly unattractive young woman. I'm afraid it affects Leonora too because we can't separate them, and besides, an English education will do them both good. Leonora will benefit, gain a bit of independence and confidence. She's far too attached to you.' He looked directly at his wife and added, 'It is the greatest gift that we can bestow on them. An English education is priceless.'

'For goodness sake, Cecil,' she protested. 'I would pay whatever it cost not to send them overseas.'

'The future lies in England. I didn't plan on staying here all my life, you knew that.'

'Are you suggesting we move to England?'

'Not now, no, but perhaps one day. I don't rule it out.'

'But I want to be here, Cecil. I want my children to be here. We belong in the Argentine. I will not be separated from them. I *will* not.' Her voice rose until she was aware that she was shouting.

'Calm down, Audrey, and try to think rationally. Look at it from their point of view. You do want what's best for them, don't you? Or do you just want what's best for you?'

'I'm their mother. *I'm* what's best for them,' she

202

exclaimed hotly. 'Oh, Cecil, I can't believe you would make such a heartless suggestion. What's come over you? Why do you want to tear our family apart?'

'My dear . . .' he began, but Audrey was too frantic to listen.

'I will not let you. Do you understand? You will have to kill me first!' she declared then added before she ran out of the room, 'I will never forgive you.'

Cecil was left alone in front of the fire contemplating his wife's reaction. He hadn't expected her to take it *that* badly, after all, it wasn't unusual for Anglo-Argentines to send their children to be educated abroad. School in England, finishing school in Switzerland, it taught them self-reliance, shaped them into independent, fearless young people. It prepared them for the real world. As much as he would have liked to appease his wife he was slightly irritated at her blinkered view of her children. Alicia was a problem but Audrey wouldn't see it that way. To her the twins were little angels whose wings were left at the marble gates of Heaven for them to pick up on their return. She didn't doubt that they were special and different and anyone who had a bad word to say about Alicia was plainly jealous. No, Cecil was determined to stand by his decision.

*   *   *

Audrey hadn't played the piano for a long long time. But now she lifted the lid and sat with a straight back on the worn tapestry stool, placing her feet lightly on the pedals. The tears fought their way through her knitted eyelashes and trembled on her chin before falling onto the ivory keys, which now translated into music the pain in her soul. With the releasing of her emotions came the long repressed memories of Louis, dragged up out of the shadowy corners of her mind, dusted off so that his face was as vivid to her now as if she had seen him yesterday beneath the umbrella of the cherry tree in the orchard in Canning Street. She pictured his sandy hair, always unbrushed and tousled, his intense blue eyes with their distant and wandering gaze, his full lips and crooked smile that she had kissed so many times and his long, pale fingers that twitched nervously by his side as if constantly touching the keys of an imaginary piano. Her heart yearned for him now with such intensity that the piano began to shudder beneath the weight of her tormented spirit. She had lost Isla and she had lost Louis, now she was on the verge of losing her children. She felt powerless. But the music had a soothing effect. She swayed on her stool, slowly moved her head from side to side, breathed deeply from the pit of her abdomen and let the anchor that attached her mind to reality lose its grip and release her into the limitless world of dreams.

CHAPTER THIRTEEN

Audrey now faced the toughest challenge of her life. Outwardly she had to support her husband when inwardly her resentment grew like a tumour on her heart. She clung to her daughters with the determination of a drowning woman, living every moment of every week, month and year as if each day were her last. England loomed on the horizon growing bigger and blacker like the dark spray of a waterfall as the inevitable force of time carried her and her children towards it and their certain doom. Yet, she knew the only way to lessen the shock of their imminent future was to talk about England and boarding school as if it were the quaint land of rolling green hills and old-fashioned villages, of Angela Brazil's novels about schoolgirls and teams, midnight feasts and adventure. She was so brilliant at weaving a colourful tapestry that even Leonora was gripped with excitement and longed to be ten.

'We're going to school in England next year,' said Alicia to Mercedes as she scooped a large dollop of *dulce de leche* from the pot on the stove with her finger. Mercedes fed the parrot sunflower seeds through the bars of his cage. '*Gracias*,' he squawked after each offering because he knew such politeness guaranteed him more.

'That's a long way to go to get an education, *niña*,' she said in her slow, flat drawl, thinking the whole idea preposterous. 'Besides, too much knowledge is a bad thing.' Mercedes always saw the negative side of everything.

'Daddy says that an English education is the best in the world,' she explained.

'Look at me,' said Mercedes, opening the cage door to allow Loro to hop about the kitchen. 'My mother taught me how to cook and my grandmother taught me how to pray. Cooking has won me many a good man, praying has earned me forgiveness for such transgressions. What more does a woman need to know? You'll marry and have children whether you know the earth is round

205

and rotating or not. Either way it won't stop turning.'

'We'll stay with Aunt Cicely in the holidays. She has an enormous house. It's a castle, I think. Probably haunted, you wouldn't like it, Merchi, you don't like ghosts.'

'I don't mind ghosts as long as they keep themselves to themselves. My late husband is the only ghost I object to because he still considers it his right to share my bed forty years after he died in it.' Loro scratched his depleted green feather coat then used his claws to climb up the stool where Alicia sat licking her toffee fingers.

'Why is Loro losing his feathers?' she asked, watching him move across to pick at the buttons on her dress.

'Because he's lonely,' replied Mercedes. She pouted her thick lips and added, 'That's no reason to let himself go. I've been lonely all my life and I take good care of myself. You never know . . .'

'Why don't you marry Oscar?'

Mercedes wasn't surprised by the child's question. It had crossed her mind many times. Not because she liked the look of him but because it would be nice to have a permanent relationship. She was getting too old to take lovers and besides, sex wasn't as good as it used to be when she had had the energy to enjoy it and a slimmer, firmer body to be proud of. It was companionship she craved nowadays.

'Because he's not rich enough to keep me and he's losing his teeth,' she replied nonchalantly.

'Perhaps he's lonely like Loro.'

'Perhaps he is, *niña*, or perhaps he's just plagued with ill health and bad luck.'

'He's ugly,' she stated, running her long fingers through her corkscrew hair. Sometimes Mercedes had to pinch herself for Alicia reminded her so much of Isla.

'Too much beauty is a bad thing. You'll learn that the hard way. You can't hide an ugly nature behind a beautiful face because it will seep into your features in the end. One must never rely on exterior beauty, inner beauty will always shine through when youth has faded.'

Alicia stroked Loro's balding back and sighed. 'I'm looking forward to going to England.'

'The grass is always greener. I know that one. Esteban took lovers but he always came back.'

'He's still there,' said Alicia and giggled.

'Yes.' Mercedes sighed. 'Perhaps if I married again he'd leave the bed free for my new husband.'

'Or haunt your house and frighten your new husband away.'

Mercedes studied the child through the narrowed eyes of a Mexican witchdoctor. 'You know your problem, child?'

'No, what's that, Merchi?'

'You're too clever for your own good,' she said, pinching the little girl on her cheek. 'You'll come to a bad end, I warn you.'

'Ouch! I hate it when you do that. I'm not a baby any longer, I'm nearly ten.'

'Shame. You were quite sweet as a baby, age has already ruined you.'

Alicia laughed and clicked her tongue. 'Will you miss me when I'm gone?' she asked.

'No,' replied Mercedes. 'Because you'll come back.'

'I'll come back for Christmas.'

'With an education to boast of.'

'I'll teach you a thing or two.'

'You can't teach an old dog new tricks.'

'You're not a dog, Merchi.'

'Perhaps not, but I am old!' She threw her head back and laughed raucously.

Alicia hopped down from the stool, pushing Loro onto the floor where he squawked in fury and began attacking her ankles. 'You know what you should do for Loro?'

'Besides putting him in a pan and boiling him for dinner?'

'You should put a mirror in his cage.'

Mercedes stood speechless with admiration, her hands placed firmly on her wide hips. 'You're a genius, *niña*, he'll think he has company,' she said. 'And your father thinks you need to be sent all the way to England to get an education!'

'No, Merchi! The shock of seeing his ugly, plucked coat should be enough to stop him picking at his feathers like that.'

'Don't judge him by your own standards, he's not as vain as you. Just lonely,' Mercedes chided, waggling her long brown finger. 'You don't need an education, child, but a short sharp smack on your bottom.'

'*Juicy bottom, juicy bottom!*' squawked Loro, taking a bath in the basin.

Mercedes pursed her lips together. 'He didn't learn that from me,' she said then narrowed her eyes. 'Oscar!'

*   *   *

Three years had passed since Cecil had announced

to Audrey that the girls were to be educated in England. Audrey had declared that she would never forgive him and she had meant it. She didn't rage at him and she didn't talk about her resentment to anyone else but Isla, whom she communicated with as she rode out over the grassy plains of the pampa, certain that her sister's spirit was present and sympathetic to her predicament. Instead, she showed her anger and hurt in the polite and formal way that she now treated him. She smiled, she talked, she hosted his dinners and his drinks parties in the manicured garden of their comfortable home, but always with the same distant reserve, as though he were no more intimate with her than their guests. She tamed her wild curls into a severe knot at the back of her head that made her face look longer and sadder and let it down only at night when she covered the piano with candles and played with a ferociousness that no one who knew her would have thought possible. Cecil noticed everything but held fast. He wasn't going to allow his wife to manipulate him. He knew he was doing the right thing for his children, for their future, and was old fashioned enough to think that it was a woman's duty to support her husband. He grew accustomed to her silent defiance until it became so much a way of life that he ceased to notice it except during the long nights when, in the large and arid bed of his exile, his body yearned for the warmth of hers and the affection that she had once shown him.

*   *   *

Finally the day of departure arrived. Cecil had

organised for the family to go by boat in order to enjoy a fortnight's holiday before starting school and Audrey was grateful that she would have that precious time with her daughters. Rose and Aunt Edna arrived at the house in the early morning armed with sweets and shiny new pencil cases filled with crayons for school and embraced the children warmly. 'Just don't forget us, will you,' said their grandmother, hugging them tightly and blinking away her tears. Edna handed Leonora an old saggy rabbit that she had had as a child, because she loved Leonora the best. 'Look after him, won't you, he was very dear to me when I was a little girl,' she said, kissing her grand-niece on her forehead.

'And don't forget to write often, we want to hear all the news so don't spare the details,' said Rose, glancing at her daughter whose face looked pale and strained.

Aunt Hilda dropped by with Nelly but her hands were empty of gifts. The twins hadn't expected anything from her but were delighted when Nelly handed them both large jars of *dulce de leche*. 'I bet they don't have this in England,' she said.

'You lucky things going to England,' said Edna with forced cheerfulness, 'they have the best of everything over there. Bring a Christmas pudding back when you come home for the holidays.'

'And some mince pies,' added Rose. *At least they'll be home for Christmas*, she thought sadly; after that they wouldn't be home until the following Christmas. She sympathised wholly with Audrey and spent many sleepless nights wondering how she was going to survive such a cruel separation, but there was no use in discussing it with Henry, for as far as he was concerned Cecil was doing the right thing. There was nothing quite like an English education.

Mercedes had refused to say good-bye to the girls for she hated open displays of emotion and considered tears and wobbling lower lips acts of extreme weakness to be avoided at all costs. So she went into town to do the shopping, leaving Loro alone in his cage squawking, *'dreadful shame, dreadful shame,'* as loudly as he could to betray his mistress's despair to anyone who would listen.

*   *   *

The sky was grey with the apathy of winter, casting the port in a gloomy, cheerless light. Audrey boarded the *Alcantara* with Alicia and Leonora hopping about her with the excitement of two small people embarking on a big adventure. Not only had they never been to England but they had never been on such a large and luxurious ship. Audrey wondered whether lambs sprung around with such enthusiasm moments before they were brutally slaughtered. The bustle of people, porters carrying heavy piles of suitcases, whistles blowing, engines roaring, families weeping and waving, embracing and kissing filled Audrey with panic. It was all so unfamiliar and disconcerting. She hated such noise and chaos and she feared for the safety of her children. But she needn't have worried for the twins were enchanted by everything and barely spared a moment to say good-bye to their father who watched with fatalistic detachment as his family climbed the gang plank and disappeared inside. Audrey had kissed him coolly on the cheek then stared into his eyes with an icy defiance as if

211

to remind him that this parting was of his own making and that she would never forgive him for it. He hoped time would thaw their estrangement and that she would appreciate the gift he had given them when the girls returned home with beautiful manners and superior educations. In the meantime the gin bottle would warm his wintry spirit.

The girls raced up and down the corridors in search of their cabin, squealing in delight. Audrey followed anxiously behind them, hating the airless smell of carpets and detergent and the claustrophobia of being in such a tight labyrinth. She was unable to share her daughters' optimism, especially as she knew the full horror of what awaited them in England. 'Mummy, Mummy, Mummy!' Alicia shrieked with excitement when they entered their cabin. 'Bunk beds, I'm going on top,' she announced quickly, throwing her bag onto the mattress and scrambling up after it. 'Let's go on deck, Leo.'

'Now wait . . .' Audrey began, but Alicia was already tearing out of the door with Leonora following obediently behind her. Audrey had no option but to go after them. She had a headache and wanted nothing more than to lie down and close her eyes, but she already saw in her mind's eye two small bodies falling like rag dolls into the water below, so she tearfully hurried up the maze of corridors, chasing the echo of their voices.

The deck was throbbing with people waving good-bye to relatives and friends, their cries rising above the low bellow that vibrated up from the bowels of the ship. Audrey discovered Alicia and Leonora at the front of the throng having pushed their way through, leaning on the railings waving with the rest of them. But their father had long since disappeared back to Hurlingham to the large and empty house that awaited him.

Audrey stood alone as the liner sailed out of the harbour and into the open sea. The horizon revealed nothing but grey mist as if they were heading for the end of the world. It was then that her mind drifted to Louis and to the misery of the life she had chosen. At once she felt out on a limb and detached, suddenly able to look back at the diminishing coastline of Argentina with an altered awareness. Hurlingham now seemed so small and insignificant when seen from her new perspective; a little puddle in comparison to such a vast sea. Louis had been right, she thought with a racing heart, she was afraid to dream. It was because of that fear that she had married Cecil and let Louis go. If only she had had the vision that he had, to see the world as it really was—an immense space of endless possibilities. Surrounded by strangers heading towards an unfamiliar country far away she dared imagine what her life might have been had she married Louis. They could have gone anywhere. They could have been happy. Never before had she been so aware of the power of free will. Looking about her she felt her spirit inflate with the intoxicating feeling of freedom. How had she been so ignorant of it before?

*   *   *

So began the two-week voyage that would take them up the coast of South America to Rio, across the ocean to Madeira then to Lisbon, finally arriving in Southampton at the beginning of

213

September. With her change of heart Audrey was able to enjoy the trip and the company of her children without thinking too much of what lay ahead. She would lie on her deck chair in the sun reading and dreaming while the twins ran wild with the other children, splashing about in the swimming pool, trying their hands at deck tennis and watching in amusement as the grown-ups played steady games of deck quoits. Audrey didn't have to worry about her children for the young were very quickly gathered up by the irrepressible Mrs Beetlestone-Magnus, Mrs B for short. An energetic woman in her late sixties with the round body of an amiable toad hidden beneath long flowing dresses that resembled floral tents, she organised painting competitions and singing contests, fancy dress parties and plays which proved so delightful that before the first week was over even some of the grown-ups were begging to be included. 'My dears,' she would say, shaking her chins good-naturedly, 'if you don't mind the humiliation of a small cameo role, the children really are very talented, you know.' And the grown-ups didn't mind at all. In fact, Mr Linton, an elderly, dignified gentleman with silver hair and a small, tidy moustache, was more than happy to stand the whole way through *Wind in The Willows* in the back corner of the stage as a most convincing willow tree.

Mrs B had an unfailing way of keeping the children under control by bribing them with sweets, which she bought from the little shop where they sold Audrey's favourite Yardley scent. 'This is what England is like,' she would say to her daughters, pointing to the old-fashioned lady on the front of

214

the bottle and they would swell with excitement and long for the end of the voyage.

There was great excitement crossing the equator and those, like Audrey, Alicia and Leonora, who had never crossed it before, had to partake in a ceremony that involved blindfolding the eyes and being covered in foam. The twins shrieked with pleasure while their mother did her best to pretend she didn't mind. It was all very hearty and Audrey found it distinctly unamusing, especially when they erected a plank and told the children to walk it. Leonora then cowered behind her mother while Alicia leapt on and had to be rescued by two of the passengers who could see from the look on her face that she was fully prepared to jump.

Every morning there was a sweepstake to guess how many miles they had travelled and the winner would receive a voucher to spend at the shop. Alicia won twice, not because she knew, she hadn't the remotest idea, but because Mr Linton guessed right every time and on a couple of occasions she peered over his shoulder to see the number he'd written down. Everyone knew she had cheated, but due to her charm and her age they liked her all the more for it. At eleven a steward would appear on deck with a tray of steaming hot Bovril or tea and cream crackers which the twins thought disgusting being used as they were to Mercedes' sweet *dulce de leche* and cake. The salty smell of the beef tea caught at the back of Audrey's throat and she winced as she watched the other passengers drink it with relish. Mrs B, busy rushing around being efficient, would pause by the tray, drain an entire cup, then hurry off to find paints or glue or one of the wayward children who had disappeared, attacking a dry biscuit with her dentures. This morning, however, Mrs B had time to sit down next to Audrey and tell her in her direct manner that not only was Alicia encouraging the other children to behave badly, but also, more criminally, that she was deliberately leaving her sister out.

'But Leonora has said nothing about it to me,' protested Audrey, who couldn't believe that Alicia would be so unkind. Mrs B looked at her indulgently; she was a mother herself and a grandmother besides, she knew maternal pitfalls better than anyone.

'My dear Audrey, Alicia is a strong little girl and very spirited. She has a charisma that draws other children to her, this she can choose to use for good or for bad. Like many children who have not yet learned to put themselves in other people's shoes she is choosing the latter at Leonora's expense. Might I suggest that you talk to her, otherwise she is going to run into a lot of trouble at Colehurst House.' Audrey lowered her eyes and the fleeting image of Cecil passed rapidly through her mind. She sighed and put down her book.

'You know, my husband despairs of Alicia's behaviour, that is why they are being sent to be educated in England.'

'Don't worry, dear girl,' said Mrs B, patting Audrey's hand with her fat, freckled fingers. 'It'll be the making of them. Nothing like it in the world.'

'But I want them at home with me,' she explained sadly.

'Oh, I know, it's hard, especially if you're not brought up with it. One just has to bite the bullet and get on with things. I have three daughters and eight grandchildren. My eldest, Sally, lives in Belgrano with her husband who was sent out to Buenos Aires five years ago on business and never came back. I've just been visiting. I try to go once every two years. When I look back at the years of boarding school now it seems to have passed in a moment. It isn't the end of your relationship, my dear Audrey, but the beginning of a new one. They'll grow up and blossom into young women and you won't miss a bit of it, I promise you. Then you'll have years ahead of you to enjoy them. You'll all appreciate each other more because of the long absence, believe me.'

'It seems so unnatural.'

'Not at all unnatural. It teaches them independence and besides, surely one wants nice English husbands for them. The Argentine is all very well but really, there's no place like England, is there?' Audrey didn't know because she'd never been there and she wanted to say that she really didn't mind if her daughters married Argentines or Africans as long as they were happy. But Mrs B believed in the Great British Empire and the superiority of its people. Her eyes shone with pride when she talked about her country and she simply wouldn't have understood Audrey's unconventional attitude.

'I'll talk to Alicia then,' she conceded, changing the subject.

'Good,' said Mrs B firmly, pushing herself up from her chair. 'Sometimes one has to be cruel to be kind. Children need to be told how to behave otherwise they turn into horrid little savages and one wants to avoid that at all costs.'

'Absolutely,' Audrey agreed meekly.

217

'Must rush, we're rehearsing *Peter Pan* at five.'

'Goodness, isn't that a bit ambitious?'

'Not at all. Not at all. These children are most gifted. If I could play the piano I'd have them all singing *La Bohème.*' Audrey didn't volunteer.

*   *   *

That evening when the twins returned to the cabin to change for supper Audrey was waiting for them with a serious look on her face. Alicia immediately felt guilty for she was fully conscious of her actions. She was unable to help herself. The power she wielded was intoxicating. 'I want to talk to you both,' began their mother. 'Sit down.'

'Are we in trouble?' Alicia asked, ready to spill some more crocodile tears.

'I believe that you're being unkind to Leonora,' Audrey said sternly. If it were true Alicia deserved the full force of their mother's scolding.

'No she's not,' interjected Leonora bravely. She glanced across at her sister who smiled at her with such tenderness that Leonora's little heart swelled with gratitude.

'I've been told that you're leaving her out of all your games.'

'I don't want to join in,' explained Leonora quickly, picking Saggy Rabbit off her bed and cuddling him.

'She doesn't want to,' repeated Alicia in all innocence. 'I'm not a beast, Mummy. I wouldn't be unkind to Leo.'

'I hope not, Alicia. You're about to start boarding school where you'll be among a large number of strange girls. You must stick together.

Blood is thicker than water, don't ever forget that. Life is very hard and you'll rely on each other for support and encouragement. Isla and I were as different as you two are but we stuck together and never let the other down. It would never have occurred to me to be disloyal because she was a part of me as you are both a part of each other.'

'I wish I had known Aunt Isla,' said Alicia, deliberately digressing.

'I wish you had too. She was a very special person whose light shone so brightly it dazzled. The world is a darker place now but still, there are other lights and you and Leonora shine just as brightly for me.'

'I'm going to miss you when we go to school.' Alicia suddenly burst into tears. She did it so convincingly that even Leonora who knew her sister's ways better than anyone was convinced that she meant it. Alicia looked up from beneath her thick lashes and blinked away large salty tears.

'I'll look after you, Alicia,' her sister soothed, placing a hand on her shoulder.

'My darling child, come here,' said Audrey, pulling her weeping daughter into her arms, stroking her hair and kissing her forehead. 'You'll be fine when you get there.'

'I don't want to go any more. I want to go home.'

Leonora suddenly wanted to go home too but she bit her lip and tried to say the alphabet backwards in her head in order to prevent herself crying. Their poor mother couldn't cope with both of them crying at once. She watched her sister in her mother's embrace and wished that she were there too. Alicia was usually so strong and confident, it was unlike her to be scared of

219

anything. Alicia's apparent crisis of confidence sent her sister into a decline. Leonora now dreaded the thought of boarding school, of England and of Aunt Cicely whom she had never met, but from the snippets that she had picked up she sounded a cold, unfriendly woman in a big, haunted house in the middle of nowhere. She didn't dare tell her mother of her fears because she knew that it would upset her. As Alicia poured her heart out Leonora wished she had kept her uncertainties to herself.

Audrey was suitably distressed and diverted, which was Alicia's intention. She blinked back at Leonora and despised her for being a martyr. Leonora smiled back sympathetically. Surely she now deserved her sister's friendship. Alicia narrowed her eyes and decided to be nice for a bit. Being nice was always a challenge and she liked challenges.

In the final days of the voyage Audrey was pleased to hear from Mrs B that Alicia was now including her sister in everything. 'Whatever you said, my dear, did the trick. They're like two peas in a pod,' she exclaimed happily, hurrying up the deck with an armful of pirate costumes for the end-of-trip play. She had offered Mr Linton the part of Captain Hook but he had declined, stating that the willow tree had been the highlight of his acting career and besides, he couldn't think of anything more beastly than wielding a nasty hook at all those dear children. 'It's against my nature,' he claimed, winking at Audrey in amusement.

The following morning when one of the youngsters ran down the deck screaming 'land ahoy, land ahoy,' Audrey's timeless voyage, between the past and the future in what seemed an

220

eternal moment, finally moved on. Gazing at the dreary sight of Southampton dock as it emerged out of the early morning mist anchored her mind and heart once more in the here and now and the painful journey that lay ahead of her. It was a joyless sight but one that aroused in the hearts of those who loved England a flutter of excitement and a sigh of relief. There was no place like home and even the dull skies and grey coastline did little to dampen their joy. 'Ah, England,' exclaimed Mr Linton happily. 'There's no place quite like it.'

'No place,' agreed Mrs B, pursing her lips together with emotion. Audrey looked bleakly out onto the country that her father and husband spoke of with such devotion and wondered what they saw in it. She remembered the story of the Emperor's New Clothes and felt like the little boy who shouts into the crowd that the Emperor is in fact not wearing any clothes at all.

'I thought it was late summer,' was the least confrontational thing she could think of to say.

'The end of the summer,' Mrs B replied.

'There's nothing quite like an English summer,' Mr Linton sighed, pulling his jacket around him to keep warm. Audrey glanced at her daughters who looked as grim as she did and felt the resentment towards her husband rise up inside her along with a sudden shiver of cold.

CHAPTER FOURTEEN

'It's all terribly quaint,' said Alicia in amusement as she followed her mother and sister onto the station platform. 'All the porters speak English.'

'Well, of course they do,' her mother replied, 'we're in England.' But she knew what her daughter meant. In the Argentine the working classes spoke only Spanish.

'I can't understand a word he says,' hissed Leonora, nodding in the direction of the porter who hurried along in front of them with a tower of suitcases balanced precariously onto a trolley.

'That's because he speaks with a regional accent,' Audrey said, trying to appear confident. 'You'll get used to it.'

'It's very misty,' Alicia giggled. 'It's like soup. If he goes any faster he might disappear into it and never be seen again.'

'I hope not, all your worldly possessions are in those suitcases,' said Audrey lightly, but her laughter caught in her throat. She stifled a sob and pulled her coat tightly about her shoulders. It was cold. A damp cold that penetrated her very bones.

Before Audrey could dwell any further on her impending loss a shiny green train appeared up the track, the metal of its carriages glinting in the dull morning light. A quiver of anticipation shivered up the platform as it drew into the station, hissed to a halt and exhaled thick puffs of steam. 'It's a dragon, it's a dragon,' squealed Alicia, jumping up and down, shouting above the screeching of brakes and the bustle of passengers who now boarded the train. Leonora copied her sister and jumped up and down too, her ankles tickled by the dragon's smoky breath.

'Come on, girls, we don't want to miss it,' said Audrey, taking Leonora by the hand and marching towards the carriages. For Leonora and Alicia the cheerless English weather no longer affected them for there was so much that was new and exciting. They threw themselves onto two seats by the window and knelt with their noses pressed against the glass staring out in wonder at the unfamiliar world that now opened up to them. Audrey took off her coat and hung it on the hook, then sat beside Leonora. 'Girls, take your feet off the seats,' she said in a low voice, eyeing the other passengers who glanced at them over the top of their newspapers with the utmost discretion.

As the train rattled through the English countryside Audrey switched her mind from the high-pitched chatter of the twins and allowed her thoughts to drift rootless and free among the happy events of the past two weeks aboard the *Alcantara*. She recalled those languid afternoons on deck, with the warm breeze brushing her skin and the light happy voices of the twins carried on the wind in carefree songs of childhood and focused her thoughts on the past in order to avoid the pain of the present. But in spite of all her efforts the present had invaded those sunny decks and images of school and partings, suitcases and uniforms rose up in her mind in the form of dark shadows until her head throbbed. Weary and emotional she was no longer able to control her thoughts and Louis' face finally emerged out of the gloomy picture of Colehurst House that Audrey had concocted from the brochure she had read and the tales she had heard of English boarding schools. She allowed her anxieties to retreat and steadied her mind's eye on his raffish face and uneven smile and felt her heart lurch with longing. Gazing dreamily out onto the misty English countryside she saw him in the dying

223

summer trees and burning fields and she heard his hollow voice in an echo that leapt across the years: 'I'm obviously a huge disappointment.' She winced as once again those words pierced her heart and flooded her with regret. This was his home. This was where he had grown up and she imagined him riding across those autumn hills and resting his eyes upon the same scenery that she was now surveying. If she had had the courage to dream the impossible perhaps she would have made this remote island her home too. She might have grown to love it. Then he was tracing his long fingers down her face and across her lips and she blushed because even in her imagination Louis took more than he was offered.

She swept a self-conscious glance about the carriage, afraid that her head was transparent and her thoughts laid bare. But she needn't have worried. An old man smoked a pipe with his whiskers hidden behind a newspaper, a thin woman with perfectly behaved children sat reading a book, complimenting them at intervals on their neat drawings and a young couple had eyes only for each other. She laid a hand on her belly aware that the butterflies that caused it to shudder with nerves were for Louis and for the chance that their paths might cross once again. She had never met Cicely, but as Louis' sister she might know of his whereabouts. Then her hand rose to rub the skin on her neck with anxious fingers for she knew if she were to see him again she would no longer have the will to resist her dreams, but would lose herself in them. And once lost, what hope had she of being recovered?

The twins noticed everything that was different

from the country of their birth. The patchwork of lush fields surrounded by hedges and fences, the hamlets of villages that resembled dollhouses with their thatched roofs and immaculate gardens, the pale, watery sky and the sun which now emerged from behind the clouds and celebrated their arrival by opening up like a giant sunflower. Everything was smaller and neater than in the Argentine and the twins tried to out-do each other by commenting on all the differences in loud, exuberant tones. Audrey pulled herself away from her daydreams to act as referee as her daughters' voices got increasingly louder and more boisterous as the journey progressed.

The train drew into Waterloo Station and Audrey struggled through the heaving crowds of passengers, holding her daughters' hands so tightly their chatter dissolved into mute curiosity as they sensed their mother's ill ease. But once in the safety of a shiny black London cab they began to comment once again on the narrow city streets, the pretty town houses and the red doubledecker buses they had only previously seen in pictures.

'It's exactly like I imagined it to be,' said Leonora. 'Can we go on one of those buses?'

'I'll go on the top,' Alicia interjected before Audrey had time to answer.

'I want to see the Queen's house.'

'I bet I can get one of those guards to move.'

'Tickle him under the nose.' Leonora giggled, 'I bet he'll laugh then.'

'Perhaps the Queen will ask us to tea in her palace when she learns that we're here.'

'I should think she'll be far too busy for that,' said Audrey and laughed, running a hand down

Alicia's long hair. 'Besides, we're going to be far too busy too.'

'What are we going to do?' Leonora asked.

'First we're going to the hotel.'

'Goodie, I love hotels!' Alicia exclaimed, although she'd never stayed in one.

'We can have breakfast in bed,' Leonora said excitedly.

'If you like, but first we have to go and buy your school uniform,' said Audrey, rummaging in her handbag for the letter from Miss Reid, the headmistress. 'They've sent us a long list of things to buy in . . . what's it called? It's a very smart shop according to Aunt Hilda who seems to know everything about London.' She tried not to think about her family who seemed so far away they might just as well have been living on another planet. 'Ah, here it is, Debenham & Freebody in Oxford Street.'

'What a funny name,' said Alicia, screwing up her nose in the same way that Isla once had. Audrey saw much of her sister in Alicia. The same mischievous look in the eye, the same confidence, but Audrey didn't see the malicious streak in her daughter that she had inherited from no one but cultivated entirely on her own. Alicia could be kind and she could be sweet, but only when it suited her. As there was no one else to play with she granted her favour to Leonora, who adored her with the unconditional love of a dog. Alicia looked forward to school where the choice would be vast and she could befriend anyone she wanted; besides, she'd no longer be under the watchful eyes of her parents. She recalled the Angela Brazil books and smiled at the fun she was going to have breaking the rules. After all, rules were there to be broken, isn't that what Great Aunt Edna always said?

'We'll stay in the hotel tonight then take the train to Dorset where Aunt Cicely lives,' Audrey continued, oblivious of Alicia's wicked thoughts.

'Then when do we go to school?' Alicia asked, unable to hide the excitement that caused her voice to tremble. Audrey frowned at her, remembering the tears aboard the *Alcantara*.

'On Wednesday,' she replied in a small voice, then pulled a thin smile at Leonora who had suddenly gone quiet. 'Aunt Cicely and I will take you together. She went there herself when she was your age and loved every minute of it.'

'We're going to love it, aren't we, Leo?'

Leonora nodded half-heartedly and Audrey instinctively put her arm around her and pulled her close.

'I'm staying with Cicely for a few weeks to settle you in. I'm allowed to take you out for the weekend after a fortnight, so you can tell me all about it.'

*   *   *

After they had settled into the Normandie Hotel in Knightsbridge they took another taxi to Oxford Street and Audrey promised them a ride on a bus after they had bought their uniform. Debenham & Freebody was throbbing with mothers buying clothes for their children, all clutching the same white sheets of paper that listed everything from pants to outdoor shoes and Aertex shirts, which Audrey had never heard of before. The girls eyed up the other children with a mixture of suspicion and curiosity while Audrey tried to find a sales lady to help her. She caught the attention of a small sparrow of a woman who was serving a tall lady in a camel hair coat. She smiled sweetly and indicated with a nod that as soon as she had finished she would look after her. So Audrey sat in an armchair and watched while the twins skipped through the department, playing chase.

'We won't be long,' said the lady in the camel hair coat, sitting down next to Audrey. 'They take forever in this shop. My Caroline'—she pronounced this as Cairline—'has two elder sisters who are both seniors at Colehurst House but most of their old things are worn through so we're having to get the essentials brand new. Quite an extravagance, it's not cheap.' The saleswoman disappeared through a door into the store room and the lady's daughter, a freckly child with thin hair and a turned-up nose, emerged from the changing room in a brown and beige uniform looking long faced and grumpy. Audrey smiled at her but she lifted her chin and stuck out her lower lip sulkily. 'Not a pretty uniform, is it?' continued the girl's mother who spoke with such a grand accent her chin practically disappeared into her neck.

Audrey nodded. 'It could be worse,' she said diplomatically, feeling the child's discomfort.

'Goodness me, it's ghastly, but at least it means they don't wear out their own clothes. With all those dogs and ponies and tearing around in the mud, I'm jolly grateful for it.'

'It's my daughters' first time at boarding school,' said Audrey softly.

The lady raised her eyebrows and grinned. 'Oh, what fun, you've got it all ahead of you,' she

228

gushed. 'It's a charming school and the gels are nice and well mannered. Diana Reid is a jolly good headmistress and an excellent horsewoman. My Caroline has been longing to go, she's the last, you see, and has had to put up with me. Jolly boring, isn't it, darling?' She didn't wait for her daughter to reply. 'I wouldn't let her go at eight like her sisters, she was a slow learner and needed extra tuition. So she's ten. Going into the second year. She's taking Teasel with her, though. Nothing in the world could split those two up, could it, Caroline? What would he do without you?'

'Teasel?' asked Audrey, assuming he was a dog.

'Pony,' replied the lady briskly. 'Caroline won't go anywhere without Teasel. If your gels have ponies they're most welcome at Colehurst House. Really, it's like a five-star hotel for horses. They're happier there than at home, the little devils,' she added, fluttering her eyelids and pursing her lips together to illustrate her amusement.

At that moment Leonora and Alicia bounded around the corner giggling loudly. 'Ah, do these two belong to you? They must meet Caroline.' The twins skidded to a halt beside their mother and Leonora placed herself on her knee throwing her arm around her neck.

'This is Leonora and that's Alicia,' said Audrey, 'and this very smartly dressed girl is Caroline.' The twins said hello politely and Caroline pulled a small smile in return.

'I like your uniform, is it like ours?' Leonora asked. Caroline's eyes came alive and her smile lengthened.

'Exactly like yours,' Audrey replied, watching the other child's expression soften.

'If you follow me I'll show you what else you have to have,' she said and Alicia and Leonora followed her at once to the changing room where they rummaged through the pile of beige shirts and heavy brown skirts.

'Charming gels,' said the lady who suddenly remembered to her horror that she hadn't introduced herself. 'I'm dreadfully sorry, I don't even know your name.'

'Audrey Forrester,' replied Audrey.

'Dorothy Stainton-Hughes, a bit of a mouthful I'm afraid,' she said and chuckled heartily. 'Where are you from? You have a most curious accent.'

'The Argentine.'

'Gosh, you have come a long way, haven't you!' she exclaimed. 'You won't need to worry about your gels now, Caroline will look after them and Caroline already knows all her sister's friends.'

'Mummy, Mummy, Mummy!' Alicia shrieked, bounding out of the changing room holding up a large pair of brown pants. 'Look at these, aren't they hideous!'

'Oh dear, Brownies are rather grim,' Dorothy agreed with a smile.

'What are they for?' Audrey asked, hoping they weren't underwear.

'They're for sport, the gels wear them over their knickers so their botties don't get cold beneath their culottes. One doesn't want one's daughters flashing their knickers, does one?' Alicia put them on her head and skipped back into the changing room, which suddenly resounded with laughter. Audrey wanted to ask what Wellington boots were, and Aertex shirts, but she was reluctant to reveal her ignorance in case she embarrassed her daughters, so she waited until the salesgirl had accompanied Dorothy Stainton-Hughes to the counter with armfuls of clothes before she began at the top of the list—one navy blue Guernsey, whatever that was.

* * *

As a treat Audrey took the twins to Hamleys where she bought them each a toy and watched happily as they ran through the departments gasping in awe at the shelves and shelves of glossy toys and furry animals. They were in high spirits having met Caroline Stainton-Hughes who had told them all about camps, pony rides and the large cedar tree which they were allowed to climb in the summer and whose branches had special names like Lengthies, Bearhug and Cruisies. Audrey recalled the austere grey stone mansion from the brochure Cicely had sent her and wondered whether a place so cold looking could really be so charming. Exhausted after tearing around the toyshop Audrey took them to Fortnum & Mason for tea and immediately thought of Aunt Edna and how much she would have loved it there in such an English tearoom spilling over with scones.

'Caroline says that when you're new you're given a shadow,' said Alicia, shovelling a large piece of sponge cake into her mouth.

'What's a shadow?' Audrey asked, glad to be resting her legs and sipping a cup of familiar Earl Grey tea. She smiled at her daughters indulgently, taking pleasure from their excitement.

'An older girl who looks after you for the first term,' Alicia mumbled through her cake.

'It does sound the most delightful school, doesn't it?' said Audrey, trying to be positive, ignoring the tightness in her chest. 'When Caroline mentioned riding ponies over the hills in the early morning I began to want to go there myself.'

'You're too old, Mummy,' Leonora said and laughed.

'I'm afraid I am. Aunt Cicely will be my shadow.'

'What's she like?' Leonora asked.

'She'd better be nice seeing as we're going to spend the holidays with her. I hope she has a big house with a garden. Do you think she has horses and a swimming pool?'

'Well, she's older than your father and was married for a number of years,' Audrey began but was interrupted by Leonora who wanted to know if she had children. 'No, sadly not.'

'Did her husband die?' Alicia asked without the slightest hint of compassion.

'Yes, he did.'

Her eyes lit up. 'What of?' she demanded, hoping for gory details.

'I'm not sure.'

'I bet it was something gruesome,' she said, forking another piece of cake into her mouth. 'People never seem to die painlessly. When I go, I hope I go in my sleep.'

'What an unpleasant conversation, Alicia dear, let's not talk about such morbid things.'

'Merchi says that death only frightens her because when she passes over into the next world she'll be faced with her husband and all her lovers and they'll all fight over her and make a mess of Heaven,' continued Alicia gleefully.

'That anxiety must keep her very busy,' Audrey

said ironically. 'You don't want to listen to Mercedes, she talks a lot of rubbish.'

'I miss Merchi already,' said Leonora.

'You'll miss her cooking even more,' Alicia added with a grin, 'I imagine school food is horrid.'

'Don't worry about that, girls, I'll ask Aunt Cicely to send you food parcels regularly. I don't want you fading away.'

'So does Aunt Cicely live all by herself?' Leonora asked in a quiet voice. She was no longer so nervous about Colehurst House but the thought of Aunt Cicely's large and empty mansion filled her with apprehension. She suddenly missed her home in Hurlingham and felt almost choked with longing.

'I know she's got dogs, because your father once said that after the death of her husband she filled the house with dogs so that she didn't feel so alone. I'm sure she has neighbours, though. There are bound to be other children around for you to play with.' But she wasn't sure. Cicely lived in the middle of the Dorset countryside and her husband had been a farmer. In her mind she envisaged rolling hills and forests like the landscape she had seen from the train.

'I bet she's just like Daddy,' said Leonora in an attempt to make her aunt sound more appealing.

'I bet she is,' said Audrey encouragingly. But in her mind she imagined a severe woman with a hard face, not unlike Aunt Hilda. To her surprise Aunt Cicely wasn't at all how they had imagined her to be and neither was her house.

*　　　*　　　*

When Audrey first saw the woman waving

frantically at the train from the car park beside the station, she didn't for one moment imagine that that was Aunt Cicely. Her pale hair was pinned up in a loose bun and wisps of it floated around her face in the wind and caught in her mouth that was open and smiling. She wore wide trousers and a man's stripy blue shirt. No, Cicely, from what she had heard, was more like her husband, elegant with an old-fashioned air of formality. So Audrey thought no more about the waving woman and turned her attention to finding someone to help unload their suitcases. The train drew into the remote country station that resembled a drawing from one of the children's books Audrey had grown up with. Bowls of overgrown geraniums hung from the awning and the red-bricked building was weathered and old. Audrey led her children onto the almost deserted platform and summoned a porter who busied himself at once with their luggage. 'Now where's Aunt Cicely?' she muttered. But the station was quiet, only a couple of passengers had got off and an old man who had no train to catch sat passing the time on one of the hard benches beneath the awning. She sighed and bit her lip. Had she got the day wrong? Was Aunt Cicely expecting them at all? Then before she could doubt a moment longer the woman who had been waving from the car park hurried onto the platform in a flurry of leaves and wind.

'Good gracious, I am sorry, Barley's got an upset stomach. I had to drop him off at the vet for a blood test.' She embraced Audrey as if she had known her all her life and patted the children on their heads, as if they were dogs. 'Was your trip over all right? It's such a long way. You must be exhausted. I've had the car cleaned especially, I didn't think you wanted to be covered in dog hairs on your first day.' Audrey looked into the feline face of her sister-in-law and felt the colour rise to her cheeks where they burned ferociously. Those pale blue eyes and crooked smile made her head spin. She hadn't for one moment expected that Cicely might resemble Louis.

'You're very kind to come and pick us up,' Audrey stammered for want of anything better to say.

'Don't be silly, I couldn't leave you to languish on the platform!' She gave a soft, gentle laugh and looked down at the twins. 'So you're my nieces. I hope you like dogs. I have eight. Well, come along then, we can't keep them waiting.' Alicia and Leonora, both overcome by the whirlwind of their aunt's presence, followed her down the platform in silence.

'Lucky I've got a big car,' she said, lifting the boot of a dusty Volvo so the porter could load the luggage. 'Goodness me, you have got a lot of things. I suppose you had to buy the dreaded uniform.'

'We had to buy everything,' Audrey replied, pushing her children towards the back seat.

'Well, they don't need much when they stay with me, just warm jerseys and socks. I don't heat the house, except for fires and in the winter it's damned cold.' She glanced down at the twins and noticed the look of horror on their faces. 'You can always borrow one of the dogs as a hot water bottle. They're very happy to lend themselves out when the need is great enough,' she added and laughed. 'Right, homeward bound!'

235

Audrey climbed into the passenger seat then, noticing something hard beneath her, she leant to one side and removed two large dog biscuits. 'Don't worry about them, Audrey, I brought them in case I needed to bribe Barley into the vet's. Fortunately Hilary Phipps turned up at the appropriate moment with her bitch and Barley was as well behaved as a lamb. He's always had a bit of a thing about her.'

'She must be a very pretty dog,' Audrey said, knowing very little about animals.

'Goodness no, a horrid smelly old thing. Barley's a young man and very picky when it comes to girlfriends. He's always been a bit in love with Hilary. I don't imagine she washes very much,' she added with a wicked grin.

'Oh, I see,' said Audrey in bewilderment. Cicely laughed, a warm, gentle laugh and Audrey thought once again how little like Cecil she was.

'How's my brother?' she asked as if she were able to read her thoughts. Audrey longed to ask after Louis, but she was afraid her curiosity might give her away. She reassured herself that the moment would come. Talking about her husband only reminded her of the bitterness she felt towards him and she had to muster all her strength to feign enthusiasm.

*   *   *

They drove down narrow winding lanes overgrown with ferns and dying summer foliage. The gentle autumn sun brushed the tops of the rolling hills and seemed to set the woods on fire. Although it was a clear day there was a distinct chill in the air, a

236

reminder that winter wasn't far away and Audrey suddenly felt a heavy wave of sadness. In the pause that followed Audrey heard Louis' voice echo once more across the years, *'Why do I feel melancholic? . . . Why? . . . Because we can't hold onto them forever. They're transient, like a rainbow or a sunset.'* And she suddenly wanted to cry. Whether it was due to the strain of knowing she was only days away from losing her daughters, or because in the face of such beauty she was reminded of her own mortality and the mess she had made of her love, she didn't know. But at that moment she knew what Louis had meant and what he had feared. *Transient, like a rainbow or a sunset.* She had given him her love and then taken it away. He had been right not to have trusted her. Her love had proved fickle. She had let him down.

CHAPTER FIFTEEN

'Home sweet home,' said Cicely as the car drove through a weather-beaten white fence into a cluster of gnarled farm buildings that all looked as if they had gone to seed. The twins sat up in the back seat and squealed in excitement as a pack of dogs ran towards them barking and wagging their tails, jumping up at the doors. Audrey suddenly thought of Cecil and how he would hate the thought of dogs scratching the paintwork of his car. The canine welcome party followed them through another gate into the gravelled driveway of the house.

'It's beautiful,' Audrey gasped, running her eyes over the windswept front of the manor where the green leaves of a wisteria clung to the worn red brick façade and coyly masked the windows like a feather boa on the body of an elegant old dame.

'It belonged to my late husband's family. Now I care for it as best I can with what little I have. Don't look too closely or you'll see all the cracks and the stains. It's survived four hundred years so I think it'll take more than my negligence to destroy it now.'

'It's just lovely.' Audrey sighed and felt her melancholia subside. 'It's such a happy house, I can feel it already. You must love it so much.'

Cicely smiled at her sister-in-law. 'I'm so pleased you think so. My parents have been trying to convince me to sell it for years. They don't understand like you do.'

'Oh, I can tell already. The girls will be very happy here and so shall I.'

Alicia and Leonora tumbled out of the car and fell to their knees, patting the dogs and giggling loudly as their wet noses and warm tongues tickled their skin. There were two Alsatians, a Springer Spaniel, a black and white Terrier, two brown dogs of no known breed and a fat little sausage dog. Barley the Golden Retriever was at the vet's. Cicely had eight dogs in total, all boys and they were her children. She crouched down as they left the twins rolling around on the gravel and surrounded her with their damp fur and heavy breath. She didn't care that they left testimony of their affection in muddy paw marks all over her pale trousers and shirt. Audrey imagined that she had put on clean clothes especially for their arrival in the same way that she had had the car cleaned, but now they had met, the immaculate veneer would be taken down

238

and normality resumed. She liked Cicely's normality a lot.

'Come on inside,' Cicely said, standing up and leading them into the porch. 'Leave the bags, I'll get Marcel to bring them in later.'

'Marcel?' Audrey asked.

'He's a young painter from France who's using a room at the top of the house as a studio. He's wonderfully gifted.'

'What a good idea to rent out a room like that, you're full of initiative.'

'Yes,' Cicely replied and her laughter was light with a hint of mischief. She led them into the hall. The wooden floorboards were covered with threadbare Turkish rugs and a vast display of flowers sat in a brass pot on an old oak table. 'My one weakness,' she said, once again reading Audrey's thoughts. 'Flowers. I can barely afford to pay the gypsies to cut the grass but I'll always find money for flowers and plants. They're beautiful, aren't they?'

'Lovely.'

'Let's all go into the kitchen then I can get you something to drink. I have a large chicken for lunch. I hope you like chicken, Panazel killed it this morning.'

'What, really killed a chicken?' Alicia asked, skipping after her up the corridor.

'Well, I do hope so, otherwise it'll jump out of the oven and run away.'

'What a funny name,' said Leonora.

'Panazel?'

'Yes.'

'Gypsies always have funny names,' said Cicely, entering the kitchen and switching on the light.

239

Panazel has a little boy about your age,' she added frowning. 'But he's a rather unpleasant little boy.'

'What's his name?' Leonora asked, patting one of the Alsatians.

'Florien.'

'That's a nice name,' she said and smiled.

'Far too nice for him, if you ask me.'

'Do they live in caravans like in the storybooks?' Alicia asked, pulling herself up onto one of the stools that stood near the Aga.

'They are traditional Romany gypsies, so they do. Beautiful, brightly coloured caravans with pretty piebald ponies. Don't ask me how they wash, though. They look pretty clean and don't smell, which is a blessing, don't you think? Nowadays you get horrid people in vans who sit on your land and refuse to get off, leaving litter all over the place. They do smell. Very unpleasant. I let Panazel and his family sit on my land in exchange for some gardening . . .'

'And chicken killing,' Alicia added with a grin.

'And chicken killing,' repeated Cicely, pulling some glasses out of the cupboard. In tune with the rest of the cluttered kitchen each glass was different and one was chipped.

'I'd hate to see a chicken being killed,' said Leonora, wincing at the thought and looking to her mother for encouragement.

'Oh, I'd love to,' Alicia cried. 'Can I?'

'Really, Alicia, I don't think you would,' interrupted Audrey, wondering where her daughter's fascination with death came from.

'I'm sure Panazel will be delighted with the company. You can help him sweep the leaves off the lawn as well if you're feeling energetic.'

240

Alicia screwed up her nose. 'I'll be exhausted after killing a chicken, I doubt I'll have the energy.'

Cicely laughed and poured iced lemon into the glasses.

'Can we see the gypsies after lunch?' Leonora asked. 'I've never seen a real gypsy.'

'Of course you can.'

'Does Panazel have a wife?' Audrey asked, watching the dogs begin to circle the kitchen like hungry sharks.

'Yes, she's called Masha and she cooks the most delicious fruit cakes. I'll bring one out for tea because Marcel loves them as well.' She paused and looked into the half-distance with misty eyes. *'J'adore les gateaux, mon amour,'* she muttered to herself in a very bad French accent.

'I thought gypsies were meant to have hundreds of children,' said Audrey, taking the glass of iced lemon that Cicely offered her when she focused once again.

'They have an elder daughter called Ravena who insists on reading people's fortunes. She says she inherited the gift from her grandmother, but they all say that, don't they?' Cicely fell into the armchair and sipped from her glass.

'Has she ever read yours?' Alicia asked.

'Yes, lots of times and she's never got anything right. Still, I pay her, poor thing, she has to live. She washes up from time to time, but she frightens the dogs so I don't like to have her in the house much.'

'They look like they're hungry,' said Leonora, patting one of the Alsatians that nudged his nose against her elbow.

'What do they eat?' Alicia asked. 'They must eat

241

a lot.'

'They do. I know, why don't you two help me feed them. After all, you'd better get used to it, it'll be one of your chores. You must pay your way the same as the gypsies.' She then smiled at them broadly and Audrey felt her heart flip over. When Cicely smiled like that she enchanted, just like Louis.

While Cicely and the twins filled eight large metal bowls with dog food, chattering happily as if they had known each other all their lives, Audrey sat and watched Cicely's face, more beautiful than that of either of her brothers. Her eyes were the same blue but they were set wide apart and slanted like a cat's. Her nose was long and straight like Cecil's but her mouth was the same as Louis', large and sensual and full of expression. When Marcel entered the kitchen Audrey was left in no doubt about the nature of their relationship for her lips curled up at the corners in the same way that Louis' had when he had first smiled at her.

'Marcel,' she exclaimed flamboyantly. 'I want you to meet my sister-in-law who's come all the way from the Argentine.' Marcel was twenty-eight years old, olive skinned with hazel eyes and thick dark hair that curled about his neck and ears. He spoke with a heavy French accent and smiled using only one side of his mouth. He wore a short artist's apron with a pocket at the front filled with brushes, which gave him the appearance of a caricature. Not to mention a large, hooked nose that could distinguish between a good wine and a moderate one. All he lacked was a beret and a string of onions to complete the look.

'*Enchanté*,' he said in a low, husky voice, taking

242

Audrey's hand and kissing it slowly. Then he turned to Cicely who seemed to buckle at the knees and looking up at her from beneath his fringe he said, '*Mon amour*, if I am to create I need to eat. My body has run out of fuel and without fuel I cannot paint. My brush is dry, my imagination is ground to a halt. When will I see what is the cause of this delicious fragrance?' Alicia giggled and showed him the dog bowl. He frowned at her, unamused, and put his hands in his hair and shook his head.

'The chicken will be ready in *quinze minutes*, Marcel. Why don't you join us for a little *vin*?' Cicely replied, now almost dancing about the kitchen.

'*Oui, du vin*,' he said and flopped into a chair. Cicely rushed to the fridge and pulled out a bottle of Sancerre.

'Would you care for some too, Audrey?'

'I'd love some, thank you,' she replied, watching Marcel strike a Byronic pose, which he believed gave him a sultry air. He observed Cicely from under his heavy brow.

'You know I met Marcel in Paris,' she said and her cheeks flushed prettily. 'He was painting in the street, imagine such a talent wasted like that? It killed me.'

'Cicely is my patron. Without her I would not have survived,' he said gravely, pouting his lips and shaking his head in order to insinuate that he had faced certain death.

'Nonsense,' she interjected and waved the glasses in the air. 'He would have been spotted by someone. Talent such as his wouldn't have gone unnoticed. But imagine how lucky I am that he

243

chose to come here, to the middle of the Dorset countryside, to work?'

'Shall we give the dogs their lunch?' Leonora interrupted, bored of stirring the bowls.

'Yes, yes, please do. Just put them outside the back door,' she instructed vaguely without taking her eyes off her young lover.

'What about Barley?'

'I'll pick him up from the vet after lunch so leave his on the freezer in the scullery.' And she pointed to the back of the kitchen.

'Cicely is my muse as well as my patron,' continued Marcel as the dogs followed the twins outside. Cicely glanced at Audrey and smiled at her almost apologetically.

'I can understand why,' said Audrey truthfully. Cicely did indeed have a rare beauty.

'She is a beguiling woman, *n'est-ce pas*?' he said, taking the bottle and glasses from her shaking hands and grinning lustfully. Audrey watched the way he looked at her. His face was like a poem, his eyelids heavy with sentiment and admiration and Cicely was transformed into a young girl again. Her mouth could hide nothing of the passion that had set her heart aflame. Audrey was in no doubt that this was a very different Cicely to the one Cecil knew. Marcel and love had changed her as only love can.

*   *   *

After lunch Marcel returned to his studio at the top of the house demanding total seclusion. 'Disturbance gives me pain, as it did the great Michelangelo,' he said melodramatically. So

244

Audrey accompanied Cicely and the twins to the paddock at the end of the garden where the gypsies had set up camp. The garden was wild and overgrown with the last of the summer plants tumbling from the borders onto the lawn. Tall trees stood with dignity like wise old statesmen, watching over the manor and valley in which it nestled as they had done for centuries, poised ready for the cycle of nature to end and begin all over again in the spring. The sky was a delicate blue across which white and grey clouds glided like surf on the sea and a crisp breeze turned cold every time the sun disappeared. Audrey was struck once again by the beauty of the place and she suddenly began to understand why her companions aboard the *Alcantara* loved it so much. She watched her daughters hover by the fence picking blackberries from the hedgerows, surrounded by the mélange of dogs and wondered whether they would one day consider this rolling countryside home. The Argentine would perhaps pale into a tender memory, as the years would inevitably separate them from their childhood and condition them to this new world. There was no avoiding it.

As she neared them she could see through the trees into the field beyond where three brightly painted, old-fashioned caravans stood on the long grass with their doors flung wide open, steps leading from their dark interiors to the ground. A cluster of muscular cart horses grazed lazily in the sunshine and a line of washing hung from the back of one caravan to a crooked stick which they had obviously found in the wood. The girls climbed over the fence and ran up to stroke the horses who continued to eat as if they hadn't noticed them.

'What a lovely sight,' mused Cicely, opening the gate. 'I love having them here because they look so picturesque. Marcel says he's going to paint them. Panazel's very proud, though. He'd hate to think of himself as a picture on a chocolate box. One has to be tactful. But between you and me it really is a quaint sight, isn't it?' Audrey agreed and followed her across the paddock.

'Mummy, isn't he sweet!' Leonora cried in delight, patting the horse's neck. 'Do you think we can ride him?'

'You'll have to ask Panazel,' said Cicely. 'There's a smaller one, a pony, but I imagine he's taken him out for a ride.'

'They're going to be riding at Colehurst House,' said Audrey, smiling back at Leonora who was angling for her mother's attention.

'Of course. Heavenly,' Cicely exclaimed, sighing with nostalgia. 'I used to spend the entire summer galloping across those hills when I was a child. They're going to adore that school. If I had daughters I'd send them there too.' Audrey wondered why she had never had children, she obviously liked them and her home was tailor made for them. But Cicely seemed to harbour no bitterness and besides, she had her dogs who now circled the caravan and horses barking loudly. The horses continued to munch on the grass, lifting their heads up every now and then to survey the scene and nod away the flies. Then just when the twins were about to sneak a peek inside the caravans one of the horses neighed loudly and pricked his ears forward as Panazel and Florien emerged from the woods that lined the end of the field leading a small piebald pony whose back was

246

laden with two large barrels of water. 'He's very handsome, don't you think?' Cicely hissed at Audrey.

'Very,' Audrey replied, watching them approach. Panazel was tall and strongly built with the rough, unkempt appearance of a man who has worked all his life with his hands and lived off the land. His skin was darkened by the outdoors and weathered by uncertainty as well as the years and he walked bowlegged at a slow pace, as if the days were long and life was long so there was no reason to hurry. His son, Florien, watched the strange people who waited for them by the caravans with suspicious eyes partly obscured behind a long black fringe. He was twelve years old and went to the school in the village when he remembered. He hated school and sat sulking at the back of the class dreaming of riding up on the hills and working with his father in Mrs Weatherby's garden.

'Good day to you, Mrs Weatherby,' said Panazel, nodding his head in respect. Florien mumbled the same then stared at the twins with eyes the colour of bark. The twins stared back at him with curiosity; they had never seen a real gypsy boy before and he was more handsome than any of the boys they had met in the Argentine.

'I'd like you to meet my sister-in-law who's going to be living with me for a few weeks while her daughters settle into their new school. They've come all the way over from the Argentine.' Panazel nodded at Audrey and Florien looked at the twins with more interest than ever. Although he didn't know where the Argentine was, he imagined it was somewhere very far away. He wondered whether they spoke English or French perhaps, he knew a bit of French from school. 'This is Alicia and this is Leonora,' continued Cicely, pointing at the girls. Florien was at once taken with Alicia whose beauty never failed to bewitch and Alicia, who recognised the look of admiration that had suddenly lit up his face, smiled at him self-confidently. 'Alicia wants to watch you kill a chicken,' said Cicely. Alicia looked at Panazel who frowned his disapproval. He thought it an odd request from someone so lovely.

'When will you be eating chicken again, Mrs Weatherby?' he asked, taken aback by the child's lofty gaze as she continued to fix him with her pale eyes.

Cicely shrugged, 'Well, I hadn't thought, really. I suppose we could have another for lunch tomorrow, we do have trillions of chickens, don't we, Panazel?'

'There's no shortage of chickens,' he said and chuckled.

'Why doesn't Florien take the girls and show them around the farm. There's so much to see and this is their first time in England.' Florien looked as if he had just been asked to recite his nine times table and blushed to the roots of his shiny black hair.

'Can we ride these horses?' Alicia asked and Florien's cheeks drained of his embarrassment for at least they all spoke the same language. He wasn't very good at French.

'If you like,' Panazel replied, 'but it'll have to be this evening for I've got work to do.' Cicely liked the sound of that, there was so much that needed doing just to keep the place ticking over.

'Florien, I'd like to see inside your caravan,' Alicia demanded and Audrey flinched at her

248

daughter's commanding tone. But Florien gazed upon her with more admiration than ever and strode towards the steps indicating with a nod that she follow. Leonora was used to being passed over but she tagged along as she always did, out of habit as well as necessity.

*   *   *

Audrey and Cicely wandered back across the field towards the gardens, the dogs puffing at their heels. Audrey was longing to ask after Louis. She hadn't stopped thinking about him since she had set foot in England. She felt his presence everywhere and was reminded of him each time she looked at his sister. Finally, her opportunity came when she was shown into the drawing room for a grand piano stood collecting dust in the corner beneath large black and white photographs in silver frames. Hungrily she passed her eyes over the pictures until Louis' face smiled out at her. And his smile held within it all his hopes and dreams, longings and disappointments, which she recognised and understood. She wanted to run her fingers over it and remember him the way he was when they had danced over the cobbled streets of Palermo in the summer of their love. So taken was she that she barely heard a word Cicely was saying.

'I gather you play the piano most beautifully,' Cicely said, sitting down on the club fender with her two Alsatians flopping onto the carpet at her feet. Audrey wrenched her thoughts away from the photograph and sighed.

'Not that well, I'm afraid,' she replied vaguely, staring into his features as if he were trying to communicate with her through the still, silent medium of the picture.

'Cecil is full of admiration. He can't play a note, not like Louis,' she said and her voice trailed off. Audrey went pale. She turned slowly and saw that Cicely's eyes were fixed on her with a mixture of curiosity and sympathy. She didn't know what to say. She had no idea how much Cicely knew. She waited with a suspended heart for Cicely to give her a clue as to where this conversation was leading. Her sister-in-law gazed at her steadily then tilted her head to one side. 'I'm so terribly sorry about your sister. I know it was a good many years ago now, but I know what it's like to lose someone, you never forget and you never really heal, you just push on because you have to.' Cicely pulled a thin smile and blinked away the image of her late husband that had nudged its way to the front of her mind.

'Thank you, Cicely,' Audrey replied in a quiet voice. Then feeling exposed standing up she went and sat on one of the sofas, folding her arms in front of her defensively.

'Cecil told me how special she was and Louis . . .' Audrey raised her eyes and frowned. Cicely took care to choose the right words. 'And Louis . . . suffered a broken heart.'

'Louis just disappeared,' said Audrey. Aware that her voice had thinned she coughed and added more steadily, 'One moment he was there, the next he was gone.' Then she focused her eyes on the carpet and bit the inside of her cheek.

'He went to Mexico. God knows what he did for all those years. Cecil wrote to me and told me. It didn't surprise me, Louis has always been a very

250

sensitive man, and fragile. Well, I'm sure you know. Then he arrived here one day last spring. Out of the blue. Not a letter or a telegram to warn us that he was turning up.' Her eyes narrowed as her sight misted and she spoke in a very soft voice. 'He looked older. Much older, as if he had been robbed of his youth. You have to remember that Cecil and I are a good deal older than him. He was always the baby and in my memory he always will be. There's still something very childlike about Louis.' Audrey felt a wave of regret debilitate her suddenly and struggled to compose herself. But Cicely continued oblivious of the torment her words inflicted. 'Louis has always been unpredictable but he's never been secretive. If Cecil hadn't told me about Isla I'd never have known what was torturing him. He didn't confide in me, in fact, he never spoke about it, even after all these years. He seemed so cut up, still. I tried to prise it out of him. I thought it would be better to let it all out rather than bottle it up. But he just played this maddening melody over and over on the piano. It's so out of tune, it made my ears throb. Only Chip, my sausage dog, could bear it. He'd sit at his feet watching the pedals move up and down transfixed.'

'Where is he now?' Audrey asked, hoping that Cicely hadn't noticed the desperate tone in her voice.

'I don't know. I'm afraid I asked him to leave.' Cicely pursed her lips regretfully and played with a strand of greying hair that had come away from the clip. 'He was just hanging around moping, playing the piano and taking off on long long walks. He's a grown up, he can't just sit around doing nothing expecting his family to support him. I don't know

251

what he was doing in South America. I think he was teaching music or something because he seemed to have earned a living. I told him to find himself a job around here. I knew he wouldn't go to our parents for help so I didn't dare suggest it.' She was trying to justify why she hadn't done more for him. 'I housed him and fed him for a few months then one day he packed his bags and left. I swear I could still hum that tune . . . how did it go?' Audrey froze as Cicely began to hum tonelessly the tune Louis had composed for her.

Then suddenly the tears were spilling down her cheeks and she was wiping them away, but she was unable to disguise her misery and Cicely stopped humming and reached out her hand. 'I'm so sorry, Audrey, I didn't mean to upset you. It must be hard hearing about Louis. He must be your last link with Isla.'

Audrey shook her head and sniffed, sweeping a hand across her face. 'I'm sorry. I'm fine, really. It's just that I haven't seen Louis since Isla died. I would so love to see him.'

'And I would give anything to find him. He left, you see, without a word and none of us have heard from him or seen him since. I feel so guilty. I just turfed him out.' Then she added sheepishly, 'He didn't get on with Marcel.'

'He seemed to rub everyone up the wrong way in Hurlingham. But I saw him differently. I understood him.'

'Isla must have been very special. Louis has never lost his heart to anyone before and I doubt he will ever love like that again. He must have connected with her in a way we just can't imagine. She must have been a very compassionate woman.'

252

Audrey was so overcome she could no longer speak.

Cicely suddenly looked at her watch and gasped. 'Barley! I've forgotten to fetch him from the vet's. You don't mind being left here, do you?' she asked, jumping to her feet. Audrey shook her head. In fact, that was just what she needed, some time alone to digest all that she had been told. Cicely smiled apologetically then rushed out of the room with her Alsatians, leaving a light smell of tuberose in the air and a heavy sense of relief. Audrey waited until she had heard the front door slam and then walked over to the piano.

Looking once again into the face of the man she had never stopped loving she was suddenly suffocated by a tremendous feeling of loneliness. She traced her eyes slowly over his features, caressing them and loving them with her tears as if he were dead and she were mourning him. He may just as well have been dead for she didn't know whether she'd ever see him again. Life was short and she had let him go. Besides, how could she explain to him that she had married his brother? If his heart was broken now such news would certainly splinter it and then what? As his sister had said, he was fragile. She cursed her own lack of courage.

Gripped by an overwhelming desire to vent her grief she sat down on the piano stool and positioned her trembling fingers over the keys. She was aware that Louis had sat on the same seat and touched the same notes only months before and her senses sharpened as she could almost feel his presence and smell his skin. Then she closed her eyes and took a deep breath. She hadn't played it

253

for years, not *that* tune, not *their* tune. But she was alone in the house and her desire to do so was too strong to withstand. Her fingers glided across the keys as if they had been eternally programmed to play that piece. With the familiar, haunting sound of 'The Forget-Me-Not Sonata' she felt the pressure lift from her spirit and her heart inflate with hope. She didn't notice a little brown sausage dog wander in and lie beneath the piano to watch the pedals move up and down, nor did she know that at the very top of the house Marcel heard the echo of her music and paused his paintbrush to listen.

CHAPTER SIXTEEN

Florien wasn't very talkative. Not that Alicia noticed, she was far too busy telling him about herself. Leonora fell naturally into her usual role, trying to be kind and put him at his ease—she was used to her sister dazzling people until their tongues grew thick and heavy and barely worked at all. She knew that was what had happened to Florien even though Aunt Cicely had said that he was a sullen boy. He was just shy, she thought, and overwhelmed.

He led them inside the caravan and watched mutely, barely able to take his eyes off Alicia. While Leonora was enchanted by the pastoral charm of the hand-woven rugs and blankets, the bunk bed that was attached to the wall and the odd photographs and pictures stuck roughly over peeling paintwork, Alicia was amazed at the small

254

dimensions of their home and exclaimed in patronising tones that she couldn't believe real people lived in places such as this. 'I mean, it's like a house in a fairy tale. You could be a family of goblins. It's very dear, isn't it, Leo?' she trilled, while her sister cringed and tried to make up for her tactlessness.

'Oh, I think it's beautiful. I'd love to live in such a pretty house and besides, you can take it anywhere you choose, much more fun than a house made of bricks.' But Florien wasn't offended, he was far too awe-struck even to hear what she had said.

'Show me the farm,' Alicia demanded, striding out of the caravan into the sunshine, which had temporarily emerged from behind a heavy grey cloud. 'Do you have lots of animals?'

Florien nodded.

'What, cows, pigs, goats?'

Florien nodded again and began to walk off in the direction of the little gate through which they had come in. Alicia turned to Leonora and said in a deliberately loud voice, 'I think he's lost his tongue.'

'Alicia . . .' Leonora protested, but her sister threw her head back and laughed.

'Or perhaps he doesn't have one.' This he did hear and he felt the heat prickle the skin on his face. He kept walking in front of them so they wouldn't notice. They followed him through a large walled vegetable garden which was old and crumbling, although parts of the ground were obviously well looked after by Panazel and Florien.

'You must work so hard,' Leonora said, hurrying to catch up with him. 'This place is enormous.'

When he didn't reply she continued, determined to show her sister that with a little encouragement he would open up and talk to them. 'In the Argentine we have to buy all our vegetables. We have a nice garden, though, and our grandmother has an orange orchard, which smells lovely in summertime. I'd like to help you in the garden, it's a lot of work for only two people.' At this Florien looked across at the eager face of this rather plain-looking girl and he felt his confidence return.

'Three people,' he said in a surprisingly soft voice, opening the gate in the wall, which led into a yard surrounded by farm buildings.

'Oh, your mother helps too? Still, three is a small number for such a big place.'

'It's all falling down,' said Alicia, rejoining them. 'Now where are the animals?'

'But it's so pretty,' Leonora commented with a sigh. Alicia screwed up her nose in annoyance. She was getting rather tired of her sister and looking forward to making new friends at school.

Florien wandered across to a fence that opened into a grassy enclosure. To Alicia's delight it was alive with chickens and one very large, proud cockerel who strode through them pecking at their feathers just to remind them who was boss. 'How do you kill them?' she asked without the slightest inhibition. Florien climbed onto the fence where he sat and looked down at her imperious face. He felt more confident at that height.

'We break their necks,' he replied nonchalantly.

'Ah, so the gypsy boy can talk!' she said. Leonora was horrified. Knowing that there was little she could do to help him she took off to explore the dusty buildings on her own.

'How do you do that?' Alicia continued, watching her sister disappear inside an old barn. Florien made a twist and pull gesture with his hands. Alicia's eyes glinted in the light just before the sun disappeared behind a cloud.

'Show me,' she said.

Florien shook his head. 'I'll only kill to eat,' he replied.

'Well, Aunt Cicely said she wanted a chicken for tomorrow.'

'I'm not allowed.'

'Don't be such a baby.'

'I can't.'

'Go on!' she insisted. 'While Leo's not here to sneak. I can assure you I won't tell anyone. It'll be our secret.'

'I don't know.' Florien shook his head and his eyes darkened as a heavy rain cloud settled above them.

'I don't believe you can do it,' she goaded. 'You're too little. How old are you?'

'Twelve,' he replied quietly, turning to watch the chickens. Alicia sensed she was winning and continued to wear him down.

'I'm ten and if I knew how to kill a chicken I wouldn't be afraid to do so. You're two years older than me and a boy and yet you're afraid you'll get into trouble. Who'll tell? I won't. We can bury it in the garden and no one will ever know. Don't you want to have a secret with me?' That was about as much as Florien could take. Alicia watched him jump down from the fence and remain a moment staring at the chickens who pecked at the grass oblivious of the boy who stood ready to kill. He slowly rubbed his hands together in preparation.

He had broken many necks before, but never with such a beguiling audience and he didn't want to make a mistake. If the chicken didn't die immediately he would have failed and he'd never be able to face this imperious girl again. He hated her yet he longed for her admiration. He could feel her eyes upon him, penetrating his skin and burning his insides so that he was acutely aware of every muscle in his body. He had never wanted to impress anyone so much in his entire life. Not even his mother, whom he adored. He crept across the yard with the agility of a cat. A few heavy drops of rain fell about him but they did not deter him. He had to concentrate. He didn't want to make a fool of himself chasing chickens around the yard. He set his eyes on one who raised her head momentarily and stiffened in terror, then he pounced.

Alicia cried out in delight and clapped her hands together. Florien felt his heart inflate like a balloon and his face broke into a triumphant smile. He held the chicken up by the neck and then with Alicia's eyes upon him he twisted it, breaking it in one swift movement.

At that moment the sky opened and rain fell in a torrent of large drops. Alicia squealed and tore her eyes off the dead bird that swung from Florien's victorious hand. 'Leo, let's go!' she shouted, running off towards the house. Leonora emerged from the barn and followed her, laughing as the rain splashed off her head and shoulders and trickled down her back. Florien was left in bewilderment, standing alone in the yard as the chickens hurried for cover. He blinked away the stream of water that cascaded down his face and shame now surfaced with his reasoning. He was overwhelmed by a wave of self-loathing. He hated that snobby little girl. He would never speak to her again. Biting his lip in anger he walked through the yard to the vegetable garden where he fell to the ground and began to dig a hole with his bare hands. He placed the warm body in the earth and covered it up as best he could. Then he wiped his hands on his trousers and made his way back home feeling lower than he had ever felt before.

*   *   *

'Florien killed a chicken for me,' said Alicia to Leonora as they cowered for cover in a windy stone folly that stood beneath an umbrella of trees in the corner of the garden.

Leonora was suitably horrified. 'He didn't!' she exclaimed, staring at her sister in disbelief.

'Don't be such a baby,' Alicia sneered. 'I told him I wouldn't tell you, so don't sneak.'

'I won't. I promise.'

'Good.'

'Did the chicken suffer?'

'Terribly,' said Alicia, smiling triumphantly. 'First he had to chase it around the yard. It ran and ran until its little legs couldn't carry it any further. It collapsed on the grass and when Florien picked it up I think I heard a gasp of terror. Then he wound his hands around its neck and squeezed slowly, very slowly, so that the chicken died a long and painful death.' Alicia watched as her sister's eyes filled with tears. She waited until they began to spill over her cheeks and then she put her out of her misery. 'Don't be silly, he killed it so quickly the stupid animal didn't feel anything.'

259

'Oh, I'm so relieved!' Leonora gasped, hastily wiping her face. 'You are mean sometimes, Alicia.'

'And you're a gullible old thing, Leo.'

Leonora smiled weakly at her sister's affectionate tone.

'What do you think of Florien?' she asked. Alicia was never happier than when she talked about herself and her opinions and Leonora was only too ready to please her.

'I think he's handsome but dumb.'

'You mean he never says anything?'

'No, I mean stupid.'

'Oh.' Leonora thought her sister most unjust but she didn't dare say.

'He'll be fun to have around though in the holidays,' she continued. 'I'll be bored if it's just you and me. Maybe he can build us a camp in the woods and we can ride those horses bareback.'

'I love the caravans. We can play in them too.'

'Perhaps,' said Alicia whose mind was now wandering back to the yard and to Florien whom she had left alone with the dead chicken. 'I wonder if he's going to bury it or own up,' she said, narrowing her eyes.

'He'll eat it, of course.'

'No he won't,' replied Alicia and laughed. 'He wasn't meant to kill it. His father will eat *him* for dinner if he finds out. I don't think he's allowed to kill animals on his own. Besides, I said if he did it, it would be our secret.'

'Ah,' sighed Leonora who already understood. Alicia had made him do it and he had been too impressed not to seize the opportunity to show off.

'He'll be furious with me now,' she giggled. 'But he won't be able to say anything without owning

260

up.'

'Poor Florien,' said Leonora, looking out onto the lawn and imagining hot summer days helping him and his father in the flowerbeds. He probably wouldn't want her to help him now.

'You had better toughen up, Leo. No one will like you at school if you're too nice.' Leonora looked across at her sister and knew she was wrong. But still, she couldn't help but admire her, Alicia was everything she wasn't. And as if Nature had heard her thoughts the rain cloud moved away and the sun came out, bathing Alicia's beautiful young face in a heavenly golden light.

*   *   *

When Barley the Golden Retriever bounded into the drawing room Audrey was sitting on the sofa with Leonora listening to Alicia playing the 'Moonlight Sonata'. 'Goodness me!' exclaimed Aunt Cicely. 'Don't you play beautifully.' Alicia grimaced. She hated it when people interrupted her. But because she didn't know Aunt Cicely all that well yet, she forced a smile and continued to play even though they all began to talk over her. 'Darling Barley's going to be fine. Nothing wrong with him at all. In fact, he's never been fitter. Must have eaten something nasty on the farm.' Barley sniffed at Leonora's feet then, without any warning, sat in front of her and placed his two large paws on her lap.

'Oh, Mummy, look!' she gasped in delight and rubbed his ears. 'Isn't he sweet.' Alicia hit the pedal with her foot and played the notes as loudly as she could.

261

'He's adorable,' Audrey replied, running her hand down his yellow back. 'He's got curly hair just like Alicia.' At that Alicia gave up playing and wandered over to pat the dog.

'He has got hair just like me, hasn't he?' she said, feeling better now that she was the centre of attention. 'I want him to put his paws on my knees,' she whined, pulling the dog away from her sister and dragging him over to the other sofa. Leonora didn't protest and Audrey simply watched with an indulgent smile on her face. Alicia sat down and commanded him to sit, which he did without any fuss and after a bit of stroking he flopped his furry feet onto her lap and proceeded to pant at her with his sweet doggie breath. Cicely raised her eyebrows, surprised that Audrey let her daughter get away with such capriciousness. There was something very disagreeable about Alicia. Cicely hoped her arrogance would be knocked out of her at Colehurst House.

*   *   *

It was especially dark in the countryside at night. No streetlights to illuminate the rooms, to creep through the gaps in the curtains and sketch reassuring streaks of gold across the floor and wall. It was a thick and heavy blackness that obliterated everything so that Audrey was left alone with her thoughts and a suffocating loneliness that frightened her. Unable to sleep in a house which still reverberated with echoes of Louis' presence she switched on the light and sat up in bed, breathing sharp, shallow breaths. Leonora and Alicia were sharing a bedroom down the corridor.

She hoped they weren't alarmed by the darkness. Cicely had turned off all the lights when they went to bed in order not to waste electricity. 'I have to cut costs wherever I can or lose the house to some vulgar millionaire with more money than taste,' she had said. But Audrey was anxious for Leonora who was likely to mind and suffer in silence, so she sneaked across the floorboards towards the twins' room, cringing as every time her foot landed a loud creak cried out in protest and threatened to wake the whole house. There were so many rooms and each door looked the same. Unsure of which one belonged to her daughters she lingered sweating in deliberation, her eyes jumping from one to the other, afraid of waking Cicely or Marcel by mistake. Finally she gave up and tiptoed back towards her room. But then another idea struck her. The light from her own room illuminated the stairs, which led into the hall and drawing room where the photograph of Louis whispered to her from the piano. She wouldn't have to play, she could just pretend. She could close her eyes and imagine. She would feel close to him and her loneliness wouldn't hurt her anymore. It would be a temporary relief.

With an aching nostalgia she was reminded of those times she would steal down the stairs at her parents' house in Canning Street to drive off to Palermo with Louis. So many secrets, she thought, no one would imagine it of her. She walked at the very edge of the steps so that the yawning floorboards made less noise. She hadn't noticed their squeaking during the day. There was just enough light to enable her to find her way to the drawing room and when she reached the photograph she could just make out his features. She picked it up and ran her thumb over the glass. In the silence of the night she recalled their dancing and their dreaming, their loving and their laughter before Isla had died and the fantasy had shattered. They had been so happy and they had believed such happiness would last forever. It could have. If only she had been braver, stronger, more courageous. Instead she had been tested and failed. She didn't deserve him. After all those years with Cecil, Cecil who was good and kind, gentle and generous, she now resigned herself to the fact that she had made a terrible mistake. The thought of spending the rest of her life with a man she didn't love, whom she had never really loved, was like renouncing one's soul to a long winter. There was nothing she could do. She had to live with her choice and be reminded at every step of her misjudgement. But without her children what was there to live for? She threw her mind across the waters to the sunny streets of her home and yet, without love, they were bare streets and an icy wind rattled through the large and empty spaces.

She put the frame down and sat on the piano stool, resting her fingers once again on the keys. Slowly at first, but then with increasing clarity she began to hear the familiar tune of Louis' gentle spirit reaching her from some far distant place where they were still able to meet and relive those moments of extraordinary tenderness.

Suddenly a bright light shone into her face. She flinched and opened her eyes. 'Oh, it is you,' said Marcel, switching off the torch. Audrey blinked through the darkness. 'I am sorry, I didn't know. I thought you were a thief,' he continued gravely. His

264

accent seemed heavier than usual. She placed her hand on her heart which was hopping about like a startled mouse. She felt she had been caught doing something wicked.

'That's all right,' she whispered. 'I couldn't sleep.'

'It is dark, *n'est-ce pas*?' he said, leaning against the piano. As her eyes adjusted she could make out that he was wearing a long dressing gown and slippers. Feeling vulnerable in only a cotton nightdress and cardigan she folded her arms in front of her chest.

'Yes,' she replied, staring down at the keyboard.

'When I first came to the countryside the nights were so dark and Cicely wouldn't have the lights on, that I thought it was the end of the world.'

'I know how you feel,' she replied and chuckled uneasily.

'When I cannot sleep, I paint.'

'In the dark?'

'I light a candle. Candlelight is always more romantic anyhow.'

'What do you paint?'

Marcel shrugged the way Frenchmen do, pouting and raising his palms to the ceiling. 'Anything that moves me.'

'Cicely?'

He looked at her steadily and then a small smile curled the corners of his mouth.

'For whom do you play?'

'For myself,' she replied carefully.

'You play with emotion,' he stated.

'You haven't heard me play,' she said and laughed nervously.

'Oh, but I have. This afternoon the melody rose

up to my studio in the attic and I paused to listen. I recognised the tune, but could not remember where I had heard it before.'

Audrey caught her breath 'It is late and I'm tired,' she said, getting up. 'I think I'll go to bed now.'

'Of course. And I am too tired to paint,' he replied in a whisper. 'I will show you to your room so you don't stumble.'

'Thank you,' she said, following him as he led the way with the torch.

'You'll get used to the darkness, in time it will cease to frighten you but will comfort you. After all, one cannot hide one's secrets in the light of day.'

Audrey closed the door of her room behind her and leant back against it. She found Marcel very creepy, as if he could read her thoughts. She bit her lip anxiously. If he had heard her playing that afternoon he would have recognised the same tune that Louis had played because, according to Cicely, he had driven them all mad with it. She knew the way she played gave her feelings away and Marcel wasn't a fool. He appeared to have worked it all out in one afternoon. She sighed wearily and walked over to the bed. Before she got in she noticed a small lump beneath the sheets. It stirred and stretched, then rolled over. Leonora opened her eyes dreamily. 'Where have you been?' she asked softly, without taking her head off the pillow.

'Darling, are you afraid of the dark?' Audrey asked, getting in beside her and gathering her into her arms.

'Yes,' the child replied. 'And I'm scared of going to boarding school. I want to stay here with you

266

and Aunt Cicely. I like Aunt Cicely and Barley.'

'I know, my love, and I wish you could stay here too. But you have to be a big girl. You'll love it when you get there.'

'I know, I'm just being silly.'

'No, you're not being silly and I understand completely. You're going to have to be very brave and so am I, because I'm going to miss you too. But sleep now, my love, and your fears will have gone in the morning.'

Leonora snuggled up against her mother and Saggy Rabbit and Audrey switched off the light. She relished the warm feel of her daughter's body pressed tightly against hers and remembered Leonora as a baby, when a seamless future stretched out in front of them, before it was marred with the dread of separation. But now she wouldn't witness her growing up, not the small changes that happen day to day. She wouldn't be there to help with schoolwork, to wrap her arms around her when she was afraid or felt hard done by. She listened to her breathing and smelt the soft scent of soap that mingled with the fragrance of childhood. Her face was warm and soft and each time she kissed it Leonora nestled closer in her sleep, safe and secure in her mother's embrace. But Audrey remained awake. At first she thought about Isla, how they had often slept like two puppies, limb carelessly draped over limb. Then she thought about Louis, but she was unable to forget her strange confrontation with Marcel. She blinked into the night and went over what he had said. He can't really have believed her to be a thief because he would have seen the light on in her room. He must have deliberately come to find her.

CHAPTER SEVENTEEN

At first sight Colehurst House looked cold and forbidding. It was a large greystone mansion set in the vast, manicured grounds of a park, surrounded by velvet green hills. Aunt Cicely said that it had once been the private house of a very grand family whose portraits still hung collecting dust on the wooden panelled walls. In the late nineteenth century it was converted into a school when the last in the family line died without an heir. Audrey remembered the building from the brochure and it looked no less imposing in reality. Tall sash windows reflected the light and a vast door within the gates of an archway yawned like a toothless old man. There was a small church on the left where the lawn rose in a little hill and a giant cedar tree which dwarfed it. The long driveway was flanked by lush fields of fat ponies and weeping willows draped their branches into an ornamental pond. The drive opened out into a gravelled semicircle in front of the mansion and was now teeming with cars. Fathers in tweeds and v-neck sweaters lifted heavy trunks out of the boots and mothers chatted to other mothers while their Labradors ran around with their noses to the ground, wagging their tails, excited by all the new smells.

Audrey's shoulders hunched with tension as she looked out onto this strange world where everyone seemed to belong but her and her children. She glanced anxiously back to the twins who sat in the rear seat staring out of the windows, wide-eyed and curious. Leonora was frightened. Her face was long and pale and with white-knuckled fingers she held Saggy Rabbit tightly against her. Alicia smiled eagerly as she observed with total confidence the unconquered territory that spread out before her. She wasn't unnerved by the sense of alienation that had gripped her mother and sister. On the contrary, she felt her distinctiveness to be her trump card which she would use to rise to the top of the pile.

'Look at all those lovely dogs,' Audrey said, knowing how much Leonora loved animals.

'There's the tree that Caroline mentioned,' said Alicia, pointing to the cedar. 'I'm going to climb higher than everyone else.'

'I once fell off at Dead Man's Drop,' laughed Cicely, 'luckily I was so round back then, I bounced.'

'And all those ponies to ride,' Audrey continued. 'You love ponies, don't you, Leonora—'

'They look very sweet,' she replied. 'It's a big house,' she added and Audrey winced at the nervous quiver in her voice.

'In the summer term they take you out on the hills in the early morning. It's heavenly galloping across them at dawn. There are the ruins of an old castle up there and we used to ride through it. Deliciously romantic,' Cicely exclaimed, getting carried away with her memories.

'I hope the house is haunted,' Alicia said as they drew up outside. 'I'll write to Merchi the minute I see a ghost.'

Alicia hurried out of the car and stood on the gravel staring in excitement at the other girls and their parents. Leonora lingered beside her mother, worrying how on earth they were going to carry the

269

trunks in by themselves. She didn't see one other mother on her own, all the girls had come with both parents. Leonora wished her father were there, dressed in tweed and corduroy like the other fathers. She noticed a couple of girls look her over disdainfully, their narrowed eyes scanning her from top to toe, then shifting to her mother and aunt. She felt painfully at odds with everyone else and longed for home. But there was no turning back. She felt her throat constrict with fear and would have taken her mother's hand had it not been for the other girls who might have laughed at her childishness.

'Good God!' Cicely exclaimed in a loud voice, waving furiously. 'Dotty Hollinghoe, of all people!' Audrey recognised the woman in a Husky and headscarf as the one she had met in Debenham & Freebody. Leonora recognised Caroline and her spirits jolted back to life. 'Audrey, come and meet Dotty, we were both here in the same year. Goodness me, eons ago!' The woman smiled a toothy smile and pushed her daughter forward.

'Cicely Forrester! What a delightful surprise. Although I'm Stainton-Hughes now.'

'And I'm Weatherby,' Cicely replied, kissing her.

'We've already met,' said Audrey, extending her hand. Although she didn't warm to Dorothy Stainton-Hughes, she felt a great relief at knowing someone and blending in with everyone else who all seemed pleased to see each other after the long summer break. She watched Caroline approach Leonora and felt pathetically grateful to the child for befriending her daughter. When she looked around for Alicia, she was nowhere to be seen.

Alicia was used to people staring at her. She was a beautiful child and unusually for a little girl of ten she was well aware of her own allure and the power it gave her. She strode into the hall and sniffed the smell of polish and old wood like a dog familiarising itself with its new territory. A group of girls crowded around a notice board which was pinned up in the entrance to the great hall where long tables formed a large square, already laid up for supper. A waft of boiled cabbage floated in as the doors to the corridor and kitchen opened and a fat cook in a white apron and hat waddled off into the shadows wielding a wooden spoon. Alicia joined the huddle of girls and saw that they were looking at lists of names typed out beneath highlighted names of writers, such as Shakespeare and Marlow, Milton and Shaw. She searched for her name and found it beneath Dickens. She was about to look for Leonora but a light tapping on her shoulder stopped her in her tracks and she turned around.

'And who might you be?' said a tall, thin woman with short silver hair and hooded brown eyes. Her tone was commanding but gentle and Alicia knew instinctively that she was someone very important.

'Alicia Forrester,' she replied. The lady raised her eyebrows and nodded.

'Ah, one of the twins. I'm Diana Reid, your headmistress,' she said in a clipped English accent.

'Hello,' Alicia said boldly, looking at her steadily. The headmistress was disarmed by the child's self-assurance. *This one's going to be trouble*, she thought to herself.

'You're in Dickens and your sister's in Milne. They're next to each other.'

'Bedrooms?'

'Dormitories. Ten beds in Dickens and eight in Milne. They look out onto the box garden. Very pleasant. Now where's your mother?'

Alicia led Miss Reid outside to where Audrey was listening to Dorothy Stainton-Hughes and Cicely reminiscing about their school days. 'Absolutely nothing's changed,' they were saying. When they saw Miss Reid they both stood to attention like soldiers, suddenly on best behaviour.

'Dotty and Cicely, you were in the same year, were you not?' said Miss Reid, looking at them as if they were still pupils of hers. They laughed and nodded. 'Do you still ride, Cicely?'

'Not really, no,' Cicely replied apologetically.

'Shame, you were rather promising if I remember rightly.' Then she looked down at Alicia. 'I found this little stray in the hall, whom does she belong to?' Audrey smiled and nodded her head.

'Me. Audrey Forrester, it's a pleasure to meet you, Miss Reid,' said Audrey, who recognised the headmistress from the photograph in the brochure.

'Please call me Diana.' She bent down stiffly to retrieve a scruffy-looking terrier who was scratching at her stockings. 'This is Midge,' she said. 'Midge gets overexcited by all the other dogs then collapses with exhaustion. I think he's just about had enough, haven't you, Midge?' Midge licked his mistress's nose and wagged his thick little tail.

'This is Leonora,' said Audrey, putting her arm around her daughter's shoulders. Leonora's cheeks flushed pink, but Miss Reid's face softened into a kind smile. She was used to new girls and understood their fear. Beneath her icy shell blazed a compassionate soul.

'Ah, the other twin. Why don't you all come with me and I'll show you to your dormitories.'

'Which are they in, Miss Reid?' Cicely asked, winking at Dotty.

'Dickens and Milne.'

'Oh, I was in Milne!' Dotty exclaimed in excitement. 'Do you remember Shoddy Hambro, she used to hide her sweets in the secret cubby hole. Do they still do that?'

'I'm sure they do. One turns a blind eye occasionally,' the headmistress replied, walking into the toothless yawn.

They followed her up the front stairs, shiny polished oak steps that creaked like old bones and Cicely recounted how she was always in trouble for sneaking up them instead of the backstairs which were for the children. 'These portraits used to give me the creeps,' she laughed, 'especially this one.' She pointed to a dark painting of an aged bishop whose cold eyes stared straight out at them. 'Wherever one looks his eyes always follow.' As they walked across the landing Audrey glanced back at the painting and saw that Cicely was right. His gaze pursued her so that when she turned away she still felt his stare on her back.

Diana Reid led them through a string of large dormitories that would once have been elegant reception rooms with ornate marble fireplaces and heavy mouldings on the ceilings. Each one was more beautiful than the last. Audrey looked at the rows of iron beds and tried to envisage what it must

273

have been like as a private home. Diana Reid stopped every now and then to greet a parent or a child and comment in her firm but kind voice on a teddy bear placed lovingly on a pillow or to quieten a cluster of overexcited girls happy to be back after the long break. Leonora stayed close to her mother while her sister strode forward asking questions without compunction.

Finally they arrived at a white-walled room with tall sash windows overlooking the Box Garden. Alicia stood on the window seat and gazed down at the maze of box hedges that sat bathed in the golden light of evening. A fat pheasant stood in the middle, pecking at the grass. She thought of Florien and the chicken and smiled. She wondered whether he shot pheasants, or whether he wrung their necks. 'You can choose your bed, Alicia,' said Miss Reid, who still held Midge under her arm.

'I'll have this one,' she replied, sitting on the one closest to the window. 'That way if there's a fire I can jump out.'

'Let's hope you won't have to,' said Miss Reid. She turned to Leonora and her expression softened. She instinctively understood the relationship between the two girls and was pleased she had had the foresight to place them in different dormitories. Leonora was clearly in the shadow of her sister who basked in far too much sunshine. 'Now, Leonora, you're next door. Come with me.' The child stepped forward, leaving her mother admiring the view with Alicia and Aunt Cicely. Miss Reid showed her into Milne where the walls were rich brown oak, darkened with age and smelling of centuries of wear and tear. 'Caroline Stainton-Hughes is also in this dormitory,' she said, watching Leonora's timid face open into a small smile. 'She already knows the ropes because she has two sisters here. She'll look after you, I'm sure.' Leonora liked Miss Reid. She was the sort of woman who commanded respect but was fair and kind. She had that rare quality in a teacher that made the children want to do well for her. Leonora already wanted to impress her.

When Audrey entered with Alicia and Cicely she was heartened to see her more sensitive daughter standing contentedly by her bed talking to Miss Reid. 'Right,' the headmistress ordered, rolling her *r* and accentuating her *t*, 'Bob and John will bring up your trunks and then I suggest, Mrs Forrester, that you leave the girls to settle in.' She raised her eyebrows at Audrey before walking briskly back through Dickens. Cicely smiled encouragingly at her sister-in-law. Audrey felt her eyes begin to well with tears and her chest compress with panic. This was the moment she had been dreading for the last three years. She had lived for this, made all her plans for this, but she had never thought about afterwards. There hadn't been an afterwards. She hadn't had the courage to envisage it. As she passed Alicia's bed she cast her eyes out of the window. It was now dark and empty, like her heart. Tomorrow Alicia would wake to the dawn breaking through that window. Tomorrow she would look out onto a different world. If she felt homesick or frightened she would have to suffer it alone. When Leonora slipped her hand into her mother's Audrey thought she would choke with grief. But she forced herself to be jolly. She couldn't show her children how miserable she was because if she broke down they were sure to follow. 'Right,' she said, imitating the headmistress's way of speaking. 'Let's go and find Bob and John.' Audrey smiled down at Leonora but she was too stunned to smile back. The reality of her situation was slowly sinking in. Her mother was leaving her here amidst all these strange people in this frightening old house. She tightened her grip and walked back downstairs in silence.

It was cold when they returned outside. Miss Reid had disappeared but two burly men in dungarees waited by the car. Leonora saw a few cars leaving up the drive, their headlights swallowed into the night. She blinked back her anxiety and stood biting her nails as her mother opened the boot and showed Bob and John the trunks. 'The first night is the worst,' said Aunt Cicely gently to Leonora. 'But tomorrow it'll be so exciting you won't have time to think of home. You'll be riding, playing netball, constructing camps down the avenue of chestnut trees they call Chestnut Village. There's so much to do. You'll be very busy. Just don't forget to write to us, will you? Your mother will want to know how you're getting on. We'll write to you too.' She didn't place her arm around her niece's shoulders because she instinctively knew that the child would disintegrate. She glanced over at Alicia who hopped about from foot to foot with impatience as if longing for her mother and aunt to leave. Cicely hoped Audrey wouldn't drag out the good-byes; it would only make the parting more agonising.

'Well, darlings, we'd better be off,' said Audrey, trying very hard to mask her unhappiness. But Leonora wasn't fooled, she heard the quiver in her mother's voice and she crumpled into tears.

'I don't want you to leave me here,' she sobbed, clutching Saggy Rabbit to her chest. Her shoulders rose and fell as her breathing was reduced to a pant. 'Don't leave me here, Mummy.'

Audrey drew the child into her arms and held her so tightly she feared she might smother her. 'You'll be fine when you settle in. Good-byes are the hardest part,' she soothed, wiping her own tears on her daughter's coat. Her child felt desperately small and frail in her embrace and it was all Audrey could do not to carry her back into the car and take her home.

'Don't worry, Mummy, I'll look after her,' said Alicia, with a hint of impatience in her voice. 'She'll be fine when you've gone.' Audrey tried to pull away but Leonora held onto her with all her strength.

'I don't like it, Mummy. Please take me home,' she begged in a voice hoarse with fear. 'Take me home.'

'You're coming out for the weekend in a fortnight. That's not very long, is it?' But nothing would console the child who was now weeping so violently she couldn't speak.

'You must leave her,' said Cicely, touching Audrey's arm. 'You'll only make it worse.' Audrey prised open her child's arms and still holding her small hand she kissed Alicia.

'Look after her, won't you,' she said in a desperate tone. 'She needs you more than ever now.'

'I will,' Alicia replied, struggling to take Leonora's other hand which held Saggy Rabbit in a tight grip. 'Come on, Leo, it's not that bad. It's going to be a hoot.'

Audrey fled without looking back. If she had she would have seen Leonora's forlorn little face staring at her in disbelief as the car swept up the gravel. Instead she threw her head back against the seat and cried. 'How could I cause my daughter so much pain? I'm a monster,' she wailed. Cicely's eyes filled with tears and she recalled her first night at Colehurst House. The loneliness and emptiness was something she would never forget as long as she lived. Although she had grown to love the place with a passion, there was nothing quite like that first night.

*   *   *

Alicia put her arm around her sister and led her inside. The older girls stared at her with curiosity and fascination while the younger ones bit their bottom lips and tried not to be drawn into her misery. They too missed their parents and wanted to cry. Leonora watched them all with dread through vision blurred with tears. The house was bustling with children, echoing with laughter and yet Leonora had never felt so alone in her life. It was like a nightmare but she was awake and her mother was now far away. She wanted to curl into a tight ball like a hedgehog and prick anyone who came close. Alicia was trying to console her but words couldn't bring her mother back, nor could they soothe the deep sense of rejection that stung like a fresh wound. She followed Alicia up the stairs like a sleepwalker and clung onto her hand afraid that if she let go Alicia too would disappear and then she really would be alone; a lamb in a field full of lions.

When they arrived in Milne a large group of girls awaited them beside Leonora's bed. They fell silent the moment the twins entered and even Alicia's heart stalled at that point. Because they had come straight into the second year all the girls of their age knew each other. Leonora and Alicia shuddered, anticipating hostility. But to their surprise the girls smiled and rushed at them with faces creasing with sympathy. Miss Reid had explained that Alicia and Leonora had come from a country very far away and that they must be looked after. So like rare creatures from another world the girls devoured them with wide eyes and questions and because Leonora was small and trembling the elder ones took her from her sister and mothered her. Alicia was only too pleased and disappeared next door with great purpose. A long-faced, freckly girl sat Leonora down on her bed and put her arm around her shoulders. 'I'm Toadie Martin, Victoria really, but everyone calls me Toadie,' she said. 'I'm your shadow and am only in the dorm down the corridor called Byron. So if you're worried about anything you can come and find me. I'm in the year above you.' She watched Leonora snivel and patted her on the back. 'Poor old you. We all felt like this the first time but it does get better. Every day will be a little easier than the one before and you're not alone because we're all here and we're going to look after you.' Leonora sniffed and dried her tears on Saggy Rabbit's soft fur. Tentatively she began to feel a little better.

Alicia returned from Dickens carrying a large pot, grinning broadly. 'Who would like a spoonful of *dulce de leche*?'

*   *   *

Because it was dark and the journey home was long and because she felt so unhappy, Audrey confided in Cicely. 'I fought Cecil over this,' she explained. Out of loyalty and duty she had never spoken to anyone of her resentment towards her husband, not even to her mother or Aunt Edna who would have understood. But now Cecil was far away and she had witnessed the reality of boarding school she felt that loyalty waver like a weakened oak tree in a ferocious wind. 'Alicia was expelled from her school because the teachers couldn't cope with her exuberance. It was nothing too serious, there are other good schools in Buenos Aires. Leonora loved it there, she was so happy. Then Cecil suddenly dreamed up this idea of sending them to be educated over here. I nearly died. You can imagine. What have I got to go home to?'

'Your husband,' Cicely replied firmly. 'You can't let this defeat you, Audrey. You can't give your life to your children because one day they'll be married with children of their own and where will that leave you?'

'A grandmother,' she stated simply.

'That's not what I mean.'

'I barely have a relationship with him any more. How can I love someone so insensitive and cruel? He has robbed me of my children.'

'It's not like that,' said Cicely in her brother's defence. 'It's hard for you to understand because you weren't brought up here. But we English really do believe boarding school to be the highest form of education in the world. It's built into the culture so one doesn't even question it. I missed my parents the first day, of course, just like Leonora. But after that I adored it and rarely thought of them at all. Cecil was at Eton and I doubt he suffered a moment of homesickness. He's thinking of his daughters and believes, I'm sure, that he's giving them the best start in life.'

'He can't love them like I do.' Audrey looked across at Cicely's profile and knew that she was sensitive enough to see the situation from both sides.

'Cecil is very English,' she said after a pause. 'He's upright and correct like Papa. He wasn't brought up to show his emotions. But that doesn't mean he is incapable of love. I'll bet you he loves his daughters just as much as you. He's willing to sacrifice his joy for their future. Don't you see? He's an Englishman and always will be.'

'And Louis? Is he an Englishman too?'

Cicely's mouth twitched as she stared out at the road ahead. 'He's in a cultural limbo,' she replied and chuckled.

'So if he had children . . .'

'He'll never have children,' she interrupted tightly. 'Darling Louis will never settle down and start a family. He's a creature of nature like the trees and the wind. Tempestuous, impulsive, irrational. One doesn't know what he's going to do next and one never has. If Cecil is too cold then Louis is too hot, but that is like comparing . . .' she floundered trying to think up an adequate analogy. 'I don't know, a horse and a donkey.'

'How can you even think to categorise Louis like that?' Audrey gasped in astonishment. 'He's ten times more talented than Cecil,' she blurted in a passionate voice. Now it was Cicely's turn to gasp.

Audrey checked herself and added swiftly, 'Cecil can't play a note and besides he's much more elegant than a horse. He's more like a Great Dane.' It was an inadequate attempt to redress the balance in her husband's favour but Cicely wasn't a fool. She continued to stare out at the road ahead.

'I don't know where Louis got that gift from, but it's not a place on earth,' she said, hoping Audrey's fervour to be on behalf of her dead sister. Then she stretched her hand across the gearbox and touched Audrey's. 'Don't hold this against Cecil, Audrey. He's giving the twins a future. Your future is with him, don't forget that.'

Audrey stared bleakly out in front of her and pictured Cecil's face growing old. Suddenly life seemed a painfully long time with little respite. She thought of her daughters going to bed in that creaky house and her stomach twisted inside her.

Why was it that everyone she loved was taken from her? First Isla, then Louis and now her daughters. She felt alone and adrift and powerless to change the course of her own destiny.

CHAPTER EIGHTEEN

Leonora lay in the darkness with Saggy Rabbit listening to the coughing and rustling of the seven other children who shared her dormitory. The sounds were a comfort for they reminded her that, as solitary as she felt, she wasn't alone. She had had supper at one of the long tables in the grand hall which resembled a scene from a medieval banquet, except there were no pigs roasting on spits in the fireplace, just a large display of dried flowers that sat collecting dust. She had placed herself next to Caroline Stainton-Hughes who announced that she'd like to be known by her nickname, which was Cazzie. Then she had turned to Leonora and told her that she had to have a nickname too. So everyone had called her Leo, like Alicia did, and they had eaten macaroni cheese and thick slices of white bread with butter in an attempt to fill the emptiness inside. One of the matrons called Sally had brought some of Miss Reid's dogs around to comfort the new girls and she had sat on the floor with Cazzie and a couple of the other children who were particularly homesick stroking them and drying their tears on their fur. But then it had been time to shower and prepare for bed. She had hung her wash bag up on the peg next to dozens of others and had suffered a sudden twisting of the gut when the name tape on her bath cap, so lovingly sewn on by her mother, had flashed at her as she expanded the elastic to put it on. Now she lay in a ball in her bed. In spite of the heavy blanket she felt cold. The mattress was hard and the springs squeaked each time she moved. She heard the head matron's footsteps followed by the light tap-tapping of her black Labrador as he followed her down the narrow corridors. She stopped at each room to shine her torch onto the beds to check that each child was where she should be then continued, the rubber soles of her comfortable shoes squelching on the wooden floorboards.

Leonora must have drifted off to sleep because she awoke in the early hours of the morning with a desperate need to use the lavatory. She lay there

283

deliberating whether she had the courage to go by herself. The light was on in the corridor and all she had to do was creep through Dickens, across the landing to the bathrooms. She was aware that the floors groaned underfoot and was afraid that she would wake everyone up. Then it occurred to her that perhaps one of the other girls was in the same predicament. 'Is anyone awake?' she whispered loudly. Her voice sounded strange as it hissed into the silence. She tried again, this time a little bit louder. But no one responded.

Finally, when the pressure in her bladder won over her anxiety she slipped out of bed and slid her feet into her slippers. She pulled on her dressing gown, tying it about her waist as she silently talked herself into braving the journey. She remembered Alicia talking of ghosts and how all English houses had them and hoped with a shudder that she didn't bump into one. The light was dim but it showed the way sufficiently for her to tip-toe through Milne and Dickens without tripping over anyone's fallen teddy bears or slippers. She hesitated as she passed Alicia's bed and peered at the pillow. Her sister was in a deep sleep, her long corkscrew curls fanning about her face and over the pillow in a silky waterfall. She envied Alicia. She doubted that her sister experienced the same emptiness, the same homesickness as she.

Each time her foot landed on a squeaky floorboard she flinched, holding her position like a statue until she was sure that she hadn't woken anyone up. Finally she crossed the landing and saw in front of her the bathroom and lavatories.

'Psssst, is that you, Mattie?' came a voice from one of the small cubicles. Leonora looked around.

'Mattie?' came the voice again, this time with more persistence.

'It's me, Leonora. I'm new,' Leonora replied, approaching the door from where the voice was coming. A girl pulled it open and smiled a long-suffering smile.

'Hello there, I'm Elizabeth,' she said with a sigh. She was an unfortunately fat child with a round face and long red hair tied into pig tails. She was sitting on the lavatory with her elbows on her knees. She looked as if she had been there for a long time.

'I'm in Milne,' said Leonora.

'I'm in Milton. I'm waiting for Mattie to come and use the loo.' Then noticing Leonora's bewildered expression she added, 'She sends me out to warm the seat up for her.'

'Oh.'

'Well, it's jolly cold, don't you think?'

'Yes, it is.'

'Where are you from?' she asked. 'You have a funny accent.'

'The Argentine.'

'Where's that?'

'South America.'

'Oh. That's a long way away, isn't it?' Then she added with a tactlessness that she was well known for, 'Don't worry, you'll speak like the rest of us after a few weeks here.'

Leonora was eager to be liked so she replied, 'I hope so.'

'Mummy says that one must speak like a lady. You're obviously a lady, but you have to learn to sound like one too. Oh, and ride like one as well, I always forget that bit. I'm allergic to horses, you see. My eyes swell up and I sneeze a lot. Mummy wants me to ride, though. All well-bred ladies ride.'

'Yes,' said Leonora, trying to be agreeable. She wondered what Alicia would make of their conversation.

Elizabeth sighed and looked at her watch. 'I must have been here for at least fifteen minutes,' she complained. Then she looked up at her new friend. 'I say, why don't you use it instead? It's nice and warm now and I doubt Mattie's going to come. She's probably gone back to sleep. She does that sometimes. I've often been here for hours expecting her to come.' She stood up and made way for Leonora. 'See you tomorrow,' she said before padding off.

Leonora watched her go and wondered who Mattie was that she was able to make another girl warm the loo seat up for her in the middle of the night. She sat down. Elizabeth had done her job well.

                    *   *   *

When the gong was rung from the Great Hall at 7 a.m., Leonora was only too happy to get up. Lying in bed only made her fearful. She had awoken to that hollow sense of homesickness that made her want to cry all over again. So she dressed with haste and followed the other girls down to breakfast. Each place had an apple on it and the smell of toast and porridge wafted up from the kitchen.

Alicia had slept well and woken with a quiver of excitement at the challenges that awaited her. When she saw her sister she was relieved to find

286

that she was pale but no longer embarrassing herself by bawling like a baby. She threw her a brief wave before taking a place on one of the long benches at another table. 'You can't sit here,' said a tall girl with shiny black hair combed into the shape of a helmet. 'You're a new girl. You have to sit at the end of the table. One sits in order of seniority.'

'But I'm in the second year,' replied Alicia, looking at the girl steadily.

She blinked down at Alicia and frowned. 'Careful, people won't like you if you're cocky,' she warned. 'I'll excuse you because you're new.' But the truth was that she excused her because Alicia's beauty was captivating and something to be greatly admired. Alicia moved reluctantly to the other end of the table where she stood beside a fat redhead, opposite a pretty blonde with a turned-up nose and dark brown eyes who looked her up and down without smiling.

'You're new,' stated the blonde.

'Yes, I am,' Alicia replied. 'I'm Alicia.'

'That's an unusual name.'

'It's Alice in Spanish.'

'I know that. You must be from the Argentine,' she said. 'Elizabeth bumped into your sister in the loo last night, didn't you, Elizabeth? She was warming the seat up for me. I hate a cold loo seat, don't you?'

'I've never thought about it. But I suppose so. What's your name?'

'She's Mattie, short for Mathilda. She's an Hon,' said the redhead.

'What's an Hon?' she asked.

Mattie laughed. 'My father's a viscount,' she said. 'I suppose you don't know what that is either.'

She sighed. 'Elizabeth will teach you about our class system over here, it's very important you know about it.'

'I know all about it. My father's a *señor*,' Alicia retaliated, knowing that neither Mattie nor Elizabeth would know it simply meant Mr.

'Good,' said Mattie, suitably impressed. 'Is he an important man?'

'Very. He's only second to the President,' she lied. Then she smiled confidently and whispered, 'The President doesn't move without my father's approval.' Elizabeth sniggered and Mattie grinned. Alicia wasn't just pretty, she was important too. Mattie was only too aware of the lack of Hons at the school, it was nice to finally meet someone on the same level as herself. At that moment Miss Reid walked in, took her place at the head of the top table and the whole hall fell silent for Grace. Miss Reid bowed her head and clasped her hands together in prayer. Leonora copied and closed her eyes while Alicia scanned the room restlessly.

'For what we are about to receive may the Lord make us truly grateful, Amen.' They all repeated Amen then sat down with a roar of chairs scraping the floor and the clattering of cutlery as the prefects began to serve steaming porridge from large cauldrons.

'I hate porridge,' Mattie complained.

'I'll eat yours,' said Elizabeth eagerly.

'Good. I'll have your toast then,' she said. Elizabeth's face momentarily clouded with regret, she loved her toast and marmalade more than anything, but her expression cleared before Mattie noticed it.

'In the Argentine we have croissants and brioche

288

for breakfast,' said Alicia, watching with a grimace as a bowl of grey porridge was placed before her.

'We have eggs and bacon at home,' added Mattie. 'Mrs Bruton makes it every morning. No one makes it quite like Mrs Bruton.'

'In the Argentine we have a maid called Mercedes . . .'

'Like the car?' said Elizabeth, catching Mattie's eye and giggling behind her hand.

'Yes, because she drives one,' said Alicia quickly, determined not to look foolish.

'The maids must be very rich where you come from. Mrs Bruton drives a little Morris,' said Mattie.

'Oh, they are. Daddy pays them very well,' she added, pouring sugar onto her porridge.

'Look,' said Mattie, leaning forward and fixing her new friend with narrowed eyes. 'I don't want to hear you say that phrase over and over again.'

'What phrase?' Alicia asked, stunned.

'In the Argentine,' she said. 'I know you come from there, so you don't have to say it. It's boring.' For a moment Alicia was lost for words. She opened her mouth to say something but nothing came into her head. She stared back at Mattie defiantly. Elizabeth giggled again. She was used to Mattie terrorising the other girls. But Alicia wasn't used to being spoken to like that. She leaned forward and fixed her opponent with arrogant blue eyes.

'Where do you come from?' she asked quietly.

'Hertfordshire,' replied Mattie.

'Oh, I see,' she said and smiled knowingly, sitting back. This irritated Mattie who frowned crossly and stuck out her lower lip.

289

'What do you see?' she asked. Elizabeth's laughter petered out.

'No, it's fine. I don't want to offend you.'

'You won't. Just tell me,' said Mattie impatiently.

'Well, no one's going to be impressed with Hertfordshire, are they? I've been to Hertfordshire and it's grey and dreary to say the least.' Alicia had never been anywhere near Hertfordshire.

'It is not,' cried Mattie.

'Merchi always says that jealousy is the greatest form of flattery. The Argentine is hot and sunny and glamorous, so I'm flattered,' she said and spooned the porridge into her mouth. Mattie looked across at Elizabeth who just shrugged her shoulders. 'This porridge is disgusting. It's cold for a start. Elizabeth, do you want mine as well?' Elizabeth shook her head, not knowing quite what to say. Alicia felt intoxicated with her success.

'Just leave it, no one's going to make you eat it here,' Mattie mumbled. She watched Alicia push her bowl to one side and help herself from the basket of toast. She admired her. Not only was she beautiful but she was clever too and unafraid. 'If you want, you can come and stay with me one weekend,' she said, passing Alicia the butter. 'Hertfordshire is really very pretty.'

'I might,' Alicia replied. 'Now tell me, do you have a camp in Chestnut Village?'

*   *   *

Leonora found her sister after breakfast in Milton sitting on a bed with the round redhead she had met in the lavatory in the middle of the night and a pretty blonde. 'Ah,' said Alicia, grinning broadly.

290

'This is my sister, Leo.'

'Hi, Leo,' said Elizabeth. 'We already know each other.'

'Oh yes, your midnight rendezvous,' Alicia said grudgingly. She hated it when her sister trespassed on her territory.

'Yes, it was nice to have company,' said Elizabeth.

'Mattie here has a really big camp in Chestnut Village and I'm going to share it with her,' Alicia exclaimed. 'Sorry, Leo, you can only join us if you know the password.'

'I don't mind,' said Leonora good-naturedly.

'How come you are both in the same year?' Mattie asked, looking from one sister to the other.

'We're twins,' said Leonora. Mattie's eyes widened and her mouth opened like a fish.

'Twins?' she repeated slowly. Leonora nodded.

'Hadn't you better get ready for chapel?' said Alicia bossily. 'All the new girls have to be in the hall in five minutes.'

'What about you?'

'I'm ready,' she replied then watched her sister expectantly. Leonora hovered a moment but the three pairs of eyes stared at her coldly. Finally, swallowing her pride she left the room, but something compelled her to linger by the door and listen. Mercedes always said that one never hears anything good about oneself if one eavesdrops, but Leonora couldn't help herself. Alicia had dismissed her like that for a reason. She was right. As soon as she had gone Mattie exploded.

'Twins!' she cried in amazement. 'I don't believe it. You're so pretty and she's so plain. How did that happen?'

291

'Well, I obviously gobbled up all the good qualities in Mummy's tummy leaving the rest for Leo,' she said. 'Poor Leo.' They all laughed raucously.

Blinded by tears Leonora ran into the bathroom, closing the door behind her. She placed her hands on the sink to steady herself then stared at her twisted face in the mirror as her body shook with unhappiness. *I want Mummy*, she thought miserably. *I want Mummy and I want to go home.* Typically, Leonora didn't blame Alicia. She blamed the girl with the mean mouth and thin lips who had said such a hateful thing. She wiped her eyes with trembling fingers and gazed in disgust upon her now blotchy red face. She was plain. She was terribly plain. But her mother thought she was beautiful. 'My darling, you're one of God's beautiful creatures,' she had often said and she knew she meant it because her mother looked into her features with an expression of the deepest, most tender love. She recalled her gentle face and yearned for it with such longing that it hurt.

There came a knock on the door. 'Who's in there?' It was the firm but kind voice of Miss Reid.

'Leonora,' she replied meekly and sniffed. Miss Reid opened the door and poked her head around.

'Just the person I'm looking for,' she said, disregarding the child's tearstained face. She had heard her sobbing. 'Now, I need to ask you a favour.'

'Oh,' said Leonora, attempting to compose herself.

'Come with me.'

Leonora followed the headmistress through the dorms and up the corridor to the front stairs. She

292

hesitated at the top, aware that she wasn't senior enough to use them. 'Come, come, don't dawdle,' said Miss Reid in her clipped English accent that masked a cauldron of emotion. 'Now, I need a very responsible, sensible girl to help me out in prayers. You see, Midge here isn't feeling very well.' She stroked the little dog's head with her long, wrinkled fingers. 'I can't leave him and I can't take him into chapel myself as I have to take the service. I know he likes you. So would you mind looking after him for me?' She looked down at Leonora with the wise old eyes of a woman who had worked with and lived for children for nearly forty years. Unmarried and childless she had devoted her entire existence to them and in spite of her efforts to remain detached she was only human and some children caused her heart to yield. Leonora was one of those.

'I'd love to,' said Leonora, taking the dog from her. She brought him to her face and kissed his nose. Midge had never looked so well, but Leonora wasn't to know that. They arrived at the foot of the stairs where the other new girls waited in the Great Hall.

'You had better go and join them. I'll come and retrieve Midge at the end of prayers,' said Miss Reid, pushing the child gently towards the others.

Leonora felt much better. The dog was a source of great comfort and Miss Reid made her feel good inside. She decided to write to her mother as soon as possible on the writing paper Aunt Cicely had given her to tell her about Midge and Miss Reid. She wouldn't tell her about Mattie, because that would upset her and Leonora was too sensitive to want to cause her mother distress. She kissed

293

Midge again and joined Cazzie who grinned at her happily.

'Where have you been? I looked for you everywhere,' she complained.

'Don't worry, I'm here now,' she replied resolutely. 'And I'm fine.' She grinned back at Cazzie, grateful for her friendship. So what if she was plain, she thought to herself, she was beautiful on the inside and that was what counted. As Mercedes always said, 'You can't hide an ugly nature behind a beautiful face.'

*   *   *

In the next couple of weeks Leonora and Alicia settled into their new school. While Leonora was immediately loved by all the girls in her class as well as those above and below, Alicia was admired and feared like a lovely demon who ensnared anyone who got close with her charm and charisma. But no one was more struck than Mattie.

Diana Reid was keeping a close eye on Alicia. She had an arrogance common in children used to being told how beautiful they are and a charisma that she didn't deserve. She looked for the weakness in people and then with the subtlety of a much older child, she gnawed on it with the slow but relentless cruelty of someone who enjoyed watching others suffer. Putting other children down raised her up and Alicia was ambitious to the point of not caring about anyone else but herself. She had many friends, but they weren't true friends, for real friendship is built not on fear but on affection and selflessness. Alicia needed to be taught about selflessness. Not an easy task with someone of her

294

nature.

Then one evening Alicia played straight into Miss Reid's hand.

'Mattie, let's go and ride the ponies bareback in the field,' she suggested to her friend. Mattie sat in the corner of their log camp in Chestnut Village. It was a large house built out of the remains of old trees that had fallen down in the storm the year before. Mattie and Elizabeth had constructed two rooms, stuffing the gaps between the logs with cut grass from the pile left from the summer's mowing behind the walled vegetable garden. The roof was made of sticks and leafy branches pulled from bushes and trees. It was the snuggest camp in the avenue and envied by all the other girls. Therefore Alicia felt it was most appropriate that it now belonged to her as well. Mattie was uncomfortable with Alicia's suggestion. Hadn't they got up to enough mischief already? They had been at school for barely two weeks. They had crept out of the house and down the fire escape in the middle of the night to dance in the light of the moon, stolen biscuits from the larder and eaten them in Library Loo and run naked through the Box Garden in the afternoon after netball. They had even tormented Elizabeth by leaving her warming not one, but two loo seats until the early hours of the morning. But riding the ponies in the field without supervision was a serious offence.

'I don't think it's a good idea, Alicia,' she said, shaking her head. 'Let's do something else.'

'I don't want to do anything else.'

'We'll get expelled for it,' she protested, imagining the wrath of her father and shuddering. She was prepared to do almost anything, punishments meant little to her, but expulsion was something she feared.

'I don't care. I've already been kicked out of one school.' Alicia laughed, throwing her head back, showing off the graceful curve of her long white neck. 'What's the worst they can do?'

'My father would kill me.'

'Of course he wouldn't kill you,' said Alicia, flashing her icy eyes at her friend, challenging her.

'Well, he'd be furious and shout at me.'

'But he wouldn't kill you.' Mattie thought about it a moment. 'Words don't kill, Mattie. Expulsion doesn't kill either. In fact, they can't do anything. I'll happily write one hundred lines or stand in the corner of the class. Those punishments don't hurt.'

'All right, let's do it,' said Mattie, suddenly infected with Alicia's bravado. 'But we should wait until after supper when it's nearly dark. That way there's less chance of getting caught.'

'Good, I knew you'd come around to the idea.'

'We had better not tell Elizabeth, she'll only want to come too and she'll fall off or hurt herself or something.'

'Yes, she's a hopeless fool.'

'But obedient.'

'Oh, we all need Elizabeths. As Merchi says, if everyone was as clever as me there'd be no servants to look after us. Thank God for Elizabeths.' They both laughed heartily.

'Let's go and take a look at the ponies and plan which we're going to ride,' Mattie suggested, leading the way out of the camp. They wandered to the field and leant on the fence. There in the midst of long lush grass were five fat ponies, as docile as cows.

'I'll ride that white one over there,' Alicia said, pointing.

'It's grey,' corrected Mattie.

'Grey then. What's it called?'

'Mr Snow.'

'Well, I'll ride Mr Snow. Which one will you ride?'

Mattie thought about it a moment then pointed to the dappled grey who was so small and round that his belly almost touched the ground.

'Lucky.'

'How appropriate. Let's hope his luck rubs off on us!'

'He's little so it won't be hard to jump on his back.'

'Good. Ah, there's the bell for supper. Not a word to anyone,' Alicia instructed and they walked down the drive towards the house.

After supper they crept out into the twilight. It had taken some manoeuvring to be rid of Elizabeth who wanted to join in. They had been forced to arrange a false meeting place where she was now waiting for them, looking at her watch and wondering where they were.

But Alicia and Mattie were climbing the fence, looking about them with the furtiveness of robbers, stealing into the forbidden, risking everything. The thrill of such naughtiness was intoxicating and their eyes shone through the half-light. 'You have to ride the pony for three minutes or it doesn't count,' whispered Alicia as they ran, bent double, up the field. Mattie giggled as she approached Lucky, who lifted his head and stopped chomping grass. Mr Snow thought he was about to be offered some nuts and neighed softly as Alicia hurried up to him.

'Shhh, or you'll give us away!' she hissed crossly. She glanced over at Mattie who was already stroking Lucky's head, ready to mount. Alicia was spurred on by a sudden twinge of competitiveness and didn't hang around to pat the animal but with a running leap clambered onto his back. She sighed with relief, she was first. Mattie scowled and swung her leg over Lucky's back, then sat leaning forward, hiding her face in his mane. But Alicia was now triumphant and, typically, she had to go that little bit further. Not content to sit and hide like Mattie, she kicked Mr Snow's barrel of a belly and instructed him to trot. 'Come on, you silly old thing, move!' But Mr Snow bent his head and began to chew the grass again as if Alicia wasn't there. Mattie shot her a look and waved her wrist, indicating that their three minutes were up. But Alicia shook her head and grinned, kicking the pony harder. Mr Snow huffed wearily as if she were an annoying summer fly buzzing about his face. 'For goodness sake, you lazy toad, move!' and she kicked him again, this time with greater force. Suddenly the pony lifted his head with a start and neighed in fury before galloping off as fast as his short legs could carry him. Alicia was delighted, if not a little shaken. She didn't see the chocolate brown Lurcher dash out from under his hooves and neither did Mr Snow. But before she had time to enjoy the ride she found herself sliding down his back. She tried to cling on but his fur was so soft and slippery she had nothing to grip onto but his mane which seemed to come away in her hands. He trotted on angrily, as if he knew that a tight trot would be sure to lose her, and she slid round his back until nothing could save her and she fell with an angry thud onto the grass. Wounded only in her pride and red faced with rage she stood up and wiped her muddied hands on her skirt. She turned to see the Lurcher lolloping jubilantly towards the gate where Mattie now stood with her arms crossed, staring at Alicia in alarm. Next to her seethed Miss Reid, her face frozen into an expression of the coldest resolve, her fingers running up and down Midge's back in long, pensive strokes.

When Alicia rejoined them, her shoulders hunched anticipating the headmistress's wrath, she was surprised if not a little relieved to find that Miss Reid said very little. 'In my study, tomorrow morning at seven thirty.' Then she stalked off down the drive towards the house, followed by her entourage of four-legged detectives. 'Don't panic, Mattie,' said Alicia, trying to sound confident, holding her chin up. 'Writing out lines never killed anyone, and expulsion, she wouldn't dare.' They wandered back to the house in silence, both alone with their fears.

The following morning they arrived promptly outside Miss Reid's office. They both hoped that whatever the punishment was they would be able to do it in secrecy. No one knew of their evening adventure and they hadn't even told Elizabeth or Leonora. Miss Reid made them both wait to prolong the agony. Then a few minutes before chapel she emerged in a tweed skirt and jersey with a string of old pearls hanging loosely about her neck. 'Come with me,' she ordered, walking past them towards the Great Hall and front door. Bewildered the two girls followed her onto the gravel towards the chapel. She stopped just before the little steps that led up to it and turned to face them. 'Now, you're going to be human trotting poles,' she stated. 'I want you to lie on the ground and all the girls are going to walk over you to get to prayers. They know what you have both done and that you, Alicia, didn't even manage to do it with competence, but fell off. No one will talk to you all day. Then you will both get up every morning at five to help clean out the stables. Not for one day, or for two, but for the whole term. Until you have learned that rules are there for a reason. My priority is the safety of my pupils and of my animals. You could have seriously hurt yourselves last night and damaged those poor ponies. What you did is beyond the pale. It will not happen again. If it does I will not be so generous. Alicia, you've been here a mere ten days and have revealed a very ugly nature. Perhaps you should use the opportunity of morning prayers to ask God for His forgiveness. As Jesus said, "Love thy neighbour as thyself." You have much to learn.' Alicia swallowed hard. She hated the idea of being a human trotting pole for all the other girls to walk over and she hated the idea of getting up to clean the stables at five every morning. It was the worst possible punishment. Miss Reid knew and was satisfied. Alicia was a special case and required a special punishment. She walked up the steps to take prayers while the rest of the girls filed out of their classrooms towards the chapel. She felt a warm sense of contentment and quietly thanked God for His inspiration.

CHAPTER NINETEEN

Audrey had spent the two weeks living for the weekend when she would see her daughters again. She had written to them every morning in Cicely's small sitting room, beside the fire for it rained continuously and was damp and cold. She felt compelled to write in order to have some sort of communication with them although she had little news to share. Alicia had only written twice, the obligatory Saturday letter they were all made to write to their parents and one to Mercedes, but Leonora had written every day.

Leonora's letters were long and poetic. She wrote about her new friends and Miss Reid, whom she liked enormously, and the rides on those fluffy round ponies in the riding school where they trotted and cantered one behind the other and jumped red and white poles. She compared the riding to the casual way they rode in the Argentine and decided that she liked it better in England because Frankie, the instructor, was kind to her and praised her in front of the other girls. She was learning to play the piano and had been chosen to sing in the junior choir. But she loved the art classes best of all and had been elected to form the art committee with three other girls. That required them to take Art Club on Saturdays and make sure that the art room was well looked after and tidy. In return they had a meeting once a week with Mrs Augusta Grimsdale who brought in tea and cakes and allowed them to call her Gussie. She wore long floral dresses and ethnic beads which wound around her neck and hung down to her waist like Great Aunt Edna's. She didn't say how much she missed her mother, because she was tactful and she didn't write about Alicia being made into a human trotting pole because she knew how upset her mother would be. Instead she painted flowers on the paper and love hearts which she spent all prep colouring in with a red felt pen. The only indication of her homesickness was the odd smudge in the ink and the odd watermark on the paper. Audrey convinced herself that they weren't tears. She had to in order to carry on.

Cicely floated around the house in her floppy drawstring trousers with Marcel's sky blue shirts flapping around her waist, reminding her of him each time she passed her image in the hall mirror. She helped Panazel and Florien in the garden, cutting hedges and picking apples, plums and blackberries until the storeroom was bursting with the gifts of autumn. She drove Audrey around the farm where the neighbouring farmer was finishing off the remains of the harvest with large green combines that resembled fierce beasts chomping their way through the linseed and spring oil seed rape. She told Audrey how the land belonged to her but since her husband's death eight years before, Anthony Fitzherbert, who owned the large estate next door, had farmed it for her. 'Farming makes little money these days, but it keeps me clothed and enables me to continue living here. I wouldn't leave Holholly Grange for anything in the world,' she had said. 'Besides, it's all I have left of Hugh.' Cicely didn't speak much about her late husband. Perhaps it didn't seem appropriate with Marcel lurking upstairs in the attic. But everyone

302

needs someone and Audrey imagined Marcel was good for her, even though it was quite obviously a physical attraction and not a meeting of minds.

Marcel emerged only for meals, which he often took back upstairs to his studio, silently placing the plate of food on a tray then disappearing without a word. Cicely didn't seem to mind. Their relationship was a twilight one, because she always came down to breakfast looking rejuvenated and shiny, like Barley after a long walk in the woods. Her eyes shone and her cheeks glowed and her smile became brazen like the scent of love that followed her around the house to remind Audrey of what she had had and lost.

There seemed to be only one photograph of Louis and that was the one that sat on the piano and tugged at Audrey's heart whenever she was able to gaze into it. But one day when she was searching for something to read she discovered a few tattered photograph albums on an old maple table in the library. Aware that her curiosity might be intrusive she took the risk of asking Cicely's permission. To her relief Cicely was only too delighted to sit with her beside the fire and show them to her personally. 'I imagine you want to see Cecil as a little boy?' she asked, settling comfortably on the sofa.

'Yes,' Audrey lied, barely able to restrain her enthusiasm.

Cicely opened the book and slowly turned the pages. There were photographs of their parents, Cecil as a child, Cicely as a little girl and their home, which was large and forbidding like Colehurst House. Audrey bit her nails with impatience. She willed Cicely to move faster through the book. She made the right comments, sighing at Cecil in his christening dress, admiring Cicely's animated face grinning out from a large black pram and marvelling at their mother's cool elegance. And then they arrived at a black and white photograph of Louis. He must have been about six months old. How little he had changed.

He had the white blond hair and soft curvy body of a small baby and yet the expression of wonder and innocence in his large enquiring eyes was combined with that dreamy, faraway look that so set him apart from everyone else. He was already in a world of his own. So vulnerable, so new, so fragile and so easily hurt. Audrey's heart remembered the grown man that she loved and then looked beneath to the child who still remained and who needed her. 'What was Louis like as a little boy?' she asked quietly. Cicely wasn't surprised by her questions because she was asking about all the photographs. But she was hesitant because she felt guilty.

'He was sweet,' she said thoughtfully. 'He really was. As a baby he was adorable.'

'He looks it,' Audrey replied, smiling tenderly at the picture. 'He really hasn't changed that much, has he?'

'Yes, that was the problem.'

'Problem?'

'He had trouble learning. He was late to crawl, walk, talk. He's never really grown up.'

'I see.' Audrey felt the palms of her hands grow moist with nervousness. She sensed Cicely was about to tell her the real reason Louis was different.

'But he really was very sweet as a baby. I

304

remember because I'm that much older than him. He was like a doll and I played with him, until he frustrated me. He had a temper.' She chuckled nostalgically, then curled a stray piece of hair behind her ear. 'I think he frustrated himself. He wanted to be more advanced than he was, as if he knew inside that he could do better but his limbs wouldn't follow what his head ordered them to do. He grew so angry.'

'Why was he like that when you and Cecil are so . . . so . . . ?'

'Normal?'

Audrey jumped at the accusation with the ferocity of a protective mother. 'Oh, I'd never say Louis was abnormal,' she said hastily. 'He's extra normal. Extra ordinary. Gifted.'

'Oh Audrey. You know so little about him,' said Cicely suddenly, sighing heavily. 'If it wasn't for the fact that Isla loved him I wouldn't tell you about him. But you're family and I won't be betraying him, I'm sure, by confiding in you.'

'Go on.' Audrey barely dared breathe.

'Because, dear Audrey, Louis was born very prematurely. Dangerously prematurely. Mama nearly lost him and suffered terrible depression while he was in the hospital, while they were struggling to keep him alive. It was dreadful. The relief in the house when he was brought home was intoxicating. It was as if a black cloud had blown away leaving clear blue sky. That was until they realised that he had, in fact, been slightly damaged. But the effects were subtle. Not scars that we are all able to see and understand, but mental fragility that is harder to accept and even harder to treat.'

'What do you mean?' Audrey asked fearfully.

305

Cicely continued as if attempting to justify their behaviour and while she spoke her voice rose in tone and texture until she sounded almost strangled with guilt.

'He was a tormented little boy. He'd have these terrible screaming fits and there was nothing anyone could do to quieten him. He'd just scream and scream with his arms out like this,' she extended her arms and waved them about. 'It was as if he was in great pain. It was horrible. Papa, who was used to being in control of every situation, was bewildered. He simply couldn't cope. So, as Louis grew into a little boy he stopped taking an interest in him. As if he wasn't there. Mama was very attached to Louis at the beginning. She felt guilty because her body hadn't held him for as long as it should have. She felt she had failed. But he was simply too difficult for anyone to handle. He rejected her. I'm guilty too,' she said and her voice cracked. 'I used to pretend that he was adopted. I used to tell everyone he wasn't related to us, that Mama and Papa had adopted him. It was awful. I don't know how I could have been so brutal. He didn't seem to mind. He used to laugh. But he must have hated me for it. I was horrid to him. Cecil was always good to him though. But then, Cecil is a saint. I'm more selfish, I admit it. I have many regrets but I'm far too weak to do anything about them. Cecil, *saint* Cecil, put up with Louis long after we had all given up on him. It was only when he started to play Mama's piano, as if he had played for years, as if he had had professional tuition, that he calmed down. I think suddenly discovering that he could communicate, that he was gifted at something, assuaged his frustration and

306

the fits stopped. But then he was lost to us all because he'd just sit and play for hours and hours, shutting us all out, alone with the music. Music is his only love. Isla didn't stand a chance, Audrey. Dear Louis, he's a tormented spirit.'

'But he's all right now?' said Audrey. She knew Cicely was wrong. He was capable of loving another human being. He loved her and music was the backbone to that love. It was what held them together. It was their means of understanding each other where words failed to express what they felt in their hearts.

'He's learned to live with it and he knows his limitations, I suppose. But he still can't cope when things go wrong. He breaks down.'

'He just needs to be loved,' she said in a quiet voice.

'But who will love him, Audrey? Who will invest that sort of time and effort in order to understand him? He shuts people out. No one can reach him. He's miles away in dreamland and the older he gets the further away he goes. One day he'll simply disappear altogether.'

That night Audrey lay awake in the darkness and cried. She cried for her daughters and she cried for Isla and she cried for Louis. She didn't know for whom she cried the most.

*   *   *

Finally Leonora and Alicia returned to Holholly Grange for the weekend. Audrey embraced them both with excitement and yet her excitement was undermined by the knowledge that once they had returned to school she was to board a plane and fly

307

back to Buenos Aires. She didn't know how she was going to do it. But she was determined that their parting should not ruin the present moment which she intended to enjoy to the full.

Alicia was so ashamed by the punishment dealt to her for riding Mr Snow bareback that she didn't mention it and neither did Leonora. She had suffered a terrible humiliation. She wouldn't even tell Mercedes, in whom she usually confided everything. Instead she went through all her teachers imitating each one with the perception of a professional mimic. They lingered in the kitchen by the Aga laughing at Alicia as she pranced up and down as if on a stage, while the dogs lay scattered about the floor on their beanbags.

To Audrey's surprise Marcel appeared for lunch and instead of taking his food upstairs on a tray he sat at the table observing those around him as if attempting to draw inspiration. He smouldered in the corner like a hero in a bad romantic novel, brooding and sulking for effect, smoking a cigarette he had rolled himself. Cicely was transformed once again into a flighty girl and flitted about the room making a greater effort with the leg of lamb while the twins barely noticed that he was there and certainly didn't care. Marcel's presence was quiet and watchful and Audrey couldn't fail to see that he was watching her. Not with the eyes of a lover, not the way he looked at Cicely, but knowingly. As if he knew her secret. As if she knew he knew and it was now *their* secret. She felt uncomfortable. Marcel hid himself up in the attic and yet everything seemed to reach him. He had heard her piano playing when she had believed she had been alone, he had deliberately found her there in the middle of the night when she couldn't sleep. Who's to say he hadn't been there in the shadows too when she had spent those precious moments with Louis' photograph? She caught his eye and frowned but he continued to blow smoke into the air, gazing at her with the eyes of an artist studying the object of his creation.

In the afternoon they took the dogs for a long walk armed with large bowls for blackberry picking. The hedgerows were brimming with fruit and the trees in the orchard were heavy with apples and plums. The air was warm and sunshine bathed the hills in a golden autumn light reminding them all of summer and how beautiful England looked when the weather was fine. Audrey thought of Colonel Blythe and how wrong he was. It didn't always rain in England. She watched Alicia run with the dogs while Leonora hung behind with her arm linked through hers, as if she wanted to hold on to her mother for as long as possible before they were parted once again. They walked back through the field where the gypsies camped to find Panazel and Masha lying out on the grass with their two children. Alicia rushed up to Leonora and tugged at her sleeve. 'Don't mention the chicken, whatever you do,' she hissed.

'Of course not,' Leonora replied. 'But be kind,' she added. Alicia scrunched up her nose. Kind was a word like nice, it was dull and in her opinion should be erased from the English language. Audrey noticed that the dogs, usually keen to bark at the horses, now kept their distance, sitting in an uneasy pack a few hundred yards away.

'Hello, Florien,' Alicia shouted at the sullen boy who was now scrambling to his feet along with the rest of his family.

'Oh, goodness me, please don't all get up,' Cicely insisted, waving her arms about as if she were instructing the pack of dogs to sit. 'There are so many blackberries in the woods, I hope you're exploiting the crop, Panazel.'

'We've helped ourselves to all the land can offer, thank you, Mrs Weatherby,' he replied, putting his cap back on.

'Ah, Ravena, you haven't met Alicia and Leonora, my nieces. They're living with me now and will be helping Panazel and Florien in the garden during the holidays. There's so much to be done.'

'I'll enjoy telling their fortunes,' she replied, exhibiting a crooked set of teeth.

'Yes please,' Alicia cried enthusiastically. 'Am I to marry someone very rich?'

'Alicia!' Audrey rebuked, ashamed at her daughter's bad manners.

'Oh, why not,' Cicely said and laughed. 'She read mine once, it's great fun. Here, let me pay you for it.' She thrust her hand into the pocket of her trousers and pulled out two half crowns. 'I'll cross your palm with silver.'

'Goodie!' Alicia squeaked excitedly. 'Why don't you have a go too, Leo?' But Leonora shook her head and looked up at her mother.

'Leonora's like me. We're a bit nervous of fortune tellers,' Audrey said, squeezing her daughter's hand as she threaded her fingers through hers.

Alicia followed Ravena up the steps into the caravan. She was tall and slim and her hair fell out of her headscarf and reached down to her waist. If it wasn't for her teeth and the sallow quality of her skin she would have been a beauty. She indicated a small round table with two chairs and Alicia wasted no time, but pulled one out and sat blinking up at the gypsy with enthusiasm. 'Do you have a crystal ball?'

Ravena shook her head. 'No, I can't afford one,' she stated. 'I read palms. Besides, my grandmother taught me and she didn't need a crystal ball.'

'Well, here it is,' she said, thrusting her hand onto the table. 'What can you see? Am I going to be rich and happy?' Ravena picked up the child's hand and studied it carefully. Alicia watched her face as she ran her eyes over every line and crease. She breathed deeply and Alicia noticed her eyelids glistening with sweat. It was hot. Hotter in the small caravan than outside where the air was warm but fresh. The caravan was quite airless and the gypsy's silence caused Alicia to sweat too, but with impatience. Finally, Ravena sighed heavily and placed her hand over the child's palm. 'Well?' Alicia asked. 'You must see something.'

'You are very blessed,' she said at last. 'You not only have great beauty but talent as well. It is up to you how you use those gifts. You will either be rich and happy or . . .' she hesitated. Alicia encouraged her by leaning forward.

'Or?'

Ravena pulled a resigned smile and shook her head. 'No, you shall be rich and happy. You'll marry a very wealthy man who you'll love very deeply. You'll live in this country and your children will be English. You'll have four children and they will all be as beautiful and gifted as you.'

'Really?' Alicia gasped happily. 'I must tell

311

Mummy.'

'I'm going to be rich and happy and have four children!' Alicia cried, clambering down the steps. 'You should have a go, Leo. She's really good.' But Leonora still hung back reluctant to know her future in case it wasn't what she wished for. As they all walked off towards the gate, the dogs leapt up and trotted after them, sniffing the ground and cocking their legs.

'Dear Ravena, I doubt she's ever got anything right,' Cicely said to Audrey, winking at her. 'At least her lies are nice lies. I'd hate to think of her frightening people.'

'Well, someone here's very happy, so it was worth two half crowns,' Audrey replied and laughed.

*   *   *

'Well?' said Masha, turning to her daughter. Ravena sighed and shrugged her shoulders.

'I had to pretend,' she confessed.

'Again?' said her mother, shaking her head in disapproval. 'Your grandmother would tremble in her grave if she knew how you're abusing your gift.'

'I couldn't tell her what I saw. Like with Mrs Weatherby, I couldn't reveal what lies ahead. Some things are better not knowing.'

'You'll lose your ability.'

'Perhaps I should give up and pick plums with Dad and Florien instead of looking into people's futures.'

'Don't be a ninny. It's what you're good at. You should just have courage, that's all. After all, we are the masters of our destinies, nothing is set in

312

stone. You could have steered her in a better direction.'

'There was no point. That child is already way off course,' she said gravely and shook her head. 'I'm going for a ride. I feel depressed.' And she wandered off to untie the pony, reflecting on Alicia's dark nature.

*   *   *

It was well past midnight when Leonora and Saggy Rabbit padded down the corridor to her mother's room. She held a candle that fought against an icy draught entering through one of the rickety old windows. She was afraid to turn on the light for Cicely hated to waste electricity. Shuddering with cold she lingered a moment at her mother's door. She knew she was meant to be a big girl and Alicia would certainly tease her in the morning—she already teased her about carrying 'that smelly rabbit' around with her everywhere. But she yearned for her mother's warm embrace, for the security of lying close to her and for the comfort of having her to herself like she had always done as a small child.

She knocked and then turned the knob. She heard the rustling of sheets as Audrey turned over and sat up. 'Who's that?' she asked, dreading for a moment that it might be Marcel, spying on her again. But then she saw her little girl's pale face illuminated in the golden flame of the candle and smiled tenderly. 'Are you all right?' she asked, shuffling over to make room.

'I'm lonely,' Leonora replied in a small voice. Audrey smiled indulgently.

313

'Come on then, my love. I'm lonely too.'

Leonora climbed into bed and blew out the candle. She curled into a ball and felt her mother snuggle up behind her, so that they lay pressed together.

'I miss you when I'm at school,' said Leonora. It was easier to speak of her fears in the darkness, when she didn't have to look at her mother's sad face.

Audrey squeezed her gently. 'I miss you too. I miss you terribly. Not a moment of the day goes by when I don't think about you both. But you'll settle in and love it the way Aunt Cicely did. She talks about it now as if she's still there. It seems a lovely place.'

'It is. I like Miss Reid and I like Gussie. Cazzie's my best friend. She's homesick too sometimes, but at least she has her sisters there and they're kind to her.'

'You have Alicia.'

'Yes,' said Leonora flatly. 'I have my sister too.' She couldn't explain how Alicia acted as if they weren't even related, that would have upset her mother too much.

'You'll be home for the Christmas holidays. Four whole weeks, imagine. We'll have a very English Christmas. I'll show Mercedes how to cook a Christmas pudding and mince pies and we'll open all our presents under the tree with Granny and Grandpa. It's not long now. Only ten weeks. They'll go very fast and you'll be home before you know it.'

'But then we'll have to leave again. I hate leaving,' she said.

'I know you do, my love. Don't think about it now. Things always seem so much worse at night.

314

You're with me now and I love you very much. Very much. Try to think of nice things.'

So Leonora tried to think of nice things while Audrey thought of all the nasty things for her. Like parting, returning home to a hollow marriage and an empty house. Like long years ahead of airport farewells and precious moments together that would go far too quickly. *Oh, Cecil*, she thought, *what have you done?*

*   *   *

The following day it rained. Leonora was unable to enjoy herself because the minutes drained away pushing her closer to the afternoon and the painful drive back to school. She clung to her mother and said very little while Alicia sat in the gypsy's caravan making Ravena read her fortune over and over again. Audrey tried to cheer Leonora up by making a small garden out of a shoebox, using moss from the roof of the house and little flowers that they hunted for in the rain under a big golf umbrella that had once belonged to Hugh. The child began to smile as she busied herself with gluing pieces on and setting a circle of aluminium foil in the bottom of the box to resemble a pond. Cicely made chocolate crispies for tea and let the twins lick the bowl, which they had to fight over with Barley, who was determined to shove his wet nose in there before them.

Parting was horrible. Leonora cried and Alicia scowled because once again she had to look after her. Audrey left quickly on this occasion having learned from the time before, but she sobbed all the way back in the car and all the way back to

Buenos Aires in the plane so that when she arrived at the airport her eyes were so swollen she was barely recognisable.

But she could never have anticipated or imagined what had taken place in her home while she had been away.

CHAPTER TWENTY

When Audrey stepped out of the car and heard the hauntingly familiar sound of the piano dancing on the air like an echo of a distant memory, she believed it to be an illusion produced by exhaustion and sadness. A cruel illusion that ripped at her heart and mocked the hope that she always harboured even though she knew her wishes were impossible wishes and her dreams nothing but mirages forged out of hopelessness. She stood there listening, not believing her ears but wanting desperately to believe. She glanced at her husband who was already opening the boot of the car to retrieve her luggage. She looked at the house and found herself walking towards it as if in slow motion, fearful of what she would find inside. *Surely*, she thought, *if Louis had returned, Cecil would have told me.* The certainty that she would have been informed clouded her mind with doubt and disappointment and yet there still remained a spark of hope.

As she entered the door the music got louder. The tune was unmistakeable. It was their tune. 'The Forget-Me-Not Sonata.' Her legs felt unsteady, her emotions raw so that she worried she might give herself away by collapsing or dissolving into tears. She heard Cecil on the path behind her and this spurred her on. She didn't dare turn to ask him who was playing the piano in case her voice exposed the sudden turbulence that had seized her spirit.

Cecil walked on up the stairs to put her suitcase in their bedroom and Audrey remained in the doorway to the sitting room, where Louis sat at the piano, his fingers floating over the keys that she had touched so often and with such wistfulness, thinking of him.

He must have sensed her there for he stopped playing and turned around. They stared at one another for a moment that seemed to defy the laws of time and hung suspended in an uneasy limbo. Within that moment each nervously watched the other, Louis in search of a flicker of affection to reassure him that she still loved him and Audrey in fear of finding anger in those faraway eyes. She felt guilty. Here she was married to his brother when she should have been married to him. But he could smell the marital discontent in the alcohol on his brother's breath and see it in the tight knot of hair that restrained Audrey's joy and her vitality and clung severely to the nape of her neck. In the fortnight that he had been there he had made a pretty damning assessment of his brother's marriage. It could all have been so different.

When Audrey managed a tender smile it was the only encouragement Louis needed. He rose to his feet and pulled her into his arms, pressing his lips to her temple, murmuring that he still wanted her, that he still loved her and that he always would. 'Louis, please,' she begged, pushing him away as

317

the stairs creaked under Cecil's feet.

'How could he break you like this?' he whispered, holding her face in his hands, his expression crumpled with compassion and sorrow. Audrey looked away tearfully. She wanted so much for him to hold her because in his arms was the only home that counted. But they didn't have time. Cecil appeared as Louis drew away.

'I wanted Louis to be a surprise,' he said, walking past his wife into the sitting room where he poured himself a strong whisky. Audrey followed him, tearing her eyes off the man she had feared she might never see again. She floundered, not knowing what to say, trying to act as normally as she could. Cecil continued seemingly oblivious of the emotions that tore through the air in razorsharp vibrations. 'It was a hell of a surprise for me, I can tell you. He just turned up one day, about a week after you'd left with the girls. No warning. Rather in the same manner that he left us.' He looked up at his brother then across to his wife. In the weighty pause that ensued he lit a cigar.

'Where is he staying?' Audrey asked, too scared to direct the question at him.

'With us,' Cecil replied, swirling the ice around in his glass. His face was grave and his jaw stiff. 'You don't mind, do you?' He looked up at her from under his brow.

Audrey panicked but shook her head. 'Of course not. Have Mummy and Daddy seen him?' Louis went and sat on one of the sofas where he could see her better. She perched on the arm of the other. He thought how much older she looked with her hair tied back. The girl in her seemed to have disappeared altogether.

318

'I have seen your parents and Aunt Edna,' he replied. 'All a little older but basically the same.'

'Henry gave Louis a dinner party at the Club to welcome him back,' said Cecil. Then he added in a softer voice, 'Rose wants to hold a memorial service for Isla, now that Louis is here, but she was waiting for you to return.'

Audrey lowered her eyes. So much had happened while she had been away. 'I see,' she replied. 'I would like that very much.' She looked at Louis nervously, playing with the handle of her handbag. 'How long will you be staying?' She focused her eyes on the shiny brown leather, not wanting to reveal how much she wanted him to stay. Cecil drained his glass and stood up to pour another. He had to muster all his strength to control his shaking hands.

'I don't know. I have no plans.'

'If he stays he'll have to marry Nelly,' Cecil joked, sitting down again. The alcohol now dulled his senses and his pain gnawed at him no longer. 'Because Nelly believes she's the reason he's returned.' He chuckled.

'Nelly?' Audrey gasped.

'Hilda's determined. Only Agatha is married and Nelly's getting on a bit.'

'We went to Hilda's for dinner the other night,' said Louis with a sigh. 'Of course, she seated me next to Nelly. Poor girl, nature hasn't been kind, has she? The girl's not unpleasant though. Not like her mother.'

This was all too much for Audrey to take in. She stood up and rubbed her forehead. 'I'm very tired,' she explained. 'Do you mind if I go and have a bath and a rest? Cecil, will you apologise to Mercedes for me, I'll go in and see her when I come down for lunch. I have a letter for her from Alicia.'

'Of course, my dear, can I get you anything?'

She shook her head and pulled a tremulous smile. 'No, thank you. I'll be fine after a sleep.' Then she made for the door but stopped suddenly and turned around, defeated. 'It's very quiet here, isn't it?' she said sadly.

Louis looked at his brother who stared into his empty glass, the ash from his cigar dropping onto the carpet.

*   *   *

When Audrey reached the sanctuary of her bedroom, she locked the door behind her and ran a hot bath. She had been dreading returning to an empty house. She could barely think about her daughters without sobbing. It had been so painful leaving them and then leaving England where she had at least been close by. But Louis' appearance had been a far greater shock than finding the twins' rooms empty and silent. She had expected a miserable homecoming, but she hadn't expected Louis.

She sank into the bath and let the water ease the tension that had knotted all her muscles in tight, painful balls of unhappiness. Why wasn't Louis furious with her? How could he sit there with her and Cecil as husband and wife and smile as if he felt nothing? What did he hope for now that he had returned? She fingered the gold band on her left hand. She was married. Everything had changed except her heart.

The bath made her drowsy and when she curled

320

up under the covers she slipped into a deep sleep quicker than she would have ever thought possible under the circumstances.

She was awoken by a light tapping on the door. She opened her eyes and glanced at the clock. It was two in the afternoon. 'Audrey, it's lunchtime,' said Cecil, trying to turn the knob. 'Why have you locked the door?'

'Did I lock it?' she asked, pretending that she hadn't meant to.

'May I come in?'

'Of course,' she replied, getting up.

'You look much better now,' he said once she'd unlocked the door. 'The colour's returned to your cheeks. Do you feel better?'

'Much,' she answered truthfully. 'Sleep is a great healer.' She opened the curtains letting the sunshine tumble into the room with the enthusiasm of spring.

'Louis has had the most amazing adventures,' he said, sitting down by the window and watching his wife make the bed.

'Really?'

'Yes, he went to Mexico where he spent eight years teaching music to children.'

'He would be good at that,' she said. Then she remembered that he was downstairs and her skin tickled with excitement.

'No, my dear, the amazing thing is that the children were deaf.'

Audrey looked at her husband and frowned. 'Deaf?'

'Exactly. I thought it sounded a little incredible myself. But he explained how he taught them to close their eyes and express their feelings through their fingers. I think they could feel the vibrations or something. He brought back a few cuttings from the local papers. He caused quite a sensation. It obviously did him the power of good.'

Audrey smiled and felt her stomach flutter with the memory of the first moment they had played the piano together. He had taught her in the same way.

'I always knew he was special,' she said quietly.

Cecil's jaw stiffened and the muscle pounded in his cheek.

'Yes, you did,' he said carefully, without taking his eyes off her. 'Well, now everyone here thinks he's special too.'

'They do?' Audrey slipped into a pair of white trousers and shirt then sat at her dressing table where she applied a little make-up and tamed her curls into a shiny chignon.

'Well, he's been elevated to the ranks of a romantic hero of old. Even the Crocodiles, what's left of them, have welcomed him with open arms. Mothers are throwing their daughters at him and he has so many invitations he's barely ever here.'

'I'm so pleased,' she said. But she felt a stab of disappointment. *How fickle people are*, she thought sadly, *if they had loved him like this when he had first arrived in Hurlingham, we'd be happily married by now.*

When Audrey stood up she noticed Cecil was watching her with a strange look on his face. She smiled at him and frowned. He returned her smile but it did little to hide the apprehension that distorted his features.

'You look wonderful, my dear,' he said jovially, collecting himself; but his eyes betrayed a sadness

322

she hadn't noticed before

'Thank you,' she replied, walking to the door.

'It's good to have Louis back, isn't it?'

'Yes, it is.' She tried to sound nonchalant, as if he were any old brother-in-law who had come to pay them a visit after twelve years.

'I think it's highly appropriate to hold a memorial service for Isla in his honour, don't you?'

'Yes.' She felt there was an ulterior motive to his questioning, but then perhaps she just felt guilty. 'Isla would have wanted it.'

'He's recovered well, though. Let's hope he finds a nice English girl out here and marries her.'

'That would be nice,' she replied tightly, stepping into the corridor.

They walked down the stairs in silence. Audrey resisted glancing across the landing to Alicia and Leonora's bedrooms and Cecil, who in the last month had accustomed himself to the emptiness, didn't even feel the urge to. Audrey felt her husband's presence behind her like a weighty shadow. She had greeted him at the airport with the same cool politeness with which she had left him and hadn't even noticed the look of disappointment that had darkened his eager face. Her kiss had been stiff and awkward and their conversation in the car had revolved very much around the children and their new school and Audrey's tone of voice had dripped with bitterness, accusing him of callousness and insensitivity. She could barely talk about the twins without crying and had only stopped when they had changed the subject to talk about Cicely and Marcel and the gypsies. Cecil hadn't ever heard of Marcel and the Cicely she had described seemed like a stranger to him.

'Have you met this Marcel fellow?' Cecil asked Louis when they had all sat down for lunch. It wasn't warm enough to sit outside, but the French doors were open and the sweet scents of the garden floated in on a fresh breeze. Louis was barely able to take his eyes off Audrey, who seemed to have blossomed in her sleep. Her eyes were no longer puffy and dull but shone with vitality and her blushing cheeks revealed that she was only too aware of his stare.

'Yes, I stayed with her last year,' Louis replied. 'Not that I saw much of Marcel. He spent most of the time in the attic painting or in bed with Cicely.'

'Good God,' Cecil exclaimed, nearly choking on his soup. 'Perish the thought.'

'Cicely's not the woman you once knew, Cecil,' he said with a chuckle. Audrey wondered how Louis could be in such good humour. Why wasn't he angry with her and bitter towards his brother? It just didn't make sense.

'She was always a paragon of old-fashioned values and phlegmatic like Papa. Can a man change a woman so much?' Cecil dabbed at the corners of his mouth with his napkin. Audrey gazed into her bowl of soup.

'Yes, a man can change a woman. He can either nurture her and love her so that she grows like a plant in the sun, or he can hurt her and let her dry out so that she withers and dies.' Audrey felt his gaze upon her once more and remembered Aunt Edna's sunshine Harry. 'Marcel doesn't love Cicely, he lusts after her, and that's very different. But it's had the same effect. She's let go of all restraint and is quite changed.'

324

'He doesn't love her?' Audrey asked without raising her eyes.

'No, I don't believe he does,' Louis replied. 'He has a roof over his head, good food and good sex. He doesn't pay for any of it. He's an artist; all he cares about is his art. No, I believe he's using Cicely.'

'I found him a bit creepy,' Audrey confessed, looking at her husband because she couldn't stare into her soup for ever. 'He crept about in the shadows, watching, listening. He was like a spy.'

'Spying for whom, my dear?' Cecil asked.

'For himself. I don't know,' she replied and then her eyes engaged with Louis' as if they had a will of their own and his were familiar, more familiar than anyone else's in the world and she knew that she didn't need to speak in order to communicate what she thought. He understood her. Slowly she felt the void inside her fill up with warm honey and she wanted to laugh because she had been so sad before and now she felt so happy. She noticed the corners of Louis' mouth quiver as if about to break into a smile and she tore herself away. Cecil sat there drinking far too much wine so that his head grew as heavy as his heart. He watched his wife and wondered whether he was just imagining an intimacy between her and his brother or perhaps the alcohol was making him paranoid, giving him hallucinations.

'My dear, I'm going into the city this afternoon,' he said, draining his glass and watching their reactions carefully with bloodshot eyes.

'You're going back to work?'

'Yes.' His tone was flat. Audrey tried to look disappointed but the shadow of a smile played

325

upon her face.

'You'll be back for dinner?' she asked.

'Back for dinner.' He then sighed heavily and stood up. 'I leave you in Louis' capable hands.' She didn't notice the caustic tone in his voice because Louis' stare distracted her.

'Oh, I'm sure Louis has got lots to do. Besides I have to unpack and I must go and see Mercedes. Mummy's coming over for tea with Aunt Edna and Hilda.'

'Good,' Cecil replied. 'I'll be off then.' He gave Audrey a kiss on the cheek. She didn't stiffen this time but frowned. He was behaving strangely. Perhaps she was being paranoid because she felt guilty. Perhaps it was the alcohol. She hadn't failed to notice how much he had drunk.

Audrey fled into the kitchen where Mercedes was washing up while Loro perched on the tap, practising the latest lines he had picked up. *'Merchi my lovely, Merchi my lovely. You smell gooooood.'* Mercedes flicked him with a wet cloth but this didn't deter him. *'Merchi, my lovely . . .'*

'Mercedes,' said Audrey as she entered.

'Señora, how are my girls?' she said, drying her hands on her apron. Mercedes rarely smiled and her intonation always dropped at the end of each phrase as if she recognised the depravity of the world and was resigned to it.

'I have a letter for you from Alicia.'

'What a good girl she is. I knew she wouldn't forget her old friend.'

'Of course not. Leonora sends her love as well.'

'Are they happy?' she asked, then shrugged her shoulders and frowned. 'How can they be happy so far from home?'

'I know,' Audrey replied, handing her the letter and nodding gravely. 'But they are happy there. Alicia, I'm sure will tell you herself.'

'Nothing can hurt Alicia, only herself. Whereas Leonora is as fragile as a feather. I know she misses her mother, I can feel it,' she said, thumping her fist on her breast.

'I miss them too. But they will be back soon. We'll all have a lovely Christmas together.'

'And then?' She walked off to the kitchen table with the letter. Loro dived into the soapy water where he splashed about with glee.

'*You smell so gooooood!*' he crowed. '*Ja ja ja!!!*' Audrey raised her eyebrows thinking he was speaking to her and wandered out.

* * *

Louis was playing the piano. A light melody in tune with the changing season that flowered outside the window. She breathed deeply and walked in. He didn't stop playing. She stood by the piano and leant on the polished surface watching his pale fingers dancing over the keys. She could smell the familiar scent of his body and was overcome with nostalgia and desire. It was as if he had never left, as if that awkward conversation in the church after Isla's funeral had never happened, as if she had never married Cecil, but married Louis and here they were together in their home. It felt so natural, as if it was meant to be.

'You're wondering why I'm not angry,' he said softly. Then he looked at her and raised his eyebrows inquisitively.

'Why aren't you angry?' she asked. He continued

327

to play for his fingers had no need of his mind or his concentration.

'How can I be angry? You love me. I'm the happiest man in the world.'

Audrey smiled and lowered her eyes. 'But I married your brother.'

'I left.'

'I missed you.'

'I missed you too. I bled for years.'

Audrey gently lowered the lid of the piano. He withdrew his fingers. She swallowed hard and her face turned solemn. 'I'm still bleeding, Louis,' she whispered, ashamed to speak of such pain.

'I know.' He stood up and drew her into his arms. She wound hers around his waist and rested her head on his shoulder. He felt warm and soft and reassuring. Then she felt his fingers pull the pins out of her hair so that her curls broke free and cascaded down her back. He scrunched them in his hand and breathed in the feminine scent that lay within them and felt their silken texture against his face. 'Oh Audrey,' he sighed. 'I've lived every minute of the last twelve years for this moment. I'm alive again.'

'Why didn't you wait for me?'

'Because I knew it wasn't going to work and I couldn't bear to be near you and not have you.'

'But Louis,' she protested, then remembered her conversation with Cicely. Louis couldn't cope when things went wrong for him. She pulled away and looked into his features. 'I never stopped loving you. You left with a part of me, the most important part of me, I was incomplete without you. Then Cecil . . . Cecil . . .'

'I know. Cecil remained constant and loyal,

everything I should have been. I left when you needed me most and I regret it. But I can't fight my nature. I can only regret it later.'

'So you don't blame me?'

'No, I don't blame you,' he said and his face creased into a wide smile. She smiled back and touched his face with great tenderness, the way a mother caresses a child, the way a woman caresses a lover. 'I ask your forgiveness.'

'You have it. You've always had it,' she laughed and wrapped herself around him again. 'I'm so happy you've come back. I need you so much. I have so much to tell you.'

'Come out to the country with me tomorrow,' he suggested. 'It's stifling here.'

'What will we say to Cecil?'

'He won't know. He'll be at work.'

'We'll have to explain where we've been.'

'Why? You barely communicate as it is. He will just presume you've been with your mother or aunt. He probably won't even ask.'

'I'll think of something,' she replied optimistically.

'Good. I met a man in Mexico who has an estancia not far from the city. We'd be there in a couple of hours.'

'Can he be trusted?'

'Trust me, my love,' he said, gazing down at her, delirious with joy. Then he kissed her. His mouth was soft and she sank against his body, holding him tightly so that their hearts accompanied the music in their souls and beat in time. It didn't feel wrong. Audrey was married and her loyalty to her husband had been unwavering. But with Louis it felt right.

'Did it ever feel right with Cecil?' Louis asked

and Audrey answered truthfully.

'It always felt like a compromise. I gave him my hand but not my heart. My heart has always belonged to you.'

He kissed her again and closed his eyes. Once more they were dancing over the cobbled streets of Palermo beneath a navy sky studded with stars. He had dreamed of holding her again and had never lost hope. While there was hope there was life. Such was the power of dreams. But the dreams were only beginning. He felt as if he could conquer the world. With Audrey he really believed he could defy gravity and fly to the moon. Nothing was beyond his reach, even a future with the woman he loved.

CHAPTER TWENTY-ONE

'My dear Audrey,' Aunt Edna exclaimed happily, pulling her niece into her foamy bosom. In the last few years Edna's hair had paled into the grey of a cygnet and she now wore it tied loosely on the top of her head so that wisps of it hung free, floating about her face and neck like feathers. She had got fatter too. After all, besides her family, what gave her more pleasure than food?

'It's good to be home,' Audrey said with a contented sigh, returning the embrace.

'Let's go and sit outside, it's a beautiful day,' suggested Aunt Edna boisterously.

'As long as you don't get cold.'

'Cold, in this sunshine? Dear girl, you must be exhausted after your journey,' said Edna, following her through the doors into the garden where Louis stood beneath the veranda in the shade. 'Hello, Louis, my dear.' Louis' face opened into a wide smile and Edna wondered why she had never noticed his charm in the days when he had lived at the Hurlingham Club.

'I had a sleep this morning,' Audrey replied. 'I feel much better. Besides, it would be a shame to waste such lovely weather sleeping all day.' She laughed lightly then gave a nervous cough for no reason. Aunt Edna narrowed her blue eyes and looked into the radiant face of her niece. She certainly didn't have the countenance of a woman bereft of her children. On the contrary, her eyes shone and her cheeks blushed. But it was her hair that most struck her aunt, for it was no longer pulled into a defiant bun but tumbled over her shoulders in those lustrous corkscrew curls for which she was so admired. For a moment Edna thought that perhaps she had been reunited with Cecil, but then she only had to watch the way Audrey and Louis behaved to know that her luminosity had nothing whatsoever to do with her husband. Suddenly everything made sense. Louis had left because of Audrey not Isla! It was obvious now with hindsight. After all, Isla had never been interested in men. Besides being too young for love, love hadn't sought her out. Edna recalled Audrey's tormented piano playing and Louis' music that drove everyone to distraction at the Club. She hoped that she was the only person with the perception to work it out.

Audrey poured the tea which Mercedes had laid out on the table and told her aunt about Colehurst House and how much the twins were enjoying it

331

there. Edna was reassured to see the light in Audrey's eyes suddenly dim with sadness as she spoke about them. 'Leonora loves Saggy Rabbit, she won't go anywhere without him. I believe she even takes him into class with her.'

Aunt Edna chuckled. 'Is that allowed?'

'Oh yes, it's a wonderful school,' said Audrey, watching Louis out of the corner of her eye. He was standing on the veranda, gazing at her with an expression of great tenderness. She felt herself inflate with excitement and was relieved when Aunt Hilda and Nelly appeared through the garden gate to give her an excuse to laugh.

'Audrey,' called Aunt Hilda joyously. 'Lovely to have you home.' Audrey was taken aback by her aunt's uncharacteristic warmth, but then remembered Nelly's infatuation with Louis.

'Hello, Nelly,' she said, kissing her pasty cheek. 'I believe the whole of Alicia's class enjoyed your *dulce de leche.*' Nelly laughed nervously and smiled at Louis, having not heard a word of what Audrey had just said to her.

'Do try a piece of cake, Hilda,' Edna exclaimed. 'Nelly, come and sit over here with me.' Nelly's small eyes darted from her aunt to Louis and then back again. Louis was still standing on the veranda and looked as if he had no intention of sitting down. She pulled a timid little smile and perched awkwardly on the edge of her chair next to Edna. Audrey played ignorant of her cousin's intention and sat opposite her.

'Isn't it marvellous that Louis has returned to Hurlingham?' said Hilda, not thinking to ask Audrey how the twins were. It was plain that she had only come to visit in order to push her

332

unmarried daughter beneath Louis' nose.

'Yes, it is,' Audrey replied carefully. Aunt Edna sipped her tea, wishing her sister would realise that it would take a very generous-spirited man to fall in love with Nelly and an even more generous-spirited one to put up with Hilda as mother-in-law. Hilda and Nelly were inseparable these days. Wherever Nelly went, Hilda followed in the shadows like a vampire, desperate to settle her daughter's future before the light of day revealed her advancing years and denied her what was every woman's right. In Hilda's opinion Louis couldn't have returned for the sole reason of paying his respects to Isla's remains, buried ten feet in the soil, no, she maintained that he had come back in search of a wife. If he couldn't have Isla, her cousin would have to do. Hilda pursed her lips together in order to restrain her ambition and cut herself a thin slither of cake.

'Louis,' she said, with a dry smile. 'You must come and see us more often. There's no point wasting away in a house where there are no unmarried girls to entertain you. Really, Audrey and Cecil must be very dull company.' She laughed but her joke had fallen flat. 'Oh dear, I don't mean that at all,' she stammered. Nelly shot her a furious look and Audrey buried her face in her teacup to hide her amusement. Louis wanted to laugh as well but controlled himself so as not to offend the shy spinster who smouldered quietly in mortification.

'Have some more cake,' Aunt Edna suggested, holding up the knife.

'You know, I think I will,' said Louis, wandering over to sit beside Audrey. 'Mercedes is a fantastic cook. I don't think I've ever eaten so well, even at the Club.'

'It was the meat I missed in England,' said Audrey. 'One doesn't realise how good it is here until one tastes it somewhere else.'

'I agree,' Hilda replied. 'One spends one's whole time hankering after England and fails to see the good that is right here, under one's very nose.'

'There's a lot that's good about Argentina,' said Louis. 'I've been all over in the last decade so I know what I'm talking about.'

'I should like to visit England one day,' Nelly ventured. Having not said a word since she arrived she was startled by the sound of her own voice and blushed a deep crimson.

'You really should,' he replied and his gentle gaze made her blush all the more. 'A woman should see the world.'

'Absolutely,' Hilda exclaimed. 'There is nothing as unattractive as a woman of limited horizon.' Then she believed she saw a glint of intent in Louis' eyes and her spirits lifted. Perhaps Louis would take her and show her the world himself. 'There's nothing Nelly likes better than adventure,' she added. There was nothing Nelly hated more than adventure. *All in a good cause*, Hilda thought, justifying her lie.

At last Rose arrived and after embracing her daughter and eagerly asking after the twins they began to discuss Isla's memorial service. 'I think, seeing as Louis has returned, it would be nice to remember her all together,' she said. 'Not a day goes by when I'm sure we don't all think of her. It would be good for the whole community to put into words what we all feel in our hearts.' Then she looked at Louis with affection and added, 'Louis

334

dear, all these years I've been wanting to ask you about your friendship with my daughter. I thought I knew everything about her but I know now that she didn't tell me everything as I had imagined. I don't mean that I should know all the details, but I would like to be told how happy she was before she died. I'm grateful to you for giving her such happiness. She always had a spring in her step but never more so than in those summer months she shared with you. I hope you don't mind me asking. I've waited until now and deliberated long and hard. But I would like to fill in at least some of the gaps.' Louis swallowed hard and avoided Audrey's anxious face that now turned towards him in silent panic. Aunt Hilda stiffened, for reminding him of Isla did Nelly's cause no good at all. The silence invaded like fog until they were all in danger of being swallowed up by it.

Louis took Audrey's hand in his. Audrey flinched and stared at him in fear. Now wasn't the moment to speak the truth. Not after all these years. He turned and smiled at her with confidence. *Trust me*, he seemed to be saying. 'Audrey was very close to Isla. I know from my brother how long it has taken her to come to terms with her death. I love Audrey like a sister and I don't want to cause her any more pain.'

'How very sensitive of you, Louis. But Audrey wants to hear too, don't you, dear?' said Rose. Audrey nodded. She felt Louis squeeze her hand and understood from his silent communication that he was holding her because he knew it was no longer appropriate to use Isla as a front and he wanted her support. But Audrey was also aware that by condoning the continuation of the charade she was embroiling herself once again in an affair. This time there was so much more at stake. She was married and she had children to think of. But she squeezed his hand back in agreement. She loved him so she had no choice.

Louis was determined to lie as little as possible so he began by praising the qualities in Isla that he had admired when he had first met her. 'She always spoke her mind,' he began and the eager expression on the face of her mother spurred him on. 'She was impulsive and wilful and always a wonderful source of joy. I never saw her unhappy or afraid. Her life was short but it was happy.' Rose seemed to want more. 'When I first met Isla, I was struck by her beauty, both your daughters are beautiful,' he said carefully. Rose looked at Audrey and smiled appreciatively while Hilda looked at Nelly and wished she could do something with that limp brown hair. 'What I admired the most, though, was the way she never pretended to be anything that she wasn't. She was exuberant and vital. She is sorely missed and always will be.'

'But when did these rendezvous take place?' Rose asked impatiently.

'At your house. She was a good backgammon player and had a sharp mind for bridge. It was an innocent friendship, Rose. One that was only beginning to flower.' Then he sighed and his face drained of awkwardness and shone with a pale translucence. Aunt Edna, who had been more interested in picking at the crumbs of cake that remained on the plate on the table, cocked her head and listened, for his voice had grown suddenly quiet and sad. Audrey felt his hand moisten with sweat. 'Love kept me here and then love drove me

336

away. Because when it was gone, I found I couldn't live without it. So I left half a man, because the part of me that contained my heart remained here, with her. I spent years in Mexico living off the memory of love, trying to find it in the eyes of other women, but I failed. Every time I failed, because the eyes that gazed back at me weren't the deep and languid pools that haunted my every living moment but the shallow eyes of strangers. You see, Rose, there was only one woman who was meant for me. God chose her for me. He led me out here for her. And the moment I met her I knew our souls belonged together. I knew she understood me like no one had ever understood me before. The most miraculous part of it all is that she loved me back. She really loved me.' He paused and lowered his eyes. Rose wiped a tear from her cheek and Edna was so moved her skin dappled all over. She glanced across at Audrey and knew that he wasn't speaking about Isla but about her. 'I tried to stay away because I knew I couldn't be in Argentina without her. So after Mexico I travelled a while before returning to England. I stayed with my sister, Cicely, and heard that Audrey had married Cecil. It was a shock because I knew it was something that I would never enjoy. Marriage to the woman one loves must be the greatest gift on earth. But it has been denied me. It was then that I decided to come back. I had to face my demons. I had to prove to myself that my dreams weren't in vain, that they meant something. So I have come back to reclaim my heart that I left here twelve years ago. So, what have I found?' He raised his eyes and looked into Rose's.

'What have you found?' she asked in a trembling

337

voice. He leant forward.

'I have found that she still has it. She has always had it . . . and she always will.'

Hilda caught her breath. 'You can't hold onto a ghost forever, Louis,' she said, darting her black eyes at Nelly and noticing the disappointment rise up her throat in the form of a rash. 'There's no point hanging onto the past.'

'But I don't think you understand, Hilda,' he said softly. 'I don't think you understand the power of dreams.'

'I do,' Audrey whispered and released his hand. She folded hers in her lap in case anyone should see that they burned. 'I understand the power of dreams, Louis. You'll always have her heart too. Always.'

Rose dabbed her eyes with a hanky and smiled at Louis with gratitude. 'That was the most beautiful thing I have ever heard anyone say. Isla was so lucky to have loved you. Thank you.'

'So,' said Edna, taking a very deep breath. 'When are you going to hold her memorial service, Rose?'

'This Saturday evening. I would like you, Louis, to read something.'

'Of course,' he replied.

'And you, Audrey.' Audrey nodded.

'I want it to be a celebration of her life. I don't want mourning. We've had enough mourning. It is time to thank God and remember the joy she brought us all.'

*   *   *

It was evening when Rose and her sisters left. Cecil

338

had returned from work to find them all talking around a cold teapot and an empty cake plate. Audrey had thanked them all for coming and accompanied them to the gate. Aunt Hilda hadn't even bothered to say good-bye and Nelly was too close to tears to speak, but Rose had embraced her warmly and said, 'Look after Louis, won't you, dear. He's very special to me.'

But Aunt Edna had whispered under her breath, 'Isla's eyes were never deep or languid.' Audrey had opened her mouth to explain but her aunt had patted her on the hand and smiled sadly. 'Your secret is safe with me, dear girl, but be careful. You're treading a path overshadowed with danger. It can only end in misery.' Then she had rejoined her sisters and they had disappeared down the road.

Cecil noticed at once that his wife had let her hair down and commented on it over dinner. 'You look lovely, Audrey. It's taken years off you.' Audrey's cheeks flushed and she thanked him. Then she fixed him with her gentle green eyes and he was reminded suddenly of the girl he had fallen in love with.

'Sometimes one has to move on,' she added softly, smiling at him. 'I'm no longer in mourning.' She meant for Louis of course, but Cecil interpreted it differently, thinking she meant for the twins. He noticed her radiant complexion and her light-heartedness and was filled with a fragile optimism. Perhaps his suspicions had been unfounded. He immediately felt guilty for having thought ill of his wife.

'I'm going out to the countryside tomorrow,' said Louis. 'I met a man in Mexico who owns an estancia west of the city. I thought I would look him up.'

'Jolly good idea,' Cecil replied jovially, feeling empowered by Audrey's good humour. Then he surprised himself. 'Why don't you go too, Audrey?' he suggested. If she was distracted she wouldn't dwell on the absence of her children.

'Oh, I have enough to do here,' she mumbled.

'Don't be silly. You've got nothing to do here. A day out on the pampa will do you good.'

She looked at Louis.

'Cecil's right. You can't sit at home all day and plan the children's homecoming. You can gallop across the plains and eat a hearty steak instead.' He laughed.

'All right,' she conceded. 'Can't you take the day off work, Cecil, and come too?' she added to be kind and because she immediately felt guilty.

Cecil smiled at her with gratitude and touched her hand. 'No, my dear, I'm afraid not. But you go and have a good time with Louis.'

'I'll bring her back in one piece,' said Louis but he glanced at Audrey and his eyes communicated so much more.

Cecil patted his brother firmly on his shoulder. 'I trust you will,' he said, then lit a cigar. 'If a man can't trust his own brother, who can he trust, what?'

*   *   *

Audrey was tired when she went to bed. The day had been both physically and emotionally draining. She remembered what Aunt Edna had said to her and wondered how she had worked it out. She

340

hoped no one else had. Then she smiled as she recalled Louis' heartfelt speech about love. She had wanted to thank him but they hadn't had a moment alone. Once they would have communicated through little white scrolls of paper hidden between the bricks of the station house. Now they had to snatch their opportunities, but tomorrow they would have all day and she looked forward to it with such excitement that she doubted whether her mind would allow her body any sleep at all. When Cecil entered the room she looked at him in surprise. He stood there, deliberating whether to leave or stay. Her expression was unfathomable but her hair was still loose and falling like springs onto her shoulders. 'I came to say good-night,' he said, hoping for a look of encouragement from her. But she sat in bed, her features staring back at him impassively. Then she lowered her eyes in resignation.

'Cecil, I'm very tired. I think it's better that we keep things the way they were before I left. At least, for tonight.' She didn't raise her eyes because she couldn't bear to see his face flush with disappointment.

'Of course. I want to sit up and read anyhow and I know how much the light bothers you.'

'Thank you.'

'Well, good-night then.' He made to leave.

Audrey was suddenly consumed with guilt. 'Cecil?'

'Yes?'

'Don't I get a kiss?'

His delight was pitiful and she felt her heart lurch for him. He walked over and kissed her gently on the cheek.

'Good-night, Cecil.'

'Good-night, Audrey. Sweet dreams.' She watched him leave. He had no idea how sweet her dreams really were.

Audrey turned out the light and curled up under the sheets. A warm breeze rustled the curtains playfully, filling the room with the scents of the garden. She wondered whether Louis was lying awake thinking of her and longed to go to him. But she couldn't risk being caught and besides, tomorrow they would have the whole day to spend as they pleased. She recalled their secret dances in Palermo, their stolen kisses beneath the cherry tree and then the heavy sense of loss when their dreams had come to nothing. She shuddered at the thought of losing him again and silently, in the quiet solitude of her room, she vowed that this time she would never let him go.

CHAPTER TWENTY-TWO

The following morning, as a flamingo pink dawn faded into a clear blue sky, Louis and Audrey set off into the countryside. With the wind catching her loose curls and dragging them through the open window Audrey looked across at Louis and knew that he had been right about the power of dreams. She had dreamed of this and her dreams had come true. As if reading her thoughts he stretched across the gearbox and took her hand in his. They didn't need to speak; they understood each other without the need to cheapen their feelings by translating them into syllables. They smiled contentedly and sat back, watching as the busy city dwindled into shabby clusters of houses and then to a long empty road that sliced through the plains, so vast and so flat that the sky was all around them and they were both filled with the intoxicating sense of freedom. Herds of mahogany-coloured ponies grazed in the long grasses, and cows roamed, lifting their heads to shake off the flies that had hatched in the warm spring weather. Audrey gazed about her and remembered her departure for England when she had looked out across the sea and seen her small world in relation to the vista of endless possibilities that stretched out before her. Looking about her now she felt once again the allure of the wide-open spaces—one could get lost in them and never come out.

'What are you thinking about?' he asked.

'How big the world is and how small we are in it.'

'And how insignificant. Sometimes one has to stand on the peak of a mountain to remember that.'

'Or gaze into an immense ocean.' He grinned at her and she felt her stomach flutter with happiness.

'It is in those views that dreams are made, my love,' he said and she turned and looked at him with sad eyes.

'I know that now. I wish I had known it before. But I couldn't see beyond Hurlingham then.'

'It doesn't matter. Nothing matters because you're here with me now.' And he told her again, 'I love you, Audrey, and I always will.'

*   *   *

La Magdalena sat like a lush oasis in the middle of

343

the fertile pampa. Out of the flat plain grew an abundance of tall trees whose branches clamoured with the song of birds. The scent of eucalyptus wafted in through the window along with the smell of horses and leather. They drove up the long dusty drive lined with leafy *paraísos*. They were greeted by a pack of dogs and Audrey remembered Cicely's dogs who were much fatter and sleeker than these skinny mongrels who now circled the car and announced their arrival by barking loudly.

They drew up under the trees and a dark-skinned maid in a pink and white uniform bustled out of the house, shouting at the dogs to be quiet and be off, waving her arms at them impatiently. '*Buen día*, Señor Forrester, Señor Ribaldo is expecting you on the terrace,' she said in Spanish, her mouth extending into a toothless smile.

The house was a white and yellow colonial building with a roof of faded green tiles. It was old and needed a new coat of paint but the walls crawled with jasmine and hummed with bees and in spite of its shabby appearance it had immense charm and character. The maid showed them to the terrace where a wiry septuagenarian sat drinking coffee. He wore a pair of grey gaucho trousers pleated at the waist and buttoned up at the ankles and a wide leather belt of glittering silver coins. On his feet were threadbare black espadrilles and the skin that was exposed above them was brown and dry like the earth. When he saw Louis he pushed himself up from the chair and grinned in delight. 'Louis, my friend! It is a pleasure to see you again.' He pulled the young man into his embrace and patted him affectionately on the back. Then he looked at Audrey with twinkling brown

344

eyes and raised his ashen eyebrows in admiration.

'And this must be the woman you spoke to me about.' Audrey blushed.

'Gaitano, this is Audrey Forrester, my sister-in-law,' Louis replied.

Gaitano nodded and his old eyes shone with compassion. 'Ah, I see. So beautiful and so beyond reach. It is always a pleasure to gaze on such beauty.' He kissed Audrey and her cheeks stung for some time afterwards from his prickly stubble. 'Come and join me for a drink. Then I will leave you two young people to enjoy my farm before joining me for lunch. My gaucho, El Chino, is preparing a delicious barbecue for you and Costanza has cooked dessert. I want today to be special. Life is a sequence of moments and this is one I would like you both to remember.'

'I'm sure Louis has told you that we met in Mexico,' said Gaitano to Audrey, sitting down and picking up his coffee cup. 'He is an unusual young man. Imagine teaching deaf children to play music? Who would dare attempt such a seemingly impossible task? Yet, deaf people hear with their hearts; there are plenty of men who hear with their ears yet are deaf to the music in their hearts.'

Audrey looked at Louis and smiled with pride. 'Louis is exceptional,' she agreed. 'He taught me to play the piano in a way I had never ventured before.'

Gaitano nodded knowingly. 'Yes, but you already felt the notes. You only had to learn to play them.'

'Perhaps.' She laughed softly. 'Do you play, Gaitano?'

The old man chuckled sadly. 'I feel the notes but

345

I am too afraid to play them. For if I were to start I would never stop. That is a great danger I face. I have seen too much in my life to restrain such emotion. This is a country of turbulence. I doubt the notes of my internal melody would be very pleasing. I will play in Heaven, if God grant me such paradise. But now, let us drink to Louis and his gift.' He raised his coffee cup and Audrey raised her glass of juice. Then Gaitano left them alone and shuffled across the park to where El Chino tended the *asado* in the shade of a eucalyptus tree.

'What a wonderful man,' Audrey said as they walked towards a small cluster of shacks where a couple of young gauchos had saddled up ponies for them.

'He's deaf,' said Louis.

'Deaf?' Audrey was astounded.

'Very deaf. Can't hear a word.'

'You would never know,' she exclaimed in admiration.

'No, you wouldn't. He's been deaf for years, although he wasn't born deaf. He came out to Mexico to meet me. A friend of his read an article about my work and sent it to him. We became instant friends.'

'But you didn't teach him to play?'

'He said he was too old. I think he feared that by giving vent to his feelings he might break down. Music does that sometimes. You hold all your emotions inside, button them up, control them and then all it takes is a simple tune to get you going. Out they pour and there's no stopping until they've been released in their entirety.'

'Poor Gaitano. Does he have a wife?'

'He had a wife and children, but his wife died

346

and his children are now living all over the world. I think he was a hard man.'

'So who looks after him?'

'Costanza and El Chino, I imagine. He's doing all right.'

Audrey took Louis' hand in hers. 'You told him about us, didn't you?'

'I had to tell someone. I couldn't tell anyone else. Gaitano always said that if I ever went back to the Argentine I was to come and visit him here. He recognised you the moment he saw you.'

'You described me well.'

'Your face was etched on my mind, it wasn't difficult.'

'Bouncing curls,' she said and laughed.

'No,' he replied seriously, stopping and pulling her into his arms. 'Long sensitive face, languid blue eyes, soft translucent skin and a full and generous mouth. The mouth of a poet.' He cupped her chin in his hand and kissed her lips. 'But the most precious part of you is inside and no one can see that but me.'

They mounted their ponies and made their way slowly across the plain. The midday sun was now high in the sky but it wasn't too hot, just pleasantly warm. All around them the pampa lay vast and flat, interrupted only by the odd cluster of trees that marked a farm, the vital water tank that rose above them to catch the rain silhouetted against the sky. Contented *vizcachas*, a type of prairie hare, hid in the long grasses, camouflaged against the earth until the sound of approaching horses moved them on. Their carefree meandering indicated that life was good on the prairie.

After a few miles they stopped beneath the

rubbery branches of a large ombu tree and left their ponies to rest in the shade. 'You know this is the only tree that really belongs on the pampa, all the others were imported and planted by settlers,' said Louis, sitting down on the grass.

'It's a fantastic-looking tree, isn't it?' she said, sitting beside him.

He drew her against him and kissed her temple. 'This moment is such a gift, Audrey. To be here with you, in the middle of this immense open space. It's like paradise. We can be ourselves and I can tell you I love you in a loud voice without worrying that I'm going to be overheard.' She laughed as he shouted it out to the sky. 'I love you, Audrey Forrester, I love you, I love you, I love you.'

'Stop!' she cried, wiping her eyes. 'You are a silly old thing.'

'But I'm *your* silly old thing.'

'Yes, you are.' Then she said in a serious voice, 'This is the way it should have been. I feel closer to you than I do to anyone else and I haven't seen you for years.'

'I know, it's as if we saw each other yesterday. That's the definition of true friendship and, Audrey, I want you to be my lover. I would like you to be my wife, but above everything else you're my dear friend.'

'I only married Cecil because I thought I would never see you again. I thought you had gone for ever, Louis. But I never stopped loving you.'

'I know, my love. Don't torment yourself,' he said gently. 'I was hurt and angry when I found out, but it was I who left you.'

'Why did you leave?' she asked, shaking her head, remembering how hurt she had been by his

348

apparent selfishness.

'Because with Isla's death everything changed. You even looked different. Distant, impassive. The fight had gone. I knew duty would come before love. I knew you couldn't go against your parents' wishes. I knew it was over.'

'But it didn't have to be. Perhaps in time,' she ventured quietly.

'No, not even in time. The irony is that now they believe Isla loved me they wish I was their son-in-law.'

'It makes me so angry. If I wasn't married to Cecil . . .'

'But you are.'

'Perhaps I could . . .'

'Audrey,' he interrupted sternly. 'I'm not going to ask anything of you now. I made that mistake before. Let's just live for the moment like two leaves in the wind, going wherever it blows. Let's not make any decisions or plans. I don't want to lose you again.'

'You won't. Oh God, Louis, you won't, I promise you.'

He held her close and kissed her, transforming into reality dreams worn thin over the long years of waiting. His kiss was tender and passionate and sad and they both recalled their conversation beneath the stars in the grounds of the Hurlingham Club, when struck by the transient beauty of the moment they were both overcome with a bittersweet sense of melancholia. But his kiss swept away the past twelve years and healed the pain of their parting and the subsequent years of loneliness and regret that had aged them before their time.

349

They galloped back to La Magdalena, their laughter carried on the wind so that birds seeking shade among the leaves of the tall plane trees flapped their wings and took to the sky and the ostriches scattered like feathers over the grassy plain. They relished the feeling of freedom as their ponies sped across the pampa and without thinking of tomorrow or dwelling on the regrets of yesterday they smiled without inhibition and shouted excitedly into the air.

Lunch was beneath the shade of a threadbare parasol on the terrace, looking out over the uninterrupted plains. El Chino displayed the barbeque that smouldered beneath the eucalyptus tree and his small brown eyes shone with pride. He had killed the cow that morning and the meat was tender and fresh, lying in neat rows on the grill. He bent over to tend to it and Audrey noticed the ornate knife tucked into his wide silver-coined belt and thought how wonderfully flamboyant the gauchos were. Gaitano handed her a round wooden plate and she chose a large slice of tender meat. 'There's enough food here for an army,' she said as El Chino placed the piece on her plate accompanied by a thick chunk of toasted bread.

'It'll feed the gauchos and Costanza,' Gaitano replied. 'But I'm hoping you'll come back for seconds. We're very proud of our herds.'

'Do you spend all your time out here?' she asked.

'I don't go to the city these days. I'm too old and I have too many memories that I would like to forget. It's quiet here and peaceful. Buenos Aires is fraught and I'm no longer a political animal. I gave that up long ago, thank the Lord. Politics brings nothing but unhappiness. Not only in this country. I opt for a simple life nowadays and I'm happy this way. Come and sit down and enjoy your food.'

Audrey liked Gaitano. She was able to talk about herself knowing that he knew nothing about the place she came from and that everything she said would remain within the boundaries of the estancia. He was fully aware that he was harbouring two illicit lovers and yet he never alluded to their affair other than to gaze upon them with empathy as if living love through them, because he had never loved like that, not even in his youth. She noticed that if he wasn't watching her lips he missed what she said, so she took care to wait until he had focused his penetrating old eyes on her face before speaking and then she would see his expression soften and his head tilt to one side and he would give her his full attention, his lips curling at the corners with affection. It was a liberation to sit with Louis and enjoy his little gestures of devotion in the open without shame. The way he would gently touch her hand, or sweep back the long springs of hair that would occasionally fall forward and cover her face. He did it naturally, seemingly without thinking, yet she knew he was just as conscious of every moment of contact as she was, because his hands burned her skin and caused it to prickle with excitement.

After lunch Gaitano disappeared inside for a siesta. Audrey suddenly looked embarrassed, as if she didn't know what to do with her hands or her eyes. The afternoon lay before them, long empty hours, and they were now alone. Louis sensed her

351

unease and understood. He threaded his fingers through hers. 'Let's go and swim, lie by the pool and sleep in the sunshine. We have the whole day and I don't want you to waste a moment of it by feeling awkward.' Audrey nodded, grateful that she didn't have to explain that she would feel uncomfortable taking their relationship any further in someone else's house, however understanding he was. She wanted him to make love to her. But not here. Once more she searched his eyes, silently asking him how he came to understand her so well, but they just twinkled back at her, hiding their troubled depths behind a sheen of happiness.

They lay entwined on the grass beside the pool that was green with algae and crumbling around the edges where once there had been neatly laid paving stones. Half overshadowed by trees and shrubs it lay neglected and forgotten for Gaitano was now too old to want to use it and only the children of the gauchos came there to play when the heat became too much. A large gardenia bush unfolded its petals to the sun and filled the air with its rich perfume while bees hummed quietly among the flowers in search of pollen to work into honey which El Chino's son, Gonzalo, collected. Audrey and Louis swam in the murky water to cool off and then chatted softly until they fell asleep in the sunshine. Their sleep was gentle and contented and when they awoke to find each other and the lengthening evening shadows they were once more filled with melancholia and the realisation that the day was now draining away and they would have to return home. As much as they tried to hold onto it the sun hovered behind the trees and the air grew cooler.

*   *   *

Costanza had laid tea out on the terrace and Gaitano had emerged from his siesta. He noticed their solemn mood immediately for having lost a sense he had gained another, finer one. Knowing Louis as he did and understanding Audrey he suggested they bring their teacups into the house. 'I have something to show you,' he said. They followed him into the dark interior of the sitting room, blinking in order to adjust their eyes to the darkness. The room smelt of mothballs and age and was lined with rows of bookshelves. But both Audrey and Louis noticed the piano almost hidden beneath piles of papers. 'This belonged to my wife,' said Gaitano, gesticulating to it. 'My children didn't want it. Will you play for me?' Audrey frowned at Louis, because of course Gaitano couldn't hear. As if sensing her bewilderment Gaitano placed his hand on his chest and smiled at her wistfully. 'I hear with my heart, Audrey. With my heart.' And he sat down expectantly.

Louis didn't hesitate. He pulled up a chair for the stool was too small for both of them and then he began to play. Gaitano threw his head back and chuckled as if he recognised the tune. Audrey sat down and placed her hands on the keys. Louis nodded to her, his face suddenly alive with enthusiasm. She took a deep breath because the last time she had played their tune her heart had been filled with concrete. Now she played it with joy and sadness together because it represented love condemned to the shadows.

Gaitano watched them with glistening eyes. How

353

he longed to hear with his ears but all he had was his heart and that was now failing him too, little by little each day. When it was time for Audrey and Louis to leave he too looked sad and he embraced them as if they were his own children. 'Please come back,' he implored them. 'Whenever you like. I'm always here.' They said they would and they meant it. La Magdalena was a refuge from their own suffocating world and they longed to return.

They drove back up the dusty highway in silence, for a heaviness had descended upon them. They tried to think of what they had to look forward to and they had to remind themselves that they still had each other. They held hands and listened to the radio as the countryside was slowly swallowed up by the buildings of the city. They left behind them the tranquillity of the sleeping pampa and their illusory freedom, and prepared themselves once again for deception. Tonight Audrey would have to find another excuse to banish her husband from the marital bed and Louis would sleep alone, tormented by the scent of her skin still clinging to his. And they would both long for each other, separated only by the walls of the house and the prudence in their hearts. But walls can be broken down and prudence can be abandoned.

As the days passed and Isla's memorial service approached, Audrey knew that it wouldn't be long before she surrendered. It was inevitable and she was ready for it.

CHAPTER TWENTY-THREE

At Isla's funeral Louis had sat at the very back of the church. Twelve years later, at her memorial service, he sat at the very front. Both he and Audrey were aware that it was because of their lies that this celebration of Isla's life was happening at all, and they both felt decidedly uncomfortable about it. Audrey tried to convince herself that her mother only needed the smallest excuse to remember her younger daughter in this way. She would have found something else to centre it around had Louis not turned up. But she knew how ill everyone would think of them if the truth ever came out. Lying about an illicit affair was bad enough but Isla was dead and couldn't speak up for herself. It was shameful, in a church of all places. Audrey stared at the crucifix that stood on the altar, bathed in sunlight that streamed in through the stained-glass window, and remembered with some consolation that she hadn't committed adultery yet, although it was only a matter of time. She was certainly on the road to Hell, but the road was a long one and she was willing to enjoy Louis now and pay for it later in which ever way God thought fit to punish her.

She sat between Louis and her husband in the same row as her parents and brothers. It was a tight squeeze as the boys were no longer children, but she didn't mind because it meant she could discreetly press her body against Louis' without anyone noticing the silent messages that passed between them. She looked at her brother Albert's handsome face. He was a man now, barely resembling the skinny child who used to make houses out of cards for Isla to destroy with one swipe of her mischievous hand. She cast her eyes down the row to her other brothers and in their growing up she noticed more than ever the rapid passing of time. As a child the years had seemed long, now they were gone before one had time to enjoy them.

Cynthia Klein had passed away the previous autumn, buried in the city next to her friend Phyllida Bates. Only Diana Lewis and Charlo Blythe remained as two fragile strings in a once formidable quartet and they were now shrunken versions of their former selves. Diana was hard of hearing, but too proud to admit it, so she just talked over people so that they didn't have the chance to speak and she didn't have the chance to listen. Her mouth had all but disappeared into a distasteful pinch of disillusionment, for if one never smiles one forgets how to and if one's thoughts are only negative one always looks glum. Charlo, on the contrary, had retained her silver dignity and at least had something to be happy about. Although the old Colonel's mind seemed at times caught in the past like a record with a scratch that plays the same music over and over, he was company and Charlo never felt alone. She and Diana rarely spoke these days because Charlo wasn't so interested in gossip as she once had been. She had found happiness and happy people are nice people. Diana had not.

Diana took a seat behind Aunt Hilda and her four daughters, muttering to herself so that no one would talk to her. She noticed Nelly's face was

356

paler than usual and the downward curve of her mouth was beginning to resemble her mother's. Diana wondered if her unhappiness had anything to do with Louis. In spite of what everyone else said about him now, she still thought as little of him as she had when he had first come to Hurlingham. Carrying on with Isla in secret was not a way for a gentleman to behave. She leaned over and looked through the congregation to where Cecil sat beside his wife. Now that's a proper young couple, she thought to herself. Audrey had always been above criticism whereas Isla had only been elevated to that happy position in death. Goodness knows what would have become of her had she lived. She sniffed and opened the service sheet. Louis was giving a reading. 'How very inappropriate', she grumbled under her breath. Then she noticed her scarlet fingers and shrunk back in horror. Blood was everywhere. She was dying. She was about to fall into a faint when she remembered that she had been painting that morning. 'Thank God!' she cried out loud. 'I'm not dead yet.' Nelly turned around and frowned at her. Hilda dug her elbow into her side and Nelly turned back.

'She's mad, Nelly, quite mad. Don't give her any attention or she'll do it again,' she hissed. Diana fanned herself. Death frightened her and the closer she got to it the more frightened she became.

As the service began Audrey caught the eye of Emma Letton who sat with her husband and three children. She suffered a sudden pain as she thought of her own children so far away and smiled sadly at her friend. Emma smiled back, a smile full of compassion for she understood Audrey's despair. It was her sister's memorial service, a reminder of her death, however well meaning and she was bereft of Alicia and Leonora. Emma shifted her eyes to Louis, who stood tall and proud next to her and couldn't help but wonder whether he had only increased the amount of stress on her dear friend's shoulders.

Audrey tried desperately to feel her sister's presence in the spring sunshine and fragrant breeze and watched the candles on the altar in case they mysteriously extinguished themselves again. But if Isla was there in spirit she made no show of herself, only in the memory of all those present as they remembered, through words and song, the ebullient child who had touched them all and then left, so suddenly, that they all still felt the ripples twelve years on.

When Louis stood beneath the nave to read a poem chosen by Rose, Audrey felt a gentle rustle of admiration sweep through the congregation, reaching her at the front of the church like a wave and causing her body to grow hot with resentment. *How fickle people are*, she thought once again, *and how fickle I was. If only I had had the courage to follow my heart.* She watched him with determination. His hands trembled as he read and he didn't once look up from the book in case he lost his place or perhaps for fear that they would see in his eyes the lies he had woven. Audrey felt her whole being swell with love and the unwavering resolve that whatever happened they would have a future together. When he had finished he returned to his place, looking at the rows of people from beneath his tousled fringe. Audrey smiled tenderly at him when he sat down and Cecil nodded his head in a brotherly sort of way, but his face was solemn. Then the two men locked eyes for a long moment so that Audrey wondered what silent communication passed between them. Suddenly Louis' face flushed and he lowered his eyes guiltily, the self-confidence at once undermined by the challenge in his brother's stare. But his sense of shame didn't last for long because he could feel Audrey's warm body pressed against his and his thoughts were distracted from the glare of his brother's scrutiny. Then it was prayers and they were kneeling with their eyes closed, trying to concentrate on what the vicar was saying, but in the darkness they could only make out each other.

It was at the end of the service, when they were filing out, that Audrey's eyes fell upon the chairs at the very back of the church, now emptied of people and cast in shadow because the sun was unable to reach then. She felt her throat tighten with the memory of that final and devastating conversation she had had with Louis. She was unable to recall it without wincing. Suddenly she felt the tears blur her vision and without caring whether Cecil was beside her or far behind her, she threw her arms around Louis. She felt him stiffen, aware that they were in public and that his brother was right behind them. 'I don't want to lose you again,' she whispered into his ear. 'I lost you right here in this very place twelve years ago and I've spent all that time regretting it. Please don't leave me again, I wouldn't survive it this time.'

Louis squeezed her and whispered back, 'I'm not going anywhere without you,' he said. 'I'll wait for you until I die if I have to.' She sniffed and pulled away. Then she noticed his eyes shift their focus to beyond her. She turned to see Cecil approaching them, talking quietly to Rose and Henry. He shot her an inquiring look and she pulled a thin smile in reply to indicate that she was fine, just tearful, but fine. He turned away and continued his conversation with her parents. But his face fell into shadow as once again he was plagued with suspicion.

*　　　*　　　*

Everyone was invited back to Canning Street for drinks and the house vibrated with celebration instead of the grief which had blackened the air twelve years before. Aunt Hilda watched Louis with resentment while Nelly felt his every move even though she was at the other end of the room. Aunt Edna's jolly presence entertained everyone in spite of the debilitating sense of nausea that gripped her every time she thought of Audrey and Louis and the potential volcano they were both sitting on and she couldn't help but notice how Cecil's hands shook as he gulped down inordinate quantities of alcohol. *He used to be such a confident, dazzling young man*, she thought sadly. *Where has Cecil Forrester gone?*

Emma Letton joined Audrey on the sofa while her children ran around draining the dregs from empty wine glasses and eating all the *empanadas*. 'You miss them terribly, don't you?' she said, placing her hand on Audrey's arm to show her support.

'I do,' she replied. 'However much I try to distract myself, I think of nothing but them. What am I to do? My life was my children and now I have nothing.'

'I know how I would feel if Thomas sent ours abroad, I'd be devastated.'

'It's the silence. The terrible silence. I feel so alone.'

'Why don't you have another child?'

'What?'

'Yes. You're still young. Try for a boy?'

'So that Cecil can send him away too? I don't think I can go through it all over again.'

'Of course you can.'

'I wouldn't want to replace Alicia and Leonora. They'd feel I was marginalising them.'

'I think they'd be happy.'

'Then you know Alicia a lot less that I thought you did!' Audrey laughed. 'She'd be furious and Leonora would be so hurt. I couldn't do it to them.' *Besides*, she wanted to add, *Cecil and I aren't even like two ships that pass in the night. We don't even get close.*

Suddenly the sound of music rose up above the chatter of voices. 'Who's playing?' Emma asked, for they were sitting down and couldn't see the piano.

'Louis,' Audrey replied.

Emma sighed in wonder. 'He plays most beautifully,' she gasped. The voices hushed reverentially as the music filled the room squeezing out the last remaining voice that continued oblivious.

'What's going on?' Diana Lewis shouted. 'Has someone died?' Charlo rushed to her assistance and led her out into the hall. 'Why is everyone staring at me, for goodness sake?'

For the first time Audrey heard Louis play something conventional, 'The Warsaw Concerto'.

361

He played it with such emotion that after a while everyone had found somewhere to sit and listen, letting the music take them to places they had never been and inspire in them feelings they had never felt. Everyone was touched by the extravagance of Addinsell and Louis' heartfelt interpretation except Diana Lewis who smouldered in the hall, unable to hear anything but an irritating buzzing. 'Why didn't he play pieces like this at the Hurlingham Club?' Charlo asked her husband in a loud whisper.

The old Colonel shrugged. 'Mighty fine young man, no doubt about it,' he hissed back rather too loudly and Charlo couldn't help but agree. He wasn't the same man who had left them in the wake of Isla's death. He was less troubled. Audrey locked eyes with Cecil who was watching her watching Louis. But she looked away. It wouldn't be long before she committed adultery and her guilt made looking at him almost too agonising. He shifted his eyes to his brother and his shoulders sagged in resignation.

*   *   *

It was late when Audrey crept across the shadows with the same silent steps that she had taken on those nights when Louis had awaited her beneath the cherry tree in the orchard. But this time she had so much more to lose. Spurred on by the dark memory of that fateful conversation in the church she trod softly so as not to wake her husband, then knocked lightly on the door of Louis' bedroom. She had to listen hard for the beating of her heart echoed in her ears against the stillness of the

362

landing and she was unable to hear anything else. She remembered the day in the countryside when they had been alone to enjoy each other and her embarrassment at finding herself in such a position. But tonight it seemed right in spite of Cecil who slept unaware that his wife was making the first decisive step away from him. She hovered at the door knowing she was wicked, trying not to think of her husband or her children but remembering Isla's encouraging grin. *'Have the courage to follow your heart, Audrey'*, she had said and her voice echoed across the years to remind Audrey that life was transient and precious and that love was the greatest gift of all. She would no longer live her life for others but for herself. Didn't she deserve it after so much pain?

The door opened slowly without creaking and she slipped inside. 'I don't want to be alone any more. I need you,' she said in a whisper.

'I knew you'd come tonight.' Louis wrapped his arms around her and kissed her forehead.

'How did you know when I didn't even know myself?'

'Because of what you said in the church. I don't want to be alone any more either.'

'I meant it, Louis. I won't lose you this time. I don't know how we're going to do it, but I won't be without you. I just won't.'

They climbed into bed and lay entwined. She thought she would be nervous, she had only ever made love to her husband, but Louis' touch was so familiar she felt as if she had been this intimate hundreds of times and that with each time it only got more loving.

His kiss was ardent yet tender and all the while

he watched her with those faraway eyes that were no longer faraway to her for the world of dreams that he inhabited had embraced her too. Her senses were overwhelmed with the spicy scent of his skin, the rough sensation of his face and the feel of his body pressed tightly against hers as if wanting to dissolve through her and into her so that their souls could join together as one. She realised afterwards that she had never truly made love before. She had often enjoyed physical closeness to Cecil in a friendly sort of way, but it had never really been about love. Love was what had happened after with the birth of her children. But with Louis she made love, bathed in it, smelt it, wrapped herself around it so that she became it. She had never in her life felt so cherished. Sex was no longer sexual but spiritual and she felt blessed that she had experienced physical love in its purest form. 'It could always have been like this,' she said as she lay against him, her hot body cooled by the breeze that swept in to witness their union.

'And it will be, I promise you,' he replied, his fingers playing with the curls that spread out across her shoulders. In the rarefied air of their love they both believed it was possible.

*   *   *

In the weeks that followed they snatched moments together when Cecil was at work or asleep in his bed. They rode out across the pampa while Gaitano watched from the terrace. They danced across the sitting-room floor when Mercedes was too busy with Oscar to notice or even care and they played the piano as the evening shadows ate into

364

the precious hours and filled them once again with that sweet melancholy, as familiar to them now as an old, trusted friend.

But as much as Audrey was dazed with love she was not blinded by it. She was aware that her husband was drinking too much. He'd arrive home in the evening with alcohol on his breath and reach for the decanter before even speaking. He no longer lingered at her bedroom door, gazing on her hopefully, ready to mend the cracks in their marriage or at least to forget in the darkness that they were there. He retreated to his study after dinner leaving his brother and his wife to play the piano together as if he knew he was being betrayed but didn't have the will to confront them. And Audrey let it go on because she knew that the moment she spoke about it their marriage would be over. She longed to run off with Louis, but the twins would be home for the holidays in a few weeks. She would have to wait until they were back at school before she made any decisions. Louis didn't press her or even ask her to discuss their future.

'Let's just live in the moment,' he said. Audrey was only too happy to oblige.

CHAPTER TWENTY-FOUR

Cicely was sorry to see the twins return to the Argentine for Christmas. She had enjoyed having them for half-term and on the odd exeat weekend. Leonora had helped Panazel and Florien in the garden, planting bulbs and picking fruit while

Alicia had insisted on bringing her friend Mattie, whom Cicely didn't much like. She was an arrogant child and sulky. Alicia would disappear with her onto the farm and get up to God knows what kind of mischief. Cicely had once caught them tormenting Florien, not that she had minded, the boy was quite capable of looking after himself, but they made an unattractive duo. They had ignored Leonora most of the time and if it hadn't been for the gypsies Cicely would have had to say something, but Leonora was quite happy playing in the caravans and listening to Masha's stories. 'I should like to be a gypsy,' she had said. 'I would love to live in a caravan and work in the garden all day. It's a lovely life.' Alicia and Mattie had scoffed, screwing up their pretty noses condescendingly.

'You're so simple,' they had teased unkindly. 'We're going to make something of ourselves, be famous, not some silly gypsy watching the world go by in a muddy field!' To Cicely's amazement Leonora continued to look up to her sister with the kind of adoration that requests nothing in return. She didn't seem to blame Alicia for her wickedness, although she was obviously hurt. She regained her composure with dignity then wagged her tail again like Barley.

Cicely had grown tremendously fond of Leonora. She was an endearing child and unspoiled, unlike her sister: as loving as Audrey was to her two daughters, she had unwittingly ruined Alicia. She had been born with all the physical advantages and yet Leonora had been given the greatest advantage of all, a beautiful nature. Cicely wasn't that unhappy to see Alicia go,

366

but when she looked out onto the garden to see only Panazel and his son pottering in the borders, her heart yearned for the plain little girl with the sensitive face and gentle smile who longed for nothing more than the simple life of a gypsy. Barley missed her too. He used to lie on the grass watching her in her muddy jeans and gumboots, waiting for her to take him on a long walk around the fields and woods. Now he seemed rootless, following Cicely instead but distinctly dissatisfied.

She had driven the twins to the airport and seen them onto the aeroplane. They had both been consumed with excitement, rushing around like a couple of young dogs. She had had to have sharp words with Alicia who had teased Leonora for taking Saggy Rabbit onto the plane in her hand luggage. 'You can be very unkind sometimes,' she had said in exasperation. 'When you're unkind you look extremely ugly.' She hoped that the fear of looking unattractive might have some effect. Alicia was very vain.

Now she was at home and the house was quiet and cold. Very cold. She lit fires and piled on the jerseys and rushed around to keep warm. Only Marcel was allowed the luxury of a gas heater for he complained he had to break the ice on the water beaker before he could put his brush into it. 'I simply cannot paint with frozen hands, *mon amour*,' he complained, gazing at her with his dark, Gallic eyes. 'And I cannot call upon you to warm me up whenever my body trembles with cold. As much as I would like to make love to you all day, my dormant creativity would torment me.' Cicely longed for the nights when his dormant creativity remained dormant, but during the day he

367

requested that he be left alone to work. What he was working on she had no idea. Sometimes she wondered whether he did any work at all.

*   *   *

Audrey, Aunt Edna and Rose were at Buenos Aires airport to meet the twins. It was a hot December day, the air heavy and sticky so that they had to fan themselves to keep cool. They stood on the roof in the sunshine and watched the plane transformed from a mere glint in the distance to the large and powerful airbus that was bringing their precious girls home. Audrey had been counting the days and writing daily, even when she knew they'd be home before they received the letters. Louis was a blessed distraction but she never forgot, not for a moment. Their little faces lingered at the forefront of her mind and her spirit quietly yearned for them even when she was in her lover's arms.

When Leonora saw her mother she dissolved into tears and threw her arms about her. The journey had been long and tiring and Alicia had sulked all the way after Cicely had told her off. Audrey cuddled her back and kissed her forehead lovingly, relieved that she smelt the same. Leonora, choked with happiness, was unable to speak. She clung to her mother like a monkey, even when she embraced Alicia and even when they set off in the car. There was nothing that was going to make her let go. She had missed her more than she had ever admitted and now she had her back she wanted to hold her, to verify that she was real and the same mother as the one she dreamed about.

Alicia cheered up as soon as she had an

audience. Aunt Edna drove and Rose sat in the passenger seat, leaving Audrey in the back with the twins. 'Froggie, our French teacher has such bad breath we put toothpaste in her cup of tea,' she said and giggled.

'Surely she can't really be called Froggie?' Audrey exclaimed, so happy to have her daughters back.

'No, she's really called Madame Duval, but we call her Froggie behind her back. She eats too much garlic. And we have midnight feasts all the time, just like in the storybooks. Leo doesn't, she's too scared. She's a goodie goodie.'

'I hope so,' said Aunt Edna. She wanted to add that it was Alicia's wickedness that got them both sent away to England in the first place.

'I heard all about Art Club, Leonora. What a responsibility that is,' Rose enthused. Leonora was snuggled up against her mother, sucking her thumb and rubbing her nose with Saggy Rabbit's furry ears.

'Gussie brings us tea and cakes on Thursday afternoons,' she said quietly. 'I like Gussie.'

'Well, she clearly likes you too.'

'I hate art. I prefer gym. I'm very good at gym, Miss Pole says so,' said Alicia. 'Do you know, there's a stable boy called Larry who speaks with a lisp? Do you know what a lisp is?'

'Of course,' said Audrey.

'He can't say Alicia, he says Alithia.' She laughed heartily. 'Mattie says he's retarded because he can't talk properly.' Leonora knew how much Mattie and Alicia teased him but she wasn't about to betray her sister. Fortunately Larry was a bit unusual, for he didn't realise they were being cruel

369

and enjoyed the attention. 'Tho, Alithia, I'll thaddle up Thalty for you,' she continued mockingly. Rose and Aunt Edna weren't in the slightest bit amused but Audrey squeezed Alicia and kissed her temple, regardless.

At home, Mercedes was waiting on the doorstep with Loro and Oscar. Alicia squealed with excitement and tumbled out of the car as fast as she could. 'My dear child,' sighed the old cook. 'You've grown an inch, I'm sure of it.'

'Did you get all my letters?' she asked, wrapping her arms around Mercedes' thick waist.

'Of course, at least they teach you how to write over there in England.'

'That's not all they teach us. I can speak French, you know.'

'What good will that do you?'

'I'll talk to Frenchmen.'

'You want to avoid those at all costs,' she said in her lazy drawl, recalling the French sailor she once tussled with in the port. It had been a short but fruitful union because nine months later Tomas had arrived with his dark skin and languid eyes and hadn't suffered from the childhood illnesses that plagued her other children. Obviously from all that garlic careering through his veins, she had deduced.

Oscar carried Loro on his shoulder, feeding him sunflower seeds to keep him quiet in case he revealed the torrid affair he was now enjoying with Mercedes at the back of the kitchen between cups of coffee. Cecil heard the commotion and stepped outside. In his hand he held a tumbler of whisky and his smile, once so dazzling and straight, was now loose and unhappy. He kissed Alicia on the

370

forehead and then Leonora, patting them both like Aunt Cicely had done the first time she had met them at the station.

Rose and Aunt Edna were aware of Cecil's drinking problem but didn't feel it was their place to get involved. Rose couldn't understand what had driven him to seek consolation in the bottle, whereas Aunt Edna knew. If Louis was going to remain in Hurlingham then she would have to have quiet words with her niece. It had been weeks since he had arrived and he was still living with them. It was most unhealthy, she thought anxiously, pitying Cecil who had loved Audrey from the day he had met her. She knew her niece was angry with him for sending their daughters away to boarding school but adultery was not a suitable punishment. It would only bring unhappiness and her children would be the ones who suffered most in the long run. She watched Audrey, so obviously happy. She was a mother first and a wife second. She wondered where Louis fit in and what their plans were. Surely they couldn't go on like this indefinitely. *Perhaps*, she thought hopefully, *now the twins are back, she'll see sense and finish the affair. Audrey is a sensible girl, she's bound to do the right thing in the end.*

Alicia disappeared into the kitchen with Mercedes while Leonora followed her mother onto the terrace with her father, aunt and grandmother. 'So tell me, Leonora, how is it going at Colehurst House?' Cecil asked. Audrey poured the iced lemon that Mercedes had left on the table and handed one to her daughter, who drained the glass thirstily.

'I like it,' she said.

'Good,' he replied. 'And Aunt Cicely?'

'I like her a lot.'

'I am pleased.'

'She has a family of gypsies living in one of her fields. They help about the garden and in the harvest time and I help them too.'

'Good.'

'They have the strangest names,' she said and her eyes shone cheerfully. 'Panazel, Masha, Florien and Ravena . . .' she began and then she told them all about her new friends and how much she wanted to be a gypsy when she grew up. Cecil half listened to his daughter while he focused his full attention on his wife. She looked beautiful. Aglow with happiness. He now regretted having sent the girls away. His intentions had been good and he was giving them the best education money could buy but it hadn't been worth sacrificing his wife. Ever since he declared he wanted to send them to England their relationship had deteriorated. He barely had a relationship at all any more. There was no doubt that she preferred the company of his brother. How far it went he could only guess at. He wasn't a fool but he was realistic. He hoped she'd come back to him in time. He'd give her all the time she wanted the same as he always had. Meanwhile he felt better with a bit of drink inside him. It dulled the pain and raised his expectations. He would have confronted his enemy in his army days, but this enemy had the one thing in his possession that he couldn't risk losing. Audrey's heart. So he'd put his head in the sand like the neighbouring ostrich and hoped it would resolve itself. Louis, who had spent the day with Gaitano in order to give Audrey time alone to enjoy her

372

children, arrived in time for supper. The twins barely noticed him until he played the piano. 'Teach me, teach me!' Alicia demanded when her mother told her that he had taught music in Mexico. Leonora, who had started taking lessons at school, showed him what she had learnt, her nervous little fingers stumbling through the music. But Louis was enchanted. 'You'll make a very good player, Leonora. Now try this,' he said, sitting down next to her and playing a chord. 'Then this,' he added, playing another and soon they were both side by side on the stool, playing in tandem.

'Me next, me next!' Alicia cried, jumping from one foot to the other. 'I want to learn how to play. Why don't I take lessons at school like Leo?'

'Because you didn't want to,' her mother replied.

'Well, I do now. Will Louis be here all holiday?' she asked hopefully.

'I don't know, you'll have to ask him.'

'Will you?'

'If you want me to,' he said and chuckled.

'Only if you teach me to play the piano,' she said seriously.

'It's a deal then. If your parents don't mind me sharing the Christmas pudding.' Audrey laughed lightly, Cecil stiffened but Leonora and Alicia were enchanted.

'Aunt Cicely made the pudding for us and the mince pies. It'll be a proper English Christmas,' said Leonora excitedly. 'Father Christmas comes all the way out here, you know.'

'I'm glad to hear it,' Louis replied. 'Have you written your wish list?'

'Wish list?' the twins replied in unison.

'Well, you have to write a list and burn it up the

373

chimney, that way Father Christmas's little helpers receive it and make sure they get you the presents you want. Only if you've been very good. Have you?'

'Oh yes!' they replied. Alicia knew she hadn't been very good, but if Father Christmas was like everyone else she had met, he would bring her presents all the same.

'Well, don't hang around, go and get pencils and paper and let's do it now. There's no time to waste,' he instructed urgently. The two girls rushed off upstairs and Louis caught Audrey's eye. She was looking at him tenderly. The way she should have been looking at Cecil. But she hadn't looked at Cecil in that way for a long long time.

*   *   *

Mercedes studied the black ball called Christmas Pudding and knitted her thick eyebrows together. It didn't look like anything she had ever seen before. It was heavy too. Like a cannon ball. Would do about as much damage as a cannon ball, she thought, dropping it onto the sideboard with a loud thud. Loro squawked in his cage, *'Te quiero, te adoro, te amo . . .'* then tried as best he could to imitate a heavy pant. That was when Mercedes lost her temper. She could cope with Oscar's declarations of love because they were touching. They reminded her of her youth when she had lain underneath the weighty body of a handsome sailor or the skinny one of a delivery boy, listening to their hollow promises, delivered with eyes closed between shallow breaths, and believing them. Now she listened to them but she didn't believe; she was

374

too old and too cynical for love. But there was nothing romantic or touching about the panting. It was too carnal, too bestial and this time Loro had gone too far.

She strode purposefully over to the cage where Loro was hopping about in a state of post-coital exhaustion. '*Ahhhhh . . .*' he gurgled.

'Loro, I've had quite enough of you!' she cried, opening the cage. 'I'll pluck you and cook you alive, you'll see.' Loro resisted as her brown hand reached in and grabbed him about his scrawny neck. Alicia's mirror idea had worked for now his feathery coat was thick and glossy again. Not that Mercedes cared; she was going to get rid of him once and for all.

There was a pot of boiling water on the stove and Mercedes dangled the terrified bird above it so that the steam engulfed him. He let out a strangled gasp, fixed her with eyes that reflected her own cruel expression and waited for death. But Mercedes was a softhearted woman underneath and was unable to inflict pain on another living creature, however exasperating. She dropped her shoulders in defeat and pulled him out of the steam. 'You are an idiotic creature. It's not right to punish you for being stupid. God created you that way. But what He was thinking at that moment, only He knows. Still, all God's work is divine, even you.' And she put him back in his cage where he shook out his feathers and sulked in the corner, trembling still.

She returned to the black cannon ball and recalled Señora Forrester's instructions. Tomorrow was Christmas and this was what they were going to eat for their pudding.

Alicia and Leonora awoke at dawn to the delicious sensation of weighty stockings sitting expectantly on the end of their beds. Leonora sat up with Saggy Rabbit and dragged the large woollen stocking up to where she could have a better look at it. Stuffed with presents all neatly wrapped up in tissue paper, it was irresistible. Alicia emptied the whole lot onto the bed then proceeded to unwrap one. 'You mustn't open them now!' Leonora exclaimed in horror. 'We must open them on Mummy and Daddy's bed.'

'I'm only opening one,' she replied, throwing the paper onto the floor. 'A hair band.' She screwed her nose up. 'I think this would be more appropriate for you.'

'Don't you like it?'

'Mummy could have done a little better than a hair band.'

Leonora was disappointed that Alicia didn't want to indulge in make-believe. She knew Father Christmas wasn't real and that her father placed the stockings at the end of their beds before he retired after dinner. But the magic of the tradition enchanted her and she wished she was still small and didn't know the truth. Alicia thought the whole event overrated. 'I don't know why they bother going through with the pretence, after all we're not children any more,' she complained.

'Because it gives them pleasure,' Leonora retaliated.

'So we have to pretend we don't know it's them to give them pleasure?'

'Yes.'

'It seems very silly to me,' she scoffed. 'But I'll do it for one reason only.'

'What's that?'

'Because if we let on we know they might stop stockings altogether and I like presents.'

'But not hair bands.'

'One wrong, lots more to go. What's the time? Can't we go in now and wake them up? It's light outside.'

* * *

It was six in the morning. Dawn had already broken, painting the sky with streaks of golden honey and the trees were alive with birds making the most of the cool morning air before the heat and the humidity of midsummer grew too intense and sent them deep into the branches to seek shade among the leaves. Audrey lay beside her husband having asked him to return in order to put on a show of togetherness for the children. Cecil was grateful to find himself invited back into the marital bed, hoping that once the twins returned to school the habit would have been established and he would be permitted to stay. Audrey knew in her heart that the children would have thought nothing of it had they found their father sleeping in his dressing room. He had often slept there and she could always have made the excuse that his snoring kept her awake. No, the real reason she had asked him back was that she needed to prevent her own nocturnal wanderings. She couldn't risk being caught with Louis by the children but she wasn't strong enough to resist him. With Cecil in her bed there was no chance of escaping down the corridor. She lamented her lack of willpower, but this was the only way. Once more Cecil was seized with doubt. Had he once again misjudged his wife?

Louis had been incandescent with rage when Audrey had told him that Cecil would be returning to her bed while the children were at home. He had disappeared to Gaitano's ranch for the day to vent his anger riding out across the pampa. Not because he envisaged nights without her, but because he envisaged nights where his brother replaced him in her arms and he couldn't tolerate what he saw as a hideous betrayal. Either the fresh country air or Gaitano's piano had assuaged his fury for he had returned that evening with his wide smile and twinkling eyes conveying once again his hope. Audrey loved him and that was all that mattered. But he too lay awake as dawn illuminated the empty space in his bed where she used to lie and he wondered how long it would be before they were free to love each other in the open.

Audrey's mind was somewhere beyond the realms of time and space when it was brought back to her room with a jolt. There was a gentle knocking at the door and then it opened to reveal two small faces aglow with excitement. The gloom of finding herself in her own bed lifted when she saw her daughters and her heart flooded with joy. She sat up and beckoned them in. Cecil groaned as the twins climbed into the space between them, pulling their stockings onto their knees, uniting them in their duties as parents in a way that nothing else could. Leonora placed Saggy Rabbit carefully on the eiderdown before pulling out the first gift. Alicia poured the contents of the stocking over her father and tore at the wrapping with impatient fingers. Cecil closed his eyes and slept through his hangover while Audrey commented softly on each present, relishing every moment, aware that soon the holidays would be over and she'd be without them again.

*   *   *

Christmas lunch involved the whole family. Henry and Rose arrived with armfuls of gifts to place beneath Audrey's tree that the twins had decorated with painted stars they had made in art class at school. Aunt Edna came with them, her chins wobbling with humour in spite of the anxiety that curdled her blood each time she saw Audrey and Louis glancing wistfully at each other across the room. Aunt Hilda must have forced Nelly to come for her face was paler than usual and her eyes red from crying. She sulked from the moment she stepped into the house, barely able to look at Louis without tears brimming in her eyes. Albert stood by the piano smoking cigarettes while Louis sat between the twins playing Christmas carols all together with six hands. The younger brothers, George and Edward, lay on their backs in the sunshine discussing girls and football for their parent's and aunts' conversations on the terrace bored them.

'I am looking forward to your sister's Christmas pudding,' said Aunt Edna to Cecil, passing a greedy tongue over thick lips.

'So am I,' he replied. 'It'll make me feel very nostalgic for home.'

'You should have seen Mercedes' face when I

showed her how to cook it,' said Audrey, laughing. 'I don't think she'd ever seen anything like it in all her life.'

'At least she didn't have to cook it from scratch,' Aunt Edna continued, her mouth watering at the thought of lunch.

'She'd have made a total mess of it, I'm sure,' Aunt Hilda interjected sourly.

'It'll be delicious,' Audrey reassured them. 'Leonora brought it all the way over from England in her luggage. It's the heaviest pudding you've ever seen. Poor girl.'

'Well, on that note, shall we eat?' Cecil suggested and Audrey nodded.

'Come on, boys, time to eat,' she shouted to her brothers, then poked her head around the door to tell the pianists. Louis looked up and smiled at her affectionately. His eyes seemed to be saying, *I wish we were alone out there on the pampa,'* and she put her head on one side and smiled back. But her heart was already being pulled in two directions.

*   *   *

They all sat around the long table that Mercedes had prepared beneath the trees in the far corner of the garden. The heat was as oppressive as Hilda's ill humour and Nelly's unrequited love, but if anyone noticed they didn't show it, but dug into the Christmas turkey with enthusiasm. Audrey rested her eyes on her daughters. Leonora sat next to Aunt Edna and her grandfather, watched closely by Saggy Rabbit who peeped out from behind the water jug. Alicia was holding forth about herself, entertaining Albert with her stories that got more

380

and more outrageous as he encouraged her with his hearty belly laughs. Audrey felt her heart inflate with love as she watched them, and then Leonora glanced at her and her little face flowered into a wide smile, the smile of a child who knows beyond any shadow of doubt that she has her mother's unconditional love.

Cecil watched his wife. He always watched her for she was the sole focus of his existence. Like a perfect apple at the very top of the tree, Audrey remained out of reach and unattainable. She belonged to him in name only. He remembered that evening on the beach in Uruguay when she had agreed to be his wife, tainted now with hindsight, for he asked himself over and over again, had she ever loved him? He drained his glass and reached for the wine bottle.

Then Mercedes walked up the lawn with a large silver dish. 'Ah, the Christmas pudding!' Aunt Edna exclaimed, rubbing her soft hands together in anticipation of Cicely's famous dessert, brandy butter and cream.

'Indeed, what a treat,' Henry agreed. 'And you brought it all the way over from England, you clever girl,' he said to Leonora.

'I helped her carry it,' Alicia interjected, keen to share the praise.

'And you're clever too,' said Rose, turning to watch the maid shuffle across the grass. When she reached them they all stared at the tray in horror. There lay the Christmas pudding, not in the tidy round ball they had all expected, but in crumbs.

'Good God, what have you done with it?' Aunt Hilda gasped for Audrey was too surprised to speak. Mercedes, who rarely blushed, turned the colour of the cherry that lay among the rubble. She frowned and shook her head.

'Señora,' she said, turning to Audrey. 'I did everything you told me to. Then as I was putting it on the tray I noticed a glint of metal. Well, I can't have one of the children choking on a piece of metal so I carefully dug it out with a knife. It was a coin. A coin of all things! In a pudding! Then I saw another, then another. In the end I had to pull the whole pudding apart, there were twenty coins. Twenty coins, *imagináte*! How they got in there is nobody's business.'

At that explanation Louis exploded into laughter. He laughed so much that he had to hold his stomach and bend over. Alicia and Leonora laughed too until everyone except Aunt Hilda and Nelly joined in the merriment. Mercedes watched them all as if they were creatures from a different planet.

'It doesn't matter, Mercedes,' Audrey reassured her, biting her lip in an effort to control herself. When Mercedes sulked she could sulk for days. 'It'll taste the same. Aunt Edna, why don't you help yourself?'

CHAPTER TWENTY-FIVE

The Christmas holidays dwindled from weeks into days until the twins' return to England was no longer a vague date on the horizon but a fixed day branded on their minds. They enjoyed long rides in the early morning, before the midday heat compelled them to seek comfort in the cool blue water of the swimming pool and played tennis in the evenings with the other children who moved around the Club in a pack. Leonora looked on them enviously, knowing that she and her sister were going to spend the Easter holiday and the English summer holiday with Aunt Cicely in England. She couldn't talk to Alicia about her fears because her sister longed to return to school and didn't seem to miss their parents at all. Her heart was surely made of stone.

While the twins took part in gymkhanas, fêtes and tournaments at the Club, Audrey's snatched moments alone with Louis were few and fleeting. Their hopes simmered in their hearts, quietly, unobtrusively until they reached boiling point and could be ignored no longer.

Louis strode purposefully into Audrey's bedroom. Cecil was at work and the house was empty for Mercedes took a siesta in the afternoon and emerged from her memories only at teatime. Audrey was putting away the clothes that Mercedes had washed, her thoughts deep in an imaginary future where she and Louis and the twins were one happy family together in the land of makebelieve. She thought Louis had gone out for the day and was surprised when his ardent face appeared around her door.

'I thought you were at Gaitano's,' she said as he drew her into his arms.

'I came back early. We need to talk and we never seem to have more than minutes these days.' Then his voice cracked and his face turned grey. 'Audrey, I can't go on like this any more.'

She gave a sad smile and ran her fingers across the frown that had dug trenches into his forehead.

'I know, Louis. What are we going to do?'

'Let's run away together. Once the twins have gone to England. We'll join them there. Start a life together, you, me and the girls. Then you won't miss them any more and you won't miss me either.' She hesitated.

'I can't break it to Cecil,' she said. 'I'll write a note, explain everything in writing. I've never been very good at communicating with him. I can't bear to see his hurt face. In spite of our differences, I'm very fond of him. I just don't love him like I love you.'

'We'll take a plane and sort everything out once we've arrived in England.' Then when he saw her face shadow with doubt he added firmly, 'You can't go on living your life for other people. One day your parents will be dead and you'll be left with Cecil and the remains of a sense of duty that will no longer matter.'

'You're right.'

'I'm not asking you to leave your children, my love. I would never ask that of you, or want to. They are the most important people in your life and I understand that. They should never have been sent away in the first place.' Audrey thought of leaving the country she had grown up in and considered home, but then before she could miss it she remembered that feeling of freedom she had felt on the *Alcantara*, gazing out onto the horizon of endless possibilities.

'I'm frightened,' she confessed, resting her head against his chest. 'I love you and am prepared to give everything up for you. But I'm still afraid.'

'I know,' he whispered, stroking her hair and kissing her forehead. 'I'm frightened too.'

'You are?'

'Yes, frightened of losing you again.'

'Oh, Louis,' she sighed. 'You'll never lose me now, I promise.'

They planned their trip and cast their dreams across the waters to England but neither dared think beyond for beyond lay a mist of uncertainty.

*   *   *

As if Aunt Edna sensed their plans she arranged to meet her niece for tea at the Club while the twins rode out across the plains with their Uncle Albert and his girlfriend, Susan. Audrey suspected nothing of her aunt's intentions and greeted her warmly. But Edna noticed the strain behind the smile and was determined to get to the bottom of it once and for all.

'So the twins fly to England in a few days,' she said, pouring them both a cup of tea. 'I shall miss them very much.'

'I can't bear it,' Audrey replied sadly. 'They won't be home for a year. A year is a long, long time to be away from home and one's family.'

'All for a good education,' Edna sniffed disapprovingly.

'I can't believe it's worth it. But I'll spend more time in England with Cicely. Perhaps I'll get a place of my own.' She hesitated, taking care to choose the right words. 'I don't want to be a burden to Cicely.'

'I'm sure you're not a burden, my dear. And besides, England is not your home.'

'No, it isn't. But it's where my children will be. I want it to be a home for them. In time they'll feel

385

more at home there than here, I'm sure of it.'

'Leonora is a charming little girl. She's very dear. I'm immensely fond of her.'

'She's a good girl,' Audrey agreed proudly. 'She hasn't her sister's advantages . . .'

'Or her nature, thank the Lord. One Alicia is bad enough,' Edna interjected warily. 'She's a little too beautiful for her own good.'

'She is very beautiful, isn't she?'

'But Leonora's got the nicer nature.' For a moment Audrey looked offended and Edna remembered that a mother's love is often blind. Audrey was unaware of Alicia's narcissism, or at least, she didn't want to know. 'Alicia's a joy, of course,' she continued diplomatically, she wasn't here to talk about the children. 'I see they've bonded with Louis.' At the mention of his name the apples of Audrey's cheeks shone crimson. She lowered her eyes and played with her scone.

'He's been teaching them how to play the piano. They adore him,' she replied.

'He's good with children.'

'He's a big child himself. He can relate to them.'

'How unlike his brother he is,' she remarked carefully.

'Yes,' Audrey replied cagily.

The conversation was beginning to grow awkward. Tact wasn't one of Aunt Edna's finer qualities, she grew frustrated with skating around issues, preferring to come clean and discuss things openly. So she took a deep breath and put her teacup down. 'What are you going to do, my dear? You can't very well go on like this, can you?'

'I don't know,' Audrey replied evasively. She recalled her aunt's comments on the doorstep the day she had returned from England. There was no point pretending she didn't know what she was talking about.

'Is Louis going to stay here?'

'I think he's planning to return to England.'

'Ah,' Aunt Edna sighed knowingly. There was a weighty pause before she continued, fixing her niece with eyes that brimmed with compassion. 'That is why you want your own home in England.' Audrey opened her mouth to respond but her aunt ignored her and continued to speak. 'You can't live two lives, Audrey. What will the twins think when they find you and Louis living together in England? They'll think it mighty odd, won't they? Will you tell Cecil or live a secret life?'

'Aunt Edna, you've got it all wrong,' Audrey protested, but her aunt tilted her head to one side and narrowed her eyes.

'Dear girl, I didn't come down in yesterday's snowstorm. I've lived too and loved. I know what it is like to love someone and lose them.'

'Sunshine Harry,' said Audrey, stirring her cup with a silver spoon.

'Dear Harry. I loved him more than life itself and I lost him. I can't get him back. I know what it is like to grieve.' She placed a warm hand on Audrey's forearm. 'Dear girl, what I'm trying to say is that one recovers and gets on with things. At first it seems as if your heart will never mend. You wander around in your own private Hell that no one else can see into. They can't believe how much you are suffering. But time is a great healer. You love Louis with all your heart and you lost him. Now he's come back again I well understand that you don't want to lose him again. But there's much

387

more at stake now. There's Cecil to think of and the children. Divorce is a very dirty word and dirt sticks wherever you are in the world.'

A tear dropped into Audrey's teacup and she spoke in a very quiet voice. 'I married Cecil because I knew it was what Mummy and Daddy expected and after Isla's death I wanted to make them happy. I did the right thing. I married him for them. But I never stopped loving Louis. I love him more now than I did then. Don't you see, I've been given a second chance?' She looked at her aunt with solicitous eyes, but Edna only shook her head.

'No you haven't. Louis is a temptation to be resisted at all costs. You will only bring unhappiness to all those who love you. Can you build your happiness on that?'

Audrey withdrew her arm and bowed her head in defeat. 'I can't live my life for other people,' she said.

'Loving is about sacrifice, my dear Audrey. You made your choice and it was the right choice. Cecil loves you. He's a good, honest man and don't tell me that you aren't fond of him too. You might not love him in the same way that you love his brother, but you do care about him. You're a compassionate young woman and I understand you. You built a life with Cecil and you have two beautiful daughters. You have a responsibility to them. Cecil sacrificed his own feelings in order to give them the best education money can buy. Now you must sacrifice your love for Louis in order to give them stability and pride. How can they hold their heads up if you have run off with their uncle? What will their friends say? How heartbroken do you think they will be? Don't imagine for one moment that

388

your actions won't affect all those around you. Bring shame upon your own head if that is what you want, but don't hurt those two innocent people. You owe them a future without shame.' Another tear plopped into Audrey's tea. She didn't want to hear any more. Her conscience had tried to tell her and she hadn't listened. She now wished Aunt Edna would go and leave her alone with her thoughts and her hopes that were fast unravelling like a beautiful tapestry of dreams.

There was a long silence while Aunt Edna asked the waiter for another plate of scones and Audrey sat staring at the tea leaves that had collected at the bottom of her cup. 'My dear child,' Aunt Edna said finally. Her voice was gentle and made Audrey want to cry again. She could cope with fury but sympathy debilitated her completely. 'When you were a little girl I imagined your future would be blessed, because you had been born with an easy nature as well as beauty. Isla, on the other hand, was sure to court disaster because she was born with a more complicated nature. No one could ever have predicted this. But I know you, my dear, and love you very much. That is why I can tell you that you won't run off with Louis. Your sense of duty is too strong and always has been. People don't really change on the whole. But your situation has. You know in your heart that you have too much to lose. I know you don't welcome my advice. I am the voice of your conscience. But I will give it to you anyway.' She placed her hand on Audrey's arm again and looked her steadily in the eye. 'Light a candle for Louis and keep it burning. But let him go and save yourself and your family from this tempest that can only damage you all. No one

389

knows what the future holds but it is in your hands to shape it, for you and your children. It is your choice. I know you will do the right thing.'

*   *   *

Audrey rode across the plains at a gallop. The wind streamed through her hair and swept away her tears before they had time to touch her cheeks. She was furious. Furious with Aunt Edna for voicing her own secret doubts and furious at herself for succumbing to them. Thoughts of Louis, her children and Cecil crowded her mind and clashed with each other in an imaginary battle of wills. What would Isla have done? She knew. Isla would have stuck her pretty nose in the air and eloped with him before any of this had happened. She wouldn't have let him go in the first place, even in the wake of her sister's funeral. She certainly wouldn't have married Cecil. But if she had she would have whipped up a scandal to beat all scandals and run off with Louis, leaving those around her to pick up the pieces and nurse their broken hearts. They'd all survive it and move on. That's what people did. They survived. Why couldn't she be more like Isla?

She heard the echo of her aunt's words and as fast as she galloped she couldn't outrun them. *'I know you'll do the right thing.'* What if she didn't do the right thing? What then? As she gazed out at the immense sky and wide open plain she felt her unhappiness lift and a dizzy sensation of determination fill her. It was still her choice. She loved Louis and had her whole life ahead of her. She wasn't going to let herself waste away in a

390

miserable marriage. She'd surprise them all. *People do change*, she thought rebelliously. *I've had enough of being the sensible sister. Oh Isla, if you can hear me, help me to be more like you.*

*   *   *

Later that day, when she sat across the table from Louis, listening to the twins recount their day at the Club, how Leonora had won the egg and spoon race and how Alicia had poured pepper in the buckets of water before the other children bobbed for apples, she knew she had made the right decision. She loved everything about him, to the extent that her spirit ached beneath the weight of so much tenderness. She loved his deep melancholic eyes that always appeared distracted for he saw the world in a different shade to everyone else. She loved the way his hands often trembled for no reason and his fingers twitched in search of the imaginary piano he played all the time. She loved his mouth that could suddenly open into a wide, infectious smile and then just as suddenly fall into misery, reflecting the turmoil of a heart not quite like others. She loved the man inside whom no one else knew or understood but her and he loved her back equally. When she focused her eyes again she saw that he was staring back at her, his face aglow with affection and gratitude because she had promised that she would never be lost to him, ever.

*   *   *

Finally the day of the twins' departure arrived.

Alicia scrambled out of bed in a fever of excitement while Leonora pushed herself further down beneath the sheets of her mother's bed and cried. She was inconsolable. Even when Aunt Edna and her grandmother arrived for breakfast armed with more gifts for them to take to England.

Cecil had said good-bye before catching the train as usual into the city and Audrey quietly fumed, wondering how he could have the heart to work on a morning such as this. But she didn't complain for Louis was there to wrap his arms around Leonora and dance with her about the room until her face blossomed into a reluctant smile. That was before the search for Saggy Rabbit.

Saggy Rabbit had disappeared and Leonora refused to leave for the airport until she found him. The whole house was turned upside down in search of the floppy brown toy that had become irreplaceable to Leonora. 'I'm not leaving without him,' she sobbed. She loved him with the intensity of a child who has spent long months away from friends and family.

'He must be somewhere,' Audrey exclaimed in exasperation. She was almost buckling under the pressure of having to say good-bye to her daughters and prepare her getaway the following day with Louis.

'Can't you buy her another one?' said Alicia to Aunt Edna.

'Of course I can,' she lied. 'There are lots where he comes from.'

'But I don't want another one. I want Saggy Rabbit. He'll be miserable without me,' Leonora wailed.

Alicia rolled her eyes. 'He's only a toy,' she said

sulkily.

'No he's not. He's my friend,' Leonora responded with a ferociousness that astounded her sister.

'I've searched her bedroom twice,' said Rose, shaking her head. 'I can't imagine where he's gone. Did you take him to the Club, dear?'

Leonora shook her head.

'I had him last night,' she replied. 'I always sleep with him.'

'He's not down my bed,' said Audrey. 'Oh dear,' she sighed. 'What are we going to do?'

'He'll probably turn up once you've gone,' said Louis kindly. 'We'll take great care of him and I'll bring him to you personally when I fly to England.'

'You promise?' Leonora sniffed and wiped her nose on her arm.

Louis knelt down and drew the trembling child into his arms. 'I promise,' he said and kissed her wet face. 'He'll be safe with me.'

So Leonora was persuaded to fly without Saggy Rabbit. Audrey, Edna, Rose and Louis stood on the roof at the airport and waved off the two little girls for another year. Edna and Rose were reduced to tears while Audrey just watched, pale and anxious, as Alicia walked across the tarmac with her arm around Leonora. Then their faces appeared in the small round window of the plane. She couldn't see that Leonora was crying, but felt sure she was and her throat ached. Louis put a hand on her back, the most he could do to comfort her without raising suspicion. 'You'll see them soon,' he whispered as the noise of the engines drowned his voice. She nodded at him mutely. If all went according to plan she would see them in a few

393

days. So why was she so unhappy?

That night she lay in the darkness beside her husband. She listened to the rhythm of his breathing and tried not to think about the hurt she was going to cause him. He had drunk too much so his breathing grew heavier until it rumbled into a loud snore. His drinking had now become a habit that he was unable to control. He didn't realise that his character was beginning to be affected by the poison that swelled his liver. He was becoming short tempered and volatile. Audrey had noticed but she had been too busy with the children and Louis to dwell on it. After all, why should she care? She was leaving him.

When Cecil left for the office the following morning, he kissed his wife on her taut cheek and mumbled to his brother in an irritable fashion, then opened the door and stepped out into the sunshine. Louis and Audrey were left alone. They looked at each other nervously, too anxious to smile. 'I'll go and pack now,' she said, biting her lip. Louis suddenly pulled her behind the door and kissed her.

'I'll meet you at the airport at midday,' he whispered urgently. 'What are you going to do about Cecil?'

'I'll write him a note and leave it in the hall.'

'Good.'

'I'm frightened,' she said in a tremulous voice.

'Me too, but you'll be fine when you're on the aeroplane.'

'I hope so.'

'It's meant to be. Audrey, my love, we're meant to be together. Love is stronger than both of us.'

'I know. I'm just so afraid.'

394

'Of what?'

'Of hurting people.'

'They'll live, Audrey. You're doing this for you and you deserve it. You owe it to yourself.' Then he pressed his lips against her forehead. 'Don't forget your dreams, Audrey, my love, and that I've built mine around you.'

At that moment they heard Mercedes' footsteps in the hall as she made towards the dining room to clear away the breakfast. They wrenched themselves apart and Louis wandered across to the piano where he sat down and began to play. Once more he played the tune he had composed for her. Audrey left him there and climbed the stairs to her room to pack in a small suitcase those things from her life that she wished to take with her. A little later she heard the door close and knew that he had gone. The next time she saw him would be at the airport. The first step towards a new life together. Without thinking any more about it she began to pack.

How do you pack for a lifetime? What do you take? Audrey didn't know. She packed some clothes, her spongebag and the sentimental things that were of no value, like photographs of Isla, the pressed flowers she had kept from her funeral and the little prayer book her father had given her as a child. She then sat on the end of her bed and deliberated how best to use the next couple of hours before she had to leave for the airport.

Suddenly she saw two brown ears sticking out from under the window seat. Her heart began to pound as she recognised Leonora's beloved Saggy Rabbit. As sweat collected on her brow she walked over to pick him up. He looked forlorn and small in her hands, which quite inadvertently began to tremble. She pressed him to her face and closed her eyes as the tears began to push through her lashes and tumble down her cheeks. She began to shake so much that her legs buckled beneath her and she fell into a heap on the carpet, shuddering with sorrow. There was no point pretending any longer. She couldn't go through with it. Her children would always come first. She had to let Louis go.

*　　*　　*

When a heart breaks it makes no noise. There are no outward signs, no rash, no bruising. Only a strange calmness that takes over when there are no more tears to shed and no more voice left to howl one's grief into the silence and a resignation that numbs one's senses like a drug, for how else would one be able to go on? People survive in spite of themselves.

Audrey sat down at her desk and began to write. Not to Cecil as she had planned but to Louis. She paused, the pen over the paper, and deliberated how to put it, knowing that however it was expressed she would break him all the same. *'Forgive my weak spirit. I will never stop loving you. Never.'* She then put Saggy Rabbit, damp from her tears, into an envelope with the letter and sealed it. With a grey face she left the house for the airport.

*　　*　　*

When Louis arrived at the airport he cast his eye across the concourse in search of Audrey. He then

396

looked at his watch. He was early. Fifteen minutes early. He was nervous. He flicked his fingers in agitation then burrowed inside his pocket for a hanky, which he passed over his sweating forehead. After a few minutes he decided to pick up their tickets from the sales desk. Anything to keep busy. As he strode over his eyes darted from face to face, expecting at any moment to see her familiar smile shine through like a sunbeam.

'Ah, Mr Forrester,' said the painted lady with scarlet lips to match her silk cravat. 'Here are your tickets and I have a parcel here for you.' Louis' face drained of colour, leaving it at once pale and fearful. The lady handed him a brown envelope. He recognised Audrey's handwriting immediately. With a palpitating heart he tore it open and pulled out the rabbit and the note. He didn't need to read it for he knew what it contained. Saggy Rabbit's doleful countenance relayed more than her note ever could. But with a vision blurred with anguish he read what she had written. *'Forgive my weak spirit. I will never stop loving you. Never.'* His throat suddenly constricted, but he was unable to contain his grief. The painted lady blinked at him in bewilderment. She had never seen a grown man cry.

CHAPTER TWENTY-SIX

When Cecil returned that night and reached for the whisky decanter, he kissed his wife on her cold cheek without knowing how close he had come to losing her. 'Where's Louis?' he asked, used to arriving home to Louis' piano playing and his wife's glowing cheeks and ill-disguised enthusiasm. Only now did Audrey notice the bitterness in his voice.

'He's left,' she replied, picking up a magazine and walking towards the door which led out into the garden. Cecil followed her.

'What do you mean, left?' he asked, imagining that he had gone to board at the Club.

'He's gone back to England.' She swallowed and took a deep breath. She had cried all day, on and off. Hoped he'd come after her, then changed her mind and hoped he'd boarded the plane and left. Only after a long bath had she managed to compose herself, ready to face her husband and the first day of the rest of her life.

'He didn't even say good-bye,' he stammered. The alcohol had already begun to corrode the eloquence for which he had once been so admired.

'Oh, he did. I gave him Saggy Rabbit to take to Leonora,' she replied, trying to sound casual. Trying to muffle the desperate cry in her voice. She wandered out into the sunshine and began to deadhead the flowers, her face hidden from view.

'Ah, you found him. I am pleased.'

'Yes, Leonora will be very happy.'

'I wonder why he left so suddenly,' Cecil mused, sitting down on the terrace.

'You know your brother better than I,' she replied. 'He left suddenly last time too.' Cecil stiffened and narrowed his eyes as he watched her wander sadly about the garden like a shadow.

'I see,' he said. His voice was a deep groan. He drained his glass. 'I don't suppose we'll see him for a while then.' Audrey blinked away a tear. She was now unable to speak. In order to avoid having to

398

talk any more she walked away from him to the far corner of the garden where she stood pretending to deadhead where there were no flowers, just ferns and evergreens. Cecil got up and retreated inside the house. She was relieved he had left her alone.

It was no coincidence; through his drunken haze Cecil knew he had an enormous amount to be thankful for.

*   *   *

Aunt Edna was the first to arrive at the house when news of Louis' sudden departure spread once again around the community. It was late in the evening and Audrey was preparing for an early night. Her aunt's sudden appearance surprised her as much as it surprised Cecil. 'To what do we owe the pleasure?' he asked, his red face breaking into a loose smile.

'Where's Audrey?' she asked hoarsely, deducing from Cecil's drunken state that she must have left with Louis as she had threatened. She clutched her neck with hot fingers and sat down.

'Upstairs preparing for bed. She's tired and missing the twins,' he stated flatly.

'Ah,' she breathed deeply with relief. 'I'll go up and see her then.'

'As you wish. You won't find her very communicative tonight, I'm afraid. She's quite done in.' Aunt Edna noticed the anger in his voice and wondered how much he knew.

She found Audrey in her room, sitting on the window seat, staring blankly out into the garden. She rushed over and drew her trembling niece into her embrace. 'Dear child,' she said softly, pressing

399

her close. 'I know how much it hurts, but you've done the right thing. You're very, very brave. No one but I knows how brave and courageous you have been.' Audrey buried her face in her aunt's bosom and sobbed. 'It will hurt for a while but in time the pain will subside and you will feel little more than a dull ache. My heart still aches for Harry. But I no longer suffer pain.'

'What is the point of living without love?' she asked in a whisper. 'What is the point of it all?'

'You have your children to love.'

'But they're not here.' Her voice was barely audible.

'You'll go and see them.'

'What? A few weeks here and a few weeks there? Who will they run to when they're unhappy? Who will they talk to about their fears and their worries? Someone will replace me in their lives. What's the point of having children if you're not going to nurture them?'

'Audrey, this is silly talk. You have to pull yourself together.' Aunt Edna gripped her by the upper arms and held her face with a determined stare.

'I can't.' Audrey looked into her aunt's compassionate old eyes. 'I just can't.'

'I know you still care about Cecil. Even if you don't realise it. My dear, he loves you so much. Just look at him. Look what you've done to him. He's drinking too much. He's losing his confidence. He was such a dashing young man. He needs you. Can't you see?'

'He's driven me away.'

'You have to make a go of it. You've got each other for life.' Audrey groaned and lowered her head. 'Don't forget that old cliché, *"it's better to have loved and lost than never to have loved at all."* I would rather have had eight years of loving Harry than a lifetime of no one special. You've lived something unique and loved to your full capacity. We can't always have it all. Be thankful for your children, some women are unable to conceive, others lose their children like your mother lost Isla. Don't focus on what you have lost, remember what you have and hold onto it.' Her face softened into a sympathetic smile. 'You can either be miserable or make the best of what you have been dealt. It is your choice. You did the right thing today, and in time you will appreciate that. Tomorrow you must set out to repair your marriage and put Louis behind you.'

But Audrey's emotions were too raw to contemplate her marriage and it was too early to put Louis behind her. When her aunt had gone she hid beneath the sheets and slept.

*   *   *

It was dark when Cecil entered his dressing room. He switched on the light and closed the door softly behind him so as not to awaken his wife who was asleep next door. He walked over to the dresser. Catching his reflection in the large oval mirror he rubbed his chin in dismay. He looked old and shabby. His eyes sagged and the whites were dull and yellowed. His skin was ruddy and coarse in texture and his mouth twisted in a permanent grimace. He clearly looked unwell. He sighed and picked up the leather-bound bible he had recently come to rely on. Then he opened one of the

401

drawers at the base of the mirror and pulled out a small key. He was meticulously tidy and everything had its place. Finally he lifted the little brown walnut box where he kept things of great importance and walked over to the armchair where he sat down. He opened the bible where it was marked with a gold ribbon and began to read. He read until the early hours of the morning and with each verse his spirits were uplifted and reinforced. But it was one verse in particular that caused him to rub his chin ponderously, sigh heavily and reflect on the last decade of his life with objectivity. That verse above all others spoke to him and stayed with him so that it became a mantra that he repeated quietly to himself over and over again. When dawn lit up the sky and the song of birds danced on the air, signalling the beginning of another day, he turned the key in the little walnut box and pulled out a folded piece of paper. He opened it and his eyes scanned what was written there. Louis' ink had faded a little over the years but his words had lost none of their potency. Taking a pen Cecil copied that verse from the bible, writing it at the bottom of the page. He studied the note a moment before folding it and placing it once again in the walnut box. He locked it then put the key back where it belonged.

*   *   *

The next couple of weeks passed slowly. Audrey took solace in the mundane routine of domestic life. She busied herself inventing tasks in order to fill the empty hours. Time dragged as if the hands of the clock were weighed down with sorrow and the skies turned grey and stormy, drenching the plain below with heavy, torrential rain. The humidity was stifling. She sweated out her pain and frustration as she turned all her energies on the silver and brass, old cupboards that needed sorting out and threw into boxes marked 'charity' all the clothes she had gathered over the years but never worn. Then she went to the hairdresser and had her lustrous curls cut short.

Finally she played 'The Forget-Me-Not Sonata' for the last time. With the ceremony of a ritual that only she knew, she pulled out the stool, sat down, lifted the lid of the piano and rested her fingers lightly over the keys. She closed her eyes and took three deep breaths. With each exhalation she felt the strain loosen its bonds and free her at least from the physical symptoms of a broken spirit. The emotional wounds, however, would never heal. Slowly her fingers began to move across the keys.

In her mind's eye she saw herself as a young girl when love had wrapped its honeyed tendrils about her heart and ensnared her for the first and only time. She saw Louis' handsome face and the vulnerability behind his eyes that belied the confidence his face projected. She imagined his wide and captivating smile, before disappointment had erased his joy and his hope, and lived once again his kiss, that melted the material world and transported her into the intangible world of shared dreams. Then once she had awoken from her solemn meditation she closed the piano lid. 'Let it collect dust,' she said to herself. 'Because I will never play it again.'

*   *   *

Just as Audrey believed she would never emerge from her dark tunnel of despair Fate endowed her with a gift she could never have foreseen. Louis' child. When she discovered her pregnancy she placed her hand on her belly and with a shamelessness that was quite out of character her face opened into a large and tender smile and her spirit, once so dead, now revived itself and quivered with excitement. A part of Louis was growing inside her. A piece of him would always be with her and, God willing, nothing would take it from her. This child wouldn't be sent overseas to be educated. She had learnt her lesson. She wouldn't allow it. Conceived with the purest of earthly love this child would be special. By God's grace she had been given another future. A future brimming with joy. She was no longer staring into an abyss, but onto a vast horizon of endless possibilities. *It shall be a little girl*, she said to herself, *and I will call her Grace.*

Only after having revelled for some time in the magic of Fortune, did she consider her husband. Then her smiling face was reduced to an anxious frown while she deliberated what she was going to say to him. She would have to tell him the whole truth. There was no avoiding it. He would know it wasn't his and she couldn't put it down to immaculate conception. She was deeply afraid. Not of his rejection or his anger, but of hurting him.

It was late when Cecil returned home. He was weary and his shoulders stooped as he walked up the path to the front door. Audrey had been so absorbed in her own troubles that she had failed to notice his. He looked broken and dejected and her

404

heart went out to him. She was standing in the hallway biting her nails when he walked in. His face didn't change expression. He just looked at her impassively as if he were tired of loving her and not being loved in return. As if he were tired of trying.

'We need to talk,' she said.

'All right,' he replied in a resigned tone. If she were to announce that she was leaving him he wouldn't have been at all surprised. He followed her into the sitting room and reached for the whisky as he did every night, barely aware of his actions, certainly unable to change the habit even if he wanted to. He sank into an armchair and took a swig from his glass. 'So, what do you want to say?' Audrey sighed. She didn't know how to put it gently, how to soften such a severe blow.

'I'm expecting a baby,' she stated without emotion. He stared back at her for a long moment giving nothing of his feelings away, except for his cheeks, which smarted red as if stung.

'I see,' he said finally.

'I owe it to you to explain,' she began.

'There is nothing to explain, Audrey.' He put his hand up, signalling for her to remain silent. She obeyed without a protest and watched as he got up and leaned against the mantelpiece above the empty fireplace. He stared into the shadows, remembering the verse from the bible and deriving strength from it. He was now faced with the unavoidable reality of Audrey's affair with his brother. His suspicions had been right all along. But she hadn't left him; for whatever reason she had let Louis go. With a shudder he recalled the morning all those years ago when he had discovered Louis' disappearance and the note he

405

had written. This was a golden opportunity to redeem himself of his own wrongdoing and assuage the guilt that had gnawed at him ever since. Audrey had placed him at a crossroad. He could continue up the current path with her and the baby, or leave her and walk alone. He had a choice. But there was no decision to be made because Cecil's nobility of character now asserted itself. He stood up and pulled his shoulders back. He felt empowered; the way one does when one's actions are selfless and good. 'We are expecting another child. We are truly blessed,' he said finally and turned to her with eyes that shone with determination. While Audrey blinked at him in confusion he walked over to her, bent down and kissed her. She flinched and caught her breath, all the time watching him in amazement, not knowing how to respond. 'Have you telephoned your mother?' She gulped and tried to compose herself. But her shame suddenly overwhelmed her and she dissolved into tears. She shook her head. 'Don't be upset, Audrey, a child is a gift. This is not a time for tears but a time for joy.'

'I'm so sorry,' she stammered. But he pretended not to hear her.

'I suggest you telephone your mother right away so that we can share our good news.'

'But, Cecil.' She attempted once again to explain herself.

'And we must let the twins know that they are going to have a little brother or sister. I'm sure they'll be delighted, or at least, Leonora will be.' Audrey knew that it was pointless trying to fight him, so she leaned back against the cushions and wiped her eyes with the sleeve of her shirt. 'How are you feeling?' he asked.

'Terrible,' she replied and sniffed.

'I mean physically.'

'No sickness, Cecil. Just sickness of the soul.'

'Why don't you have an early night, I'll sleep in my dressing room. You'll feel better in the morning.' He walked towards the door then turned and looked at her steadily with dull eyes that had once sparkled with love. 'Some things are too painful to face, Audrey. So if one pretends hard enough one might be fooled into believing they haven't happened.' He lifted his chin and continued in a very quiet voice, 'You are carrying my child, Audrey. There is nothing else to discuss. Our child and we will bring him up together. I don't want to speak of this again, ever. And I don't want to see my brother for as long as I live, in this world or the next.' Audrey watched him walk out and suddenly remembered to breathe.

She didn't know whether she'd ever love her husband but from that moment on she deeply admired him. He must have known about the affair all along. He had never confronted her. He had always treated his brother with courtesy. Now he had done the noblest thing of any man she had ever known; he had elected to bring Louis' child up as his own. Audrey wept again, this time out of gratitude.

*　　　*　　　*

Grace was born at The Little Company of Mary in town, like her sisters and her mother before them. But unlike any baby the doctor had ever seen, Grace was born with a smile hovering on her pretty pink lips and a knowing look in her wise eyes, the

407

eyes of an old woman who has seen all that the world has to offer. She didn't scream like Alicia or whimper like Leonora, she just watched her mother with curiosity and held up her little white hand to touch her face. Audrey took the hand in hers and kissed it as the tears tumbled down her cheeks and dripped off her chin onto the newborn body of her baby. 'Shall I call in your husband?' the doctor asked. But Audrey shook her head.

'I would like some time alone with Grace,' she said. 'Just a few minutes, then you can call him.' The doctor left her sitting up in bed, mesmerised by the features of her child that were a perfect reflection of the man she loved. 'You're more special to me than anyone else in the world,' she whispered and the child blinked up at her contentedly. 'You will never know who your real father is, but that doesn't matter because your gentle spirit is a part of his and always will be. You will carry his memory in your smile and in your eyes, which are so like his and you will be happy because I will love you for the both of us. For the both of us, my love. And Cecil will love you too, in his own way. I will never disappoint you, Grace, or let you down as I have let down your father and your half-sisters. That is my promise.'

When Cecil laid eyes on the baby he noticed at once how like Louis she was and he knew instinctively that little Grace would always be a stranger to him, just like her father. Grace had the same disconnected expression in her eyes and something more, something that Louis had never had, a knowing look that was quite unsettling, as if she could see into his soul. Cecil shook his head and chuckled out loud. How could a baby, no more than some twenty minutes old, be endowed with so much awareness? It was impossible, he was mad to have imagined it. He pulled away and looked at his wife. She smiled at him tentatively but Cecil didn't return her smile. He asked her how she felt and then went to telephone her mother. He still loved Audrey to distraction but she had destroyed his trust and made a mockery of his affection for her. What tormented him the most was the question that now gnawed at his heart: had she ever loved him? He didn't dare ask her in case she confessed that she never had.

*   *   *

Grace was indeed a special little girl. Alicia and Leonora returned to Argentina only once a year at Christmas time so their small sister grew up effectively an only child, indulged by her mother and tolerated by her father, spoiled by her grandmother and great aunt Edna who were delighted to have another child to love. As Grace grew into a willowy, ethereal little girl with the long white hair of an angel and the light foot of a garden spirit, Alicia resented her charm and bullied her, but unlike Leonora Grace was resilient to her taunts. She simply smiled at her sister with pity as if she could see into the dark corners of her nature and foresaw the struggles that lay ahead. Leonora wanted to love her, but Grace was remote. She didn't need friendship, just the air to breathe and the garden to play in, for she told how it was filled with fairies. Leonora wasn't immune from jealousy either and suffered seeing her baby sister swept up into the arms of her beloved mother, who used to have eyes only for her. When she returned to England at the end of the holidays she would think of her mother and suffer a different kind of homesickness. For now home wasn't the same as it had been, for her mother's attentions weren't reserved exclusively for herself and Alicia. Grace was different and those differences might as well have been as wide as a sea for as much as Leonora tried she was unable to reach her.

So Grace grew up in the rarefied air of Hurlingham where her mother took her for picnics beneath the fragrant eucalyptus trees, rode out over the plains and chased ostriches at Gaitano's ranch, La Magdalena. She taught her about the wild prairie hares and the plants and flowers that grew on the fertile plains of the pampa and listened while her daughter told her of the spirits that accompanied her along her path of life. 'We all have an angel who looks after us,' she told her mother. 'Mine is tall with brown skin and feathers in his hair. He's called Totem. I have many friends in the spirit world and am never lonely.' Audrey believed her for if she ever lost something about the house she only had to consult Grace who would ask her angel and the missing object would be found immediately. She would hear her talking in her bedroom after she had been tucked up in bed, her voice recounting the day's events and her opinions as if she were sharing her room with a friend. But Grace didn't have any friends, only her mother and the spirits that seemed to occupy her imagination.

Grace was a natural pianist and exasperated the tutor who came every Monday evening because she would begin a piece, following the score punctiliously before suddenly digressing, allowing her fingers to wander off as if they had a mind of their own. She had a talent for playing by ear and it would take the tutor a few moments before she realised that Grace was inventing it as she went along, but in the same key and style as the original. She could imitate Mozart, Bach and Beethoven to perfection then just as quickly change to something all her very own, 'the music of spirits' she would call it because she claimed that they danced around the sitting room as she played. The tutor would shake her head with impatience and claim that spirits didn't exist to which Grace would reply, 'That, my dear Miss Horner, is because you can't see them.' And once she threw her head back and laughed to the horror of poor Miss Horner who simply didn't understand her strange pupil. 'There's a little creature over there in the corner grinning at me now because of my impertinence. Let's step this up a bit and get his little feet moving!' Miss Horner only lasted a few months and when the next tutor arrived Audrey took care to tell her daughter to keep her 'little friends' to herself, because not everyone understood her like her mother.

Grace was a happy child. She laughed a lot because nothing seemed to frighten her. She instinctively sensed that unkind people were unhappy people; whether bitter, jealous or full of hate, these emotions were usually bred in misery and self-loathing and she didn't retaliate with aggression but compassion, which was unusual for a small child. She wasn't besieged by the normal doubts that trouble children for she always had her angel friends to ask and Audrey was always there.

She was self-sufficient and independent, often disappearing for hours just like her mother had done when she was young, returning home with a smile and a carefree toss of her long curly hair.

At night after her mother had tucked her up in bed and kissed her good-night a lovely spirit would always appear with long bouncing curls and a smile that was at once tender and mischievous. She would sit on the side of the bed and run her hand down Grace's little face, all the time gazing upon her with love. Grace adored this time and would relate her thoughts and ideas and the spirit would listen patiently before sending her off to sleep with a soft kiss on her forehead.

Cecil looked at Grace warily for she seemed to see right through him. He took to hiding the bottles of alcohol and drinking vodka which didn't linger on his breath, because she would study him with those large, all-seeing eyes of hers and say, 'Daddy, if you smiled a little more you wouldn't need that medicine you're always taking. A smile cures everything.' Cecil never felt close to Grace because she seemed not to need him. And through his drunken vision she constantly reminded him of Louis.

Audrey also thought of Louis each time she gazed upon the countenance of their daughter. She wished that he could see the divine being they had created together, and she had to constantly remind herself that she should be grateful for the little part of him that she had been allowed to hold onto and not to wish for more. She cried when she was alone and when she was at the theatre, for in the darkness when no one could see her the tears came readily and willingly. As the orchestra played she

412

remembered Louis and his love of music that Grace had inherited and she felt close to him there, in spite of the fact that they had never visited the Colón together. She bought herself records of sad tango songs that she played when Cecil was out and Mercedes was sleeping. She would close the curtains and dance about the room imagining herself in Louis' arms beneath the violet jacaranda trees in the spring days of their love.

Grace grew up accustomed to her mother's sudden bouts of melancholy. She would hide in the corridor and watch her through the crack in the door or if it was closed, through the keyhole. She loved to observe her solitary dancing. There was something dark and alluring about the secrecy of it for she would go to great lengths to check that she was alone, and the romance of it touched her very deeply, for her mother often cried as she danced and her tears were mysterious, for as much as Grace tried to ask her spirit friends about the cause of such unhappiness they were not forthcoming with an answer.

Audrey didn't know she was being watched and she didn't realise how much of an impression her dancing had on her small child. Grace never asked her why she danced because she knew that if she admitted she had witnessed it her mother would stop dancing altogether and instinctively she knew she had to dance. It was a matter of survival.

But the most fascinating of all was the little silk-bound book that her mother kept hidden in her underwear drawer. When she took it out and opened it, her pen poised above the page, Grace would strain her eyes to read what she wrote there. Her mother's face would turn pale and her eyes would often glisten like they did during her dance of tears. She would sit thinking for a long while and Grace would watch her until she could barely contain her curiosity.

Then one day, while her mother was out and Mercedes was baking a cake in the kitchen, she crept into her bedroom and opened the drawer which contained the secret book. There it lay beneath satin camisoles and stockings. With trembling fingers Grace picked it up. She felt at once the heavy vibrations of sadness and disappointment that clung to it and sent her own spirit spiralling into a decline. She breathed deeply and tried to detach herself; sometimes her gift ran away with itself. It was an exquisite little book. The silk was luxurious reds and greens woven into pictures of blue flowers and shone in the light like the hair of angels. It was soft to the touch and bound with a green cord that was knotted at the ends before spraying out into silky tassels. She sat down on the window seat and slowly untied it. For a moment she almost lost her courage. She knew she shouldn't be prying into her mother's private world. If she had wanted Grace to see the book she would have shown her herself. But her curiosity spurred her on. She opened it to find that the first page contained a strange title that she was unable to comprehend. 'The Forget-Me-Not Sonata.' She frowned and stared at the words written neatly in her mother's hand, but they still meant nothing to her. Of course she knew that a forget-me-not was a flower and the flowers woven into the silk on the cover of the book could well have been forget-me-nots. But she instinctively felt there was a deeper significance that was hidden from her. She turned the page, hoping that the following words would enlighten her, but all she saw were the dots where her mother had attempted various times to start a sentence and a smudge from a tear. She sighed in disappointment and turned back to the peculiar title. 'The Forget-Me-Not Sonata,' she read. What did it mean?

PART III

CHAPTER TWENTY-SEVEN

England 1971

Florien sat beneath one of the apple trees in the orchard, watching the evening sun bathe the top of the wall with bright golden light. The rumble of the combines in the distance was carried on the wind bringing with it the smell of smouldering fields and decaying foliage and the pale watery sky reminded him of winter and the colourless months to come. He chose an apple out of the basket beside him, full of the fruits he had picked for Mrs Weatherby's larder, and bit into it. His father always said that the apples already nibbled by wasps and bees were the best of all and he was right, for this apple tasted sweeter than any he had ever eaten and it was riddled with little holes from hungry insects. His mind wandered lazily to Leonora and Alicia Forrester.

Leonora had helped him all day. He liked her. She was now a somewhat buxom seventeen year old with a small waist and large swollen breasts and bottom. Her face had lost some of its plainness and now began to reflect her gentle nature in a wide, disarming smile and soft blue eyes. She didn't seem to care very much how she looked. She tied her brown hair into a pony tail and hid her figure beneath loose shirts and jumpers, preferring to dirty her hands in the mud of the garden than waste time applying makeup and painting her nails. He could talk to Leonora. She was kind and sympathetic. He could tell she admired him. He saw it in her shiny eyes and in her cheeks that blushed easily. Alicia was entirely different. It was she who now dominated his thoughts night and day. With the allure of the devil she enchanted him with her mocking grin and sharp wit, putting him down one moment, encouraging him the next so that he didn't know what to make of her.

At night he lay in a sticky sweat, her angular features branded on his mind so that it fumed with frustration and love and hate and all the conflicting emotions she managed to stir up in his heart, leaving him confused and ashamed for caring for her like he did. He wanted to throw her up against a wall and make violent love to her so that she no longer smiled with conceit or looked at him through the narrowed eyes of a temptress sure of the power she wielded, quite able to turn him to stone with a flash of her lively blue eyes. Then he wanted to make love to her with tenderness, to melt her steely spirit and discover a compassionate and gentle human being beneath her hard outer coating. He longed to hear her sigh in wonder at her own capacity to love and share pleasure. He dreamed of discovering a vulnerable young woman with fears and hopes like any other. But Alicia wasn't like anyone else. She appeared not to feel.

Alicia had no desire to help in the garden. Nature bored her and so did the gypsies. They were provincial and poor. She was going to marry a Duke at the very least and live in an enormous mansion. Aunt Cicely bored her too and made her help in the kitchen, which she hated because she didn't like getting her hands dirty with flour and chicken flesh. She saw that Marcel was sponging off her aunt, who was still so enraptured by him that she was unable to tell that he was using her. When Cicely wasn't looking she flirted with him in the hope of proving her theory, but much to her humiliation Marcel, who was closer to her in age than to her aunt, just smiled ironically and dismissed her advances with a fluid wave of one of his paintbrushes. 'Little girl, if you want to seduce someone, go and seduce a gypsy, they'll be grateful, after all they only have turnips to talk to,' he said in his heavily articulated French accent. Alicia vowed that she would have her revenge. *How dare anyone speak to me like that?* she thought angrily. But perhaps he was right; it would be fun to seduce a gypsy.

Alicia knew Leonora adored Florien and that made her plan all the more enticing. She watched them planting together, chatting away about the weather, the soil and the harvest, laughing with the ease of old friends and the thought of slipping in between them was just irresistible. She noticed Florien's desire for her, he was a man after all, and most men were not like Marcel. She knew she could have anyone she wanted. She was confident of her appeal. She lay in the autumn sunshine, biting a bar of chocolate, watching her prey knowing that he knew he was being watched. That in itself was enough to send a tingle of excitement up her beautiful body.

She had not yet had sex. Virginity was a hideous word, reeking of inexperience and vulnerability. She wanted to get rid of it as soon as possible and Florien was very attractive. He was tall and strong with black shiny hair and dark suspicious eyes that smouldered beneath his fringe. He was sulky and taciturn, quite the moody hero of the Mills & Boon books that got passed around at school, but he was sadly lacking in the most important area. He was poor and unlikely to become rich, even less likely to become famous and simply unable to acquire a title or status of any worth. That made him good for only one thing.

'It's a magical evening, isn't it?' she said, sitting beside him on the grass, taking an apple out of the basket and biting into it. He didn't reply, just looked at her blankly. 'Where's your little helper?' she asked.

'Leonora?'

'Yes, the garden gnome, where's she?'

'Gone to the garden centre with Mrs Weatherby,' he replied, wondering what she wanted, for her eyes glistened with intent.

'Not more bulbs, surely?' She laughed and noticed to her delight that his sullen expression softened a little. 'You spend all day on your knees, digging away in the mud. Can't she ask you to drive a combine or something a little less manual?'

'I like working in the garden best. Driving a combine is very dull.'

'It's more manly though and you're a man.' He averted his eyes. He was used to her flirting with him and then squashing him like a summer fly. He was in no mood to be humiliated. 'Give me your hand,' she asked suddenly.

He chuckled and shook his head.

'What do you want with it?'

'I want to feel it.' She laughed again. 'Don't be shy, I won't bite it.' He had no option. He gave her his palm. She took it and ran her fingers lightly over the rough surface. He felt himself grow hot as he couldn't help but imagine what it would feel like to have her fingers caressing the rest of his body like that. 'There, you have the hand of a farmer. It's deliciously coarse. Can you feel my soft skin with it, or is it too hardened to feel?' His cheeks throbbed with embarrassment and he pulled his hand away, fighting the excitement that strained at his trousers. He took another apple in order to do something with his hands.

'You're being silly,' he retaliated, biting into it.

'I'm not. Really, I'm not, Florien. I'm curious. When you make love to a woman, can you feel with those hands of yours?'

'That's none of your business.' He was astonished by her boldness and titillated at the same time.

'If you were to run your hands over my body, would you feel how soft my skin is? I take a lot of trouble with it. I rub oils into it every night after my bath and only wear silk to sleep in. Here,' she said, thrusting her arm at him. 'Feel how smooth it is.'

'What are you playing at?' he retorted angrily, frowning at her with his dark eyebrows. 'I don't want to feel your skin. Keep it to yourself.'

'Surely you don't mean that.' She looked hurt. 'I know I'm being foolish, but love does that, doesn't it? So I'm told. I've never been in love before.'

Florien couldn't believe what he was hearing. Her words suddenly put a whole different complexion on the situation. He looked at her steadily, disarmed by her apparent vulnerability. She gazed back with limpid eyes and smiled sweetly, like other women smiled and he felt his heart swell with joy. His mind told him to be cautious, but the blood was already pumping through his veins at such a speed that he didn't hear the small voice of reason. 'I've never been in love before, either,' he said impulsively, lured into a fragile sense of security.

'I've tried to ignore my feelings, Florien, because I know Aunt Cicely would kill me. She would say I'm too young for love. But I want you. I want you now.' She bit her lip because she knew her little speech was clumsy. From the books she had read, and tired of, women spoke of love like that. Of this ridiculous battle with their feelings. So she had moved a little too swiftly onto sex, she presumed, but Florien was too surprised by her declaration of love to notice.

'I love you too,' he replied, turning to her swiftly and taking her hands in his. 'I've tried to ignore my feelings as well, but your face torments me as much by day as by night. I can't seem to get you out of my head. You're just not like anyone else. You're wonderful.' Alicia was amused by this sudden outburst. She only wanted to sleep with him and here he was almost proposing. She had opened the door an inch and he had blown the whole thing off its hinges.

'Where shall we go then?' she said, suppressing a giggle.

'What?'

'Where shall we go, to be alone?' she repeated, hoping she wasn't taking this too fast. How men put up with the tedious rituals of courtship she couldn't imagine. She was very aware that she was taking the lead and behaving like a man, which Florien probably wouldn't like so she decided to speak once more of love. 'I love you, Florien, and only you. I want to be close to you. To feel your heart against mine, your body next to mine. I want

424

to give myself to you. I want you to claim my innocence and make me a woman.' She was delighted with her speech this time and even more delighted by the gypsy's response. He jumped to his feet.

'Come with me,' he said, taking her by the hand. He led her up the orchard to a door in the wall that opened into the cluster of barns and outhouses. She smothered her laughter and tried with some success to act the part of a vulnerable young girl in the first flush of love. Florien was so astonished by his own good fortune he didn't notice the cracks in her performance.

He led her to a barn filled with hay bales. Golden beams of light entered through the holes in the wood and caught the tiny straws of hay, setting them aflame with the red and amber rays of sunset. With a pounding heart he climbed to the top where the flat surface of bales lay beneath the timber roof of the barn, giving them a secret, sweet-smelling bower in which to discover each other undisturbed. Then he turned around and held her by the shoulders. 'Are you sure?' he asked, his dark eyes caressing hers with tenderness. Alicia pulled a small, girlish smile and nodded. She tried to imagine how Leonora would reply. Mutely, she deduced unkindly and continued in the same vein.

Florien knew what he was doing. He had slept with enough girls to know his way around a woman's body and yet he was nervous. So nervous that if it hadn't been for the exquisite undulations of Alicia's pale body he might not have been able to perform. She lay on the hay with her eyes half closed while he kissed her and undressed her, stroked her and admired her and like a cat in sunlight she stretched and sighed and purred with the enjoyment of a woman with a large capacity for pleasure.

She was sure of her allure and unlike other girls she showed no apprehension or inhibition, but abandoned herself to him with a mouth half twisted with amusement. Florien was too busy feasting on her and his good luck to notice the contemptuous glint in her eyes. He was sure that she loved him, for why else would she give him such a precious gift? Her virginity. She had chosen him and he felt glorious.

Alicia discovered that she enjoyed sex. Not only was it physically pleasurable but it was another wonderful power game to be played and won. She was amused at how easy men were to seduce. She had already worked out that beauty was a formidable weapon in a world obsessed with image, but now she realised that sex was the atomic power of such warfare. Men lost their minds because of it. They were weakened by their own carnal longings and she despised them for their fragility and intended to exploit it for her own ends. As she lay there in his arms, while he kissed her forehead and caressed her hair, telling her how lovely she was and how much he had enjoyed her, she fantasised about the wealth and status she was going to acquire with her beauty and her body. The wide smile of a satisfied cat crept across her face.

*   *   *

Florien was mortified when Alicia had to return to boarding school. 'Only another year,' she taunted him. 'Then we'll have the whole of our lives to

426

spend together.'

'I'll never love another like I love you, Alicia.' He took off the Saint Christopher pendant he always wore about his neck. 'I want you to have this,' he said, gazing at her with dewy eyes.

'What is it?' she asked, screwing up her nose. 'Is it pretty? Let me see.' She held the gold necklace in her hand and decided that she liked it very much.

'It will bring you luck.'

'Goodie,' she exclaimed, lifting her thick hair so that he could place it around her neck. He clasped the little chain then kissed the white skin that was usually covered with curls. She giggled.

'I really do love you,' he said and sighed happily.

'I know, Florien. You're terribly sweet,' she replied glibly.

'When will you be coming back?'

'In a few weekends' time. Then there's half-term, then the Christmas holidays and I'll be flying back home. You'll have to find somewhere else for our loving when the hay bales go.'

'Don't worry, I'll find a cosy place. We'll keep warm together in the wintertime.'

'Yes,' she replied, trying to muster up a little enthusiasm. She didn't much like romantic talk and knew she wasn't very good at it. But she was aware that if she didn't play the game he'd think less of her and perhaps wouldn't make himself so available. Besides, she had noticed Leonora's forlorn face which made the game all the more worth playing.

Leonora had indeed noticed Florien's ill-disguised ardour for her sister. She was hurt because she genuinely adored him and longed for

427

him to reciprocate her feelings, but as usual she didn't blame Alicia. She accepted her sister's superiority in every field and bowed out gracefully. Alicia was beautiful and talented and charming, everything that she wasn't, and she was devoted to her. If Alicia wanted Florien she'd be pleased for her and do all in her power to assist the relationship. However, her generosity of spirit came at a price. She wasn't immune to the unhappiness it caused, for once again she was left out, ignored, isolated. She yearned for home and the security of her mother's unconditional love while at the same time she knew she was meant to be a grown-up who shouldn't need her mother any more. Besides, Audrey had a somewhat unusual seven year old to take care of. If it weren't for Aunt Cicely, whose affection for her was almost as unconditional as her mother's, and the garden, fields and woods where she felt the strong presence of a higher power, she would have felt very alone in the world.

Leonora loved taking Barley and the other dogs for long walks around the farm. The wide expanse of fields that opened out before her and extended into soft undulating hills filled her spirit with courage and prevented her from feeling sorry for herself. Out there beneath the sky she questioned the meaning of life and death with the cycle of the seasons and she learned that happiness is in accepting things the way they are and not trying to fight them. For winter melted effortlessly into spring and spring blossomed easily into summer to finally subside with grace into the rich red and golden palate of autumn. *What will be, will be*, she thought and such resignation had its own rewards.

She decided she wasn't going to waste her life chasing the material world, for what could give her more pleasure than this ever-changing panorama? She knew instinctively that nothing was important but love and life and she could get all that in the Dorset countryside. Her future lay with Nature for it was there that she felt at home. She was too humble to expect Florien's love but she dreamed about it all the same. She sometimes imagined living the life of a gypsy, working in the garden, planting, picking and potting. She'd love more than anything to build a home in a prettily painted caravan, own a few sturdy horses and have enough children for games around the camp fire. Now with Florien's infatuation with her sister her dreams seemed little more than the smoke that rose above the woods from the burning fields beyond. But she tried not to yield to her breaking heart; as long as she was in the countryside, she conceded, she'd never be unhappy.

Once the autumn term finished the twins returned to the Argentine for the Christmas holidays. Florien disappeared behind his fringe to sulk and Aunt Cicely was left once again to miss Leonora's earnest face and quiet company. She didn't miss Alicia at all and neither did Panazel, Masha and Ravena; only Florien tossed and turned in his hot bed as his dreams burned holes in his pillow.

*   *   *

Grace was now seven years old and was beloved by everyone in the community. She played cards with old Colonel Blythe, now so ancient he had ceased

429

to count the years and although nearly deaf he often heard that strange melody which had once penetrated his psyche and never left him. He now had a heart as soft as marshmallow and wasn't ashamed to show it. Grace danced for Charlo in a white tutu Great Aunt Edna had made for her out of silk and netting and reduced large audiences to tears as her fingers glided fluidly over the keys of the piano. But nothing entertained people more than the 'trick' she performed with objects. 'Show your sisters what you can do,' said Audrey proudly.

'She's terribly clever,' Aunt Edna gushed, buttering a scone. Edna was now so fat there was only enough room for her alone on the sofa, so Audrey sat in one of the arm chairs and the twins on the club fender.

'You're not still talking to fairies,' said Alicia meanly.

'Of course I am,' the child replied and shook her head at her sister. 'They're constantly talking to me. If you listened hard enough you'd hear them too.'

Alicia rolled her eyes. 'So what's this new trick?' she asked with a heavy sigh.

'She'll take an object from someone she doesn't know and tell you all about that person,' said Edna, getting very overexcited at the thought of her great niece's strange gift.

'Do show us, Grace,' Leonora exclaimed kindly. 'What can we give her?' she asked her mother. 'There's no point giving her anything that belongs to us.'

'I have something that was given to me,' said Alicia, removing the pendant that hung about her neck.

'My dear, how pretty!' Aunt Edna exclaimed. 'But don't say a word, not a word. Grace will now tell us all about the person who gave it to you, won't you, Grace?'

Grace took the necklace in her little hands and closed her eyes. She concentrated on emptying her mind of all thoughts. She had a gift for blocking the world out so she didn't even hear Alicia's cynical commentary. Slowly images began to appear before her like pictures on a large screen. 'I see a lovely green field with pretty caravans and some horses,' she began. Leonora gasped and knew immediately whom the necklace belonged to. Alicia's cheeks stung crimson but it was too late to stop her now. 'The caravans are painted. They're gypsy caravans I think, like the ones in Granny's book of fairy tales. I'm hearing the name, Florien. What a funny name that is. He's got dark hair and brown eyes and is looking very sad. I feel his unhappiness. Poor Florien, he's not happy at all. I now see a barn with hay in it. It's lovely and warm and bathed in a golden light. It must be sunset. It's very pretty where he lives, there are hills, not like here.'

'All right, I think that is enough!' said Alicia. But Grace ignored her and continued in her delightfully innocent way.

'Florien's in love with Alicia and he's missing her. His heart is on fire. He can't eat or sleep or do anything at all. He just sits and looks miserable.' Then she laughed and opened her eyes. She looked directly at Leonora who had turned as pale as a ghost.

'Don't look sad, Leo, you're going to be very happy.' Leonora frowned and blushed with embarrassment. No one spoke but they all looked

431

from Alicia to Leonora. Alicia tried to swallow but her throat was dry. Grace's gift had shaken her so that now she trembled with fear and amazement. She grabbed the necklace and began to wind it around her fingers. 'Well, so what if Florien is in love with me,' she retaliated. 'I only took the pendant as a present. I don't love him back.'

'My dear child, of course he's in love with you. You're a very beautiful young woman,' said Aunt Edna with a smile. 'I take it she got it right?'

'She's never been wrong,' said Audrey, pulling Grace into her arms and kissing her face. 'You are very clever, my love.'

'If you can read the future, who am I going to marry?' Alicia challenged, regaining her confidence. But Grace shook her head, leapt off her mother's knee and skipped out into the sunshine.

'She won't abuse her gift by reading fortunes,' Audrey said. 'She learned her lesson after she told Nelly she'll never marry. Nelly hasn't spoken to her since.'

'But it doesn't stop her mother from introducing her to every young man who comes to the Club. Such a humiliation for the poor girl.' Aunt Edna sighed.

'I don't believe in Fate,' said Alicia with a toss of the head. 'You make your own future and I know exactly the way I want mine to be.'

Audrey looked at her wistfully. 'I once believed that, my dear, but one can't always have everything one wants.' She caught her aunt's eye. Edna smiled with compassion. She was pleased that she had convinced her to stay with Cecil all those years ago and she knew Audrey was too. It had been a painful sacrifice, but it had all turned out for the best. After all, beautiful Grace had been born out of their reconciliation and Grace was a very special little girl.

CHAPTER TWENTY-EIGHT

Cecil and Audrey were like two characters in a play. They performed in public with finesse and removed their masks only when they were alone. Only Grace knew the torment that both parents suffered. She watched her mother's dance of tears and observed her father's secret drinking because she had the ability to creep around the house with the light step of a cat and hide in the shadows. But her psychic powers were unable to pick up the reason for their distress, which was unusual because Grace was very gifted. God obviously didn't want her to intrude into her parents' private pain.

Her father's ill humour and sudden bouts of fury failed to affect Grace. She seemed detached, as if suffering was something experienced by other, more earthly people. As if she controlled her emotions rather than letting them control her. She required nothing of him. She didn't want bedtime stories as Leonora and Alicia had done. She preferred to lie in the dark and sing to herself, talk to her spirit friends, or sit looking at the pictures in his collection of National Geographic magazines. This unsettled Cecil, who failed to understand his youngest daughter on any level. What frightened him the most, however, was the expression on her face when she looked at him. Her head on one side, a sympathetic smile and eyes that gazed at him with total understanding. 'Daddy,' she had once said after he had shouted at her for spying on him. 'Your anger only hurts yourself, you know. If you didn't drink so much of that witch's brew you'd be a lot happier.' Cecil had shaken his head in exasperation before storming out of the room, leaving the child sighing with the weariness of a patient old lady.

'Mummy,' she said later, when she found her mother reading in the garden. Audrey put down her book and held out her arms. Grace climbed on to her knee and snuggled up against her. 'Why is Daddy so unhappy?' Audrey suddenly looked defeated. Grace had never asked such a question.

'He's not so unhappy, my love. He just lets life get on top of him sometimes.'

'He *is* unhappy. That witch's brew is turning him into a monster. I don't like the way he shouts at you.'

'Oh, I don't mind. I'm used to it.' She stroked the child's hair and kissed her wide forehead.

'I don't like to see you sad. You are sad sometimes, aren't you?'

'Everyone's sad sometimes.'

'I'm never sad.'

'You're very lucky.'

'Why am I different?' she asked suddenly.

'You're not different, my love, you're special.'

'But no one else I know can see fairies and spirits.'

'You're very gifted. God has opened your inner eye and enabled you to see the world of vibrations. Don't be afraid of it. You're very fortunate. You'll

434

never feel alone.' Then she smiled as she recalled Isla's funeral when the candle flames went out. 'I had a sister once called Isla. She died when she was a young woman. I was very sad because I loved her very much. At her funeral I felt her presence there in the church. I couldn't see her but I most certainly felt her. Then, as if it frustrated her not to be seen, she blew out two of the candles on the altar. That was typical of Isla, she was a very naughty girl. So, you see, you're not so very different. Isla showed herself to me that day. You are lucky, you see spirits all the time. I only "saw" Isla once.'

'What was Isla like?' Grace asked.

'She had long fair hair that fell over her shoulders and down her back in shiny, bouncing curls and sparkling green eyes. Her mouth was always twisted into a naughty smile and she laughed a lot. She would have loved you.'

'I think she's the lady who comes and sits on my bed every night. She strokes my face and kisses my forehead. She's very pretty and kind. I look forward to seeing her when I go to bed.' Audrey didn't doubt her daughter, she had witnessed too much of her strange gift to be sceptical. She blinked as her eyes began to sting with tears and wrapped her arms tightly around her daughter.

'Of course your spirit friend is Isla, my love. She's watching over you. I wish I could see her too,' she said in a husky voice. They sat there entwined for a long while as Audrey remembered her sister then cast her thoughts to Louis. When she looked down at her child's face she saw that she was sleeping.

435

*   *   *

Once back in England Alicia enjoyed toying with Florien's heart. It was a new game and greatly entertaining. She'd lure him into the barn and make love to him with tenderness, whispering all kinds of promises and declaring her love with tears and sighs then later ignore him, only to pick him up again a few days later when it suited her. Florien trod water in this cruel sea, allowing the waves to batter him about, but he didn't drown for calmer waters were always just on the horizon and he longed for them so much that he kept afloat.

Leonora watched quietly as Florien grew paler and thinner. She didn't tell him when he planted the wrong bulb in the garden or when he gave the chickens the pig feed because she understood. She was tormented and distracted herself. She knew what Alicia was up to because she had seen the numbers of boys she had flirted with in the Argentine, leading them all a merry dance like the pied piper of Hamelin. She longed to tell him and put him out of his misery, but she was Alicia's sister and as their mother always said, 'Family must stick together. Blood is thicker than water.' And Leonora was as loyal as a faithful dog. As usual she didn't blame Alicia. After all, it wasn't her fault that God had made her beguiling and lovely. She pitied the men who lost their hearts to her and she didn't blame them either. She accepted Florien's infatuation as inevitable but her heart yearned for him still.

The year passed by quickly and soon the twins left Colehurst House for the last time. Audrey expected them to return to the Argentine but to

436

her surprise and sadness they both wished to remain in England. Leonora because she loved Florien and Alicia because she felt that society was superior in England and there weren't any rich Dukes or Princes to marry in Hurlingham. Then Henry died.

It happened suddenly. A heart attack in the middle of the night and he had died in his sleep, without any knowledge of it. Rose was devastated. Henry had been her soulmate and she had loved him all her life. Cecil, Audrey and Grace went to her at once and found Aunt Edna and Aunt Hilda keeping her company in the dining room where she was holding a candle-lit vigil. When Grace saw the body of her grandfather lying there on the table she smiled at her grandmother and said, 'He's with Isla now, isn't he?' Rose was grateful for the child's faith and burst into tears again.

'You're so right, my dear. How happy that makes me to think of them together. It won't be long before I join them both. What joy it will be to see them again,' she said, wiping her tears.

'I wish he had taken Herbert with him,' Hilda hissed to Edna.

'It's always the people one loves the least who go on and on and on,' Edna replied. 'Dear Henry was a good man. I understand exactly why God wants him back. I'm afraid your husband will be around for some time.' *And so will you*, she thought wickedly. She was getting much less tolerant in her old age.

After Henry's death Cecil decided the time had come to return to England. This time Audrey's response was very different. 'It is for the best,' she said. 'After all, the twins have made their home in

437

England and we must be a family again. All together. Grace barely knows her sisters, which is a great shame.'

'I'm so pleased you agree,' he replied seriously. He rarely smiled these days.

'I shall miss my mother and Aunt Edna and Hurlingham. But it won't go away and besides, travelling is getting easier all the time. I think I could grow to love England.'

'You will love England. It is a beautiful place. I think we need a new start, Audrey.' She looked up at him and pulled a thin smile. He was right, they couldn't go on like this, making each other miserable. Audrey with her memories, Cecil with his drink. 'I won't drink another drop from the moment we arrive in England,' he said.

Audrey lowered her eyes. 'And I shall leave my memories behind.'

They both stared at each other in amazement. That was the first time they had communicated in many years.

Death often bequeaths a surprising gift to those left behind. An appreciation of life. So it was with Audrey and Cecil. They both sat together at the funeral and thought how many funerals they had been to and how each one had affected them profoundly. Audrey remembered her father whom she had adored and hoped that Grace was right, that there was life after death and that he was with Isla and Aunt Edna's Sunshine Harry in some wonderful paradise. She flinched when Cecil took her hand. It reminded her of that time, all those years ago, when he had first taken it during the performance of *Giselle* at the Teatro Colón. This time she didn't ignore it. She squeezed it, then her eyes glistened with tears. It was time to give Louis up for ever. She would leave the Argentine and all those memories behind. The cherry trees and the station, the Hurlingham Club and the cobbled streets of Palermo, Gaitano's ranch and his silent understanding that continued to keep Louis' memory alive. Happiness was up to her and she had a choice. She could either live in the past and be miserable or try to recapture the fondness she had once felt for her husband. Spring always follows winter, she thought and although it was cold outside, spring wasn't far away.

It was time she admitted that Cecil's drinking was her fault. With her help he could stop. She looked across at him, her eyes filled with compassion and squeezed his hand again. How noble he had been. He had remained with her when she had broken her marriage vows and then done what few men would have the courage to do, bring up another man's child as his own. As far as he was concerned Grace was his third daughter and he had always treated her the same as the twins. How could she fail to appreciate all of that? 'I've hurt you so much,' she whispered.

His eyes flickered with emotion, but he put his finger across his lips, 'Shhhh,' he cautioned. 'We'll be overheard.'

'I want to start again.' This time he nodded at her then looked away. The alcohol had dulled his senses so that now he wasn't sure whether he was imagining or hearing those words for real. 'I want to earn your forgiveness,' she continued in a loud whisper. Cecil was too moved to reply.

*   *   *

439

There was one thing that Audrey had to do before they left for England. Taking Grace with her she boarded the train for the city. 'Where are we going?' Grace asked, staring happily out of the window.

'To a very special place that I want you to see before you leave.'

'Will I like it?'

'Yes you will. It's a nice place, a magical place. I'll take you for an ice cream afterwards if you like.'

'Yummy,' she enthused in excitement. 'I can't wait to see the gypsies.'

'Well, Daddy's bought a house very near to Aunt Cicely so you can see them as often as you like.'

'I'm going to like England very much,' she said. But she kept a fear to herself. For the first time in her life she felt apprehensive. Not about going to live in another country, that was a thrilling prospect, but she worried that the spirits might not go with her. She didn't ask her mother if there were spirits in England because she knew she wouldn't know the answer. And she didn't want to ask her spirit friends in case they said no, for then she would be very sad to leave them. She would just have to wait and see. But the possibility that Isla might not be there at night to kiss her to sleep worried Grace very deeply.

Audrey and Grace arrived in Palermo. It had changed since the days when she had danced there with Louis. The small tavern was gone and in its place a restaurant now served lunch. The square was still as it was, the same jacaranda trees about to burst into flower with the arrival of spring, the same dilapidated buildings that surrounded it with

440

the same dusty windows. But they stared at her with the eyes of strangers, for many years had passed and they failed to recognise her any more. Only the ghostly music of the tango floated on the air from a gramophone somewhere, or was it just the wind rattling through old memories?

Grace didn't speak while her mother stood in the middle of the square, her thoughts lost in another era. She looked about her and wondered what was so special about this part of the city. It was old and worn and sad. She sensed the vibrations and her heart flooded with melancholy. The square was draped in a mist of nostalgia and Grace knew intuitively that it had something to do with her mother's dance of tears. She looked up at her and saw that she was crying once again. But she still didn't want to ruin the moment. Crying was very healing, that's what her grandmother often told her. So she let her cry and wandered off to puff like a train into the cold winter air and watch her breath rise up in a cloud of steam.

Audrey stood very still and remembered. For the last time she recalled what it had felt like to dance in his arms in this very square. To feel the bristle of his skin tickling her forehead and temple, to hug him close and live in the moment. Not in the past or in the future but in the now. 'Oh, Louis,' she sighed out loud. 'I will never stop loving you but in order to live I must let you go.' There followed a heavy silence and then the elusive music of the tango began to play again. 'Grace, can you hear the music?' she asked her. Grace came slipping back and cocked her head to one side. She frowned.

'What music?'

'That music? Can't you hear it?'

441

'There's no music playing, Mummy,' said Grace and she laughed, skipping about the square once more, puffing like a train. Audrey smiled for she still heard it and later when she went to bed she heard it again. Only when she arrived in England did it stop and she knew an old life had ended and a new one begun. It was time to start again.

*   *   *

The moment Grace set foot in England she searched around the airport for spirits. She saw none and her heart stumbled. She was suddenly overcome with a pain she had never experienced before, panic. Like a dog chasing its tail Grace spun around and around desperate to see some sort of smoky being. She saw nothing but people with suitcases and they looked very real indeed. Cecil waved at Aunt Cicely who was waiting for them behind the barrier to drive them down to Dorset. Grace was now quite tearful. She blinked hard, trying to disguise her misery. She wished she had had the courage to ask them; at least then she would have been prepared. She would have had the opportunity to say good-bye.

'Hello, Grace, I'm Aunt Cicely,' said Cicely, bending down. The child extended her hand. Audrey frowned. It was most unlike Grace to look so sad.

'Are you all right, my love?' she asked in a concerned voice. Grace's mouth turned down and she looked past Aunt Cicely and extended her hand to the man who was now smiling at her. Aunt Cicely looked beside her then back at Grace.

'Pleased to meet you, Uncle Hugh,' said Grace
442

without smiling.

'Hugh?' Cicely gasped and looked at Cecil.

'My dear, who are you greeting?' Cecil asked. Suddenly Grace's face was transformed into a wide, excited smile.

'You're a spirit!' she exclaimed, laughing at Hugh. Hugh just smiled back then disappeared. Grace looked about her. 'Totem!' she cried, clapping her hands together. 'Oh, Mummy, I thought I'd left them all behind. I'm so happy.'

Audrey put her arm around her daughter and smiled down at her. 'I'll explain later,' she said, winking at her sister-in-law.

'I think you had better,' she replied, a little shaken. 'If she's seen Hugh I dread to think who else she's going to see in my rickety old house.'

That night, Audrey kissed her youngest goodnight and ran a hand down her soft cheek. 'We'll move into our new house the moment it's ready, my love, then you'll have your own bedroom.' She smiled tenderly at the little girl who had brought her so much happiness and felt her body glow with love.

'I'm so glad the spirits have come with me,' she said, grinning up at her mother.

'But of course they have. They fly about the place with no difficulty at all, crossing an ocean is nothing for them.'

'I know. But I still worried about it.'

'You should have told me.'

'I will next time I have a worry.'

'Good, because that's what I'm here for.'

'I really love you, Mummy,' she said suddenly, looking straight into her mother's eyes. Audrey caught her breath for Grace wasn't a sentimental

443

child. She bent over and wrapped her little girl in her arms.

'Oh darling, that's the nicest thing you've ever said. I love you too, very much.' They held each other for a moment while Audrey silently thanked God for the gift of Grace and Grace enjoyed the warm cocoon of her mother's embrace. Then Grace laid her head back down upon the pillow.

'I hope Isla kisses me goodnight too,' she said. 'You once had long hair like hers, didn't you?'

'Yes, I did. But I'm too old for hair like that now.'

'You're beautiful.'

'So are you. But you've got a rare gift, my love, because you're even more beautiful on the inside.' She hesitated a moment, remembering that that was what Cecil used to say to her.

When she left the room and closed the door she hovered a moment until she heard Grace's voice greet her spirit friend. 'I knew you'd come,' she said. 'Because you know I need you.' She smiled to herself and sighed. She loved all her three children and yet, there was something about Grace that made her love her more intensely. Alicia and Leonora were young women now, but Grace was still a child and would always be childlike. That she had inherited from her father. She wasn't made for the material world and Audrey felt it was her duty to protect her from it, for as long as she was able.

She went downstairs to where Leonora and Alicia were talking to Aunt Cicely and their father in the kitchen. Leonora was lying on a beanbag with Barley, who gazed up at her with the opaque eyes of an old man. He had even grown white around the nose and eyebrows. Alicia slouched in

444

the armchair by the Aga, drinking Coca Cola and eating a packet of crisps. She looked up at her mother when she entered the room and suddenly remembered Mercedes. 'Mummy, was Merchi sad to say good-bye?' she asked.

'You know Mercedes,' Audrey replied, raising her eyebrows. 'She never liked to show emotion. But I think she was sad. Mind you, she was old and it was time for her to retire and rest a little. You know she's living with Oscar now.'

Alicia laughed heartily. 'That doesn't surprise me. He always had the hots for her. What happened to that hideous parrot?'

'Oh, Loro.' Audrey chuckled. 'I'm afraid he died.'

'How did he die?' Leonora asked from the beanbag. She paused her hand over Barley's head and he began to nudge it with his wet nose.

'He fell into a pot of boiling water.'

The girls both stared at their mother with shock. Cicely stopped stirring the Bolognese sauce and turned around. 'What a hideous way to go,' she said. 'Reminds me of the pheasant that flew in here one evening. I found him roasting with the chicken. Of course, it would have been a bonus had he been plucked first.' Cecil looked at his sister quizzically. Cicely never used to be this fanciful. When he later met Marcel, who deigned to descend from his attic studio for supper, he understood why she had changed. Later when he looked at himself in the mirror he realised that he had changed too, and not for the better.

He climbed into bed with his wife and they both lay staring out into the darkness and into their future, which now seemed suddenly frighteningly

445

uncertain. 'I was brought up in an old house like this,' he said. 'We used to play hide and seek, though Papa used to call it 'Cocky Ollie' for some reason. The house was a labyrinth of corridors and little rooms here and there, it was a magical place for Cocky Ollie. You could disappear for hours and never be found.' He wanted to add that Louis often hid somewhere so brilliant that they were still searching for him long after the game had finished. Then they stopped bothering and just left him until he came out on his own, hungry and sleepy, having missed supper and his bedtime. But he didn't want Audrey to think of Louis. That was behind them now. He took her hand and remembered what she had said in the church. She didn't withdraw it.

'Tell me more about your childhood, Cecil,' she whispered. While he began to paint a vivid picture he felt her edge closer until their bodies were pressed tightly together like they had often been in the early days of their marriage. As she revealed the quiet stirring of her affection, Cecil's confidence began to grow. He was suddenly reminded of the man he had once been and with a fiery determination he vowed to find that man again. He was still there somewhere, beneath the broken pieces of a once formidable soldier. He could hear the distant echo of the accolades heaped upon him after his glorious successes in the war and he began to emerge from a long and wintry hibernation.

He rolled over and kissed her. At first Audrey was stunned. She lay a moment without moving, her body frozen with panic. But little by little she warmed to his attentions until she finally surrendered the long war of resistance. She wound

446

her arms around his neck and became his wife once again. And with his gentle loving she was reminded of all the reasons she had married him in the first place and why she had grown so fond of him. He held her with reverence and made love to her with the tenderness of a man who, in spite of all the pain and humiliation, had never allowed resentment to destroy his love. He had always hoped that if he resisted acknowledging her affair it might go away. His instincts had been right.

CHAPTER TWENTY-NINE

'I don't love you anymore,' said Alicia to Florien. She watched his face turn grey with disbelief, leaving only his ears to throb as the blood from his cheeks drained into them, betraying his anguish. He was speechless. He had been on the verge of asking her to marry him.

Since leaving school Leonora had taken up employment with Aunt Cicely. In exchange for gardening she boarded and lodged for free. Although her parents had bought a house only twenty minutes away in a small village by the sea, it was more convenient for her to continue living with her aunt. Alicia had spent one year at finishing school in Switzerland, learning how to ski, speak French and the fine art of seduction, of which she had had no little experience with Florien in the barn in Dorset. Rich, handsome men from all over the globe came to study at Le Rosay in Morges and there was more on their minds too than algebra.

Florien waited. He sulked behind his fringe,

spoke little and barely smiled at all. Even Leonora was unable to reach him. Each day her heart bled. Drop by drop as she watched his dark gypsy eyes gaze through her to Alicia, who was constantly in his thoughts, mesmerising him with her dark allure. She pretended she didn't notice when he ignored her or when he snapped at her but later she curled into a ball on her bed and licked her wounds like a dog. She knew she should leave and go somewhere else where she wasn't reminded every day of his rejection, but she couldn't. She might not have his love but she had his company and that was better than not having him at all.

She wanted so much to talk to her mother about her aching soul, but she knew she wouldn't understand. She had never loved like this nor longed like this and besides, it had been years since she had confided in her. The lines of communication between them were no longer as open as they had once been. Grace had taken her place.

When Alicia returned, tanned and more beautiful than before, she picked Florien up as if he were a pet she had left with the neighbours. They made love once again in the barn and in the pool house until Alicia bored of the tedium of those places and preferred to take him into the woods or the fields and make love there beneath the sky. Once again Florien emerged from his sulk, his eyes blinked away the dust and shone and his smile lit up his face and turned his cheeks a healthy pink. He noticed Leonora because his spirits lifted and he suddenly noticed everything around him. But he wasn't thinking of her when he talked to her or when he laughed with her. He was drunk with love and his happiness was because of Alicia.

But Leonora's spirits lifted too. It didn't matter that it wasn't because of her that he now chatted jovially and chuckled for no reason. If he was happy then she was happy too.

The countryside bored Alicia. There was nothing to do. So she moved to London where she stayed with her friend Mattie, in her parents' spacious apartment in Kensington. Mattie didn't dare ask for rent, she knew her friend would baulk at the suggestion. Alicia was used to being given whatever she wanted. She had that effect on people. Even shopkeepers found it hard to take money from such a beautiful young woman and often gave her discounts. She knew when to be gracious but the rest of the time she didn't bother trying. Her moods swung from excitement to irritability with no prior warning. There was no reason for her petulance. She lived off her adrenaline. Without thrill she sunk into boredom and lashed out at the people closest to her.

It would have been easy for Alicia to finish with Florien. She saw him only at weekends or for a little longer in the summertime when the weather was too stifling to remain in the city. London was brimming with eligible young men in search of beautiful wives and Alicia was entertained like a princess. She toyed with them all, taking her pleasure when she wanted it, avoiding their calls when she had tired of them. But Florien remained a constant fixture in her changeable life. She began to grow fond of him in spite of herself. The more his confidence grew the bigger his personality became. She discovered that there was more to him than the smouldering dark looks of his gypsy heritage. He was witty and playful, intelligent and perceptive. Alicia's love was all used up on herself so she didn't have much left for anyone else, even Florien. But there was something about him that drew her to him so that she found herself returning to Dorset most weekends like a homing pigeon. While in the arms of her more sophisticated city lovers she always resolved to leave her country friend. Yet, she had never seemed able to. Until now.

'I'm sorry, Florien. I just don't love you any more,' she repeated. It was springtime, the woods vibrated with the clamour of birds and the vitality of growing foliage and plants, giving them a soft mattress of bluebells to lie on. They hadn't made love for Alicia felt uncomfortable. She desired Florien, but he was too poor. It was as simple as that.

'Yes, you do,' he retaliated, shaking his head, unable to come to terms with her sudden change of heart. 'I'm not grand enough for you, that's all.' She listened to him speak with his coarse country accent and cringed. She could never share her life with him for his was going nowhere. She envisaged private yachts and aeroplanes. The fast life of the rich and famous. The open road of the privileged. Holidays on the French Riviera, skiing in St Moritz, shopping in Paris. She gazed at him with regret. She would miss him, but he was right. He wasn't grand enough for her.

'Florien, it's not that. You're lovely but we're just not right for each other. I want to spend more time in London. It's not convenient.'

'I'll come up to London.'

She laughed. 'And stay where?' She placed her

450

hand on his but he withdrew it. 'It's been a lovely affair. We've enjoyed each other. All good things come to an end.' He looked at her with dejected eyes and she realised that she was being flippant. She adjusted her face to reflect his and sighed heavily, the way women do when they don't know what to say.

'You have no idea how I feel, Alicia. I love you. I can't live without you.' His throat shuddered as he swallowed while the weight of emotion on his chest began to suffocate him. He looked at her with glassy eyes and the corners of his mouth twitched as if he was trying his best not to cry. 'I thought you were capable of feeling. But now I realise that I was wrong. You don't feel like other people. You're too selfish to allow yourself to be touched because you can't bear to be vulnerable or to suffer pain. But I've been touched by you and now I can't live without you, in spite of your faults.'

Alicia shrugged. 'What do you want me to do?'

'I was going to ask you to marry me,' he said in a small voice, reflecting on the magnificence of the spring day that had seemed such a perfect setting for his proposal.

'Well, I've answered,' she said, growing impatient with him. 'I can't say I'm sorry any more because there aren't any other words for sorry. Sorry, sorry, sorry.'

She stood up and brushed down her jeans, adjusting the silk Hermès headscarf that one of her suitors had given her.

'So this is it?' said Florien, blinking at her in astonishment. 'This is what I get in return for loving you like I do?'

'What do you expect?' she asked, putting her

hands on her hips and shaking her head with irritation.

'I don't know, but not this.'

'Well, if you don't know, how am I supposed to? God, Florien, I've just finished our affair, what do you want, a medal?' He reeled back as if she had struck him. 'I'm going back to London now. Marry Leonora, she's more your type and, unlike me, she *wants* to be a gypsy,' she said, stomping off through the bluebells.

'I thought we had a future together,' he protested, following her.

Alicia spun around, her eyes blazing. 'Look, Florien. I have never loved you, okay? I desired you. I enjoyed you. You're a good lover. I've had many. Don't think for one moment that while I was in Switzerland or in London I was saving myself for you. No, I took lovers when I felt like it. Lots of them. They all fulfilled me in the same way that you did. The only difference was that I liked you. You were more than a body, Florien. You made me laugh. We had fun together. But that doesn't mean I want to spend the rest of my life with you. It's the seventies, for God's sake.'

Florien watched her stride through the trees until she was out of sight. He stood there with his mouth agape and his eyes bulging. He had never felt so humiliated in his entire life. So used and so discarded. He was too furious to cry so he let himself go like an enraged animal in a cage, kicking the surrounding trees and pounding his hands against the bark. Finally when he was sweating and exhausted he collapsed onto the ground and put his face in his hands and wailed. His whole body felt hollow, as if she had scooped out his insides with a spoon and left only his skin. He hated her with all his strength and yet hate is love's other face. When he had calmed down he realised that if he had loved her before he was now entirely consumed by her.

Florien retreated into his gloomy world. He no longer smiled and Leonora was once again cast aside. She knew what had happened although neither Alicia nor Florien ever mentioned it. He was so miserable that she found herself hoping they would patch up their differences and get back together, then at least he would be happy and he would notice her again. But the weeks rolled on into months and soon a year had passed and they had seen nothing of Alicia.

The following year when the bluebells once again occupied the woods like a vast blue army Florien began to speak again. He remembered the day Alicia had spurned him as if it were yesterday and the wound was still raw and bleeding. But his misery was damaging his health. He'd grown pale and thin and his glossy black hair had begun to fall out. Then one day he was shaken from his stupor by his own, haggard reflection staring miserably back at him from the mirror. He gazed upon the strange face in horror, scrutinising his now bearded chin and the haunted look in his eyes. If Alicia were to see him now she wouldn't recognise him. What's worse, she would despise him for having let himself go. If he wanted to win her back he would have to shave, scrub up and look as if he was enjoying life without her. No one respected a man who didn't respect himself.

Leonora was shocked when next she saw him. Not only was his face smooth and clean but he was smiling. 'Let's take a look at what we planted last autumn,' he suggested, walking with her around to the back of the house. Leonora felt uncomfortable for surely her sister was back, why else would he have made such an effort? He hadn't smiled in a year. But she soon realised that the sudden change in his appearance as well as his humour were entirely his own initiative. He must have decided to get on with his life.

Then, just when Leonora was beginning to enjoy her deepening friendship with Florien, Cicely announced that the gypsies were leaving. 'But Florien hasn't mentioned it to me,' she exclaimed in astonishment.

'That's because he's still dreaming of your sister,' Cicely replied, pursing her lips. She was awed by the masochism of the men who took her on. They were no match for Alicia; she was stronger and more resilient than any of them. She would always have the advantage for she didn't have a heart to be broken.

'When did Panazel tell you?'

'This morning.'

'Where are they going?'

'I don't know. They've been here for years, perhaps they want a change of scene.'

It was late evening. The sun was sinking over the ripening corn fields and the warm kitchen smelt of steak and kidney pie. Leonora was in her usual place on the floor with the dogs, having changed out of her muddy gardening clothes for dinner. They waited for Marcel to emerge from the attic. 'Do you think Florien will go too?' Leonora asked, trying to hide her sadness, but her voice cracked. She coughed to disguise it, then got up and poured herself a glass of water.

'He's an adult. I'm sure he can do what he wants,' Cicely replied, straining the peas. 'He likes it here, doesn't he?'

'Yes, I think he does. He's certainly been a lot happier in the last few months,' she said.

'I wish I could say the same for Marcel.' Cicely sighed. 'He's been broody for so long I can't remember the last time he smiled.' She wandered back to the Aga, glancing at the clock.

'Marcel is always broody. That's the way he wants to be seen. He's like a caricature,' said Leonora and laughed. 'But he's very handsome.'

'You know, initially I fell in love with him for his looks. It was hard not to. But then, as I got to know him, I realised that a very tender man dwelt beneath that smouldering Gallic exterior. It's an unconventional relationship. He's young enough to be my son. He'll probably run off with someone his own age in the end, but I have enjoyed him immensely.'

'Don't say that, Aunt Cicely,' Leonora exclaimed. 'He's lucky to have you. He should be worrying that you're going to run off with someone your own age.' Aunt Cicely chuckled.

'Goodness me, I'm almost sixty!'

'And you're still young and attractive. Love doesn't stop just because you're sixty. Daddy's in his mid fifties and love hasn't dried up for him and Mummy. I think it just gets better as one gets older.'

'You're so positive, darling,' she said, then shook her head. 'Let's start. If broody Byron upstairs can't come down on time for dinner he's going to find his food has grown cold.' Then she looked at

455

Leonora and grinned wistfully. 'I like the person I am when I'm with him and that's half the battle.'

They started to eat in silence, Leonora worrying that Florien might leave with his family and Cicely quietly fuming over Marcel's absence from the dinner table.

In all these years he had never let her see any of his paintings. 'My elusive creativity,' he would say, locking the door behind him. She assumed it was because of shyness, but lately she had begun to wonder whether he did any painting at all. He had grown sullen and distant. At least Florien had snapped out of his mood; Marcel was still so tightly wrapped in his ill-humour, she could hardly make him out.

Dinner was finished and Leonora went to bed. She didn't sleep much for her mind was like a flour mill, grinding all her hopes into dust. If Florien were to leave, what would become of her? In the morning she came down to breakfast to find the dogs in a state of excitement, chasing each other around the kitchen table. She frowned and fought her way through to the biscuit tin, then threw them one to quieten them down. When her aunt appeared with swollen eyes and blotchy skin she realised something serious had happened. 'He's left me,' she wailed, crumpling into the armchair beside the Aga. 'No wonder he didn't appear for dinner. He's left the attic empty but for a painting leaning against the wall. I haven't looked at it yet, I can't bear to.'

'Are you sure he's gone?' Leonora asked, crouching down beside her and placing her arm on her aunt's.

Cicely smiled cynically. 'Darling, he's packed his

456

bags and gone, there's no doubt about it. He hasn't hopped off on holiday, I can assure you.'

'But didn't he give any indication that this was on his mind?'

Cicely shook her head and squeezed out a few more tears. 'We've hardly spoken recently. He's been so grumpy. I just thought that if I ignored it, it would go away. It did. All of it.' She chuckled sadly. 'What a fool I was to believe that he loved me. He didn't love me at all. He loved my cooking and my washing machine. I was convenient.'

'Don't be hard on yourself, Aunt Cicely. You were much more than that. He's a rat.'

'Yes. I wish I had known that. But he made me feel young again and attractive. After Hugh died I felt like an old woman. A stiff, conventional old bag. Marcel was like the Prince in Sleeping Beauty, one kiss and I came alive again.' She took a deep breath then looked at her niece with weary eyes. 'What is it with me? My lovely gypsies are leaving me too.'

Leonora made her aunt a cup of coffee while she snivelled into a hanky. She suddenly looked her age, as if Marcel had taken her youth with him. She wondered where he had gone and why he had left so suddenly. 'Didn't he leave a note?'

'Nothing.'

'Perhaps he left a message in that painting,' Leonora suggested, pulling a chair nearer her aunt and sitting down.

'Do you think so?'

'Well, why else would he leave it? He took all the others, didn't he?'

'What others? I doubt he's painted much in all the years he's been sponging off me. What he did

457

up there is nobody's business.'

'When was the last time you saw him?'

'At lunch yesterday.'

'He didn't say a word,' she recalled.

'Not a word.'

'But he was always grumpy. He never made conversation, just delivered monologues.'

Cicely laughed into her coffee. 'You know you're very sharp, Leonora. Alicia might have all the beauty but you've got all the wit.'

'Thank you,' Leonora replied, wishing that God had been a little fairer in distributing the beauty; perhaps if she were prettier Florien might have fallen in love with her instead.

'You know what else?'

'What?'

'You're getting better looking every day because your nature is beginning to show in your features. Alicia will end up looking as sour as her heart. You watch. Beauty only lasts beyond youth if one's got the character to match it. I'll confide in you now, because I'm drunk with grief. I've never liked your sister. She's a nasty piece of work and always has been.'

'She's not a bad person. She's just selfish. But I love her all the same,' Leonora protested.

'I know you do. The mind boggles . . .'

'She's my sister. We were sent away together, she was the only family I had.'

'Poor old you.'

'Not at all. She's beautiful and gifted.'

'What's that got to do with it? She's unkind and selfish. She's been horrid to you and you've always taken it. She'd sell her own grandmother if she had to and she'd sell you too!' But Leonora just smiled the smile of someone entirely confident with her own judgement. *She's bewitched you too*, thought Cicely. Then her skin began to crawl.

She ran upstairs to the attic leaving Leonora sitting in front of the Aga, patting a very aged, nearly blind Barley. With a heart suspended with anticipation she hurried as fast as she could to Marcel's small studio, terrified of what she would find. She turned the doorknob and walked inside. The room still smelt of him, that sweet scent of France mingled with the strong blend of paints and paper, dust and stale air, because he had rarely opened the window. She stood a moment, surveying the room, seeing him working there still in the dawn light that tumbled in through the glass. Her eyes rested on the painting that lay against the wall. It was large, painted onto hard canvas. She bit the skin around her thumbnail, scarcely daring to breathe. She feared she knew what was on it. If Leonora was right and Marcel had left the painting in order to communicate a message to her, then she prayed her fears were unfounded. Slowly she walked towards it.

With trembling hands she pulled the canvas from the wall and let it drop on the floor. She caught her breath. There in delightful abandonment was the luminous body of Alicia, as naked as the day she had been born. Cicely turned cold at the sight of her niece. She didn't question her innocence or presume for one moment that the painting might have arisen out of Marcel's imagination. A work of fantasy. She looked back to when Alicia had left and realised that it coincided with Marcel's declining humour. Could Alicia have seduced Marcel as well as Florien? Why not

Panazel as well? In her aunt's mind Alicia rose up like Medusa, her hair a writhing mass of snakes and her eyes capable of enchanting anyone who dared look into them. She could have coped with Marcel leaving her for a younger woman eventually, but to leave her because of Alicia was more than she could take. With one kick her foot shot straight through the canvas, transforming Alicia's beautiful, self-indulgent face into a ragged hole.

CHAPTER THIRTY

Florien didn't want to leave with his family. He knew that if he went away he would never see Alicia again and his spirit still burned in its own hellish inferno, ignited that day in the hay bales when they had made love for the first time. From the moment he had shaved off his beard he had silently vowed to himself that he would win her back. However long it took and whatever he had to do to achieve his goal, she would come crawling back begging forgiveness. And he would forgive her.

But while Florien focused his thoughts and intent on Alicia he failed to notice that little by little his heart was slowly yielding to Leonora. Leonora who was always there. Leonora, whose affection was as unconditional as one of Cicely's dogs. He took her friendship for granted and felt so comfortable with her that he barely noticed her, like an old blanket whose warmth he could always count on. She rode out with him over the Dorset hills, shared the sunrise and the sunset and enjoyed the delights of the ever changing countryside. She understood him, but most of all she made him feel magnificent.

*   *   *

Florien sat in the tractor by the side of the field waiting for the combine to be ready to unload. The heat was insufferable. It was midday and not a cloud marred the clear perfection of the sky. He had taken his shirt off and his brown back and chest glistened in the sunshine but he was still hot and longed for a swim in Mrs Weatherby's pool. Then he heard the familiar bell on Leonora's bike as she arrived with a basket of cold beer. He thought of leaving and his heart lurched. How he'd miss the sound of Leonora's companionship. She climbed up and handed him a can, withdrawing a packet of biscuits from the pocket in her dungarees. She didn't smile. Instead she gazed at him with her large, sad eyes and asked in a tentative voice if it was true that he was going to leave. 'I'm afraid so,' he replied flatly, watching her carefully. 'Dad wants to move up north.'

'But it's so nice here and you're happy, aren't you?' Her eyes began to glitter with tears.

'I love it here. I don't want to go,' he said, opening the can.

'When is Panazel planning on leaving?'

'After the harvest.'

'Can't you stay?' He looked at Leonora's long, sensitive face and he felt a strange stirring in his heart, like the slow thawing of ice. He held her in his gaze for a long moment. For the first time ever he actually saw her, not as plain, but as endearingly

461

beautiful and he wondered why he had never noticed before. She lowered her eyes as the intimacy of his gaze sliced away her confidence. He had never looked at her like that before.

'You know, it's only when you're about to lose something that you realise how much it means to you,' he said in a very soft voice. He wiped the sweat from his forehead with a dusty rag. Leonora assumed he was talking of her aunt's farm.

'You're part of the place now,' she replied.

He looked up at her from beneath his thick lashes. 'I didn't mean Holholly Grange,' he said, but he didn't smile. He was too stunned and confused by such an unfamiliar rush of emotions.

Leonora's face suddenly turned the colour of a beetroot. 'I . . . I'll bring you some more beer later. You're needed,' she stammered, indicating with a nod that the arm of the combine was out, ready for his trailer. He turned the key and the engine began to rattle like the guttural chuckle of an old man. She stepped down and mounted her bicycle. As she cycled back up the farm tracks she wondered what he had meant if he hadn't meant Aunt Cicely's farm. He couldn't have meant her, could he?

By the time she arrived back at the house she had convinced herself that he couldn't possibly have meant her. He had been sick with loving her sister, how foolish to have imagined, even for a brief moment, that he might have grown fond of her. She shook her head to rid it of such optimism then set about weeding the borders and cutting the sweet peas for Aunt Cicely's kitchen. There were beans of every type to be peeled or podded and raspberries and rhubarb to be picked. With her help Aunt Cicely's vegetable garden had flourished

462

into a veritable cornucopia and little gave Leonora more pleasure than to work there in the sunshine, listening to the restful murmur of the combines and the light chatter of birds. But now her mind spun with all sorts of thoughts and dreams and disturbed the languid tranquillity of the afternoon. If Florien were to leave he would take all that she loved about the place with him. Nothing would look as beautiful ever again for even when the skies were grey the countryside vibrated with loveliness because he was in it. She couldn't bear it. For the first time in her life she envied and resented Alicia. She had had his love and she had thrown it away.

* * *

As the harvest progressed Leonora worked hard in the garden, but she always made time to take Florien cans of cold beer and biscuits and would often sit with him in his tractor while he drove to the farm to dump the corn. She was aware of a change in him, but she didn't want to harbour any hope that their friendship might be developing into something more profound. He never spoke of Alicia and he now looked at her with his eyes focused and alert, not through her to the shadowy image of his former lover. He took time with her. He asked her about herself, her feelings, her dreams and her memories of the Argentine. And for the first time he really listened.

Then one night as the harvest drew to a close, she lay beside him staring up at the stars as the campfire flickered and finally died, recounting the golden days of her early childhood in Hurlingham, the homesickness she suffered at Colehurst House

463

and the passion that she had discovered she had for Nature. 'I don't want to be anywhere else. A city would choke me to death.'

'Me too,' he agreed. 'I hate the fumes and the noise.'

'The chaos, everyone running everywhere without any time for anyone else.'

'I've always lived in the countryside. I'd be lost without it.'

'Where will you go, Florien?' she asked and felt again that familiar pain in her chest.

'When I was a boy we roamed from farm to farm in Yorkshire. Now Dad wants to go back.'

'But why?'

Florien sighed heavily. 'He's stayed with Mrs Weatherby for many years because he likes her and the work has always been good. But, you know she's going to sell the farm.'

'I didn't know that,' she gasped in horror.

'She won't have told you because it doesn't affect you. She'll keep the house but that neighbour of hers who farms it for her now wants to buy it. He's a big landowner. You only make money farming if you have a lot of land. Your aunt's plot is very small.'

Leonora fell silent and gazed bleakly up into the glittering black sky above her. 'Marcel left her,' she said in a quiet voice.

'I know. She looks miserable.'

'She is.'

'Why did he run off then?'

'Probably for the same reason that your father wants to move up north. A new scene.'

'He was young enough to be her son.'

'But she loved him.'

'Love is strange, isn't it?'

Suddenly Florien felt something he had never experienced before. It wasn't the intense burning of Alicia's demonic aura or the insistent demands of possessiveness that had constantly pulled at him but something gentle and warm and sad. They lay side by side in silence while he tried to work out what it was that had come over him and Leonora contemplated an uncertain future. Tentatively he took her hand.

Leonora barely dared breathe or blink in case she ruined the moment. She closed her eyes and assured herself that he was offering nothing more than his friendship. She dared not presume anything more. She held his hand back, swallowing the longing that rose up her throat in a desperate cry. But like Saint Paul on the road to Damascus Florien had seen the light. It filled him up, made him want to laugh with happiness, prostrate himself in humility, yield to it in awe and he rolled onto his side and gazed into her features. Then he kissed her. Leonora was so stunned she lay as still as one of the logs on the fire.

When Florien pulled away and looked down on her face he noticed it had opened like a sunflower. In the golden light of the diminishing fire she looked beautiful, as if his kiss had transformed her like the kiss of a prince in a fairy tale. She smiled up at him, a smile that was at once tender and shy and her love empowered him so that he felt as strong as Hercules. While Alicia had emasculated him Leonora filled him with confidence so that when he kissed her again he didn't doubt her affection but knew she gave it with all her heart. And this time Leonora responded by wrapping her

465

arms around him and kissing him back.

'Oh, Leonora, I've been such a fool,' he exclaimed after a while, brushing his lips across her temple and smelling the scent of nature that clung to her hair.

'You're not a fool at all,' she murmured happily.

'Not any more. I'll never be a fool again.'

'Oh, yes you will. Life is a learning curve, don't think you've graduated yet.' She laughed lightly as he nuzzled his bristly chin into her neck.

'How could I have missed you, Leonora? I just don't understand.' He shook his head and looked into her eyes. 'You've always loved me, haven't you?'

She nodded.

'And I always will.'

'I love you, Leonora. I thought I loved Alicia, but now I know the difference.' He took her hand and placed it on his heart. 'The difference is here.' Overcome by a desperate need to make up for the time he had lost and to reassure himself that he would never be without her, he asked her to marry him. Much to their surprise his proposal felt entirely appropriate.

'Yes, I will marry you,' she replied, blinking away her joy. 'I can't believe this is happening to me. I've loved you for so long, I've grown accustomed to it being unrequited.'

'You'll never feel that again. I'm going to dedicate my life to making you happy.'

'Oh, Florien, I don't deserve you.'

'How wrong you are. You've been kind to me from the moment we met as children. I'll never forget your kindness. Besides, we both love all the same things. We love the countryside, the garden,

Nature, dogs, horses. We love this beautiful old house of your aunt's. We love the wide-open spaces and the freedom that being a gypsy gives us. We can go anywhere we want to. All we need is our caravan and our horses. We hate cities, smog and noise. You see, we're two sides of the same coin. You're not a gypsy, but I'm going to make you one.'

Leonora was so full of happiness she felt she might explode at any minute. 'When will you ask for my hand?' she asked.

'What?'

'You have to ask my father's permission.' Florien suddenly turned cold. He saw his dreams dissolve before his very eyes. Her father would never allow her to marry a gypsy. Leonora read his thoughts. 'Daddy will give you permission. The way Alicia carries on he'll be thrilled that at least one of us is settling down. As for the gypsy life, if I'm happy he won't mind how I live.' She wanted to add that she barely knew her father, having only ever seen him for a few weeks every year. He no longer had any influence over her.

'Are you sure?'

'Of course I'm sure. The person to worry about is not Daddy, but Alicia.' At the sound of those words Florien's heart warmed up again.

'Do you think she'll mind?'

'I'm afraid she will. She's very possessive. Even if the two of you no longer love one another, you were her love once. She'll be mortified.'

'What should we do?'

'Nothing,' she replied in a determined voice. Florien wanted her to elaborate but Leonora was too loyal to say a word against her sister. Instead she said simply, 'We must both be very kind.'

467

'She'll come down and see you, won't she?' he asked hopefully.

'Of course she will. The minute she hears she'll be down. She's just come back from Antibes where she's been with her latest man. I can't remember his name because they change so often. No point remembering really. If she's had a good time she'll be happy for us. If she's grown tired of the poor man, she'll be furious. Let's hope she's happy. Alicia's always better when she's happy.'

The thought of Alicia with another man caused Florien to go rigid with bitterness, but he was careful not to let his anger show. He recalled her words, said so carelessly in the woods, *I took lovers when I felt like it. Lots of them.* And they still festered somewhere at the bottom of his pride. He hoped his engagement to her sister would hurt her. He hoped she'd regret letting him go. He hoped she'd want him back, because it was now too late. He didn't want her; but he wanted revenge.

The following morning Leonora borrowed Aunt Cicely's car to drive to her parents' small house on the coast. She had left her aunt consumed with curiosity for she had never seen Leonora's face so pretty and glowing with happiness. She guessed it might have something to do with Florien. Only a man had the power to make a woman glow like that. She knew. She had glowed like that once. Now when she looked at herself in the mirror she resembled a dusty old reptile. But reptiles were survivors.

Leonora drove down the little winding lane that meandered its way through the village like a gentle stream. The houses were pretty with painted white walls ablaze with roses and butterflies, honeysuckle and bees and crying gulls hovered in the sky above the sea beyond where there were fish to eat and cliffs to nest in. The air was fresh and tasted of salt. Cecil and Audrey's house stood at the end of the village, set apart from the other cottages, beside a narrow sandy path that led down to the beach. The village was quiet, only a fat ginger cat lay sleeping on one of the window sills in the sunshine.

When Leonora's car drew up outside the house Grace came bounding out like one of Aunt Cicely's dogs. 'Gracie,' Leonora laughed, wrapping her arms around her little sister. 'Why aren't you at school?'

'I had a tummy ache and Mummy let me stay at home,' the child replied, smiling up at Leonora with mischievous blue eyes.

Leonora shook her head. 'You're very wicked,' she said. But she didn't care that her mother overindulged Grace because *she* was getting married. She strode into the house and out through the sitting room into the garden. When Audrey saw her she knew at once that something dramatic had happened. Like Aunt Cicely she recognised that radiance as the hue of love. She put down her secateurs and stood up to greet her.

'You look wonderful, darling. What's happened?'

'You had better sit down,' said Leonora happily, joining her mother on the bench. 'Where's Daddy?'

'He went into town to buy some equipment, he's going to make Grace a playhouse.'

'Well, I'll tell you then. I can't wait, I'm too excited.' Audrey leaned towards her and took her hand, anticipating her news.

'Florien asked me to marry him,' she said and

her eyes filled with tears. 'I'm so happy, I don't know what to do with myself.' Audrey gathered her daughter into her arms and hugged her so tightly they both had to hold their breath.

'Oh darling, that's the most wonderful news,' she exclaimed, feeling tearful herself.

'I can't believe it.'

'You love him very much, don't you?' she said, pulling away and caressing her child's face with eyes that glittered with an autumnal light.

'I love him so much it hurts.'

'I know. But it's an exquisite pain. The most blissful feeling on earth. It's the closest one gets to Heaven down here and no one deserves it more than you.'

'I'm so happy, Mummy, I want to cry all the time. Is that natural?' They both laughed and Audrey recalled the intensity of emotion she felt when Louis had claimed her heart for the first time, and with a sudden twinge of nostalgia her body longed for him.

'It's the most natural thing in the world. You are so blessed, my darling. You are going to marry the man you love. You can't imagine how many people never experience true love. They go through life searching for it until it becomes the driving force of their very existence. But it eludes them. Life's a gamble and you can suddenly be dealt a most surprising card when you least expect it.'

'I never expected Florien to love me back.'

'You were patient and your patience has been rewarded.'

'Did you feel like this when you met Daddy?' Leonora asked. She had never spoken to her mother about her relationship with her father, but now she was about to marry she was curious.

Audrey paused. 'Your father is the most noble man I have ever met. He's a good man. An honest and kind man. I knew he was right for me. I knew I'd be very lucky to be loved by him. When one is young one yearns for adventure and excitement, but what I have learned in my life is to appreciate the quieter qualities that often go unnoticed. Our love for each other has never been fireworks, but it is a deep and tender love. Your father is a good man.' Leonora wanted to tell her mother of the overwhelming, intoxicating feeling that filled her up with bubbles, but she worried her mother wouldn't understand.

When Cecil returned from town Grace was waiting for him in the driveway, sitting in the sunshine playing with the garden spirits who danced about the pale roses that grew up the front of the house. He saw Leonora's car and raised his eyebrows at Grace.

'Leo's in the garden with Mummy. She's got some news for you.'

'Good news, I hope,' he said, heaving the box that contained the playhouse out of the back seat.

'Of course. I've always said Leo will be happy.' She stood up and wandered over to him. 'Is that my house?'

'It certainly is.'

'It's flat.'

'It won't be when I've finished with it.'

'You're so clever, Daddy.'

'Your aunt Cicely always had a playhouse as a little girl. You can lock your spirits up in it.' He chuckled and walked past her into the hall.

'Spirits can walk through walls, silly.'

471

'Wish I was a spirit.'

'You will be soon because you're very old.' Cecil laughed at the child's frankness. Ever since the move to England had exorcised the ghosts of the past and brought a sobriety that had cleared his vision, he had grown to love Grace in a way that he had never believed possible. He didn't struggle to understand her, he accepted her differences and learned to wonder at them instead of fearing them. Because she went to a day school in town he was able to help her with her homework. They sat together at the kitchen table while Audrey cooked supper, discussing the kings and queens of England, arithmetic and biology. She was fascinated by everything and the more he told her the more she wanted to know. She had a vast capacity for learning and never tired of it. Finally Cecil had found a role that suited him; he didn't believe in her garden fairies and spirits but he could satisfy her demand for knowledge. With great pleasure and pride he watched his little girl grow under his tutelage; only Audrey was aware that he also grew, in confidence, for Grace's special magic touched him too.

When Leonora told him her news he put down the box and patted her firmly on the back. 'What good news,' he said but he couldn't hide his unease for his voice was flat. Audrey understood his concerns immediately and couldn't help but imagine what the Crocodiles would have made of it. But Louis had taught her the value of love and she would fight for her daughter. She was confident, however, that she wouldn't have to.

'Cecil,' she said, smiling at him reassuringly. 'Leonora and Florien love each other. They've grown up together and their life at Holholly has given them a common ground.'

'I love him, Daddy. I always have,' said Leonora.

'They're destined to be together, Daddy,' Grace added in her carefree way, hopping from one foot to the other, with one eye on the flat box. 'I've known it for years but I made a promise not to read people's futures after I read Nelly's. Trust me, I know.'

'I'm only thinking about your future, Leonora. You're from two very different backgrounds. Have you thought long and hard about it?'

'I don't have to,' she said and smiled broadly at her mother.

'He's a gypsy,' Cecil said, rubbing his chin with his hand.

'And I'll be a gypsy too. Daddy, I'm happy, what more could you want?'

Cecil looked once again at his wife. He dropped his shoulders and shook his head. 'My dear Leonora, I wouldn't be doing my duty as your father if I didn't raise the question. If you're happy, then I'm happy. You have my blessing.' When he smiled one could still detect the shadow of a once dazzlingly handsome face.

'Thank you,' Leonora cried, embracing him. His opinion mattered much more than she had realised.

'Can I be bridesmaid?' Grace asked, hovering about the box.

'You and your fairies,' said Leonora.

'Goodie. I'll dance down the aisle in my ballet dress.' Audrey grinned at Leonora who laughed at her sister indulgently.

'I'm going to be a gypsy,' she said. 'I'm going to

live in a pretty caravan in the middle of a field.'

'In my day the man asked the girl's father for her hand in marriage,' said Cecil.

'Oh, Cecil. It's the seventies for goodness sake,' Audrey replied. 'Everything was so different in our day. Florien's a gypsy. They probably have their own codes,' she added, imagining that they would want to wed in the woods like the hippies.

'He's too shy to ask for my hand. But he wants your blessing too.'

'You have it, darling,' exclaimed her mother in delight. 'You have both our blessings. No one deserves to be happy more than you.'

At that moment Grace burst out laughing. They all turned and looked at her in surprise. 'What are you laughing at, my love?' Audrey asked.

Grace rolled her eyes. 'Alicia's coming home today and she's going to be very very cross.' Then she turned her animated little face to her father. 'Is this box going to remain on the ground or are you going to build me a palace, Daddy?'

CHAPTER THIRTY-ONE

Grace was right. Alicia was furious. But she was much too cunning to reveal her anger to her sisters and parents. Instead she congratulated Leonora by embracing her, albeit coldly, and then drove over to Aunt Cicely's house to confront Florien.

'You don't love her!' she said in a mocking tone when she found him at last in his tractor awaiting the long arm of the combine. A glint of triumph sparked in his eyes as he looked upon her livid face.

'Yes, I do. I love her more than I ever loved you,' he said. He suppressed the desire to grab her by her shoulders and kiss her petulant mouth, for her skin was moist with sweat and brown from her recent trip to France. Her blue eyes sliced through him and in spite of the ugliness of her character they bewitched him still. He averted his gaze and stared out into the cornfield where the combine moved sedately through the golden sea of wheat.

'You still want me, don't you?' she said and smiled spitefully. 'You can still have me if you like.'

'I don't want you, Alicia, I had you when I was a boy and then I grew up.' She laughed contemptuously and he cringed inside. She still had the ability to make him feel as small as one of those grains of wheat that were strewn over the floor of the tractor. He recalled the day she had made him kill the chicken and he suffered the same sense of humiliation all over again. 'Don't flatter yourself,' he retorted at her laughter.

Her expression softened and she edged nearer. 'I don't need to, Florien,' she said quietly. 'You're more handsome than I remembered. You're stronger too. Working on the farm does you good. Let's not talk about love.'

'I think you had better leave,' he said weakly. But in one swift movement she was astride him. She laughed again as she felt his excitement through his jeans.

'You don't want me to,' she giggled, wriggling about on top of him. 'You can't hide lust, Florien.'

Florien was now so humiliated the only way to assert control was to take her brutally. He roughly grabbed her neck and kissed her. She responded triumphantly, turned on by his fury and his force. She knew the power of her allure but to have it proven in small conquests such as this never ceased to excite her. She didn't care that she was stealing her sister's fiancé, for no one else's feelings meant anything to her. She thought only of her supremacy over Leonora and all the other women whose men she had stolen. She felt omnipotent and her mouth twisted into a conceited smile. She rose up on her knees to allow him to unzip his trousers and laughed with pleasure as he swept aside her panties and thrust inside her. Florien felt even more humiliated as she rode him hard, writhing about on top of him like a fiend. He couldn't control her or the warm, tingling feeling that conquered his limbs and drugged his mind so that he was aware only of the climax ahead and an overpowering desire for Alicia. She had wrapped her arms around his head so that his face was now buried in her breasts, which dripped with sweat inside her white shirt. He inhaled her scent and ran a tongue over her skin, tasting salt and perfume and something animal that belonged exclusively to her. Only after it was over did he feel guilty. But the arm of the combine was out and he was compelled to start up the tractor and drive unsteadily across the field. He looked back to see Alicia skipping happily over the stubble towards her car, her long brown legs shining beneath her blue mini skirt and her curls bouncing in the breeze. His heart was still pounding and his groin ached. His body was satisfied but he felt a tremendous wave of guilt and remorse.

As Alicia drove up the track towards the main road she spotted Aunt Cicely coming the other way, having been to the village shop to drop off the new-laid eggs. She pulled over on to the grassy verge to allow her aunt to pass. She bit her lip, hoping that she wouldn't stop to talk. But when Aunt Cicely saw her she stalled the car and threw open the door. Alicia took a deep breath.

'I think you've got some explaining to do, young lady,' said Aunt Cicely crossly. Alicia was struck at how her aunt had aged for she stared at her with the hooded eyes of an old woman.

'If it's about Marcel . . .'

'Of course it's about Marcel.'

'I didn't ask him to come out to France, he just turned up on the beach,' said Alicia, shrugging her shoulders.

'He turned up in France?' Aunt Cicely gasped.

'Don't ask me, he was your lover. Look,' she said in an almost patronising voice, 'he tried to seduce me on various occasions when I was living with you. I was a child, for God's sake. I rebuffed him every time. The next thing I know is I'm on the beach in Antibes with my friends when he turns up, swearing undying love and all that nonsense.'

'*My* Marcel?'

'Yes, *your* Marcel.' She sighed wearily. 'I told him to go home. I didn't want him.'

'So what did he do?'

'I don't know. I assumed he'd come back here to you.'

Cicely hesitated and stared out across the fields. 'I'm sorry he's gone,' said Alicia. 'But I assure you his departure had nothing to do with me.' Aunt Cicely thought of the painting that now had a brutal hole in the place where Alicia's face had once smiled out.

'I'm sorry,' she apologised tightly. She didn't
477

trust Alicia, but Marcel was an artist, fantasy was his job. She had no alternative but to give her niece the benefit of the doubt. She looked down upon Alicia's beautiful face. It was a cruel, unforgiving beauty. 'I don't suppose he said where he was going.'

'No. But you don't want him back, Aunt Cicely. He's useless and I doubt his paintings were any good. Did you ever see any of them?'

'Unfortunately I did,' she replied. 'He left one behind but it's going on the bonfire as soon as I get my hands on some matches. Wonderful news about Leonora and Florien,' she added, changing the subject. She noticed that Alicia betrayed a very unattractive smugness in the half-smile that crept across her face.

'They're perfectly suited,' she said. 'Leo's always dreamed of being a gypsy and living in one of those hideously small caravans. You couldn't swing a cat in them. Still, if it makes her happy. Horses for courses and all that.'

'Yes.' Aunt Cicely didn't like her tone. 'What about you?'

'No one special,' she replied. 'Until I find Mr Wonderful, men have their uses.' She chuckled, thinking of all the exotic places she had travelled to thanks to the fat chequebooks of her lovers. Aunt Cicely raised an eyebrow but Alicia only laughed. 'It's the seventies,' she said, as if that excused her louche behaviour.

'Well, don't have too much fun, or the important things in life will pass you by.'

Alicia rolled her eyes. 'You and Mummy!' She sighed heavily and shook her head. 'Life has never been so good.'

As she drove off she pictured the love-sick Marcel turning up on the beach in Antibes. What a ridiculous sight he had been. She would have slept with him had he not rejected her the year before. He had missed his opportunity. The fool. She had flicked him away like one would a harvest fly and he had begged her to reconsider, professing undying love, claiming that he couldn't eat or sleep because of her. 'My life is a mess,' he had said in desperation, turning to walk back up the beach. 'I have left your aunt, who I loved, for a mirage.' And because of the painting he could never go back.

*   *   *

The wedding was set for 29th October. Audrey dusted off her sewing machine and made Leonora the most exquisite dress out of ivory silk, embroidered with daisies and ivy and a fairy costume for Grace who was to be bridesmaid. Panazel gave his son one of his caravans so he and his bride could start their new life together in the middle of the field where they first met and Aunt Cicely promised to keep them on after she sold the farm, for the grounds of the estate needed looking after and she felt too old and uninspired to do it herself, now that Marcel had gone and left her all alone again.

No one knew of Florien's clash with Alicia in the tractor and no one wished it hadn't happened more than he. He went out of his way to avoid her. But his guilt pounded against his conscience like a pestle on a mortar.

Leonora was so happy that her face acquired a beauty all its very own. Not the sharp, all-

479

consuming beauty of her sister, but a softness of the features and a serenity of expression, an altogether quieter beauty.

As the summer gave way to autumn Audrey took long walks along the beach. Grace was at school and Cecil now worked in the nearby town for a small investment firm. He earned little compared to his salary in Buenos Aires, but living was cheaper in England. She reflected on their new life. To her surprise she discovered that England was an easy country to love. The undulating hills and patchwork fields were so green and vibrant, the sunsets a luminous flamingo pink and the sky a delicate watery colour, as if the rain had washed the blue away. Little by little such a gentle landscape captured her heart. She was close to Cicely and saw Leonora all the time and Alicia now came down to visit most weekends. She missed her mother, though, and the loss of her father still hurt. She often thought about Aunt Edna and she missed her too. But she had been a small sacrifice for the restoration of her marriage. She could never have made it work out there where her aunt knew too much and was a constant reminder of her weakness.

In the fresh English air she had been given a second chance. She had made an effort to forgive her husband for sending the twins away when they were little and she had been rewarded. She couldn't pretend that she never thought of Louis. Yet, Cecil was a good man. She knew she had done the right thing. Every day brought her closer to him and took her a little further away from Louis, so that the pain of leaving him was now a dull ache that she could choose to ignore. She had kept her vow not to play 'The Forget-Me-Not Sonata' again and although there were times when her fingers fidgeted for those notes still so familiar, the fact that she refused to indulge them was an important part of the healing process.

She no longer danced and she had locked her little silk book away for ever. Only Grace was a constant reminder of Louis, but as far as Cecil was concerned she belonged to him and Audrey's admiration for her husband grew as she watched them together, both so very different and yet united as father and daughter. 'Her head's in the clouds with angels and other such nonsense,' he would say, 'but I don't have to understand her to love her.' And Audrey loved him for loving her.

*   *   *

The morning of the wedding arrived. Leonora awoke tingling all over with excitement, Florien felt sick with guilt and nerves and Alicia climbed out of bed unable to believe that he was actually going to go through with it. She had enjoyed him that day in the tractor. But now the reality of his imminent wedding hit her between the eyes and her head spun, causing her to sit down to overcome the nausea in her stomach. She was certain of Florien's love for her. She had held his heart from the first moment they had met and she was sure she could keep it until she was ready to give it back. Only she wasn't ready to give it back. Today he was going to be united in wedlock to her sister. She ran to the bathroom and threw up.

Leonora bathed and dressed in the gown her mother had made and even Alicia, whose face was

481

as grey as the October sky, had to admit that she looked beautiful. Grace skipped about the room in her fairy costume, irritating Alicia by tapping her on the back with her wand and pretending to turn her into a toad. Cecil appeared at the bedroom door in a suit and rested his eyes proudly on his family. 'You look lovely, Leonora,' he said, kissing her on her forehead. 'It will be an honour to walk such a pretty bride down the aisle. I hope Florien knows how very lucky he is.'

'Oh, Daddy, of course he does,' she replied and laughed lightly. 'I'm very lucky to be marrying him.' Alicia bit her tongue. She knew she could ruin everyone's day with a few well-chosen words.

'Grace, stop spinning around, you're making me dizzy. Tell her, Mummy,' she complained. Alicia wasn't used to Leonora being the focus of everyone's attention and she didn't like it a bit.

'Grace, why don't you sit down for a few minutes,' said her mother gently. 'You'll wear yourself out as well as the carpet.' Grace promptly plonked herself on the bed, but waved her wand one last time at Alicia.

'Bad fairy,' she hissed, narrowing her eyes.

Alicia blushed. 'When I get married, I'm going to have a big wedding,' she said quickly. She didn't trust Grace's gift. It was as if the child could see through her and read all her dark secrets.

'If you marry the prince or duke of your dreams you probably will,' said Audrey and laughed. 'Our Leonora wants a simple wedding, don't you, darling?'

'Just the family,' Leonora replied. 'Sad that Granny and Great Aunt Edna won't be there. Nice of them to send a telegram though. Mercedes sent

482

an odd message.'

'What did she say?' Alicia asked. As far as she was concerned, Mercedes had been *her* friend.

' "I always knew you'd be happy." '

'What does she mean by that?' Alicia retorted sulkily. 'That I won't be?'

'Of course not, my dear,' interjected Audrey.

Cecil shook his head but ignored Alicia's self indulgence. 'When you get married, Alicia, she'll probably send you the same message,' he said, straightening his tie in the mirror. He looked at his watch. 'Right, I think it's time for you all to go to the church. Leonora and I will follow.' Leonora smiled at her father. It didn't matter that she felt she barely knew him because today was her wedding day and he was going to give her away. Audrey nodded, looking at his perfectly polished shoes and pressed suit. He looked as sleek and dashing as he had looked at her eighteenth birthday party in Hurlingham, just older. His hair was now grey and his eyes betrayed the emotional turmoil of the last decade in the encroaching lines and in a certain weariness that caused his eyelids to droop. He was still handsome though. More handsome, in fact, than he had ever been, because now a depth of experience replaced the once glossy surface of a complacent army officer. Age had softened him around the edges and fate had humbled him. He looked up and caught her watching him. She smiled with tenderness which he mistook for pride. Unlike his brother he had never been able to read Audrey's thoughts. But he smiled back, suddenly emotional at the sight of his little girl who had grown into a young woman while he had been elsewhere. Then Grace nudged him with her wand and his wistfulness evaporated. 'Don't forget me, Daddy,' she said brightly. 'I'm coming down the aisle too.'

* * *

Alicia tried to catch Florien's eye but he pointedly ignored her. She sat in the front pew with her mother and Aunt Cicely, barely able to take in the flowers and the candles for the sickness in her stomach. She willed him to look at her, but his guilt was too much. Here, before God, he was about to make vows to love and honour Leonora. The Ten Commandments hung in large gold letters over the nave. He felt the words burning into his soul. He lowered his eyes and beads of sweat collected on his brow and nose. He had done a terrible thing and he hated himself more than he hated Alicia. Then the organ began to play and Leonora appeared in the doorway on the arm of her father, followed closely by Grace and her magic wand. He looked up timidly. He watched her approach, her face hidden behind a diaphanous veil embroidered with lilies. He could sense Alicia smarting with jealousy in the pew opposite, willing him to back out, which made him more determined than ever not to be distracted.

Then Leonora was beside him. With sweating hands he lifted her veil. To his surprise his fear left him. He gazed upon the young woman who had always been his friend and a warm tenderness flowed through his veins. She looked up at him with eyes that sparkled with love and he smiled down at her, silently wondering how he could have been such a brute to betray her trust.

484

Alicia watched them. She wouldn't have recognised love if it had slapped her around the face, but she knew then that she cared desperately for Florien. Suddenly in those few moments when the bride and groom exchanged vows to love one another until death parted them, Alicia realised that her feelings hadn't been solely about sex and possession. Yes, she had desired him and yes, she hadn't wanted anyone else to have him. But she felt something more powerful and uncontrollable than desire. Feeling sicker than ever and a little lost she sunk into the wooden bench and bowed her head. She had never believed he would go through with it.

*   *   *

After the wedding Alicia left for London without saying good-bye to her sister and her new husband. She couldn't stomach it. She called one of her rich lovers as soon as she arrived and after dinner passed a feverish night in his bed, trying to prove to herself that Florien didn't matter.

Florien settled happily into married life but the shadow of Alicia lingered in the corners to remind him of his betrayal and his lust which had never completely died. Leonora had been hurt that Alicia hadn't said good-bye and was saddened that for some reason she hadn't come down to Dorset to see them. But she never said a word against her. She made excuses and laughed off her sister's carelessness. Florien wondered how generous she'd be if she knew of Alicia's betrayal. He didn't have the heart or the will to tell her, even though confessing would have made him feel better.

When Florien was on the point of despairing that his obsession with Alicia would never abate, Leonora fell pregnant. He relished her growing belly and the bounce in her step that conveyed her happiness. He grew protective. Worried that her work in the garden might damage their child he forbade her to carry anything that weighed more than a chicken. Audrey began to knit baby bootees from her mother's own patterns that she sent her and Rose, after having vowed never to knit again after the war, made an exception for Leonora and started clicking those needles once more. Grace put her hand on her sister's stomach and foretold the birth of a little boy. No one doubted her, so the bootees were knitted in blue.

When Audrey told Alicia the news she fumed for a week before she could muster up the courage to drive down to Dorset to congratulate her sister. She arrived at her aunt's house and made her way around the back to the field where Leonora's immaculately kept caravan stood, a picture of pastoral simplicity. To her surprise she wasn't met by Leonora but by Florien who was busy weaving a Moses basket for his baby. He was so engrossed in his work that he didn't notice her until she was almost upon him, casting a cold shadow across the grass. He looked up and his face suddenly flushed crimson. 'I came to see Leo,' she said crisply. 'Where is she?'

'At your parents' house,' he replied, blinking up at her in bewilderment.

'I suppose I should congratulate you too. How did you do it?' She looked down at him loftily.

'What?'

'Were you thinking of me when you made love to

486

her?'

Florien put his tools down and stood up, astonished by her sudden outburst.

'Go back to London and take your bitterness with you,' he said.

'Perhaps I'll go to Mummy's house and tell them all about our secret rendezvous last summer. Or would that ruin your happy marriage?'

'What do you want, Alicia?' His question startled her, because she didn't really know.

'I thought you wanted to have your cake and eat it,' she retorted defensively, her face softening into a sly smile. 'You haven't forgotten what it feels like to make love to me, have you?' She was pleased to see a spark of desire glimmer in his eyes like the dormant embers of a fire.

'I'm very happy with Leonora. You and I were over a long time ago.'

'But you still dream about me.' Florien was disarmed by the sudden change in her tone. She was right, he did still dream about her. He often awoke in the early hours of the morning drenched in sweat and self-loathing that he could allow this monstrous woman to possess him like she did.

Florien shook his head and sat down again. Picking up his tools he began to work on the basket. 'I think you should go,' he said quietly, without looking up at her. 'You've outstayed your welcome.'

'I'll be back,' she said with a giggle and she walked back down the field aware that his eyes were on her and the glimmer in them was brighter than ever.

*   *   *

487

In March Leonora and Florien moved into Aunt Cicely's house for the caravan was too cold and cramped for the mother-to-be and there was no telephone in case she went into labour in the middle of the night. Aunt Cicely's house wasn't much warmer but at least it was larger and all their meals were cooked for them. Cecil had managed to persuade them to rent one of Aunt Cicely's cottages once the baby arrived. 'A caravan is no place to bring up a child,' he had said. Leonora had been disappointed until her mother had suggested she put the caravan in the garden for the child to use as a playhouse. 'Grace adores the little house Cecil made for her,' she added.

*   *   *

'I think I'm in labour,' said Leonora to Florien. It was six in the evening and she was running a hot bath. She placed her hand on her naked belly and smiled up at him. 'I've had mild pains all day, but now they're coming more regularly. Every four to five minutes. I've been counting.'

'Shall I call the midwife?' Florien asked, panicking that the baby was due imminently and not having the courage to deliver it himself.

'Tell her labour has started, but it'll be hours yet,' she replied calmly. 'All first babies are slow in coming, so I'm told.'

'Should you have a bath?'

'Of course,' Leonora grinned at him lovingly and touched his anxious face. 'I'm fine. I'm excited. Our baby is announcing himself.'

'Well, I hope he doesn't come before the

midwife!'

'He won't,' she said, patting her stomach. 'He's a long way off coming yet.'

'I'll tell Aunt Cicely and call your mother, too.'

Leonora climbed into the bath and let the warm water ease the pain of the contractions. By the time Audrey arrived they were coming every three minutes. Leonora had been taught how to breathe with the pain and panted away on the bed, holding her mother's hand, while Florien paced about the bedroom in a state of nervousness until the midwife arrived. Mary was a soft-spoken, spongy-bodied Irish woman with a wide-open face and reassuring smile. 'There now, nothing to worry about, I'm here and it's all going to be all right,' she said in dulcet tones. When the waters finally broke Aunt Cicely and Audrey left the room at Leonora's request. They patted her on her hand and wished her luck, both looking as worried as she. Florien was about to leave too when Leonora's frightened voice called him back. 'Don't leave me, Florien. We're going to go through this together.' So Florien stayed. At first he felt powerless. The contractions intensified and each time he watched his wife's body seized by agonising spasms he held onto her, desperate to alleviate her suffering but knowing there was nothing he could do but give passive support. However, as labour progressed he soon felt needed as she gripped him around his middle and cried out into his shirt. He wrapped his arms around her head and stroked her hair, feeling as never before such intensity of love and despair. 'You're so brave,' he said, kissing her temple. 'You're so brave.' The hours passed rapidly as they lurched from contraction to contraction until she was barely able to breathe as the tail end of the last merged with the beginning of the next.

If the contractions had been bad, nothing could have prepared them for the hour and a half of pushing, for as eager as the child was to break out into the world, he was too busy chewing on his fingers to notice that they were holding him up. Leonora pushed and prayed and cried out in desperation while Florien wept, visualising out of fear the death of them both. When the little boy finally appeared, all red and blue and shivering, they both wept again, overwhelmed with awe and reverence for the miracle of life.

Mary wrapped him up in a towel and placed him in the arms of his mother. Florien was still trembling from what had most certainly been the most harrowing experience of his life. He sat on the edge of the bed and placed his finger in the grip of his son's tiny hand. 'Look, my love, he's holding onto me.' Leonora's face flushed with surprise and joy for Florien had never called her by anything other than her name before.

'You called me "my love",' she said, leaning her head against him.

He nuzzled his face into her hair and kissed her. 'That is because you are my love,' he replied in a hoarse voice. 'I have never loved you as much as I love you now. But more than that I admire you. You were so brave and strong. You've brought my son into the world and we shall love him and care for him and give him the best that we can give. I don't think I'll ever be the same again.'

'Nor me,' she whispered, bending to kiss the baby's damp face. 'Nothing will ever be as important to me as my child.'

'What shall we call him?'

'What would you like to call him?'

'Panazel, after my father.'

Leonora smiled. 'Little Panazel.' She sighed and kissed him again. 'You shall be blessed with your grandfather's name. You're a very special little boy.'

*   *   *

The next time Alicia wrenched herself out of her frenetic social scheming to drive down to Dorset, Leonora and Florien had settled into their new cottage. Little Panazel was asleep in his Moses basket in a bedroom that smelt of lavender and talc and Leonora was bustling about the house transforming it into a warm home. Florien met her at the door which he was painting white. To her dismay her brother-in-law smiled at her with the coolness of a distant friend. The glimmer of desire was now extinguished, never to be rekindled, and Alicia knew that Leonora had somehow managed to conquer his rebellious heart. 'Go on up and see him,' he said with a smile. 'He's the sweetest of all God's creatures.'

'I hear you're calling him Panazel,' she said.

'After my father and grandfather. Although he no longer lives in a caravan he's got gypsy blood running through his veins.'

Leonora was delighted to see her sister and embraced her heartily, throwing her arms around her and squeezing her. 'Where have you been?' she cried. 'You must come up and see Panazel.' Alicia followed her sister up the stairs, noticing at once that she was far from getting her figure back. She still looked as if she were pregnant. This gave Alicia a small feeling of satisfaction, but it was short lived. The moment she laid eyes on her nephew she felt as if a hand had suddenly gripped her about the heart. Crouching down she looked into the basket. Sleeping with the contentment of a well-loved baby, Panazel was more beautiful than any other baby she had ever seen. His skin was pale and translucent, glowing with a delicate sheen. His eyes were closed but she could see the rich brown eyelashes that were sweeping and long and his lips were generous and pink, breaking every now and again into a subconscious smile.

'He's adorable,' she said in a low voice. 'You're so lucky.' For the first time in her life she realised that Leonora had everything that she wished she had for herself. Mercedes had been right and her words came back over the decades to remind her of her own delusions. *'Leonora will find happiness because her features won't deceive anyone.'* Alicia's features had deceived many, but no one more than herself.

CHAPTER THIRTY-TWO

The following eight years were a joy for Leonora, a blur for Alicia and a continuous adventure for Grace, who was enchanted and curious about everything her small world had to offer. When she announced that she had won a place at Trinity College Dublin no one was more surprised than her mother, who had always believed her to be more interested in fairies than academia.

'Philosophy has a lot to do with fairies,' replied Grace, smiling at her mother in amusement.

'But it's so far away,' she lamented.

'A short plane ride, Mummy. I can even fly home for the weekend.'

But Audrey's concerns weren't only for the distance. Louis lived in Dublin.

'Trinity College Dublin,' enthused Aunt Cicely, who was now Mrs Anthony Fitzherbert after marrying the neighbouring landowner who had bought her farm the year after the gypsies left. Anthony, a jovial, kind-hearted man who always wore tweed and cashmere, had given her back her youth, her belief in love and her much beloved farm. She now smiled with the resignation of a woman who has walked through the flames of love and emerged with her heart singed but still beating, grateful for the affection of a less passionate but truer man. 'How utterly wonderful. Dublin's a beautiful city. You'll love it.' She paused from brushing one of the dogs to pick the hair out of the bristles, which she then tossed onto the grass. 'Makes good nesting material for birds. Shame the nest-building moment has passed. They're all flying about now.'

'Have you been there?' Grace asked, stretching out on the lawn to sun herself.

'Yes, twice in fact. To see your Uncle Louis.'

'Uncle Louis?'

'You know, that odd uncle of yours that no one talks about.'

'The one who taught Leonora to play the piano?'

'Yes, that's the one. The mad one.'

'What's he doing in Dublin?' Grace had always

493

been aware that her father had a brother, but his name was rarely mentioned and there were no photographs of him anywhere, except the black and white print on Aunt Cicely's piano.

'He was Director of Music for many years. He's retired now. Lives in the College. Grace and favour and all that.'

'What does he do all day?'

'Shout at people, I suspect.' Aunt Cicely laughed, recalling his rudeness and began to brush the dog again. 'He's a cantankerous old thing. But if you're interested, you can pay him a visit. Surprise the life out of him.'

'Why doesn't anyone see him? He's family after all.'

Cicely sat back and stared into the half-distance, trying to find the right words. 'He fell out with your father. Many years ago. Before you were born. I don't know what it was about. He was living with your parents in the Argentine at one time. He loved your mother's sister, Isla, who died rather tragically of meningitis at a very young age. I don't think your mother's ever got over that. Come to think of it, I don't think Louis has either.'

'Is he older than you and Daddy?'

'No, eight years younger than your father. If Cecil's sixty-five now, Louis must be fifty-seven or thereabouts. But he seems much older. He's had a rather unhappy life. He's not like other people. But perhaps you'll soften him up. It'll do him good.'

'Didn't he marry?'

'I never believed it was possible to love just one person for your entire life. I never subscribed to that kind of romance. But,' she sighed heavily and a little wistfully. 'Louis has loved one woman all his

494

life. He's never got over her. He never looked at another.'

'That's so sad. Everyone deserves to love and be loved back. Without that the world wouldn't turn.'

Aunt Cicely laughed. She never quite understood Grace. 'You can go and cheer him up. You two will get on like a house on fire, you're both up there in the clouds somewhere. Funny you haven't already met.'

'Mummy doesn't want me to go.'

'That's because your sisters were sent away to school over here. Your mother suffered terribly over that, but your father believed he was giving them the best education money could buy. He was right too. If Leonora hadn't come here she would never have met Florien and look how happy they are. That little Panazel is a dream. I could put him between two slices of bread and eat him up. Utterly charming little fellow. Mischievous too. I love him to pieces. His brother and sister are adorable as well, but I'll always have a soft spot for Panazel. He was born in my house, you see. So I feel I have claim to him.'

'You know Alicia's never going to be happy,' Grace said darkly.

Aunt Cicely paused her brush again. 'Darling, you mustn't say such things.'

'Oh, I would never tell Alicia, or Mummy. I made that mistake once when I was very little with my cousin Nelly. She never spoke to me again. But I just know that she won't. She's chasing the impossible. Reaching for a cloud that she can never hold on to. Not even Alicia can pin down a cloud.'

'I'm sure she'll settle down one day.'

'Oh, she'll have many lovers. But no one will be

good enough. She'll always be discontent. It's beginning to show on her face.'

Once again Grace was right. Alicia's personality was beginning to seep into her features like a canker, pulling them down and drawing in her mouth so that she looked constantly pinched. Still beautiful but cold. Whereas Leonora grew more lovely as each day passed. She wasn't slim or glamorous but earthy and radiant like a ripe peach. She brought up her three children with love and enthusiasm, teaching them about God's great garden that was so close to her heart. They helped her gather the apples and plums, blackberries and sloes to sell in the market in town and in the summertime they'd picnic by the side of the cornfields so their father could jump down from his tractor and join them before racing off to unload the combines. Their life was simple, but they had everything that they needed and the most valuable possession of all they had in abundance: love. By comparison, Alicia had nothing.

*   *   *

Audrey worried the moment Grace was out of her sight. 'She's not like other children, Cecil, she's a child in the body of a young woman,' she said the night after Grace had left for Dublin. Cecil put his book down on the bed beside him and turned to face his wife.

'She's much more resilient than you think. She isn't all fairies and angels, you know.'

'Oh, I know she's not completely in the clouds, but she's childlike. I don't believe she's ready for the real world.' She reached for her pot of hand

496

cream from the bedside table.

'She has to give it a try, for how else will she know,' he replied, taking off his glasses.

'I just want to protect her from everything.' She pulled an apologetic smile to show that she was aware of her weakness.

'And you wanted to protect Alicia and Leonora from everything too. She's our youngest, it's natural that you want to hold on to her.'

'Do you think it's that I don't want her to grow up?'

'You missed the twins growing up. That was my fault,' he added in a quiet voice.

'Oh, Cecil. I'm not blaming you for anything. That's all water under the bridge.' She patted him on the hand. 'No, there's something so ethereal about Grace. I feel she needs me more than the other two ever did.'

'You know, Audrey,' he said, shaking his head at her fondly. 'You and Grace have a very touching relationship, but to tell you the truth, she's stronger than Alicia and Leonora put together.'

'You think so?'

'I know she is. Look at her. Her beliefs are unwavering. She knows there's a whole world out there waiting for us when we die. Although I'm not certain of it, it's very comforting at my age that she's so sure. That gives her a huge advantage over everyone else. She's never needed anyone because she's so content in her own skin. That's a blessing. She's not vulnerable. She's unconquerable. She'll never do anything that goes against her better judgement just to fit in, or do something silly because of some foolish infatuation. No, I believe that Grace is somehow closer to God than the rest of us, that's why she's childlike. It's as if she's aware that life is a stage. She doesn't take it too seriously. I never thought I'd say that about Grace, she used to baffle me to the point of despair. But I've grown to understand her over the years. She'll do all right. I really believe she will.'

Audrey looked at him with eyes that revealed in their gentle expression the admiration she felt for him. It never ceased to astound her that he truly loved Grace as his own child. 'You've put my mind at rest. I shall sleep well tonight.'

'And so shall I. Because, my dear, if you're happy, I'm happy.' She kissed him on his weathered old cheek and knew that he meant it.

But that night she dreamed about Louis for the first time in many years and awoke with the 'Forget-Me-Not Sonata' ringing in her ears.

*　　　*　　　*

Grace settled into her college with the ease of someone who considers life a wonderful adventure. With childlike curiosity she searched for the good in everyone, disarming her fellow students and tutors with her directness and the unique quality that made her stand apart from the others, what her mother called her 'otherworldliness'. She floated about the university with the same air of detachment that had isolated her from fellow classmates at school and although she was well liked she didn't make close friends. She seemed not to need anyone.

Grace thrived at Trinity College. She had an unquenchable thirst for knowledge, soaking up new information with the enthusiasm of someone who's

498

been deprived of education all their life. She found university so stimulating that at night she could barely sleep, not because of her spirit friends, who often kept her up with their games, but because her mind was whirring with all the questions she wanted to ask and she could barely restrain her impatience. She joined the Don Juan Society who met every Thursday evening in a pub to discuss poetry over beer and cottage pies and the Olivier Society where she discovered a natural talent for acting. Her parents weren't surprised, she had acted all her life. But her gift earned her more notoriety than her stage performances. After astonishing a few students with the accuracy of her readings she was besieged wherever she went by people thrusting their watches and bracelets at her so that she was forced to limit herself to two readings a day. She refused to look into the future, having learned a sharp lesson from her cousin Nelly.

After a few weeks in Dublin Grace decided to go and pay a visit on her reclusive Uncle Louis. It wasn't hard to find him. Everyone seemed to know of him. 'You're his niece?' they laughed in astonishment when she asked after him. 'He's as nutty as a fruit cake. Except when he plays the piano, then he's a god.' Their comments made her all the more curious.

Following their directions she found his flat situated in an old courtyard of great beauty that probably hadn't changed for over one hundred years. The door was small, built into a weathered brick wall and surrounded by an abundance of late roses that seemed to grow better there than anywhere else. She held her breath and knocked.

No reply. She waited, put her nose to one of the roses and sniffed it. It had an extraordinarily sweet fragrance. Finally she heard a shuffling noise, then the sound of feet and the unbolting of the door. She envisaged an ogre but what she found was an old man with long grey hair that fell about his shoulders in unruly rats' tails and the softest blue eyes. He didn't look mad at all.

'What can I do for you?' he asked in a deep voice that crunched like gravel. He looked at her quizzically as if he had met her somewhere before and was trying to place her.

'I'm your niece, Grace Forrester,' she said confidently. 'Audrey and Cecil's daughter.' He stared at her as if he were seeing one of her spirits for the first time and his pale cheeks glowed as if suddenly bruised.

'Cicely told me they had had another daughter,' he mumbled, shaking his head in astonishment and rubbing his chin with his fingers. 'You had better come in then.' All the while he led her up the narrow wooden staircase he kept turning around to look at her again. 'You're the image of your mother,' he said wistfully when they reached the sitting room on the first floor. It was small and dark with a thin layer of dust that covered everything. He seemed nervous for he flicked his long fingers on his knees and his mouth twitched at one corner.

'Am I?' she replied, noticing how his eyes suddenly looked sad. 'I'll take that as a compliment.'

'Oh, I mean it as a compliment. The greatest compliment a man can give. I admire your mother. More than you'll ever know.' Grace removed some loose bits of manuscript from the sofa and sat down. 'Excuse the mess, I don't often receive visitors these days.'

'Why not? I hear you play the piano beautifully. You should share your gift.'

'Do you play?'

'Yes,' she replied brightly. Anyone else would have been unsettled by the intense way that he looked at her, but Grace wasn't afraid of anyone. She found him compelling for she sensed a deep unrest in his soul and knew instinctively that she could somehow make it better.

'So how is your mother?' he asked, sitting down on a chair that only had three legs; the other was made out of books piled one on top of the other.

'She's well. Not very happy that I've come all the way to Dublin to study.' She gave a gentle laugh that was so innocent and charming Louis found himself smiling too. He couldn't remember the last time he had smiled. His face had set into a grimace that had become a comfortable habit he was frightened of breaking. But Grace disarmed him. When he smiled his whole face changed, as if he had turned on a light and transformed the dank little room into a conservatory. And it felt good. His smile caught Grace off guard and very little caught such a gifted clairvoyant off guard.

'Does she still play the piano?'

'Never.'

'She once played, you know.'

'Yes, she did. Leonora plays though and remembers you teaching her in Buenos Aires. She's married a gypsy called Florien and has three children.'

He shook his grey head and rubbed his bristly chin with his hand. She noticed how the tips of his

501

eyelashes had been caught by an early frost.

'How time flies. It's only with children that one becomes aware of the rapid passing of the years. If it weren't for them I'd feel the months withering away slowly. But no, I am old and the years have left me behind.'

'Goodness, Uncle Louis, you're not old. You only look old because you're unhappy.'

Louis smiled again. 'You didn't inherit your boldness from your father, that's for sure.'

'I say what I think. There's no point in hiding the truth, as long as the truth is always motivated by love.' He frowned. Her uniqueness was compelling.

She looked around the room and saw the piano hidden beneath disorderly piles of manuscripts.

'Did you enjoy being Director of Music?' she asked.

'I enjoyed teaching music,' he replied with a sigh. 'Nothing gives me more joy than music. It's the rules and regulations that go with an institution of this sort that grate on my sense of freedom. But it paid the bills and has given me a roof over my head ever since.'

'You never married?'

'You ask a lot of questions.'

'I'm curious, Uncle Louis. You were a handsome man when you were young. I've seen your photograph on Aunt Cicely's piano.'

'She can't play a note.'

'Well, I've never heard her play, to be honest.'

'That's because she can't, the old stoat.'

'The names she calls you are much worse,' she said with a giggle.

'I bet they are. Has Marcel left her yet?'

'Goodness me, you are out of date!' she gasped.

'Marcel left her, which was no bad thing, and she married the farmer next door. Anthony Fitzherbert. You'd like him.'

'Why would I like him? You don't even know me.' His face turned irritable again as if to challenge her.

But Grace smiled indulgently. 'I know. But I feel I do.' Louis stared at her with his chin loose and floundering. Grace held his eyes with an expression of compassion and understanding that was a direct reflection of her mother's.

'So, what can you play?' he asked, getting up stiffly and shuffling over to the piano.

'Anything you want. But I find sight-reading boring. I tend to improvise for fun.'

'You do, do you?' he said slowly. 'Show me how.' So Grace sat down and lifted the lid. Louis handed her a manuscript. She placed it on the stand and began to play. She put little feeling into the notes at first, following them mechanically. Then all of a sudden she closed her eyes and allowed her fingers to follow a different course, in the same style as the original. Louis was astounded. He knew no one else who could play like that but him.

When she finished, his eyes were moist with tears. 'I'm an old man and you've just given me a lot of pleasure,' he said huskily. But then he looked at her with that strange intense stare and asked in a very quiet voice, 'How old are you, Grace?'

'Eighteen,' she replied.

'What month were you born?'

'October.'

'October,' he repeated slowly, nodding his head. 'October.' The truth hit him between the eyes and he had to sit down.

'Are you all right, Uncle Louis?' she asked.

'Play some more. Anything. You play so beautifully, it breaks my old heart,' he choked gruffly, waving his long fingers at her. 'Just play.'

So she played. Sensing his unhappiness she let her empathy direct her fingers so that the music mirrored the heaviness in his soul and enabled him to let go of it, little by little. It was only the beginning of a healing process that would take many months, but Grace was very gifted and when she left the house he felt strangely lighter. 'Your roses are beautiful,' she said as she departed. Then she opened her inner eye and saw the flurry of spirit entities who danced among the branches. She laughed. 'They like your music,' she added. 'No wonder the flowers grow better here than anywhere else.'

'Who do?' he asked.

'The spirits,' she replied, as if everyone could see them. He shook his head and watched her skip off with a bounce in her step. It was painfully obvious. She wasn't Cecil's daughter at all.

*   *   *

Louis retreated into his house. His little sitting room still smelt of her, the sweet scent of youth and optimism that mingled with the tang of lemon. He sat at his piano and placed his fingers over the keys, breathing heavily, his mouth set once again into its habitual grimace. Then slowly, as if to reflect his enduring patience, he began to play the tune he had composed for Audrey. He closed his eyes and the frost that had caught on the ends of his lashes glistened with sorrow. Over and over he played it. So that he would never forget or give up hope. No wonder Audrey had been able to survive the years without him; for Grace was the part of him he had left behind.

That night he dreamed. He couldn't remember the last time he had dreamed. He had lost the will many years ago. But that night he dreamed of Grace. He was sitting in a field full of buttercups. The gentle evening sun bathed him in a warm golden light and he felt at peace. And Grace was with him, her laughter like the bubbling of a nearby stream that filled him up inside until he was so light that he was hovering over the grass. Half of him wanted to stay on the ground, the other longed to fly. And Grace kept on laughing and laughing, filling him up and up and up . . .

In the morning he awoke, not with the usual heaviness of spirit that made getting out of bed the hardest part of the day, but with an enthusiasm that had been lost somewhere over the years along with his dreams and his smile. He hoped that Grace would visit him again. He hoped so very much. He bathed and shaved and splashed himself with an old bottle of cologne that was sticky with dust and neglect. It was hard to find a clean shirt, but at the very bottom of his drawer he found one that was slightly too small but washed and ironed by the housekeeper who came weekly. Then he emerged into the early morning sunshine to go to the corner shop to buy the papers and some milk.

When he returned Grace was sitting on his doorstep in a pair of faded denim jeans and a bright yellow shirt. Next to her was a basket full of food. 'Good morning, Uncle Louis,' she said brightly. 'I'm taking you on a picnic. It's a beautiful

505

day and I've bought bread and pâté, a bottle of wine and some tomatoes.' Louis was so taken aback that he didn't know what to say. Grace didn't wait for him to respond. She stood up and followed him through the front door. 'I don't have lectures today, but I have lots of things I want to ask. I thought, perhaps you wouldn't mind helping me.'

'What are you reading?' he asked.

'Philosophy,' she replied.

'Ah, there are never satisfactory answers in philosophy, only questions.'

'But isn't it exciting to discover just how many questions there are? We could go on asking questions for ever. Can we go and sit in a field somewhere? It's going to be a warm day. An Indian summer. We had better make the most of it before autumn sets in. By the way, I like your cologne.'

Louis found Grace refreshingly unpredictable. With a small smile tickling the corners of his face he drove his old Morris Minor into the countryside where the roads were narrow and winding and the small green fields lush and inviting, lined by the grey stone walls that had withstood centuries of wind and rain. Grace entertained him with her stories of the Argentine, reminding him of the hideousness of Aunt Hilda and the neediness of her daughter Nelly, until he laughed out loud. 'Do you miss it?' he asked, wiping his eyes.

'I thought I would when I left. But I belong here now. I'd like to go back one day. Of course it will all be very different. Granny died some years ago then Great Aunt Edna. Great Aunt Hilda is still alive somewhere, she's so old she's probably petrified, quite literally. People's personalities end up in their features, there's no avoiding it, so she

506

must be set in stone by now. But I'd like to go back just to remember it.'

They found a little wood that bordered a stream and sat down on the rug that Louis had found in an old trunk in his hall. The sun shone through the leaves creating moving patterns on the grass like a kaleidoscope. Grace kicked off her shoes and stretched out her legs. 'Can you see all the wood spirits?' she asked, then laughed with childish delight. 'This is a beautiful place. How clever of us to find it.'

'Anyone else would think you were mad,' he said and chuckled. 'People have considered me mad all my life.'

'Have they?'

'Yes. Nowadays people are far more tolerant of those who are different. In my day everyone had to be like everyone else. It was all very rigid.'

'I've been different from birth. None of the other children had spirit friends like I had. Of course they all had them, we all have guides, but they couldn't see them. People are afraid to believe in what they cannot see.'

'Which is silly considering we're surrounded by things we cannot see which are proven by science, like radio waves.'

'Have you ever wondered where the world comes from? Why are you *you*? If you weren't you, who would you be? What would you be? Would you *be* at all?' When her uncle frowned at her again, this time in amusement, she continued with haste, her eyes wide with excitement. 'Most people are too caught up in the world to wonder at it. They take the rain and the sunshine for granted without wondering why. Why, when science has invented all these clever machines to give us more time, like dishwashers and washing machines, do we have less time? Do you ever take a moment to lie on the lawn and stare up into space and question eternity? Do you?'

Louis chuckled. 'You really are full of questions.'

'But I don't have the time to answer them,' she replied in frustration.

'Well,' he sighed indulgently. 'Let's start with the first question, what was it?'

'Have you ever wondered where the world comes from?'

'Ah, that's a hard one. Open the bottle of wine, there's a good girl. It'll oil the cogs in my mind and get them turning, they haven't turned for many years.'

Louis and Grace lay on their backs gazing up at the mobile of leaves that shimmered above them as the breeze tickled their spines and sent them dancing. They questioned their existence with the fervour of ancient philosophers and the humour of students embarking on an existential journey for the first time. The wine loosened their tongues and their throats and they laughed with their bellies until they ached with happiness. When the evening shadows began to lengthen Louis looked at his watch and realised that it was already time for supper. 'I should have bought two baskets, one for lunch, one for dinner, then we could have set up a tent and continued all night,' she said, packing the picnic away. Louis loaded the boot of the car and was about to get in when she handed him a small cluster of yellow buttercups. 'These are "happy-making" flowers,' she said with a grin. 'Put them on your piano to remind you to play happy tunes.'

He took them from her and recalled his dream and her laughter that had filled him up. He hadn't felt this full in a long time.

CHAPTER THIRTY-THREE

As the cold autumn winds whispered through the shortening days and the Indian summer of their picnic dissolved into morning mists and frost Grace's relationship with her uncle grew in depth and strength. She was elusive by nature and didn't bond easily with other young people but in Louis she discovered a soul mate, someone whom she could relate to, someone who saw the world as she did. They lay under the stars and questioned eternity, they went to concerts and cried in the same places, they sat together on the piano stool and played the same music instinctively, composing the tunes as they went along, laughing when they clashed, which they didn't do very often, and smiling when they blended with such perfection that their music might just as well have been composed by the angels themselves. Grace cooked for him, badly, but he didn't mind for he loved her company. His grimace was worn away by so much gaiety and the spontaneity that had once captivated the heart of a reticent young woman returned to enchant her daughter.

Then one day she heard him play a piece of music she had never heard before. She was lying on the sofa in front of the fire, preparing an essay, while Louis tinkered away on the piano. It was early December and the rain was almost turned to sleet, rattling against the window panes with icy fingers. He played quietly so as not to interrupt her studies. They had spent the morning discussing the subject and working out a strong argument so that all she needed to do now was read some theory. She liked to lie reading while he played, and often she would join him for a break, taking her place beside him on the stool without speaking. But suddenly he began to play a haunting melody of such beauty that she felt her whole body ripple with shivers as if the window had opened to let the winter in. She put down her book and concentrated her attention on the music. Then she turned onto her side and watched him, her large joyful eyes melting with sorrow. Of all the tunes he had played this he played with the most drama. It was as if the vibrations consumed him so that he became the notes he was playing. Grace watched transfixed, trying to work out what he was thinking and why this piece of music was so different from every other piece she had heard him play. Finally, she got to her feet and walked softly to his side where she put a hand on his shoulder. When he felt her hand he opened his eyes and blinked, as if disturbed from a deep sleep. His hands stopped and he breathed deeply, slowly waking up. The colour returned to his face and his mouth extended into a sheepish smile.

'That's the most magical piece of music I have ever heard, Uncle Louis. Who did you compose it for?'

Louis hesitated, thinking very carefully of what he was going to say. He remembered her comment that it is always better to tell the truth if one is motivated by love. But he loved her too much to tell her the truth. It wasn't his place. If Audrey hadn't told her then he had no right to.

'It rained like this the night Isla died,' he said sadly and Grace believed she understood.

'The night she died?' she asked softly.

'The night she died,' he repeated. 'The night I left Argentina a broken man.'

'Oh, Louis,' she whispered, feeling the full force of his sadness. 'I'm so sorry.' She sat beside him and wrapped her arms around him. As she wiped a tear on his jersey she suddenly realised that she wasn't so very different from other people after all. Louis had taught her how to empathise. She no longer felt that she was watching the world through a pane of glass. She no longer felt detached. She felt it all as if she had suffered too.

'Why do I feel so melancholy?' she asked. Louis put his arms around her and squeezed her with so much tenderness that it almost overwhelmed him.

'Because beautiful things always make us sad,' he replied with a strong sense of *déjà vu.*

'Why?'

'Because we can't hold onto them for ever.'

'I've never felt melancholy before. Your music has touched me, Uncle Louis. I'm trembling.'

'There's more than earthly forces at play here, Grace. There's magic in it, I tell you.'

'And I believe you. Will you teach me how to play it?'

Louis pulled away and looked at her gravely. 'If you promise me you won't play it at home.'

'Why?'

'It'll be our secret tune, Grace. Just promise me that.'

'I promise,' she said. 'Our secret tune.'

511

When Grace returned home for the Christmas holidays she knew instinctively that she shouldn't speak of her friendship with her uncle. She told her parents about her courses and the professors who brought her studies alive. She told them of the concerts and theatre she had been to and the weekends she had spent in the countryside. But she didn't mention the friend she had shared it all with. She only told Aunt Cicely because she had to tell someone.

To her horror Grace saw that her father was getting old. She had never noticed it before but time was catching up with him. He was thinner too. His cheeks were drawn and the bones looked severe beneath the skin. He was pale and his eyes no longer shone. She wondered how he could have deteriorated so fast without her noticing. Had she really been so detached, so blinded by her hidden world of spirits as to have missed her own father fading away right in front of her?

Cecil had been retired now for eight years. He pottered about the garden, read books on military history and accompanied Audrey on walks up and down the beach. He enjoyed his grandchildren, who came to visit daily with their mother and enjoyed a deepening relationship with his sister and Anthony Fitzherbert who was much more to his taste than the moody Marcel. He had enjoyed his retirement, but now he was weary. He wished he believed in life after death with the same certainty as Grace. The end still frightened him. He hadn't feared dying in the war. As a soldier he had been prepared to sacrifice his life for his country. He had thrown himself against the icy gates of death but had returned a hero having escaped the unknown, believing such victory rendered him immortal. Now old age had withered his courage as well as his bones.

'You look decidedly peaky,' said Cicely to her brother as they sat in her sitting room beside the fire, waiting for Audrey and Grace to come in from their walk around the farm.

'I'm just weary, that's all,' he replied, puffing on a cigar.

Anthony put down *Farmers Weekly* and leaned forward to stoke the fire that was sending smoke out into the room. 'It's the cold. Stops the circulation at our age,' he said cheerfully.

'Honestly, darling, you're a good ten years younger than Cecil. Cecil's a dinosaur.'

'Thank you, Cicely,' replied Cecil, chuckling lightly.

'I'm sorry, darling, I should save my venom for that other mad brother of mine. Isn't it nice that Grace loves him so much.'

Cecil pulled the cigar out of his mouth and frowned. 'Grace hasn't mentioned anything about Louis to me,' he said, puzzled. 'I knew she would go and see him but . . .'

'My dear, they've become firm friends. They go to concerts, picnic together. She spends more time with him than anyone else. She says she doesn't need any other friends. She must have brought the best out in him because the last time I saw him he was a grumpy old sod.'

Cecil chewed on the end of his cigar. 'What else did Grace say?' he asked thoughtfully.

513

'She probably doesn't dare mention his name. I'm afraid I told her that you two fell out all those years ago.'

'You did?'

'Well, of course I did, Cecil,' she explained, feeling guilty, as if she had betrayed a secret. 'It wasn't right to let her go to Dublin without knowing that her uncle lived there. They have the same name. He lives in the college and from what I hear he's extremely well known there. Someone would have introduced them. Was I wrong?'

'No, no. You're right. Besides, he's her uncle. Blood is thicker than water and all that.' He chuckled again and puffed on the cigar but inside he felt weak with jealousy. Louis had stolen his wife's heart and now he stood poised to take his daughter's too. He swallowed hard and felt a shortness of breath that caused him to cough.

'Really, Cecil, you don't look very well at all.'

'Change the record, Cicely,' he snapped unintentionally, then spotted Audrey and Grace walking past the window. 'Ah, they're back. Good.'

'We went for such a long walk. It's dark outside,' said Grace happily, her cheeks glowing from the cold. 'Mummy, tell Daddy about the sunset. It really was magical.'

'Up there on the hill. I promise you it flooded the land with treacle. The sky was red as if it were on fire,' said Audrey. Cecil noticed that her eyes were raw and watery. There must have been a bitter wind.

'And pink too,' added Grace.

'And pink. It was as if God was putting on a show especially for us.'

'How wonderful,' he exclaimed with forced

514

enthusiasm. 'I wish I had been up there with you.' Then he put his arm around Grace and kissed her temple. She looked at him in puzzlement. He wasn't a demonstrative man and such a gesture took her by surprise. Audrey saw it too and her expression suddenly clouded with sorrow, but she blinked her emotions away and followed them out into the hall.

'Why don't you come for dinner tomorrow night?' said Cicely. 'No point walking around the farm until dark and then having to go home and cook. I'll do a chicken.'

'If a chicken's on offer I'll say yes for Mummy and Daddy,' said Grace with a grin.

'We'd love to,' Audrey replied, still shaken by Cecil's tender kiss on his daughter's temple.

As Cicely watched them drive away she turned to her husband and said, 'I don't think Cecil's at all well.'

'No, he doesn't look good.'

'I hate secrets,' she said suddenly. 'I really hate secrets. Cecil and Audrey have far too many. I don't know what I'm allowed to say and what I'm not.'

'Darling, don't think about it. Cecil wasn't cross.'

'He was hurt. God knows why. He wasn't possessive like that about the twins.'

'Grace is different, anyone can see that. He just doesn't want his cantankerous younger brother getting close to his precious little girl. If he fell out with him as you say, it's only natural.'

'Well, pooh to all that,' Cicely exclaimed, walking down the passage to the kitchen. 'He'll get over it. He'll have to. Louis and Grace are two of a kind.'

515

Alone on the hill Audrey had asked her daughter about Louis. Her curiosity had finally got the better of her. Grace's reply had taken her as much by surprise as Cecil's tender kiss later.

'At first he was a sad old man, plagued by the past, a prisoner of his memories. But little by little he lightened up. Now he's my best friend. We do everything together. We laugh all the time, discuss philosophy, play the piano and chill out. I know Daddy fell out with him, but that doesn't have to affect me, does it?'

'Of course not,' Audrey replied, putting her hands in her pockets and hunching up her shoulders. 'I'm glad that you make him happy.'

'Oh, I do. He didn't smile much at the beginning.' There was a pause while Audrey wondered whether it was healthy to question her daughter further. Perhaps it was better to leave Louis in the past with the 'Forget-Me-Not Sonata' and her silk-bound book. But she tried to envisage him old and could not, so she persisted.

'What's he like?'

Grace laughed. It seemed an absurd question seeing as he had lived with them in Buenos Aires, according to Aunt Cicely. Had he changed so much?

'He's got long grey hair. He doesn't brush it very much. It's a bit messy. He tries to look tidy but does a hopeless job,' she said with a smile. She was delighted she was able to talk about her friend at last. 'He's tall and strong, like a bear. A lovely, cuddly bear. He's not bony like Daddy, he's soft.

He has these amazing blue eyes that go from looking sad to happy in a moment. You never know what he's going to do next. He'll suddenly cry over a piece of music then laugh a minute later at something I say. But as much as he laughs there's something very sad about his old eyes. His lashes are white, they glisten as if they're frozen, like icicles. He's a gifted musician. He plays so beautifully. I study in his sitting room while he plays. He composes, you know. Like I do actually, except now he writes a lot of it down. It's a hobby of his. He said he was never disciplined enough as a young man to write down what he makes up. He's very gifted.' She sighed, remembering him fondly. 'He's not at all like Daddy and Aunt Cicely.'

'No, he's very different,' her mother agreed, but Grace didn't detect the wistfulness that caused her voice to crack.

'I'm glad I met Uncle Louis. He's very kind to me.'

Audrey was too moved to speak. She stared out over the valley that lay before them, her face bathed in the golden light of sunset. When Grace turned to her she noticed that her mother's eyes were streaming with tears.

'Oh, Mummy. The view?' she asked, linking her arm through hers. Audrey nodded because the lump in her throat had muted her. 'Beautiful things always make us melancholy,' she continued, squeezing her mother's arm, without realising the significance of her words. 'It's because we can't hold onto them forever.' Overwhelmed by memories, Audrey's shoulders shook. Grace assumed her mother's tears were in response to the magnificence of the sky. 'We must tell Daddy about this view. He'd love it. What a shame he didn't want to come with us.' But Audrey was grateful for this moment alone on the hill with her daughter. It was a private moment in which Cecil had no place. She gazed out over the darkening valley and pictured Louis' face as Grace had described it. She knew she would never see it for herself.

*   *   *

The following day Grace believed herself to be alone. Her father had driven to the garden centre to buy some poinsettias and her mother was visiting Leonora and her grandchildren. She sat down at the piano, feeling as guilty as a schoolgirl about to break the rules, and rested her fingers on the keys. She remembered the promise she had made to Louis, but, she reassured herself, she was alone and her fingers were just itching to play it.

Quietly she began to play the poignant tune he had taught her. Softly at first in case her mother should return without her hearing, or her father come through the garden with the plants. But slowly the notes wound around her like tentacles of ivy until she was aware of nothing but the expanse of dreams that opened up to her like the view on the hill. She couldn't help but close her eyes and let the music carry her. And she flew, far away, to an unfamiliar place where she knew she didn't belong, but for which her heart yearned. She saw the vast plains of Argentina where a young man and woman were galloping in chase of ostriches. It was sunset and the pampa was bathed in a rich amber colour beneath a vast golden sky. The beauty of it caused her eyes to swell with tears. There was something moving about the couple. Their joy was grounded in sorrow. She felt their hopes and sensed their dreams as if they were her own. She tried to search deeper into her vision but suddenly instinct caused her to withdraw her fingers from the keys. She opened her eyes as her mother's hand threw down the piano lid in fury. Grace was so shocked that she burst into tears. She looked up at her mother, whose face was as white as death. 'I don't ever want to hear you play that piece again. Ever,' she shouted. 'Do you understand?' Her hands were trembling as she rubbed them together. It was as if she had scalded herself touching the piano. She stared down at her daughter with fear. When she saw her own fear reflected in Grace's eyes she too dissolved into tears. She placed her shaking fingers over her mouth and dropped onto her knees. 'I'm sorry. I'm so sorry,' she whispered, frightened by the ferocity of her reaction. 'I didn't mean to hurt you. I'm so sorry, Grace.

'Oh, Mummy. What have I done?' Grace sobbed, throwing herself onto the floor and wrapping her arms about her mother's body. 'I'm sorry too.' They sat in each other's embrace while 'The Forget-Me-Not Sonata' still rang in their ears. Finally Audrey took her daughter's face in her hands and swept away her tears. She shook her head and pursed her lips together in resignation.

'Your father is dying, Grace.'

Grace's eyes widened like a startled animal caught in the headlights. She sat staring at her mother in disbelief. She had noticed how thin and pale her father was. But she hadn't imagined that his health was failing.

'He's dying?' she repeated, hoping that perhaps

she hadn't heard correctly.

Audrey nodded. 'He's riddled with cancer, my love. We're losing him.'

Grace held her mother close and buried her face in her neck. 'Why didn't you tell me?' she asked. 'How long has he been ill?'

'Two months. Years. I don't know for sure. But it's everywhere. He hasn't got long. We didn't want to frighten you.'

'But, Mummy, he's my father. You should have told me.'

Audrey pulled away and sat back on the carpet. 'My love, your father is a proud man. He doesn't want everyone fussing over him. Least of all me.'

'Do Alicia and Leonora know?'

'I haven't told them yet.'

'Well you must. My God, we should all be here for him. It's only after people die that we realise how much we love them. We mustn't wait until then to show him how much he means to us all.'

'Darling, you're so sweet,' she mused, noticing how she had grown less detached since she had gone to Dublin.

Grace read her mother's expression. 'It's not right to be so heavenly minded as to be no earthly good,' she replied with a wry smile. 'Louis has taught me that.' Audrey curled a stray curl behind Grace's ear and smiled at her with tenderness.

'Don't mention your uncle to Daddy, my love. He's weak.'

'I understand. It's okay,' she replied. 'Will you tell him that I know about his illness?'

'I'll tell him.'

'And tell the twins. I don't care how proud he is. The least we can do is be there for him now.'

Audrey nodded and embraced Grace again.

'Play something else, my love. Something less sad. That tune just set me off. I'm sorry.'

'I'll play something positive,' she said, sitting down on the stool once again. 'Positive vibrations will make Daddy better.' She wondered why it was that her sixth sense had failed her.

* * *

But the months rolled on and nothing could make Cecil better, not even Grace's music nor her prayers. His health deteriorated like trees in autumn that shed their leaves one by one until their branches are bare and lifeless. It was meant to be. Destiny had brought him to the end of his journey and the world of spirit awaited him. But he was afraid.

'I wish I could see the other side like you do, Grace,' he said from his bed. 'Then I would be certain of it.' Audrey fluttered about him, nursing him with all the love and tenderness she could muster while Grace sat beside him on her mother's side of the bed, trying to explain to him that death was simply going home.

'Life is like a play. Death is only stepping off the stage, shedding your costume and returning to where we belong. It's not oblivion. Trust me. I know.'

'I've always thought you a little batty, Grace. I wish I could trust you.' He chuckled then coughed and winced.

'Oh, Daddy, does it hurt a lot?'

'Not so bad, Grace,' he replied. 'Your mother's magic pills dull the pain most of the time. I shall

521

die on a high.'

'Too many cigars,' said Audrey, picking up his tray of tea and heading for the door. 'I've got my father to blame for that.'

'Cigars have nothing to do with it,' he said gruffly. 'I'm an old man, that's all.' He coughed again. 'Audrey, stay a while, there's something I want to tell Grace.' Audrey went pale. She had suspected this moment might come and her heart lurched, not only because she dreaded her daughter's reaction but because she knew now that death was very close. The tray began to shake in her hands as she turned and put it back down on the dressing table. She forced a smile and went and sat on the arm chair that stood beside the bed.

'What do you want to tell her, my love?' she asked, the muscles in her neck straining as she tried to mask her apprehension. The last few weeks had drained her of energy and emotion. She felt weary. But she knew by the light in his eyes that he wanted to tell her the truth.

Cecil took his daughter's hand in his and looked at her with battle-weary eyes. He had spent many months deliberating whether or not to tell her the truth about her parentage. As much as it had hurt when Cicely had told him about her friendship with Louis he had forgiven his brother long ago. Now he was dying he wanted to leave everything settled. No more secrets. 'I'm about to depart,' he began dramatically, not knowing how to break it to her. Hoping, perversely, that such a revelation might make her happy. Audrey lowered her eyes in apprehension. 'Your mother and I haven't always been happy,' he said carefully.

'I know that, Daddy,' Grace laughed. 'Every

marriage has its ups and downs.'

'But your mother lost her heart to another man just before you were born.'

Grace narrowed her eyes and looked at her mother's bowed head. 'Go on,' she said in a quiet voice.

Cecil sighed and his white cheeks stung with colour before draining just as quickly.

'She had a brief affair during which time, my dear, you were conceived.'

Grace blinked at him in horror. She suddenly felt isolated, as if she didn't belong to anyone. 'So, you're not my father?'

Cecil shook his head. 'Not biologically,' he replied, trying to state the facts without letting the tearing of his heart interfere with the delivery. Grace's eyes shone and she visibly shrunk back.

'Then who is?' she asked.

Cecil looked at Audrey. She lifted her head and cast it on one side, apologetically.

'Louis,' she replied in a small voice. 'Your uncle Louis.'

*   *   *

Grace climbed slowly off the bed and walked over to the window in silence. She thought of her uncle and now understood his sadness. He had never loved Isla. He had loved her mother all along. She appreciated the tragedy of their affair immediately. Suddenly her mother's dance of tears made sense. She understood her father's drinking as a result of his unhappiness. Their frostiness as they had struggled to come to terms with their situation. Their mutual understanding as they had buried the past and resolved to move to England and make a new start. It was all suddenly very clear.

No wonder Louis and she were so alike. *He's my father*, she thought in disbelief. *He's my father and he knows it. He's known it all along.* She sighed heavily and leant against the window pane. Audrey stood up and walked over to her husband. She took his outstretched hand and smiled at him through her tears. But neither spoke. They knew what the other was thinking. Cecil felt as if he had just given his daughter away and Audrey squeezed his hand, knowing how much that had cost him. They watched to see what Grace would do next. But she just stood by the window looking out. Thinking it over. Coming to terms with such a shocking revelation. But to her surprise, as much as she tried to feel something, she felt very little but surprise. It didn't change anything. She was still standing in her parents' bedroom where her father lay in bed dying.

She turned around and looked at her parents who hung suspended in a limbo, waiting with trepidation to see what would happen now they had let the demon out. Grace shook her head. Cecil caught his breath.

'Louis isn't my father,' she said nonchalantly. 'You'll always be my Daddy. The fact that Louis is my biological father makes no difference to the last eighteen years. You raised me as your own daughter and loved me. I love you as my father. You're all I've ever known. I don't want another one. You're the only father I'll ever have.'

Audrey's shoulders began to shake like they had done that day on the hill and Cecil smiled at his daughter in a way he had never smiled before. His

524

face flushed with pride and gratitude and he held out his hand to her. With glistening eyes she took it and pressed her lips against it. 'I love you, Daddy. I love you so much it fills me up inside like warm honey,' she said and her voice croaked so that she couldn't go on. They stared at each other with total understanding, for love is a bridge that can join even the two most dissimilar human beings. Then his eyes wandered past her and he smiled with recognition. Grace followed the line of his gaze and saw at once the watery forms of a woman and man who had come to take her father across to the other side. 'Not yet, Daddy. There's so much more I want to tell you,' she sniffed. 'Why is it that now I'm losing you I realise how much you mean to me?' Audrey frowned at her, then looked down at the contented countenance of her dying husband. Grace watched in fascination and sorrow as her father's spirit sat up in bed and moved into the outstretched arms of his mother and favourite Uncle Errol. He turned and grinned at her, understanding now as she did that the world of spirit awaited everyone. She wiped her face with her hand. 'Bye, Daddy. We'll meet again one day,' she said softly and watched him fade into sunlight that now beamed in through the frosted window.

Grace's legs were trembling so much she had to sit down. She saw the empty shell of her father lying on the bed and was almost surprised to see it there. Audrey sat stroking his hand, shaking her head in disbelief. 'It was so fast. He was quite well this morning,' she said, a frown now etched in deep lines on her troubled forehead.

'He's gone, Mummy.' Grace sniffed and smiled at her mother. 'Look at his face. Doesn't he look happy?'

Audrey caressed his features with loving eyes. 'I've never seen him look that happy, ever.' She fixed her daughter with solicitous eyes. 'I'm sorry.'

'Don't be sorry. As I said, my life hasn't changed. You can't alter the past, even with a revelation like that. So you loved Louis. That's got nothing to do with me.' She smiled again. 'Let's not tell the twins. No one needs to know but you, me and Louis.'

'Louis?' Audrey asked.

'He knows,' she stated simply. 'I know he knows. What I find most surprising is that I didn't know. I seem to know so much about everyone else, but nothing about me.'

'God works in mysterious ways,' she said, kissing Cecil's hand. She pressed her lips to his skin that still felt warm and soft. 'God works in very mysterious ways.'

CHAPTER THIRTY-FOUR

October 1984

'I feel cheated,' Alicia said, sitting with her arms folded in the chair her father had always sat in. 'I mean, you had barely told me that he was dying, Mummy, and then he was gone. Gone. I never got to say good-bye.'

'Neither did I,' said Leonora sadly.

'That was the way he wanted it. He didn't want anyone to fuss over him.'

'Well, I still feel cheated and desperately sad,' Alicia continued, wiping a large tear away with her glove. Grace rolled her eyes. Alicia had often told her that she had never felt close to him. As a child he was always working, then when they came to school in England she had only seen him once a year at Christmas. 'Hardly the recipe for a close relationship,' had been her exact words. But now of course, the opportunity for melodrama was too much to resist. She sat in her black funeral suit as if she were dressed for a London cocktail party. She was still single, still searching for that elusive dream and still getting nowhere.

Alicia had always been beautiful, but her youth had hidden all manner of evil behind the softness of her flesh and the flawlessness of innocence. As her youth had fallen away so the dark contours of her nature were revealed little by little in the sharpness of her features and the thinning of her once generous mouth. She still possessed an icy beauty. The chiselled, stony looks that turn heads and incite admiration. But bitterness had warped her and sucked the juice out of her face, leaving her dry and formidable but less able to bewitch.

Leonora, on the other hand, whose loveliness had always shone from within, now glowed with a mellow beauty, for her nature had softened the features that had once been plain. Grace admired her for she was happy. She didn't yearn for more than she had or covet what others had; Florien and her children were all she needed along with the velveteen fields of the Dorset countryside. According to Grace, her one flaw was her blind devotion to her twin sister. However much Alicia grew into a grotesque parody of herself, Leonora still saw her the way she was as a child and nothing she could do could change that. She would always

527

admire her.

And what of her? Grace sat dressed for her father's funeral but as far as she was concerned he wasn't in the coffin that awaited burial in the churchyard, but free to fly with the power of thought in the world of spirit. She knew, she had seen him depart and she had said her good-bye. Since then she had thought a lot about Louis. It didn't seem odd at all that he was her biological father. They were so alike. In a way she was pleased. She already loved him as a dear friend, now he was closer to her than that. But nothing could change the past eighteen years and the immense goodness of Cecil, who had raised his brother's child as his own, in spite of the adulterous love that had brought her into the world. She would miss him.

*   *   *

'Ah, Florien,' said Audrey as her son-in-law entered the sitting room.

'Hello, Audrey,' he said. His tone was sympathetic. He nodded at Alicia briefly before turning to his wife. 'Leonora, the children are in the car. Are you ready?'

'We'll see you there,' she said to her mother and sisters who were waiting for Anthony and Cicely to collect them in their car. When they were gone Alicia turned to her mother.

'Someone should tell Leo to lose a bit of weight. She'd look much better if she lost a few pounds.'

'Darling, Florien likes her that way,' replied her mother.

'And so do I,' Grace added. Alicia sat back with

a sigh. She didn't feel comfortable in the same room as her little sister, there was something in her eyes that spooked her.

Finally Cicely tumbled in, hobbling on her high heels. 'I'm sorry we're late, I tripped over one of the blasted dogs. Sprained my ankle. Still, the show must go on. Are you all ready? You look like a trio of blackbirds.'

Audrey stood up stiffly. She felt old although she was only in her early fifties. But she felt old in her bones and old in her heart. Cecil had been such a large presence in the house, now that he was gone it felt empty, even with her daughters around to fill it. It echoed with his absence and was cold.

'It's a beautiful day for the funeral,' she said.

'Isn't it lovely,' Cicely agreed, limping out into the hall.

'Daddy's here in spirit,' said Grace. 'I can feel him.'

Alicia sighed with impatience. 'For God's sake, Grace, he's dead.'

*   *   *

The sky is almost too enchanting for a day such as this, thought Audrey as she watched the coffin being lowered into the ground. *Surely this is the kind of beauty Nature reserves for saints.* It was as if Heaven opened her arms to welcome him home. If she were sensitive enough she was sure she would hear the sound of angels singing and celestial trumpets. But there before her was the humble body of Cecil Forrester and no one but she and God knew the magnitude of his virtues.

Audrey released Grace's hand and stepped forward, holding her silver head high with a dignity that had supported her through many tumultuous years and dropped a single white lily into the grave. She whispered a hasty prayer then raised her eyes to the shrinking sun that descended behind the trees casting long black shadows over the churchyard. It was at that moment that the colour suddenly returned to her cheeks and her fingers touched her neck in an effort to loosen the skin that now seemed to choke her. At first she feared he was one of Grace's ghosts, for his silhouette was outlined against the sunset and he appeared to float through the trees towards them. She squinted her eyes in an effort to see him better. Then her heart plummeted taking her breath with it and for a moment she thought she might faint away. He had come. She bowed her fevered head and stumbled backwards to where Grace extended her arms to steady her. Interpreting the widow's sudden wilting as a natural expression of her grief, the Vicar concluded the burial with a hasty benediction then tactfully left the family to their sorrow.

'Are you all right, Mummy?' Grace whispered to her mother. Audrey shook herself free and searched anxiously through the trees. Grace followed the direction of her mother's eyes and frowned. 'What do you see?' she asked, bewildered because as much as she squinted her eyes she saw no one and spirits always revealed themselves to Grace.

'Go and comfort Alicia, dear,' Audrey said,

patting her daughter on her arm distractedly. 'I'm fine, I just need a little space,' she added hoarsely, walking away with a purposeful rhythm in her step. Grace glanced at her sisters who stood the other side of the grave. Alicia had stopped crying. Her audience had dispersed so there was no longer any reason to perform. Leonora pulled a thin smile when she caught eyes with Grace and indicated with a shudder that it was getting cold and dark and was time to leave. When Grace reached them Leonora was staring across at their mother in bewilderment.

'Who's that man she's talking to?' she asked. The three sisters looked through the blue dusk at their mother who was standing some distance away at the other end of the churchyard, talking to a man they thought they recognised.

'God knows,' Alicia sighed, shrugging her shoulders. 'But she better not be long, it's cold.' She pulled a cigarette out of her handbag and attempted to warm herself up by lighting it.

'Do you know who he is, Grace?' Leonora asked. Grace brought her long white fingers up to her lips where they traced the line of her mouth in wonderment.

'That's Uncle Louis,' she replied slowly. Alicia exhaled with impatience.

'Oh, I remember him. The mad uncle no one ever talks about,' she said, clipping her consonants with efficiency. Alicia hadn't the patience to dither or to think about anyone else but herself. 'Let's go over and find out if he really is mad.'

'No, leave them,' Grace said. 'They have a lot of catching up to do.'

Leonora looked at her sister in puzzlement, but

531

Alicia was only too happy to leave the churchyard and return to their mother's house. She laughed throatily. 'That's fine by me. I'm cold. I really don't care about mad Uncle Louis. Let's go home and warm up. Aunt Cicely and Anthony will wait for her.'

*   *   *

When Louis Forrester stepped across the shadows towards her, Audrey felt the long years dissolve with the mists and placed a hand on one of the gravestones to steady herself. He wore a plain suit beneath a black coat and hat, which sat crookedly on his head, and he walked in the same unique way, with a slight dance in his step as if he were constantly hearing the melancholy rhythm of the tango, echoing still from another life, long ago when he was young and had someone to dance for. As he came nearer, Audrey recognised the gentle expression in his blue eyes and the longing behind them, barely disguised, as if at the sight of her he was no longer able to suppress feelings that had only grown stronger with the slow passing of time. And now, there he was, as if he had stepped across the decades, bringing the memories with him, in his smile and in his smell and all that had changed were the naïve expectations of youth, swallowed up into the deep furrows that marred his forehead.

He stood a moment staring into her features, devouring the details of the face he had carried with him during the lonely days of waiting which had rolled from years into decades until finally they had become so many and so long he had lost track of them, but never of his goal. Now the waiting was over.

'You're not angry,' he said, taking his hands out of his pockets and letting them fall against his coat where he flicked his fingers together apprehensively. Audrey blinked at him with her soft eyes and he noticed how age had robbed them of their definition but not of their tenderness and he wanted to hold her against him and dance the way they had done when they were young and their music undiscovered.

'Cecil was a good man,' she said. She noticed his lips twitch and wished she hadn't said it. But she didn't know what to say. She was no longer certain of how she felt. 'I'm getting old.' She sighed in an effort to excuse her tactlessness.

'So am I,' he replied and the corners of his mouth extended into a small smile. 'But I haven't forgotten how to dance.' Then with an impulsiveness that had conquered her timid heart all those years ago he took her cold hands in his and stepped closer. They both flinched at the startling sensation of physical contact and stood staring at each other not knowing where to go from there. Audrey lowered her eyes anxiously, thinking of the husband she had just buried, unable to ignore the shame she felt as the feeling of Louis' warm hands ignited the spark in her heart, that in all the nineteen years they had been parted, had never gone out.

'Have you forgotten how to dance?' he asked softly. Audrey raised her eyes that were now glistening with tears and her pale lips trembled because suddenly the past confused her. It had once all been so clear.

'I haven't forgotten,' she replied and her voice

was a whisper that was carried on the wind. 'I just put my dancing shoes away for a time.'

He sighed as the years fell away and once more they were united, beneath the red *ceibo* trees and violet jacarandas in the leafy plazas of Buenos Aires, moving to the internal melodies of their love.

*   *   *

'Hello Louis,' said Cicely, staggering up to them. 'From what Grace tells me you don't shout any more.' Louis shook his head at the memories that had come alive there and smiled at his sister.

'I'd never shout at Grace,' he replied, turning to settle his watery eyes on Audrey once again. 'Grace is special.' Audrey didn't avert her eyes, she wanted to tell him by her expression that Grace knew. She had so much to tell him. But Cicely persisted.

'Why don't you come and stay with me at Holholly Grange?' she asked. 'Anthony has never met you.'

'I'm booked into a bed and breakfast,' he replied. 'There's plenty of hot water and heating there.' He grinned mischievously.

Cicely didn't take offence. She shrugged her shoulders. 'As you wish.' She looked from one to the other. 'Well, let's not stand here getting cold. There's tea back at your house, isn't there, Audrey?' Audrey nodded. 'Well, good. I'll give you both a lift.'

Audrey sat in silence while Cicely asked her brother all about Dublin. She watched his profile, barely able to believe that he was sitting there beside her. It didn't matter that they weren't alone for they were almost touching. After so many dreams they were once more united but this time it was different. For the first time in their lives, the road ahead was open to them. They had entered the realm of endless possibilities. She knew he was thinking the same thing. That was why he had come.

When they arrived home Leonora was passing the canapés around and pouring everyone tea. Little Panazel raced about the sitting room with his brother and sister, scrambling between the legs of the guests, unaware that a funeral was a solemn occasion. To him, death was like the changing of the seasons and not worth questioning. He'd miss his grandfather like he missed the summer, but he was too young to know about mourning. Alicia stood smoking beside the fire, her face still half hidden behind the veil, her eyes watching Florien without wavering, like the eyes of an old lioness who watches her prey longingly but knows she can no longer run fast enough to catch it.

Grace had been waiting for her Uncle Louis. She had barely been able to concentrate on anything else. She had watched the door, shrinking in disappointment each time it opened for someone else. When finally he entered she rushed up to him with unrestrained enthusiasm. She was about to throw her arms around his neck when something pulled inside her—a sudden feeling of unease as her instincts told her it was not appropriate in her father's house on the occasion of his funeral. He sensed her retreat and placed a hand on her arm instead. 'It's good to see you, Grace,' he said. She smiled at him warmly, grateful that he understood.

'I hoped you would come,' she said.

'We had our differences, but Cecil was my brother.'

'I know. I'm sure he's pleased that you've come too. Nothing brings people together like death.'

Louis nodded and removed his coat and hat, placing them on a chair. 'I wish I had known about his illness earlier.' He sighed, flicking his fingers nervously.

'He didn't want that,' Grace replied. 'He wanted to die with dignity.'

'Cecil was a man of huge dignity.'

'He was.'

'Were you with him when he passed away?'

'Yes, I was,' she said, looking at him steadily with her deep, knowing eyes. 'He tied up loose ends as dying people do.' He nodded again with understanding. Then his face unfolded like a sunflower that is turned towards the sun. They stared at each other as if suddenly seeing their own reflection for the first time. For a brief moment the world about them seemed to move in slow motion as they hung suspended in time, gazing into the other's features in astonishment. Neither knew what to say because not only did such a revelation open the cobwebbed box that contained the secret past, but because their real relationship was unmentionable in that house. Finally Louis spoke in a deep voice that was barely audible, even to Grace.

'He was a good man,' he said and no one but Grace, Louis and Audrey knew how good he had been.

*   *   *

When the house was finally emptied of guests and Aunt Cicely had been helped out by her husband, wobbling on her heels because of her sprain and because she had consumed far too much wine, Audrey asked Louis to stay for dinner. 'It will just be you, me and Grace,' she said. 'Alicia has returned to London, she finds the countryside suffocating and Leonora has gone home to put the children to bed.'

'I would like that very much,' he said, gazing deeply into her troubled eyes.

'I'd like to have a bath and change, the cold has penetrated right through to my bones.'

'Of course. Grace will keep me company.'

Audrey left him in the sitting room and climbed the stairs. She felt heavy as if her legs were made of something more solid than bones and her joints ached. But nothing ached as much as her heart. She rubbed her forehead in confusion. Louis had come for her. It was what she had dreamed of and no one knew better than she the power of dreams. Without knowing why she wandered into Cecil's dressing room. His smell lingered as if he were still alive. It clung to the walls and fabrics and conjured up in her mind the face of the man she had struggled against for so many years until, by the very force of her will and perhaps something much greater than herself, she had grown to love him as she had never believed possible. It wasn't the obsessive love that she had felt for Louis, but a quieter love born out of respect. He was gone but his presence was so strong she had to sit on the bed and savour it. Such an intense reminiscence might not last forever, even memory fades.

Then she began to go through his things. Cecil

537

kept everything. Boxes of coins, drawers of old letters, piles of leaflets, books and souvenirs all tidy and orderly according to his nature. This room had been his nest and she had never disturbed it. Now she picked each item up, turned it over lovingly, remembering him in all the odd things he collected for his vibration was alive on even the smallest coin. There were peso notes from the Argentine, his ticket from their first date at the Colón, a map of the city of Buenos Aires, the silver pen her father had given him on the morning of their wedding and old newspapers, all worn and creased as if he had handled them a hundred times. She smiled with tenderness as her fingers traced them with nostalgia, brushing off the dust and the years, reliving the past all over again. Then she came across a polished walnut box. It was solid and heavy and shining as if new. This was obviously something of great importance because it was on the chest where he could reach it with ease. She tried to open it but it was locked. Her curiosity was now aroused and she searched for the key. Cecil, being a military man, kept everything in its place and sure enough, in the small drawer at the base of the large oval mirror, not far from the box, lay a silver key. With trembling hands she now opened it to find an old piece of yellowing paper folded neatly inside. Excited by what was without doubt a secret she put the box down and unfolded the note. When she saw what was written on it her heart stumbled and her body was gripped by an icy chill. It was written in Louis' unmistakeable hand and dated 24 June 1948, the day of Isla's funeral.

Cecil, why do women torture us so? I gave my

heart to Audrey and she took it. We loved with the abandon of two people whose destinies are prewritten in the stars. We sailed against the tide hoping that the winds would change and we would be free to love one another openly, but who would have predicted such cruel winds of change? Isla has died and taken Audrey's heart with her. Shame on me that I resent Isla for such an untimely departure. I cannot be in Argentina if Audrey is unwilling to belong to me. The pain is too much to bear. I will throw my dreams into the waters and return when the tides change to favour me once again. Until that blessed time I shall wait restlessly in some Mexican city where Audrey's loveliness is unknown. Forgive us that we led you such a merciless dance, we never meant to hurt, only to disguise. You and I are both victims of love. Louis.

Audrey's feverish eyes were then drawn to the phrase that Cecil had written beneath:

And when ye stand praying, forgive, if ye have aught against any: that your Father also which is in heaven may forgive you your trespasses
                                        Mark II v25.

She stared at it as a hot feeling of shame crept up her spine and soon her vision was so blurred that she could no longer read. Cecil had known about their love affair right from the beginning. He must have known too, when she returned from settling the twins into boarding school and Louis was waiting for her playing the piano. He must have accepted it but never given up. What caused her the most pain, however, was the fact that he had chosen to forgive. Her husband's nobility touched her once again but this time it left an indelible print.

It was at that moment of awakening that 'The Forget-Me-Not Sonata' resounded through the house from the piano downstairs. With its haunting undulations and hypnotic repetitions the notes penetrated Audrey's spirit and caused her head to spin. She put her hands to her ears to block out the melody that had been a musical expression of their love but now had no place in their lives. It only insulted Cecil's memory. Cecil who had never stopped loving her, even during the months, years, when she had dreamed of his brother, conceived his child and planned to leave him and start a new life on the other side of the world. 'The Forget-Me-Not Sonata' now accentuated his goodness, his patience and his pain and tears of regret burned her cheeks. Yes, he had deserved such a magnificent sky, such flamingo pink and slashes of red and gold. The soul of Cecil Forrester was more than deserving. Yet, he deserved more. He deserved her faithfulness. She hadn't honoured him in life, but she could honour him in death. Louis' self-indulgent love suddenly seemed pale compared to the deep love of her husband.

With faltering steps she hurried down the stairs as the music got louder and louder, the notes ringing in her ears like a scream. When he saw her livid face and flaming eyes he stopped playing and a frown darkened his face. She handed him the note. Grace watched from the sofa, barely daring to breathe. He read it and the silence was as loud as the music had been. Then he raised his eyes, at once heavy with a dreadful sadness. He understood. Cecil's death hadn't liberated them, it had set them apart for ever. How could they resume in the shadow of such self-sacrifice?

He stood up and slipped into his coat, placing his hat crookedly on his head as was his custom. Then he walked over to her without taking his eyes that were once again distant, but no longer forlorn, off her anguished face. And he took her in his arms and kissed her cheek, savouring for the last time the scent of her skin and the proximity of her body that had once moved with his to the internal melody of a love that they had believed would never die. He caressed her features, though he need not have taken the trouble for hers was a face that he would never forget. Then he departed. They heard the door close and shivered as a cold wind swept in, leaving them alone. All that remained was the tension in the air and an almost tangible sense of loss.

Grace looked at her mother then at the door, her face solemn and anxious. When she turned back Audrey nodded at her slowly, without saying a word. Grace needed no other encouragement. She sprang up from the sofa and ran out into the road. 'Louis!' she shouted after him. 'Louis!' Her voice was carried on the wind and he stopped and turned around. He saw her running through the darkness and his face crumpled into a tremulous smile. He looked so grateful to see her that she threw her arms around him. It had begun to drizzle and his coat was wet against her face. 'This isn't the end, Louis, but the beginning,' she said, pressing her cheek against his shoulder. 'Spring always follows winter, doesn't it?'

Louis was too moved to speak. He placed his hand on her head and kissed her forehead, aware that his tears were falling into her hair. Then she pulled away and looked at him with the eyes of a child. 'What you started with Mummy continues with me. I love you. You're my father now.' Louis swallowed the ball of emotion that had caught in his throat. There was so much that he wanted to say, but words eluded him. He ran an unsteady hand down her face, aware that the last time he had cried had been the moment at the airport when he had realised Audrey was lost to him for ever. Now his tears weren't shed in sadness but in joy. Grace was his child. She would never leave him. They stared at each other for a long moment, unable to find the words to express what they both felt. So Louis began to hum a tune. Grace listened in delight until she was able hum it too. Tentatively at first then with confidence as it became more familiar. In the velvet darkness of the empty street they held each other close and hummed together a new sonata; a sonata for the future that began now with their first deliberate steps across the wet pavement.

* * *

When Grace returned home her mother was sitting on the piano stool, her fingers stroking the keys that still vibrated from the music he had played. She sat down beside her and leant her head against her shoulder.

'The Forget-Me-Not Sonata,' she said.

Audrey nodded. 'How could you know?' she asked, for the name was hers alone.

'I used to watch you dance through the crack in the door. I called it your dance of tears. I never knew why you danced. But I instinctively knew never to mention it. I was afraid you might stop and I so loved to watch you. Then one day you brought out an exquisite little book bound in silk. You wrote something down then tried to write on the next page, but you were never able to. One day you were out, I could no longer contain my curiosity, so I found your little book and opened it.'

'The Forget-Me-Not Sonata.' Audrey smiled wistfully.

'A few dots and the smudge of a tear.'

'I never wrote it.'

'But perhaps you will one day.'

'Perhaps I will.' Then she sighed heavily and softly closed the lid of the piano. She turned to her daughter and looked at her with eyes that brimmed with compassion. 'But it won't be Louis' story. It will be Cecil's. I will write "The Forget-Me-Not Sonata" for him.'